NAZI TARGET NUMBER ONE . . .

'Harvis hung up a large map of the city of Tehran with the significant landmarks plainly marked. He was calmer now, beginning to feel the w

"You landed here, M

Shah's palace."

Callahan shot from

Russian embassies!"

They were opposite

"How far are they fr

Harvis answered, "A

Callahan looked trou

Russkies are cosy neighbours. But what about us? Say hello to our first big headache, gents."

"What do you mean?" Gordell asked.

"It's a summit meeting. They're calling it the Tehran Conference. Code name, Eureka. For the first time in the war the Boss gets together with Churchill and Stalin. So what's the big question? Which one of The Big Three travels those four miles? For one week *in the open*. Going to whose embassy to talk?"

He paused to let Gordell and Harvis absorb this. "There's only one answer. The Boss is the Nazi number one target. That's how we operate, men." '

William Copeland

Five Hours from Isfahan

PANTHER
GRANADA PUBLISHING
London Toronto Sydney New York

Published by Granada Publishing Limited
in Panther Books 1978

ISBN 0 586 04320 9

First published in Great Britain by Hart-Davis,
MacGibbon Ltd 1976

Granada Publishing Limited
Frogmore, St Albans, Herts AL2 2NF
and
3 Upper James Street, London W1R 4BP
1221 Avenue of the Americas, New York, NY 10020 USA
117 York Street, Sydney, NSW 2000, Australia
100 Skyway Avenue, Toronto, Ontario, Canada M9W 3A6
Trio City, Coventry Street, Johannesburg 2001, South Africa
CML Centre, Queen & Wyndham, Auckland 1, New Zealand

Made and printed in Great Britain by
Richard Clay (The Chaucer Press) Ltd
Bungay, Suffolk
Set in Linotype Times

This book is for FLORENCE . . ,

An evil disposed man is a captive in the hands of an enemy (namely, himself); for wherever he may go he cannot escape the grasp of that enemy's vengeance.

– *Saadi The Gulistan*

NIGHT FLIGHT, NOVEMBER 1943

They flew in the night, the German commando team, travelling two hundred and seventy-five miles per hour through a star-filled sky under a bomber's moon. It made for perfect visibility and flying weather.

The Nazi warriors, pride of the Fatherland, were not being carried in one of their own German transports, for their mission was one of deception, camouflage, and destruction. They were flying in a captured British Lancaster bomber with four Merlin engines, so named, not for the magician of King Arthur but for the bird of prey.

After it had been downed in a raid over Germany, the metal bird had been repaired, but its markings were unchanged. Now in the service of the enemy, it bore the British Air Force insignia with the standard Bomber Command green- and earth-coloured upper surface and yellow underbelly. *A for Alfie* was painted on the nose of the plane. The English crew that originated it had been killed, and the meaning of the nickname now lost for ever.

Under the control of a German crew, the present passengers of the Lancaster were twenty-two men with parachute packs, who sat quietly opposite each other in total darkness. Two of the commandos were foreign guides. The German soldiers disapproved of non-Aryans, but necessity bred temporary tolerance. As members of Hitler's *Herrenvolk*, these Nazis distrusted their inferiors, and the guides would be watched despite their collaboration.

The Germans were SS men, once Hitler Youth, the most dedicated and deadliest of the Führer's soldiers, all in their late teens and early twenties, perfected products of the Nazi period of paranoia and peril, the ten-year-old Third Reich. Their racial attitudes had been drumbeaten into them. They had no reason to doubt their superiority. Reason had been arrested and thrown into a concentration camp.

Only men with their upbringing in National Socialism would have been entrusted with this dangerous errand for Hitler himself, who had issued the order for a 'personal mission of the highest degree'.

It meant the mission was expected to encounter enormous adverse odds. Yet the chosen German commandos each had fought for the chance. It was understood that when they returned to the Fatherland, the Führer would decorate and promote them personally. Just before take off, he had named the team Wolf Pack, which was a distinction because it was an animal Hitler favoured and identified with. The commandos were both honoured and inspired.

At the inception of the mission, the Führer had charged Colonel Konrad Zenner, the leader and trainer of the team, with the crucial necessity for it: the massive flow of the matériel of war from the United States.

Speaking in the isolation of his headquarters, Wolf's Lair, Adolf Hitler had raged at Franklin Roosevelt. 'With his aid to the English he was my sworn enemy even before I declared war on the United States. Each time Germany was near winning the war he has come to the rescue of our enemies with his machines and food,' he told Zenner.

'The first time was after the defeat of France, when we had London burning and the English on their knees. What saved them? Roosevelt's supply ships. When we were ready to take Egypt and make the Mediterranean a German lake, who delivered the British from defeat? Roosevelt's military aid. What prevented us from crashing the gates of Moscow and a victory at Stalingrad? Roosevelt and his lend-lease of trucks, guns, and medicine for the Bolsheviks!'

After that meeting Colonel Zenner had, under careful scrutiny, collected his men and then worked with them at a hunting lodge near Berchtesgaden. Coming from different sections and social strata in Germany, the young men melded into this fighting machine with goose-stepping precision, a tribute to the political efficiency of Hitler's dictatorship.

Now the quiet men in the plane with the colonel, who at twenty-five was the oldest, were silent killers, able to shoot, swim, run, crawl, and sabotage with more skill than any single group of soldiers in the service of their country. There was *esprit de corps* and a conviction of invincibility. They entertained no notion of risk or danger.

Since they had been instilled early with the idea of fearless defence of their Fatherland in the Hitler Youth, these commandos still retained a schoolboy concept of heroism and a sense of immortality. Separated by design from timid families and cowering churches, they had no respect for parents, nor feared God, recognizing only Adolf Hitler as their highest authority. He was their conscience, his creed their will. Their faith in the Führer and patriotism for Germany made these warriors doubly invulnerable and was the source of their courage. It was the best possible soldier's pay.

Thus, if death came, it would be sad and grievous but not a moment for regret. They would have fallen in a cause in which they believed with all their hearts. For, they would reason, heroes don't die. They join the great German pantheon of mystic and legendary heroes and live for ever.

The Nazis huddled wordlessly in the unlit interior of the plane; they had been aloft for a number of hours and were spoken out. Words, however, were not the strong points of these young men, being creatures created for movement, not thought. Logic was the enemy of spirit. It led to isolated individuality and cold loneliness. Transmitted shoulder to shoulder in the darkness, the warm communal bond was better.

Of necessity these Germans in the British plane had been cleared through a Luftwaffe corridor in Nazi-occupied zones. So far they had passed over hundreds of miles of Allied enemy territory without being challenged, mostly because they flew at night. If radio contact had been made, the pilots were prepared with perfect English. The commandos, too, understood enough of that language and Russian, which was a priority.

They had crossed many borders and were now approaching the drop area, far from comfortable skies.

Their destination was Iran, the land now occupied by the soldiers of England, Russia, and the United States.

1

'Nice shot, Volodya!'

Captain Peter Harvis had lost the point and the game as he rushed from the backcourt to the net too late to return a delicately executed dropshot by the Russian ambassador. It was his partner, Philip Gordell, the American ambassador to Iran, who offered the compliment to their opponent that was also an implied criticism of Harvis because he had disregarded their game plan.

Sir Henry Bolt said, 'Lovely, partner!'

Ambassador Volkoff beamed, 'Thank you, gentlemen!'

The doubles match was even now after six games, and an embassy clerk, waiting for the game to end, found an opportunity to deliver a written message to the British minister. Sir Henry excused himself and left the clay court in the compound of the British embassy at Tehran, promising to return promptly.

It was a welcome respite from a tenacious competition, and Volkoff and Gordell moved to a table behind which stood a white-jacketed Iranian steward ready with iced tea. Harvis wasn't thirsty and sat down to stretch his legs, just as a nimble locker attendant handed him a towel. A ballboy in his teens, but small for his age, gathered up the tennis balls.

It was a nice way to spend a war, Captain Harvis thought. At the moment, he couldn't conceive of anything he'd rather be doing in the midst of the Second World War than performing at his favourite sport. Perfect weather, too, this Friday morning, late in November 1943. And coincidentally, one year since he had been transferred from the Pentagon to the assignment of Intelligence Officer at the American embassy in Tehran. He decided to dedicate the remaining hours of the day to celebrating his Life, Liberty, and Pursuit of Happiness. His inalienable right. There was nothing like Old Glory's red, white, and blue hedonism. Let others agonize over war aims. Captain Peter Harvis knew what he was fighting for: three manservants for tennis.

Unfortunately, Harvis couldn't dress the part. Before he went overseas, his wife had neatly storaged his tennis gear for the duration, racket covered and in a press. Now he had to appear like a parvenu in an ill-fitting grey sweat shirt and matching sweatpants over his lean, six-foot body, for which he had to bribe a venal supply sergeant. He wore black-topped sneakers with greyish rubber soles bought from a Navy officer. He was playing with an old Wright and Ditson racket borrowed from the ambassador that was the wrong weight. At least he was protected against the wintry day.

In elegant contrast, Ambassador Volkoff and Sir Henry wore creased white flannel trousers, tennis sweaters, and freshly whitened Dunlop shoes. The Europeans used English rackets. The American ambassador wore starched white ducks, his old college cardigan, and Keds. His Spalding racket was an heirloom. All three were about the same age, in their late fifties, while Harvis was twenty-five. He enjoyed himself on the court, as if rest and recreation were his wartime duty. But the middle-aged statesman went at the game as though the Grim Reaper were on the other side of the net with a tennis racket instead of a scythe.

Harvis' youth wasn't necessarily an advantage, he had discovered. The tall Englishman had once reached the semi-finals at Wimbledon and was lob-proof. The rotund Russian was a quick retriever who had spent a czarist exile teaching the game for a meagre living in Berlin. They were a complementing team and played winning doubles. Gordell, like Harvis, had been on his college team. At their age, the young captain hoped he would be in as good shape.

It was impossible not to think metaphorically about the game, Harvis thought. The Americans would win easily, or barely lose, depending on their errors because they were better singles players. They moved aggressively, gambling on smashes and drives, all kinds of fancy stuff, to the accompaniment of Indian war cries. But the ball always seemed to come back from the less demonstrative Allies. They played for time and percentages, wisely aware that errors outnumbered placements ten to one. The diplomatic dinkers used lobs, slices, and soft dropshots. They let the Americans beat themselves.

We're national stereotypes, Harvis concluded, smiling.

This match was an occasion. They hadn't played in a month because of a shortage of tennis balls in Tehran until the dozen showed up in the American diplomatic pouch ordered by Gordell for Allied relations. Dunlop had gone to war. The Russians had somehow managed to survive czarism, Bolshevism, and the Nazi attack without the manufacture of tennis balls. The American way of war was unthinkable without sports equipment, it came to Harvis, as he imagined a baseball-playing GI pitching hand grenades.

I'm a tennis bum, he thought with vagrant unease.

'Pete, what have you got showing today?' Ambassador Gordell asked him from across the court.

One of Captain Harvis' duties was to arrange screenings for the embassy staff of pertinent material from the Army Information Service. He had scheduled one for after lunch.

'It's called *Since the Casablanca Conference*,' he replied. 'Right down your alley.'

'Does it have shots of the conference itself?'

'Could be,' Harvis said. 'But I'm not sure.'

'I might be in it.' Gordell was excited. 'I'll be there if I don't get stuck for lunch with those Congressmen investigating lend-lease.'

Harvis had only been with the American embassy about a month and a half when the ambassador had returned from the Casablanca Conference. It was a first realization that his new job had put him close to people and places where wartime history was being made.

One morning eleven months earlier, Ambassador Philip Gordell had invited his staff to seat themselves informally about his large office, a diminishing of a diplomatic distance usually maintained. His mood was in sharp contrast with the routine ritual of his weekly orientation sessions in the conference room of the American embassy in Tehran. The ambassador had just returned from the Roosevelt–Churchill meeting held from 13 to 24 January 1943 in Morocco. The afterglow of the great event remained, and Gordell's urbanity had been banished for the special briefing occasion.

As the ambassador prepared to speak, Betty Lanteri, his twenty-four-year-old secretary, sat poised to record his words. Taking the roll, Betty found none of the twenty-two Americans on the staff absent; even those on sick call had made the effort. Only the Iranian employees had been excluded. At first glance, however, she had not seen a certain favourite.

Attempting anonymity, Captain Peter Harvis had taken a seat in a far corner of the office. He had arrived hung-over and hungry, having barely made the briefing by missing breakfast. He caught the secretary's searching eye, and she acknowledged his presence with a nod. Look intelligent, her wrinkled brow seemed to admonish, you're the Intelligence Officer. I hope she knows I can listen with my eyes closed, Harvis told himself...

The President of the United States and the Prime Minister of Great Britain, with their staffs, had met at the Anfa Hotel, in a sumptuous suburb of villas, owned by wealthy French colonialists, who had been temporarily dispossessed. The hotel was on a knoll overlooking the Atlantic Ocean. There was a magnificent view of the blue water, the red soil in which green palms grew, and the white buildings of Casablanca, French Morocco. Ambassador Gordell had used a map as he described the scene for his staff, making it seem like a review of a spectacular pageant of knights and kings on an African encampment. He had been invited to attend because one of the main topics of the conference was to be the flow of American supplies to the Soviet Union that passed through his jurisdiction in Iran under the lend-lease programme. It was a milestone in Gordell's diplomatic career.

Harvis was sleepy, but it was hard not to react to the ambassador's enthusiasm. He was positively protean, the captain observed. Philip Gordell had left Tehran wrapped in his usual ennui and returned rejuvenated. He must have slipped off to a Swiss spa....

Among the people Ambassador Gordell had met at the conference was Major-General George S. Patton, he told his staff. Only two months before, the entire area had been under the control of the Vichy French. Operation Torch, the code name for the massive Allied attack on North Africa, had cleared the way after hard fighting. There had been three task forces commanded by Lieutenant-General Dwight D. Eisenhower, striking at Casablanca, Oran, and Algiers. It was General Patton who had made the successful landing against stiff resistance at Casablanca, then became the proconsul of Morocco, and played host to President Roosevelt and Prime Minister Churchill.

Pausing as though he had mental reservations about his next words, the ambassador shrugged off caution. He told them Patton was a 'brilliant soldier, but a dumb politician', who fraternized with the defeated French Fascists and continued their pro-Nazi policies. The embassy staff made appropriate sounds and shook heads at this misbegotten affair of state.

Now there's an eye-opener, Harvis thought. Gordell was a consummate diplomat who rarely dealt in extremes. Political generals were his sore point, however, ever since his difficulties with the commanding general of the Persian Gulf Command.

Harvis had often heard the sarcasm he reserved for military men who fancied themselves politicians.

Ambassador Gordell was now offering 'Georgie' S. Patton as War Exhibit No. 1 of how to win battles brilliantly and lose the peace stupidly. The general, he said, was an uncouth clown, who designed his own uniforms, like Göring, and drove a big Packard with special horns to announce himself. He was a martinet, rattling pearl-handled pistols, and going in for military pomp and lavish parades. Patton rivalled the local sultan for splendid living and champagne parties. His foul language was 'atrocious', and his ideas were 'atrocities'. He was a dewclaw.

It was not the typical bloodless diplomatic jargon, Harvis thought, loving it like the rest of the staff. He was thoroughly awake now.

After diverting himself with this deviant portrait, Gordell went on to proclaim Operation Torch a military success, coming as it did with the Russian victory at Stalingrad and the American triumph at Guadalcanal. Next was Rome, then Berlin.

However, the Allies were still pursuing the enemy even while the conference was in progress. Roosevelt and Churchill were meeting within bomber range or a surprise raid by Nazi commandos. So American fighter planes, reinforced by radar-equipped British night fighters, scoured the skies. The Navy had special surface patrols in the nearby Atlantic. General Patton's Armoured Corps ceaselessly roamed the area. Anti-aircraft batteries were on a twenty-four-hour alert.

Then the ambassador repeated the words that were to make Casablanca part of contemporary history, the words first uttered on the veranda of the hotel at the final press conference: 'Unconditional surrender'.

The President had made the phrase seem like an afterthought, Gordell reported. Churchill appeared quizzical, as though hearing it for the first time, straining to hear Roosevelt's words. However understated, the announcement had the effect of an apocalyptic thunderbolt from the clear blue African sky among the assembled correspondents. They now had the biggest story of the war.

The President of the United States had issued the first official declaration of the ultimate Allied objective in the war against Fascism. There could be no negotiations with Germany, Italy, or Japan through traditional diplomatic channels, no more of the ancient behind-the-scenes-bargaining. The world was warned it was to be a battle to the bitter and bloody end.

Add another first, Harvis thought. He's also placed himself on Hitler's shitlist in the first position. Unconditionally.

The code clerk asked, 'How did the President look, sir?'

What a silly question, Harvis thought. The most powerful man in the world has just told us–we are going to beat the Fascist bastards into the caveman era. 'Mr Gable, what do you and Miss Lombard have for breakfast?'

The ambassador was complimentary. 'That was an excellent question. The physical and mental condition of our leaders is of vital importance in politics,' he pointed out didactically. 'The President arrived in high spirits. It might interest you people to know it was the first time any President has ever used a plane to travel outside the United States. In fact, no President has ever taken a plane inside or outside the country, on official or unofficial business.'

'Hey, that's one for the books!' someone declared.

'However,' Gordell said gravely, as if he had been following his own rules of close observation at the conference, 'when it was over, the President seemed tired. There were deep hollows under his eyes. Of course, he was still mourning the death of his mother. He wore a black tie and crepe on his sleeve.'

The code clerk wasn't so dumb, and I learned myself a lesson, Harvis thought. If FDR died tomorrow, what would we do? It was hard to imagine any other leader for this war. Keep him out of draughts, for chrissake!

Another person asked, 'Is there any truth to the rumour there was a plot to get him and Churchill at Casablanca?'

'Mike Callahan, the President's bodyguard, is an old friend of mine,' Gordell told them. 'Roosevelt never arrives anyplace without a prior checkout by Mike and his Secret Service men, who have the authority to requisition anything. Or anybody. There were a thousand officials and three thousand servants among fourteen villas. Mike put a barbed wire fence around us. He had mine detectors run over the ground, buildings searched for listening devices and time bombs, and the houses of the President and the Prime Minister were tested by Geiger counter.'

'Did they find anything?'

'It seems there were some plots boiling,' Gordell conceded. 'Nothing happened, of course. But it was always a possibility.

You remember, the Germans staged an air raid on Casablanca three weeks before.'

Harvis had read the intelligence report on the Luftwaffe bombing of the poorest section of Casablanca, killing hundreds in a search for Patton's fuel dumps. He wondered why they had chosen a genuine high-risk area for the conference. There had to be a strong reason. The place was known to be infested with French Fascist agents with plenty of German money in their pockets, who remained after their armies had retreated and been captured. Dangerous detritus. Also nearby Spanish Morocco, supposedly neutral, on the orders of Generalissimo Francisco Franco from Madrid seemed to be shooting all aircraft except those bearing swastikas.

'Now it can be told.' Gordell spoke low in mock revelatory style, drawing laughter. 'Mike Callahan turned the swimming pool outside the President's bedroom into an air-raid shelter with the help of the Army engineers. He had them cut out armour plates from a bombed-out French battleship and then used cement and sandbags. Hard-boiled Callahan would tear down the Chinese Wall to protect the Boss.'

Look at the old conservative hamming it up, Harvis thought. He's had a shot in the ass. What else happened in Casablanca, Phil baby? Come to think of it, what do these movers and shakers of worlds do after hours? Bring on the girls. . . .

'Besides the big brass, who else was there, sir?'

'Three sons.' Gordell grinned. 'Randolph Churchill and Elliot and Franklin, Junior.'

'Well?'

'No comment.'

Down goes the diplomatic mask, Harvis thought. Then he spoke out, as if to keep himself alert. 'Did they do anything out of line, sir?'

'Some kids don't know when to keep their mouths shut,' Gordell said, then cut off the subject. 'But I do.'

Chips off famous blocks, Harvis thought. Rich, too. Their old men were making footprints on history. How does a son follow in those giant steps? How would these poor little rich guys make out?

'Why didn't Stalin show up?'

'Two reasons,' the ambassador explained. 'First, the Red Army was counter-attacking the Nazis, and second, we all knew what he'd talk about: the second front.'

That's why they gambled on a place like Casablanca so near

a battlefield, Harvis reasoned. To entice Stalin into meeting with them away from the Kremlin.

'Did you meet the two French generals, sir?'

It was the ambassador's inquiring secretary, and Harvis wasn't surprised. He and Betty Lanteri had been trying to unravel the tangled skein of French politics from the incoming State Department papers. They were a complicated jumble of plot and counterplot.

'I met our man, General Henri Giraud, but I was more impressed with the British candidate to run the French show, General Charles de Gaulle, when he arrived. He and Churchill had some sort of understanding,' Gordell reported. 'It was an experience just to shake hands with the man, a tall giant. He seems to be looking over your head into history. Possessed by one idea, France personified. But he comes off like a prima donna, which is not the best political stance. He doesn't come hat in hand. France is defeated, but he believes it's a privilege for the Americans to help her and him.' He added a personal note: 'He and the President didn't get along. Too bad, I say.'

The opinion was pretty far out on a limb for the ambassador, Harvis thought. Gordell was a party-line diplomat. He was tempted to expand the point to back up Betty but couldn't rouse the energy.

The ambassador summarized the various important points and decisions in their regard made at the Casablanca Conference, then commented that it would have been considered historically as an interim meeting of war chiefs if not for the momentous statement of President Roosevelt. Even as the Commanders in Chief conferred, Operation Torch was in progress against the Germans and Italians and promising to send General Erwin Rommel back to Hitler in defeat. At the same time, the Russians at Stalingrad had General Friedrich von Paulus and his Sixth German Army trapped. Besides increasing supplies and organizing new plans for the different battlefronts around the world, immediate preparations had to be made for taking Sicily. The expectation was that Italy would collapse, thus becoming the first member of the Axis to surrender.

'It's the end of Benito Mussolini,' Gordell ventured.

There was a quip: 'We'll soon be getting our macaroni direct from Rome.'

The visa officer just made a lousy joke because I'm starved, Harvis thought. And I should say something, but it's close to lunch, and my head aches, too. He had been lounging comfortably but brought his lanky six feet to an upright position and with another effort stood up. He would make himself unpopular because the ambassador appeared to be finished.

'Sir, may I ask a serious question?'

'Mr Ambassador,' Betty Lanteri reminded her boss dutifully, 'it's almost twelve, and you have an appointment with the Shah for lunch.'

Harvis was aware that the Iranian ruler would be anxious to hear about Casablanca. Mohammed Reza Shah Pahlevi was new and young, but intelligent and eager to enlarge his knowledge of world affairs. Harvis considered retracting his question.

'Oh, yes,' Gordell said. 'See me later, Pete.'

It was an indication for the meeting to break up and chairs began to shuffle. Some of the hungrier audience skipped towards the door. Captain Harvis had begun something he intended to finish.

'It isn't only for me, sir.'

'I'm sorry, Pete,' the ambassador said, respecting his young aide's judgment. 'Go ahead, of course.'

The staff returned to their places but not without some muffled grumbling at their twenty-five-year-old intelligence officer, who apparently wasn't hungry.

'Is it possible that President Roosevelt made a mistake?' Harvis asked tentatively, suddenly becoming a focal point. 'Could the idea of unconditional surrender have been an inspiration? Or an unfortunate ad lib?'

Gordell was pleased with this scepticism, among some murmurs at what seemed like *lèse majesté.*

'Why does that occur to you, Pete?' the ambassador asked. 'There was nothing I said—'

'You said Churchill looked like it had just been sprung on him.'

The ambassador chuckled with the recollection.

'That comical homburg slipped back on his head, and he took the perpetual cigar out of his mouth to let his jaw drop,' he said. 'Then I heard him say, "Perfect! I can see Goebbels and the rest of them squeal!"'

Gordell repeated the quote with an English accent, and the staff enjoyed the mimicry. It was a good time for Captain Harvis to grin and retire, but he was just warming up to the subject. He was the newest addition to the embassy and hadn't yet established himself. They would be uncertain if he were being rash, displaying a conceit, or honestly searching. By now Harvis wasn't even sure about his own motives.

'Either way, sir,' he said, 'I'm really concerned about the implications.'

'Tell us, Pete.'

Harvis felt he had been forgiven for delaying everyone's noontime dates by the way they had quieted down.

'Well, it seems to me it might convince the German people they'll be wiped out, and so they'll fight to the last man,' he said. 'In that way it'll prolong the war, and a lot of people will die unnecessarily.'

'You've got something there, Pete. And I've got some notes on that aspect I should have mentioned.' Gordell began to rearrange his papers, while the people in the room maintained a respectful silence. His secretary caught the eye of the captain and winked approvingly.

'Of course, I wasn't privy to the deliberations of the President's inner circle. Actually, my contact with him consisted of a quick handshake and a wave from that famous cigarette holder,' Gordell confessed regretfully, giving up his rummaging for the moment. 'But my educated guess would be that he was trying to avoid the kind of disputes that took place at the end of the First World War when the Germans claimed they surrendered on the basis of Wilson's Fourteen Points.'

Because he was arranging for a German refugee to lecture to the embassy staff, Harvis had lately done some reading into German history, including a valiant effort to reread Hitler's *Mein Kampf*, which failed. He saw it now as a psychiatrist's transcript of an incurable case. Anyway, it was a time not for reading the Führer but destroying him. Beyond books to bullets.

'What about the Versailles Treaty, sir?' Harvis suggested. 'Didn't that muddle things, too?'

'It certainly did. And I'm certain Mr Roosevelt would agree with us that if there weren't a Versailles Treaty, there would be no Adolf Hitler,' the ambassador observed. 'There's probably only one way to treat that – that—'

'Monster from the German deep,' Harvis supplied.

'Thanks,' Gordell said, then found the paper he was looking for, 'but let me quote our President directly: "Peace can come to the world by the total elimination of German, Japanese, and Italian war power.... The elimination of German, Japanese, and Italian war power means the unconditional surrender of Germany, Italy, and Japan. That means a reasonable assurance of future world peace. It does not mean the destruction of the population of Germany, Italy, or Japan, but it does mean the destruction of the philosophies in those countries which are based on conquest and the subjugation of other people.'

'Thanks, Mr Ambassador,' Harvis said. 'That clarifies it for me.'

There was some scattered appreciative applause.

'That's it,' Gordell said, ending the meeting. 'I'm hungry. Betty, call the palace and tell them I'm running late.'

The embassy staff began to file out of the office. Captain Peter Harvis left with the others, thinking he had seen his duty and done it for the enlightenment of his fellowmen, thereby doing a good day's work. He had earned the right to go directly home to sleep. And eat.

Sir Henry Bolt returned after twenty minutes, having spent less time on his British embassy business than he should have because he was anxious to continue the tennis game. They got into position, and the doubles match picked up from the last score. It was the Russian ambassador's turn to receive from Captain Harvis.

'Okay, Pete,' Ambassador Gordell said. 'Let's blow these Allies off the court!'

As Harvis prepared to serve, he bounced the ball a few times to recover his concentration. Oddly, three words forced themselves up from his unconscious: folly, transparency, and retribution. He wondered why. Perhaps they were the tail side of the words from the Preamble of the American Constitution he had assumed as his motto for the day.

Nevertheless, at the end of his first year overseas, it was a nice way to spend a war.

2

It was dawn in Iran, somewhere north of Tehran, when the first team of commandos, five Germans and one Iranian guide, jumped from the British Lancaster bomber named *A for Alfie*.

Standing in the open doorway of the plane, Colonel Konrad Zenner watched the six parachutes with the dangling men float earthward until he could no longer see them. As he moved away, two crew members closed the door, and the colonel sat down with his remaining sixteen men. It was the first drop of the mission that had actually begun four months before in Berlin, back in July 1943. He thought about it:

Sitting erect in the chair, the broad six-foot-five frame of SS Captain Konrad Zenner placed him at eye level with the short and frail Reichsminister of Enlightenment and Propaganda, Joseph Goebbels, who couldn't stand still. They sat in the front room of Goebbels' villa at Wannsee, a lake suburb, fifteen miles outside Berlin, near Potsdam. Why he had been brought here in the minister's black Mercedes instead of the scheduled meeting at his office had not been explained to the captain. It would have been tactless to ask.

Captain Zenner had come directly from the Kharkov front, where he had fought with the SS Leibstandarte Division that had recaptured the city from the Russians, and the midday ride in the Mercedes through Berlin had been his first view of the damage done by the enemy bombing that morning of the city in which he had been born and reared. It was the second raid in two days. The depressing sights had not placed Zenner in the best mood for this important meeting, as he swivelled his head to keep the lame Reichsminister in view. Goebbels bobbed up and down about the room, pacing nervously. The captain found himself more fascinated by the famous man's physique than his words.

He can't be more than five feet tall with a head that's out of proportion, Zenner thought, being himself a man self-absorbed in his own body through the heightened awareness that comes from war or an Eastern philosophy. Goebbels' deformed foot attracted him, so that Zenner had to force himself to concentrate on the vital little man's cadaverous face, which reminded him of starving peasants he had seen in Poland.

He had his own dietary laws and declined the offer of a cigarette and brandy, much to the Reichsminister's surprise and curiosity. 'Like the Führer,' Goebbels commented as they exchanged some preliminary pleasantries. 'He believes more than ever that meat eating is harmful to humanity.'

The captain was one of four men suggested by Reichsfuehrer SS Heinrich Himmler for a personal assignment to Adolf Hitler that would involve 'exceptional danger and a unique risk'. Zenner had not been told he was to be screened by one of the founders of the Third Reich, and he was properly impressed. He had read all about the brainy PhD from Heidelberg, organizer, writer, strategist, political leader, who as Gauleiter of Berlin had turned that city's colour from red to black. Hitler hated the imperial city of rich cosmopolites, witty intellectuals, sophisticated pleasures, proletarian internationalism, extravagant wealth, and miserable poverty. The Führer spoke to the middle class, the petite bourgeoisie, and the nationalists, while Goebbels had the language of Berlin down pat, from the gutter to the Gods.

The meeting between them was 'under four eyes', except for the discreet valet taking inventory of the valuables to be moved to a safe place because of the enemy bombing. Captain Zenner was a baleful man these days, and his basilisk eyes missed not a detail of his surroundings, like a combat veteran searching for enemy surprises. The household goods were arranged, Oriental rugs, carved furniture, Gobelin tapestries, lamps, cut glass, silver, porcelain, linen, china, pictures. Frau Goebbels and the six children were in their country place, Lanke. Everyone knew of Goebbels' official residence in Berlin across from the Chancellory. The captain speculated disrespectfully on how many more pieces of property he had accumulated, as his awe of the minister cooled rapidly.

'We will talk about Roosevelt at Casablanca, Aristotle in Greece, and Field-Marshal von Paulus in Stalingrad,' Goebbels lectured in rich, melodious tones, orienting the meeting. 'Last night I read a book by one of our best journalists who got out of America just in time. It was a perfect picture of American life, business, culture, and politics. Roosevelt is one of the worst enemies of modern culture and world civilization. If we don't succeed in definitely defeating the enemy, made up of Bolshevism, plutocracy, and lack of culture, the world will be in for the densest darkness. We are actually carrying in our hands the torch that brings light to humanity. So it is no surprise to me when the President of the United States commits a stupid blunder at the conference in Casablanca. But understand, Captain Zenner, you are here because the Germans also made a mistake in Morocco.'

The initial flattery Zenner had felt with the invitation to exclusive Lake Wann was not to last because of a soldier's endemic rankling resentment of civilian luxury that also reeked of political hyprocrisy. Goebbels as Minister of Propaganda controlled the publishing houses and motion-picture industry that publicized him as a man of simple tastes, the son of a humble workingman, who was dedicated to the cause in the Spartan style of Hitler.

But he was cynically collecting his share of the loot like Göring and the rest of them, Zenner thought. Serving real coffee when even ersatz was hard to get. And chocolates. Both worth more than money these days. There was no rationing in this swanky villa with the proffered plates of meats, cheeses, and fruits, like a coloured relief map of the occupied countries. Maybe it was a gracious effort to treat one of the troops, but it had the opposite effect on the captain, who had lately fought house to house with the enemy.

'When I joined the party of National Socialism, I put behind me the decadent intellectualism of my university days and have since been guided by the ideas of the Führer,' Goebbels proclaimed. 'History begins in Germany with Hitler. But there are still some pieces of gold to be mined from the past, like the sayings of Aristotle.'

It wasn't only the house that fed his bitterness but the whole area, Zenner thought. On a similar hot day in July his father had taught him to swim on the nearby Wannsee beach where the Berlin crowds came on Sunday. There was boating and sailing. Who could forget his thrilling first ride on a steamboat? And the day during the Depression when his father spent a suitcase of inflated paper marks to buy beer and pretzels for himself, pigs' knuckles and sauerkraut for his mother, and pancakes for young Konrad....

'When there is unrest and trouble from his subjects, a ruler must invent terrors,' Goebbels went on. 'Find some plot against the state, whisper the wells are being poisoned, the food contaminated, the daughters ravished, high officials about to be assassinated, the treasury undermined, the farmers robbed and their crops destroyed, military secrets being given away.'

There was no stopping Zenner's memories: My father said that's what the Reichstag fire was all about.

'Find anything that will arouse the people to a pitch of excitement against some common evil,' Goebbels stated. 'Then invent a terror to destroy this enemy of the state.'

The man uses his vibrant voice like an instrument, Zenner thought. He had heard Goebbels at mass meetings and over the radio, but up close he was even more the suave charmer who made one forget his imperfect, un-Aryan image. He seemed all head and words and bones without flesh. Studied manners. Yet he was the brains and the Führer the heart of the movement. Hitler told them what to do, and Goebbels told them what to think.

Two sides of the same bad penny, Zenner heard his father say again. But, as always, his old man was only half right. There was only one man who mattered, anyway. One Reich, one people, one leader.

'The Jew served his purpose as a devil,' Goebbels continued. 'Now he's gone from the country, and Germany is pure. When I consider how Berlin looked in 1926 when I came here, and how it looks now with Berlin free of Jews, I get a feeling of achievement.'

He said that matter-of-factly, Zenner thought, like an idea used and discarded. While even now he reacted to 'Jew' and boiled up at the circumcised scum of the earth, Goebbels suggested a salesman who could switch to an opposing brand and sell it with equal conviction. It was probably how he acquired this high-class house with five servants, a valet, and a male secretary, including the beautiful young woman who had danced across a hallway. The big shots of the party had done well with the confiscated property of the Jews. The Reichsminister didn't need them anymore.

We are led by failures who seek revenge, his father had said. The bottom dogs are now the top dogs. Draping a uniform on an underprivileged person creates instant authority. The insignificant achieve significance. And profiteers, black-market operators, and embezzlers wear brown shirts. Shut up with your treasonable talk, Zenner snarled inside to still the voice in his head. He'll see it in my face and I won't find out why I'm here, away from the ministry, 'so we can talk without being seen'.

'We are in this war from which there's no turning back, so we must march on together, Captain Zenner. But new terrors are necessary. At Casablanca Roosevelt gave us a perfect one: unconditional surrender. All his life our Führer prophesied what the Bolsheviks had in store for us. Now it comes from the mouth of Roosevelt himself: All Germans will be sent to Siberia as slaves,' Goebbels said. 'In the First World War it was the French colonial blacks who occupied us. This time it will be President Roosevelt's American niggers.' He grimaced his disgust. 'Words are weapons. From his arsenal of democracy Roosevelt placed in my hands ammunition of incalculable value. The equivalent of a battle won!'

Goebbels was speaking through him, as to a roomful of reporters, Zenner thought with annoyance. The Reichsminister had seen his party file. He didn't have to be harangued. He was an SS captain, tattooed with Hitler's truths on skin, brain, and heart. Devoted to an ideal, he had taken a blood oath, loyal unto death.

'Roosevelt compounds his foolishness by trying to separate the Nazi party from the German people. He believes in the myth of the "two Germanys".' Goebbels' voice was suddenly strident. 'How ignorant the man is! Roosevelt knows we were voted into power in the same fashion – and at the same time – as he was. Ever since then the German people have been behind their leader. Their adored Adolf! They placed him where he is. He depends on them. They trust each other. Because Hitler is the voice and the soul of Germany!'

Then he faced Zenner, modulating into intimacy. 'You know the Wedding district of Berlin, of course, Captain.'

The captain ran a finger down the scar on his right cheek that some thought resulted from the traditional student duel. 'That's where I got this —'

His parents weren't aware fifteen-year-old Konrad was a recruit of the Hitler Youth until he came home with a slashed face after a Berlin street brawl against a Communist youth club in the Red political stronghold. They thought he belonged to an athletic association. After that Adolf Hitler became a member of the family. 'The camel in the tent,' his father said.

Goebbels mused for a moment. 'Once when we Nazis were nobodies, not a deputy in the Reichstag, they tried to kill me when I organized a meeting among the Red rats. But times change.' He grinned. 'Yesterday I went back there after the barbarian British had bombed the district. Back to Acker Street, which was once one hundred per cent Red, where they had thrown beer bottles at me fifteen years before,' Goebbels said with infinite irony, then spoke as though he had been to a coronation, with the ruins like triumphal arches.

'I stood in the soup kitchen and participated in the feeding of the people. The men and women workers each received me with an enthusiasm that is as unbelievable as it is indescribable. The fire fighters were still pouring water on the smoking buildings. I told them the dirty bombing by the enemy of helpless people in Berlin was bad, but it would be worse if the Slavic-Asiatic hordes overran all of Europe. The Russians are not people with culture like the Germans but an inferior conglomeration of animals. We must save ourselves and all world civilization from these beasts in human form. Our people understand the meaning of "unconditional surrender" when Stalin claims he will take ten million workers for five years for reconstruction at the conclusion of peace. He will remove production facilities and the workers with them for reparations. When I told them our captured soldiers at Stalingrad and all our men would not return home but remain in captivity as forced labour, it was a terrible thought to every woman and mother. Our people would rather defend the last remnants of our walls than accept such shameful peace.'

He continued expounding: 'Bombing breaks buildings but not the spirit of people. We will never lose the war because of morale. Or through the revolt of the masses. In the First World War the Bolsheviks made a revolution in the German Army by calling it the Kaiser's War. If I had been there, it would not have happened. Today our soldiers fight with great discipline and courage because they believe in the Führer. Hitler thanks God for giving him Germany, and the Germans thank God for giving them the Führer!'

He wasn't there to exchange ideas, Zenner knew. But he thought it would be wise to offer more than approving sounds and facial expressions. Even the old stuff.

'In *Mein Kampf* the Führer told the world and taught us Germans the war against the Bolsheviks was to the death,' he affirmed by rote. 'The Führer has always said he would never capitulate as we did in the last war. Roosevelt is a fool to think otherwise.'

'You of the Waffen SS understand, Captain Zenner,' Goebbels emphasized significantly. 'Certainly better than the Wehrmacht. They need your kind of education.'

He had repeated the right thing, Zenner congratulated himself. A parrot, his father described him, and told his mother to feed their son crackers.

'Look!'

Zenner's thoughts were broken by the shout of the Iranian guide that reached him over the roar of the Lancaster's four engines. He had pulled aside the blackout curtain to gaze on the scene below them. They were passing over the capital city of his country, and the Iranian was overcome with emotion.

'How beautiful!' he exclaimed. 'It makes me want to cry!'

The commandos were amused with their excitable guide, and those nearest the window rose to share the view with him. The colonel ignored them, still looking inward, thinking of what it had cost him to lead this mission. Goebbels had exacted a pound of real flesh and blood when he had forced Zenner to break the last link to his father and mother.

He had done what he had to for the Führer. But Goebbels seemed to have more significance in Zenner's life as a Nazi than Hitler himself. Which was strange, he thought, because he hated that twisted little man now.

There was the sound of moving vans arriving outside the house. Goebbels excused himself and limped across the room to check the valet's shipping receipt. His possessions were important to the Reichsminister.

Zenner shifted in his seat, feeling trapped. Thoughts and ideas were burdensome in a time of action, unless they led to an action. Like the second mistake at Casablanca Goebbels was dangling before him. He was sure everything said had some bearing on the matter because every word and gesture of Goebbels seemed automatic like a windup doll.

It was hard to imagine how he had idealized this man in his teens. For it was Goebbels who had inspired young Konrad to snatch an armful of his father's favourite volumes from his beloved library and throw them on the great bonfire of books, 10 May 1933. 'Remember, my son,' his father had called out, 'Germany is the land of Mephistopheles, Faust, and the Pied Piper of Hamelin.'

Now ten years later, at twenty-five, Zenner could still see the flames of the funeral pyre of books before the hawklike face of Joseph Goebbels as the great orator made the unforgettable speech that seared his soul for ever. He had marched at midnight in the torchlight parade to the square at Unter der Linden where thousands of students had gathered. To the books they had brought were added the truckloads collected by storm troopers. The words rang out.

'It is a strong, symbolic act.... The past lying in flames. The future will rise from the flames within our hearts.... Let the un-Germanic spirit of these books burn.... Brightened by these flames our vow shall be: the Reich and the Nation and our Führer, Adolf Hitler. *Heil! Heil! Heil!*'

Today Berlin itself was burning after the air raid. The Reichsminister of Propaganda, who didn't look a day older, now lived off the fat of the land, his valuable booty put underground for insurance. When Goebbels made that famous speech, he owned little more than his eloquent words. Now nothing was said without his permission on the radio, the press, or film. Starlets got ahead by visiting his villa.

Times change, Zenner thought. But not for me. Or my father's tears.

Then Goebbels hobbled towards him, as if to accept the captain into his trust. Zenner stiffened in the chair, his huge body alert, impaled by the dark, piercing eyes of this crippled, strange, and powerful man.

'Captain Zenner,' Goebbels began, then noticed the black wound badge the captain had earned at Stalingrad. He touched it by way of acknowledging his achievement. He also wore an Iron Cross and the Roll of Honour clasp. 'It wasn't the German soldier who lost the battle of Stalingrad and died for the Führer and the Fatherland. It was the weak and cowardly Field-Marshal von Paulus who would not follow the Führer's orders,' he continued in coarse candidness. 'After Stalingrad our Führer doesn't believe in the generals of the Wehrmacht any longer. These monocled "gentlemen" of the old school make him sick with their fawning and faithlessness. They cheat and disappoint him and show their disloyalty in many ways. When they give him figures and statistics, he now is convinced they are lying. The Führer says they are opposed to National Socialism because they are reactionaries. His faith is with the revolutionary new breed of soldier like you, Captain Zenner. Men of the Waffen SS who understand and believe in what the Führer desires for the German people.' His voice lowered to an undertone. 'Captain Zenner, I didn't meet you in my office because the Wehrmacht has spies everywhere. The Führer has suspicions that they are plotting against him. We are taking the necessary precautions, of course. But you will say nothing—'

'I swear it.' Zenner restrained an urge to stand up. 'I'm ready to defend my Führer with my life!'

Goebbels put a hand on Zenner's shoulder. 'I know your family history. Your loyalty is unquestioned. I'm leaving nothing unsaid because you must understand why the Führer will require extraordinary means to win the war. For that he will need extraordinary men.'

Zenner felt calm assurance, as if already chosen, and some of his characteristic swagger came back. There was behind him a career of success that justified arrogance. He was Aryan blond and blue-eyed, big and athletic, and so he had been pushed upward through leadership schools and the intense indoctrination courses in blood and soil, racial theories, and living space beyond the borders of Germany, matriculating at the élite SS school in the medieval Wewelsburg Castle founded by Reichsfuehrer SS Heinrich Himmler. The coming of war was like a graduation exercise he had studied towards. He cheered the announcement. Then came medals and wounds in special paratroop and commando units, including time with action groups, fighting Russian partisans, Polish patriots, and Jewish guerrillas. As one of Himmler's promising young SS guards he participated in the revenge for the assassination of Reinhard Heydrich by the Czechs. Tracking the murderers. And Lidice. Captain Konrad Zenner had never failed an assignment. He was Goebbels' extraordinary man.

'Stalingrad was a hard blow, we cannot deny. We need more courage now and stronger nerve. If correctly led, the German people can survive the strains of war,' Goebbels pursued with imperial frankness. 'Today the front lines are consolidated. With the present stabilization the Führer is preparing a counter-offensive of decisive proportions. It will be a massive effort on all levels, ground, air, sea, and diplomatic. We will have a great fleet of submarines with new magnetic torpedoes. There will be fourteen-ton rocket bombs to destroy the cities of Moscow, London, and New York. We do not fear the American soldier, Captain Zenner. Only their factories. We will reach them with the aid of German science, which has never ceased working for the Führer for a moment's rest. They will soon complete research in the realm of atomic destruction like the world has never seen. Believe me, Captain Zenner, whichever side produces a revolutionary novelty of destruction can end this war in twenty-four hours. Think if such an immense weapon had dropped on Casablanca.'

He was inside the secret bunker of GHQ, and Zenner hung on every word. The hint of an arms race that could dramatically reverse the war was exciting. Every German citizen spoke of the 'wonderweapons' that would soon be unleashed on the enemy.

'I have never doubted our victory,' he asserted. 'I was always confident the Führer would come up with a miracle.'

'If only the Wehrmacht had men like you, Captain Zenner. To me the only complete human being for our time is a Nazi,' Goebbels said with lordly hauteur. 'That's why I spoke so much – to add to your faith and confidence. An important part of the counter-offensive will be the use of terror – "unconditional" terror like never before. You are here because you understand that weapon.'

'I've done my share of killing,' Zenner said, thinking again of Lidice. When he had bragged about it, his father had said Konrad killed a world. 'Maybe too much.'

He saw instantly they were the wrong words from the way Goebbels' wide mouth twitched. Zenner had revealed a flaw in his armour. It had been a slip of his usually guarded tongue which in itself was a weakness in the highest security echelon. He blamed his father.

'Hitler has told me he desires the future of the Fatherland to be in the hands of the young heroes of today. Men without mercy or pity, having broken with tradition. Supermen of the white Aryan race who are beyond good and evil. Strong men who rule by terror alone.' Goebbels reviewed him sharply. 'But you still have some religion left. Some lingering sentiment. A touch of regret.'

Zenner's tension snapped like a limp puppet of this master manipulator of men, with his lost chance. It was work for Hitler himself, and he didn't measure up. Let the assignment and what the Germans should have done at Casablanca remain mysterious. While in Berlin, he should see a certain woman; that would make the trip worthwhile.

'I've heard men like me are supposed to have the gleam of pride and the independence of a bird of prey because of our special training,' Zenner said carelessly. 'But I was raised a Catholic like you, Dr Goebbels. And the war isn't over yet.'

Goebbels burst into laughter of genuine glee. Just then his uniformed aide hurried in with a telegram. He lingered a moment to observe the reactions of his superior, then returned to the office. Zenner could see the message was of sobering importance as Goebbels folded the paper but didn't put it away. Then he stood off, momentarily oblivious to Zenner, as if to organize his thoughts on the serious matter.

If the Reichsminister's humour was favourable or not, Zenner couldn't determine. He had spoiled things because he hadn't been able to perform the trick of thought control he had named Zenning. He had got the idea from a book in his father's library on Japanese Zen, a name of amusing appeal. He had adapted some of the methods to his needs; he could empty his mind or concentrate on a single thought. However, it demanded isolation – not the presence of a Minister of Propaganda. It explained why his father's dissension ran rampant in his head. And out of his mouth to expose the damning weak spot in his character. Memories were not a knapsack one could leave in the barracks....

Goebbels shattered the reflective interlude.

'Captain Zenner, I'm certain you have been asking yourself about the second mistake at Casablanca besides President Roosevelt's. Ours, eh?'

'I've been curious,' Zenner replied prudently.

The Reichsminister launched into his thesis.

'It was good weather in Morocco on that date. Perfect for flying and fighting. So they sat there, the President of the United States and the Prime Minister of England, their general staff, and assorted so-called statesmen, like mechanical targets in a shooting gallery. Why didn't we eliminate them in a blitzkrieg attack? Why didn't we wipe them off the face of the earth with one gigantic blow?'

Zenner thought it wasn't the kind of event one advertised in a newspaper or on the radio, but he remained tactically silent. A man of few words, he had already said too much.

'We knew it was coming beforehand,' Goebbels said. 'Our counter-intelligence reported the North African undertaking they called Operation Torch as well as the meeting at Casablanca well in advance.'

Zenner couldn't hold back. 'What happened?'

'These facts were sabotaged among the Wehrmacht bureaucrats and not reported to the Führer with sufficient clarity.'

'Criminals!' Zenner hissed.

'If the proper measures had been taken this would not have happened.' Goebbels held up the telegram. 'The enemy has just invaded Sicily!'

It was bad news, and the captain looked it.

'I must prepare a message for the people of Germany,' Goebbels said urgently. 'Captain Zenner, you have my permission to see the Führer at once at Wolf's Lair. He will give you the personal orders to organize a group for which we have no name. Perhaps the secret would be better kept anonymous. Your mission will be what the Führer has designated as "direct diplomacy". Good luck.'

Bringing his big body happily out of the tiresome chair, Zenner gave the Nazi salute with prodigious pride and gratitude. Then, as he turned to leave, Goebbels halted him with his siren voice and a gesture of familiarity, as though affairs of state could be suspended for the moment.

'I laughed because you struck so close to home,' Goebbels explained with polite consideration. 'At your age I had the same difficulties with my religious father and mother.'

Zenner began to seethe. His disillusion and mistrust of the man returned in a rush because he was reopening a closed subject in his file. The Devil's Disciple, his father had named Goebbels. For once his opinion coincided with his old man's. What was the goddamned clubfooted dwarf's idea?

Zenner said evenly, 'They aren't a problem anymore to me.'

Goebbels was amiable and righteous. 'What you did took great courage and love for your country,' he said. 'There is no place for defeatism in time of war, and I have dealt harshly with the offenders.'

Zenner had not communicated with his parents before returning to Berlin from Stalingrad, wounded and dispirited. There was a Jew occupying his room, his father's former law partner before the Nuremberg Laws. He was an illegal, somehow having escaped deportation. The SS captain had gone into a rage. The Jew was taken off to his doom, but his father was implicated and imprisoned. His wife had insisted on sharing the blame and joined her husband in the concentration camp.

'You had no choice but to have them arrested. It was your patriotic duty,' Goebbels buttressed him. 'If you would like to release your father and mother now, I'll arrange it for you.'

It seemed like a friendly offer, Zenner thought. He was being handed a chance at redemption. His violence had been fired by defeat, but he hadn't anticipated the outcome of the terrible scene. Now he could be calmly contrite. Yet this might be a final test of his fidelity and toughness by the Reichsminister, a cunning runt. The Lord giveth with one hand and taketh away with the other.

'Giving shelter to a Jew is punishable by death, isn't that so, Dr Goebbels?'

'We behead people for that.'

'So my father got off easy,' Zenner said. Goebbels knew his father was against the regime. 'Let them stay in the camp.'

Goebbels smiled and raised his arm. '*Heil Hitler.*'

Captain Konrad Zenner returned the salute and went out of the house to the waiting Mercedes that would take him to his first meeting with his idol, Adolf Hitler.

Four months later in the sky over Iran, having been jumped in grade by Hitler himself, Colonel Konrad Zenner congratulated himself. He was shed of all human ties, responsible to only one person in all of creation, his Führer. He was on an important military mission for his Fatherland. A German couldn't be more favoured and lucky.

3

Captain Peter Harvis sat in the darkened conference room of the American embassy with other members of the staff viewing a 16-mm film entitled *Since the Casablanca Conference.* It was after lunch, after the tennis game, and he was entertaining afterthoughts.

Is this me, a poor boy, living like the rich with more money than I can spend?

Is this me, a shy boy, having all kinds of women with a wife on the other side of the world?

Is this me, alive and well in Tehran, with my best friend dead and buried at Pearl Harbour?

Thank you, my country, 'tis of thee. God bless America for making war so that I can live like a conqueror.

In the flickering dark Peter counted his blessings after one year, taking stock of himself in a foreign country, called Iran. Or Persia, as he preferred it. He had met citizens of the land who insisted it had begun thousands of years ago as Iran and should still be so, as if to throw off some outside influence. But the name Persia was more poetic to Harvis and maintained the historic continuity of myth and illusion because words have power. They can win love or lose wars, he knew.

Persia was plangent. What did Iran say? The other name spoke volumes.

On the screen before him the first six months of the Second World War in 1943 was unreeling. The end of Operation Torch and the beginnings of Operation Husky, other American military actions around the globe, and Allied battles. Fresh from a tennis court, Harvis possessed the insouciance of a civilian as he observed other members of his country's armed forces on land, on sea, and in the air. The Persian Gulf Command patch on the shoulder of his tunic might as well have been a country club emblem on a blue blazer. After he had perceived the resortlike aspects of his overseas assignment, he had written his wife, 'Baby, I have upgraded myself to Detached Service with the rank of Tourist First Class. . . .'

The staff members in the room were glum, reminded by the scenes on the screen that the world was burning while they fiddled in Iran, the most noncombat of war zones. From previous experience with these films produced by daring combat photographers, Harvis knew when the lights went up, the audience would return unchastened to their Persian delights. He would do the same.

Everyone realized it took all kinds of people to make up an army and win a war. So don't bitch or gripe, Mac. And don't volunteer, for chrissake.

The city of Tehran was like an enormous nightclub offering Harvis every conceivable pleasure, ancient or recent, for a nominal charge. With a cast of characters from all over the world in colourful costumes, performing any human arrangement, kindly or corrupt.

It was a long way, in countless ways, from the middle-America of Moreno, California, his hometown.

His sense of being the pampered guest of an Eastern Midas-rich potentate (a paid vacation abroad) was reinforced by the perfumed arrival of Betty Lanteri, the ambassador's secretary. She took the seat beside him in the back row of the conference room, then gave him a kiss of antic affection. They were forced to whisper.

'Haven't seen you all morning.'

'I was fighting the war,' he replied.

'What front?'

'Tennis court, British embassy.'

'Mighty stylish foxhole,' she observed. 'No wounds, I hope.'

'Tennis elbow,' he said. 'Threw my service off.'

'I'll check Army regulations to see if that could be considered a service-connected injury.'

'I like that.'

'I like you.'

They kissed, then held hands like lovers in a movie house. It transformed the newsreel of the war, a flicker of disasters, into just another Hollywood product.

'Who's the star?' she asked.

'Alan Ladd.'

'I expected Clark Gable.'

'I tried to get Humphrey Bogart.'

'War is hell.' She sighed.

'Semper Fidelis!'

'I want my money back.'

'Sorry, no refunds.'

She said, '*C'est la fucking guerre.*'

Her style of speech never failed to startle him since the day they had met, one year ago. On the day he arrived from the

Pentagon Betty Lanteri became the second woman in his life and his first infidelity, a new plateau of love. He was unpacking in his Tehran apartment when she walked in with material from the embassy library, including *The War Department Guide to Spoken Persian.*

'This stuff is worse than useless,' she had said, tossing it aside, then adding with mock coyness: 'It was just a silly lovesick girl's device to gain entrance to the privacy of a handsome young man.'

She was a language and political science major from Barnard and Columbia, already in Iran for two years. Harvis recognized her as the typical female intellectual with glasses he had gone to college with, the ones who got the grades. They wore cotton stockings in boycott of Japanese silk, picketed the German consulates against Nazi aggressions, protested Mussolini's attack on Ethiopia, and weren't popular with the boys.

'I had to beat the other broads in the office to you,' she confessed. 'They're prettier, but I'm smarter. Besides, I want to lay an All-American type for a change.'

Harvis retreated from the sexual assault, pleading the need for a shower and a shave after the long flight from the States. The moment he was stripped Betty entered the bathroom. She took a long, leering look of admiration and began to undress. He froze.

'I'll scrub your back,' she said facetiously.

Harvis learned later she was a four-syllable woman at the embassy and a four-letter one in the bedroom. The ambassador leaned heavily on her abilities. But Harvis had never heard a woman use such words. He wasn't inhibited at home, but his wife only allowed herself an 'Oh, shit!'

'When I take off my clothes with a man, my brains go to my ass,' Betty said. Her body was not as beautiful as his wife's. 'Zoftig,' she described herself, being Rubens-round.

An explosion on the screen erased his reveries as Harvis was brought back to the deadly reality of the words and pictures.

The Second World War was still in progress.

Then Betty reached over and grabbed him playfully in the groin. He let go a startled gasp that was overwhelmed by the doomsday narration and battle sounds of the newsreel. She had timed it to the winning of the Battle of Stalingrad by the Russians. There was a synchronized few bars of upbeat music, an orgasm of notes.

'For chrissake, Betty,' Harvis said, his eyes on a screen filled with death and destruction. 'Can't you see what's going on? People suffering —'

'Live, darling,' she said, nibbling on his ear and opening his tunic. 'For tomorrow we die.'

Betty's lips moved irresistibly southward from his neck, following the trail of her sensitive fingertips. By the time the war on the screen had progressed from the Battle of the Bismarck Sea to the victory parade on the streets of Tunis, Harvis began to surrender to passion. At the Allied invasion of Sicily he was pathfinding for Betty's hand to his brass belt buckle, when the door of the conference room burst open, throwing a beam of light across them. There was a hasty shifting of bodies in the glare from the hallway.

Ambassador Philip Gordell squinted into the half-dark room, calling out, 'Captain Harvis!'

'Yes, sir!' Harvis responded, buttoning up.

'The Russians have caught six German paratroopers in their zone,' Gordell announced dramatically. 'We're invited!'

'Coming, sir,' Harvis said.

'Well, almost,' Betty corrected, then gave him a friendly finger to encourage his exit.

Gordell said, 'I need you, too, Betty.'

Betty followed Harvis out. 'I am your slave,' she said low in Persian at his back.

'I am your servant,' he muttered in Persian over his shoulder. They enjoyed practising the country's traditional politeness.

The projectionist stopped the film. The sensational news had formed the embassy staff into groups. What were Nazi commandos doing in Iran?

'Hey, don'tcha know there's a war on?' someone asked.

4

The second Nazi paratroop team had left the British Lancaster. It was now the turn of the last six commandos to jump to the earth of Iran. Their broad-backed leader almost filled the doorway of the plane, as he looked out to a sky strewn with scattered clouds, off which the sun reflected. He glanced at his watch, then beckoned them forward.

Colonel Konrad Zenner gave each of his men a farewell pat like a diploma from the master, as they flung themselves into the cold air. He watched them out of sight, smiling down at this last team, as if he had tossed a bouquet of flowers to the people of Persia, instead of seeding the arid landscape with war.

He was left with three men, his own bodyguard. As the crewmen closed the plane door, the colonel sat down opposite the trio, two Germans and an Iranian. Alone now, this unit exchanged grim smiles, anticipating their time to leave the big bomber for this last leg of the long flight.

Yorck and Sepp were the colonel's 'twins', both twenty-two, though they were physically as unalike as a polar bear and a wild boar. Their minds matched. Twenty-three-year-old Reza, the guide, was a middle-sized, dark, and fervent Iranian tribesman. They made up his hard core, Zenner's prize pupils.

He could depend on them, Zenner thought, rubbing the gold medal he wore beneath his uniform. It had a diamond in it, a special gift from Hitler. He had vowed never to remove it as long as he lived. The contact generated a glint in his blue eyes that reflected the Führer as his guiding light, as if the Nazi catechism revolved in his mind in perpetual emotion.

Only the Hitler cause could have brought together a quartet of such diverse backgrounds, Zenner thought, forced to continue his unpractised reflection on the long flight. Yorck was from a Junker family of proud Prussian landed aristocracy, having a long name with a 'von' and an 'auf' in it. Zenner's father was a lawyer and middle-class, which by Germany's rigid custom would have the colonel defer to these heel-clicking snobs with lengthy pedigrees from feudal days. At the same time, Zenner reminded himself, he was brought up to look down on someone of peasant origins like Sepp. His third man, Reza, was royalty, the wealthy prince of a tribal family that went back to Iranian antiquity.

Because the social barriers were insuperable, Zenner would not have met such men before the Third Reich. Hitler had created a classless society. But though they were equal now in a common crusade, the colonel's authority was unquestioned. He was on top; he expected Germanic obedience below.

He was indebted to the Reichsminister of Propaganda for his present eminence. Again his thoughts returned to what he had been forced to give Goebbels in exchange for the privileges he now owned. How did he come to despise a man to whom Zenner owed so much? Although he advertised himself otherwise, the Reichsminister was a greedy, licentious hypocrite, Zenner decided. The Führer was exactly the opposite.

5

The German prisoners seemed unreal to Captain Peter Harvis, like actors eerily out of the newsreel he had watched in the embassy only minutes before. It was as if the bad guys had parachuted from the screen into the laps of the audience. The captured Nazi commandos were being held in separate cells in the Russian stockade for further interrogation. An extra company of Russian soldiers provided guard duty.

Harvis was part of an eight-man delegation of Allies, four diplomats, each accompanied by an aide. He didn't know General Ibrahim, of Iran's Foreign Office, but Harvis had played tennis that morning with the others: Ambassador Volodya Volkoff, the host; Minister Sir Henry Bolt; and Ambassador Philip Gordell. He saw no hint of that sweaty informality now.

With them were British Major Sam Skeene, thirty, an angular man with a bitter vision of battle still in his eyes; Russian Colonel Boris Artukin, thirty-five, a grinning giant in a constant state of survivor's glee; and mustachioed Major Ali Mirza, from the Tehran police headquarters. He was a plump man, about forty, a composite of Persian paradoxes.

Each of his friends had a mannerism that Harvis considered a nervous tic by which he could chart their tensions. The Englishman had a habit of rubbing his knuckles, the Russian laughed too much, and the Persian was never without his worry beads.

'Persia bores me,' Skeene had told Harvis.

'This is paradise,' Artukin said when they first met. 'I have been rewarded for dying so many times in the war.'

Mirza thought his country to be the whole world.

Harvis had left Washington with neither expectation nor desire of seeing the enemy up close. He measured the success of his career in the Army by the distance from the front. He had requested an overseas assignment only when the opportunity of Persia had presented itself. It was about as far behind the battle as one could get and still be in a 'war zone'.

Now the sight of the paratroopers both fascinated and sickened him. They were five Germans and one Persian, all in their early twenties. Only the Persian had been spared a merciless beating after interrogation by the Russians.

Harvis spoke low, covering his revulsion, to Gordell. 'They must have talked their heads off.'

'It was either that or lose their heads,' Gordell replied, adding sagely: 'Maybe they kept their mouths shut.'

'That would be simple sadism.'

'Don't be simpleminded.'

While the young Nazis were immobile bloody lumps strewn around their cells, the Persian prisoner moved behind his bars like a caged cat, even as they looked at him. He was the last one in the line of captives. The delegation paused to confer.

'Well, did you learn anything?' Ambassador Gordell asked Volkoff. 'It appears as if you had a "talk" with them.'

The Russian ambassador glared at Colonel Artukin. 'They learned nothing!'

'We are not finished, sir,' Artukin defended himself.

'Major Skeene studied engineering in Germany,' Sir Henry offered. 'He has the language. You'll crack them, won't you?'

'I'll do my best, sir.' Skeene nodded optimistically.

General Ibrahim indicated the Persian prisoner. 'He will talk to Major Mirza,' he said confidently.

Mirza smiled reassuringly.

'Gentlemen,' Volkoff said, 'we shall leave the field to the experts.'

The diplomats retired for cocktails at the Russian embassy. Artukin went to work at once, opening the Persian's cell. The national belonged to Mirza.

'He would not even give us his name,' Artukin said. 'A Persian clam!'

Mirza entered the cell.

Harvis edged up to witness. Artukin and Skeene were already prospectively peering at the nearest Nazi prisoner, like meat merchants.

'What is your name?' Mirza asked.

The Persian was barely twenty, younger and smaller than the German soldiers. His uniform was still Berlin clean, paratroop boots shining. It was plain he had no intention of responding to Mirza.

The major began another question, then changed his mind. The prisoner's lips were set into silence. Mirza shot an embarrassed glance at Harvis, who had been joined by the other two men; then he pushed the prisoner out of the cell.

'It will be better in my office,' he declared.

Artukin pantomimed a disemboweling knife.

'Open up the clam and swallow him, Ali!' the Russian encouraged cruelly.

The Englishman pointed his finger like a gun barrel.

'If he doesn't talk, we'll shoot him with the rest of these Nazis,' Skeene threatened ferociously. 'Bang, bang.'

Harvis knew these were not idle words to intimidate the young Iranian. He understood now that the excess of Russian soldiers represented a midnight firing squad. They were like salivating bloodhounds scenting a kill. He couldn't breathe this air of brutality.

'I'll go with you, Ali,' he suggested eagerly. 'Just to watch you work.'

Mirza put him off politely. 'Thank you, Peter. I will call you when it is time.'

Then the major marched off with his prisoner.

Harvis had moved forward without expecting a rebuff. Artukin slyly put a restraining arm around the clumsy American. He wriggled free.

'Lay off, Boris.'

'You should watch us work, Petroushka,' Artukin insisted craftily. 'We have business to finish.'

Harvis didn't budge. 'They look pretty finished to me.'

Artukin guffawed and winked knowingly. 'I saw by your face you did not approve of the appearance of these Fascist scum of the earth.'

Skeene took malicious pleasure. 'I thought you were getting seasick. I was about to shout "man overboard".'

Harvis reddened, feeling like a boyish bungler. They had caught his involuntary reflex to the sight of the bloodied commandos that had turned his stomach. Artukin had detained him to turn the screw in a bit of barracks humour.

'Okay,' he said. 'But didn't you lay it on them a little more than the rules require?'

Artukin turned to the Englishman in exaggerated hurt. 'He does not like my work. What do you say of it?'

'Colonel Artukin, I think you very much improved their looks,' Skeene affirmed in an official manner. 'The military ideal of a handsome Nazi is a dead one. I'd say you came fairly close to perfection.'

The Russian made a theatrical bow of gratitude. 'Thank you for the compliment, Major Skeene. You are a man of great knowledge in such matters.'

They formed a brotherhood of battle that could never include him, Harvis thought almost enviously. Admirable men. But not when they treated him like a junior partner.

'You guys had it, all right,' he conceded graciously. 'You have to get even. But it's not for me.'

'Someday I will tell you what they did to my mother and my sister and my wife and my children.' Artukin grinned crookedly. 'But you would not want to see me cry.'

'After Boris dries his tears, I'll do a striptease and show you what these bloody beasts called SS men did to me with a cigarette when I was a prisoner,' Skeene advised him earnestly. 'Hatred helps a lot. Especially when they withhold information we need.'

'What are they, mechanical men?' Harvis inquired seriously.

'No, Petroushka,' Artukin said. 'They are animals we must teach to speak.'

Then Artukin opened a cell door and went inside. Skeene followed him. After a moment, Harvis joined them. Maybe this wasn't a perverse humour they were playing with his nerves, but basic training.

'*Achtung!*' Skeene commanded.

The German lay on the floor with his back to them. When he rolled over, Harvis saw his swollen eye and the dried blood from a broken nose. He got to his feet with a kind of dull defiance, attempting to twist his cracked lips into a smile. What guts, Harvis thought.

'How many men were in your plane? And who was your leader?' Skeene demanded in German.

The Nazi gathered himself together and stood at attention, eyes straight ahead. It was his way of facing death, knowing silence meant execution, Harvis realized. It made a moment of impasse in the cell that was like the stillness of doom.

Skeene thumbed the knuckles of his left hand, as if to keep from striking the German. Artukin made laughing sounds in his throat and lit a cigarette.

The wordless scene was absurd, Harvis thought. There was a slow intransigent inevitability of the movements now that was maddening. The commando was Hitler's finest, one of the ersatz God's chosen people, choosing to die. Harvis had no doubt this German, about his own age, would take the secret of his mission to the grave.

Skeene held out his hand, and Artukin gave him the cigarette. 'Take off your clothes,' he commanded the German.

Flinching himself, Harvis saw the soldier shudder. Skeene's

intention was plain. He intended to do unto the enemy as they had done unto him. Probably in the same place, Harvis thought in horror. An eye for an eye, a ball for a ball.

The German ignored the command.

Only moments before Harvis had approved of revenge for the Englishman's torture in the prison camp, but now protest welled inside him. Yet it was a kind of rough justice, this vengeance, and Harvis quelled his words. He stood holding his breath now, poised like a frightened deer.

Then Artukin cheerfully ripped off the prisoner's uniform.

At the same time Harvis became conscious of the closeness of the cell. The oppressive lack of space. He tried to withdraw imperceptibly, as if disavowing himself from this barbarism, but he was already against the wall. There was no exit.

Perspiration gleamed on the German's body, naked now in the cold cell. It was his first sign of fear, Harvis thought. Not of death, but of the burning cigarette. More irrationality and improbability beyond his reason, Harvis thought nightmarishly. He was afraid he'd make a fool of himself and run.

Harvis began to sweat, too.

Skeene smoked now, savouring each puff, slowly scouting the German's wet skin.

Harvis thought suddenly that Skeene was prolonging the agony to test him as well, though their eyes didn't meet. He sensed Artukin was observing him, expecting what? This must be what they meant by exquisite.

The German didn't waver anymore, taking his eyes from the cigarette, looking beyond the Englishman.

Skeene inhaled for the final time, almost finishing the cigarette, then reached out to rub the burning ember on the prisoner's testicles.

Harvis broke and fled from the cell.

A scream chased him into the night.

6

Harvis went to a bar to rid himself of the taste of shame. The drink didn't wash it away. Then he drove fast and far to outdistance it. Speed couldn't shake it. Finally, he felt there was only one way to release it. Betty Lanteri was already in bed when he called.

She said, 'Come right over, darling.'

Harvis drove to her apartment with the comfortable realization that she had dominated his sex life after their first night. Except for a period when Artukin involved him in his collection of wild-breasted exotica, they had been constant. There was a special situation with a certain Iranian girl he didn't count. But Betty was aware Tehran had whores from everywhere, black, brown, white, yellow, and golden girls like the promise of Moslem heaven.

'Don't bring me a dose,' she had said reasonably, and that ended it. She was not jealous. It wasn't love she felt for Harvis, just an affectionate friendship.

'Screwing is all that matters. Words lie. A man and a woman coming together is true communication,' she had told him. 'Knowledge is power in bed.'

Betty had a theory that sex was a man-and-woman comedy act performed for their own joyous applause. A routine to be improvised or improved by studying the masters of the art. Sometimes it was a hit, sometimes a flop. But you never gave up working on the act. Or looking for the right partner. It belonged to the happy mask side of the theatre, strictly for laughs.

To increase her general knowledge of Middle Eastern mores and language, Betty Lanteri was translating from the Arabic into English *The Perfumed Garden*, by Shaykh Nefzawi. Harvis had never heard of this sixteenth-century book of erotic techniques and delights.

'It's a how-to manual,' Betty had informed him. 'Do you realize our English–American position is culturally backward?'

Harvis laughed. 'Even his fucking name sounds dirty!'

'Don't ever use that obscene word in regard to sex again!'

'Fucking?'

'No, dirty!'

They practised what the Shaykh preached. The coital positions were called manners, and there were twenty-five of them, each designated with an Arabic name. The ninth manner was *Lebeuss el djoureb* (fitting on the sock), and Betty bought the required pantaloons for the seventh manner, *El kelouci* (the somersault). All of which made for hilarious antics, and they joked about 'good' or 'bad' manners.

Harvis would be bringing back sexual souvenirs to his wife in California he wasn't sure she would accept; they had been reared and gone to school together. Their lovemaking had been blissful ignorance.

As he approached her apartment, Harvis could almost feel Betty's presence like a force field. He was a one-woman man who had never experienced such female, honest advances. There had been no time to consider his unfaithfulness or to be conscience-stricken. He told himself later it was what men did overseas; he still loved his wife. It hadn't entered his head to replace her with anyone. But that first night Harvis, flattered, excited, and overeager, failed Betty.

And now she was waiting in bed as Harvis took off his uniform. But from the moment they embraced, he knew it would be bad for him, almost like their first night. The healing he hoped for in Betty's arms wasn't taking place.

Much too soon, Harvis went limp inside her; then he rolled away. Dazedly she lay there, passion unspent.

'What's the matter, darling?'

'I guess it was mind over manner,' he said.

'What do you mean?'

'I keep thinking about the Germans.'

She flared. 'Now I have one more reason to hate the bastards. The lousy spoilfucks!'

'I'm sorry.'

She sat up and glared down at him, cheated. 'You came charging in here like a bull loaded on Spanish fly.'

'I thought it would help.'

'I don't mind being used, as long as I get my fair share,' she told him. 'Tit for tat.'

He angered. 'I said I was sorry.'

'Shove it.'

Harvis left the bed. With his inadequacy there returned the full humiliation of the flight from the stockade. He went into the bathroom and started the shower. He didn't stay long. When he came out, towelling himself, Betty had turned on the light and put on a gown. She had two drinks waiting, the fires inside her subsided.

The shower hadn't helped. He passed the drink and picked up his wristwatch from the bedstand.

Betty raised her drink in a toast. 'Here's to peace on earth and in bed.'

Harvis stood staring at his watch, unhearing.

'You act like you lost it for ever,' she said. 'What's one fizzle among so many fireworks?'

Incongruously, Harvis strapped on his wristwatch. He wore nothing else.

'Pretty soon, at midnight, those five Germans will be up against a wall in front of a Russian firing squad.' He took the drink now and tasted it. 'I'm missing my first execution.'

'Weren't you invited?'

'Do you think Colonel Artukin and Major Skeene would let me off?' he said. 'They're teaching me the trade.'

'Why didn't you go?'

'Only six hours ago I couldn't take their beating. I need a hell of a lot more time to take their shooting. Maybe for ever.'

'It's war. Trite but true.'

'That's what Boris and Sam call it,' he told her. 'For me it's still cold-blooded murder.'

He drank up, casually naked. He knew she was looking at him, longingly again. But he began to put on his clothes, knowing her regrets. That was what he liked about her. He chose to come; he was choosing to leave. She made no claims that would appear like female clinging.

Betty probed. 'Why are you sorry for them? I'm not. After all, they are the enemy.'

'Sons of bitches, but brave ones. You won't believe what they went through without spilling their brains.'

'You mean, you still don't know why they came to Iran?' She was the ambassador's secretary now.

'Just name, serial number, and *Heil Hitler*!' Harvis raised his hand in the Nazi salute.

'That's serious business,' she said.

'I still can't believe it,' Harvis said.

The ethics of torture and his response to their act were suddenly the least part of his experience. What motivated a man who appeared to be his opposite number in the enemy camp?

'Dropping behind the lines into enemy territory has to be for special people, I'm sure.' Her words sounded like a reprimand.

'Aren't you being carried away, Captain Harvis?'

'I'm not a glory seeker,' he declared. 'But a man can't help wondering if he has the same kind of guts.'

'To do what?'

'These were not German draftees,' he said. 'They were volunteers.'

She was impelled out of the bed.

'I consider them programmed murderers.' Her office tone went up. 'Certainly not heroes!'

Harvis stopped knotting his tie, reflectively. He had never seen her so agitated. Of course, there was the sexual frustration. But there were things he had to work out.

'I suppose you have to ask yourself if they're Nazi fanatics or German patriots,' he said. 'It's still a question of belief. Faith in a cause.'

'That democracy is decadent,' she said. 'That there's one pure white master race. That everyone else in the world is shit-coloured and should be shot or enslaved!'

'That's the part that bothers me,' he admitted. 'For those ideas they were willing to be tortured and die for the Führer. You have to see it to believe it.'

She confronted him clinically. 'Don't you believe you have it? This all-fired faith in a cause.'

'I'm not sure I could do what they did for it.'

'Don't you think we're in the right in this war?'

'Sure, we're on the side of the angels. And we're undoubtedly dealing with the devil,' he said. 'But that's what they think. It's right versus right.'

'Bullshit!'

'The German church backs them.'

'God is on the side of the one with the most firepower,' Betty said. 'I've had a sneaking suspicion you're a very disgustingly moral character, Peter. Fuck off, chum.'

'You're not so immoral yourself, baby,' he bantered.

'I can't think of anything more immoral than a man and a woman arguing philosophy in a bedroom,' she told him with disgust. 'You've got your balls and your brains mixed up today!'

She walked out of the bedroom for the support of a drink. When she came back, Harvis was ready to leave. Completely dressed, he still felt naked, having exposed so much of himself beneath the skin. Before Betty, as with Boris and Sam.

'Good night,' he said, getting up a smile.

She raised her glass in farewell. 'May your shadow never grow less,' she said in Persian.

He bowed slightly, matching her Persian. 'May your kindness never diminish.'

She was her own woman, not the dependent kind, Harvis thought, as he went to his jeep. Not like his wife.

7

The nuance and malevolence of Colonel Zenner's imagination and the infinite detail with which he had worked out his plans were evidenced when he and his men landed at the target area in the hills of Shiraz. The underground had everything he had asked for and more, even to a hole dug in which they could bury their parachutes, helmets, and the heavy German Army uniforms necessary for the flight, leaving nothing incriminating.

There was a small tent with which to protect the portable radio equipment, weapons, explosives, food, ammunition, sleeping bags, clothes, and other commando gear. Now the team wore cotton tropic clothes and sweaters, exchanging paratroop boots for lightweight rubber-soled shoes, appearing like travellers.

The underground was in contact by radio, operated by expelled Germans, who stayed behind after Iran declared war on the side of the Allies. They were helped by Iranians who hated the English and Russians and loved their country. There were citizens who hated all governments, including their own, and loved money more. The Germans had plenty to spend, particularly towards those Iranians and foreigners who collaborated out of sympathy with Fascism. The success of his mission was dependent on the loyalty and ingenuity of his local sympathizers, and Colonel Konrad Zenner had every reason to feel confident.

The first setback came at midnight.

The colonel had arranged for a test contact with all the stations on the underground network, including the commando teams in their hideouts. It would be necessarily brief, a checking out of signals; the orders would come later. There was hardly room for two in the tent, Yorck, the radio operator, who sat on a stool, and Zenner, holding a flashlight. The huge colonel had to hunch over.

Reza and Sepp stood with quiet attention outside the tent opening. The campsite had been selected by the Iranian, who was born in this part of the country, two and one half hours by air from Tehran. The city lights of Shiraz, visible below them, dwindled as the night progressed.

Then Yorck broadcast: 'Wolf Pack Number One, Wolf Pack Number One.' There was an interval while he received the signal from the message centre. What he heard forced a gasp from Yorck that alarmed the others. He signed off, removed his headset, then turned and cleared his throat, but still spoke huskily.

'They caught Wolf Pack Number Two. They've been shot. They have the Iranian in jail.'

There was stunned silence as the colonel left the tent, followed by Yorck. They looked to their leader.

Zenner's tone was without a trace of emotion, unhesitant, and positive. He had lost comrades before in this war; he knew all about death. And he knew his men.

'The Germans didn't talk. They died thinking of the Führer and the Fatherland,' he said, looking at the Iranian.

'You're thinking my countryman will tell them everything,' Reza said. 'No?'

'They'll squeeze him.'

'Can he take torture?' Reza made a grand shrug. 'I don't know if anyone can, Colonel. But him I don't know anything about, only his name. You ordered all of us not to talk to each other.'

Dubious thoughts could grow from discussion, and Zenner had not permitted it during the training period. He had left them time only for food and sleep. Foreigners were a weakness, but a necessary evil, and the commandos had orders to shoot the guides at the slightest provocation.

'What do you think he'll do?'

Reza threw up his hands, expressively.

'Who knows? Everyone knows all Iranians are different. You looked in Germany for an Iranian guide, and you found him. With me, I looked for Germans and found you.' The distinction was important to him. 'We are different in our reason for joining you. He came for money. I came for politics.'

Sepp said, 'If you talk, I'll cut your tongue out. Before I kill you.'

Reza remained unruffled.

'I know, Sepp. Before you kill me, Yorck would cut off my balls. The colonel would put a bullet between my eyes. I'm sure my countrymen understood what you Germans will do to a treacherous guide. Then why is he alive? If Wolf Pack Number Two didn't trust him, he would be dead.'

It was a telling point.

'Get some sleep,' the colonel directed.

8

In the morning Harvis sat in his embassy office and typed his report of the previous day's activities.

Ambassador Philip Gordell relied on his written work as part of his communiqués to Washington, and Harvis weighed each word. For a long and discouraging time the ambassador had been convinced the State Department took little notice of his explanations, cautions, warnings, comments, and recommendations. Whether it was his new intelligence officer or the changing importance of Tehran, attention seemed to be in his direction these parlous days. Gordell liked the fresh interest his young aide expressed in the country and combined it with his experience in the embassy's representation. Mostly they had a colloquy at work. The ambassador never permitted their business to intrude on the tennis court.

It was Betty Lanteri who organized Gordell's final ideas on paper and read what Harvis handed in first.

'You have literary talent,' Betty had commented. 'Have you ever done anything?'

'The book and lyrics of a college musical,' he told her. 'I adapted an idea from George Bernard Shaw in the style of Gilbert and Sullivan and copying *Of Thee I Sing*. I'm not a cheap crook. I steal from the best.'

'My kind of show was *Pins and Needles*,' she said. 'Did you ever hear of *Meet the People*?'

'I made a special trip to Los Angeles to see it.'

'Ever tried serious stuff?'

Harvis shrugged it off. He thought what he had written was immature but 'serious' enough after reading Anatole France: 'Certain truths particularly hard for hierarchies, established order, common sense – one must present them with extreme nonchalance.... I am taken for a jester, for a juggler, for a sophist.... I have spent my life wrapping dynamite in little fancy packages.'

'What's serious?'

Meanwhile, Harvis had begun collecting material the moment he landed in Iran. Being here was an accident of war, and his departure was just as unpredictable. He retained copies of his reports, wrote detailed letters home, and clipped publications. A book? A play?

'What do you think of F. Scott Fitzgerald?' Betty had asked.
'Why?'
'Just testing.'
'I sent away to Brooks Brothers to get button-down shirts like his, that's what I think.'
'That figured, Mr Gatsby,' she said contemptuously. 'Your clothes model is a whore in Hollywood.'
'He died there in 1940.'
'He was dead before he arrived.'
Betty Lanteri had a special aura about her, coming from New York City, the publishing centre. She was ethnically rooted there; one parent was Italian, the other Jewish, both of them professionals. As with books, Harvis was an omnivorous reader of magazines, popular, little, literary, radical. Enviably, she had been reared in the midst of what Harvis had read about three thousand miles away.
Greenwich Village. Free love. Union Square. The Yankees. Costello's saloon. The Algonquin Hotel and its Round Table. The Empire State Building. Madison Square Garden. The subway. Fifth Avenue. Metropolitan Museum. The jazz joints. Broadway, The Theatre Guild, Theatre Union, Group Theatre. Carnegie Hall. The Statue of Liberty. The parades. The rallies. The lectures where American literary giants slugged it out. Visiting European men of letters. Writers' Congress. John Dos Passos himself had signed Betty Lanteri's copy of *U.S.A.* Once at a party a famous author had made a pass at her, but his wife had made an hysterical scene. Another well-known writer was a homosexual she had discovered after taking him home. It was doubly disappointing because he was a 'proletarian' author, her favourite category. All others, of course, were bourgeois sellouts.
Harvis hungered for this sort of gossip.
The city girl countered his curiosity with questions about California. She thought Harvis was a 'Huck Finn living in Steinbeck country'. (*Grapes of Wrath* was the *Uncle Tom's Cabin* of our time!) One day in the future Betty planned to arrive in San Francisco and be met by civilian Pete Harvis. They would drive to Monterey, Yosemite, Los Angeles (not Hollywood), San Diego, and Tijuana. A real 'Thoreau-back'.
'My wife wouldn't understand,' Harvis told her.
'You mean you haven't told her about me?'
She was baiting him, Harvis hoped. Betty Lanteri was a genuine door slammer out of Ibsen, nobody's back-street con-

cubine. If New York was his idea of reality, she yearned to get away from the city. She'd show up in Moreno sure as hell.

'Worry not, sir,' Betty said mischievously. 'I want to marry a man smarter than me.'

And now, as Harvis wrote about the German prisoners for the ambassador, reporting the cruel interrogation and their execution, he considered what to extract for his own literary use. He withheld his desertion from the inhuman cell; his emotional disasters didn't concern the State Department. However, he did type it out honestly for himself, diary-style.

Yesterday was a ride down a rampaging rapids. He was lucky to make it to shore. Soaked, then all wrung out, leaving nothing hidden, not a secret crevice in his soul.

Then balm had arrived in the mail that morning in the form of a baby-powder-scented letter from his wife. It contained a new picture of their son, Jeff, now one year old. Everything else dissolved into insignificance, as he feasted his eyes on the photograph.

Until this moment he hadn't felt like a father. He had been generously given a two-day furlough for the birth of his son, but Jeff arrived underweight, an incubator baby. He glimpsed him through a hospital window and left the next day for Iran. It had been unreal. Truth would have been in the touching. There followed a span of ocean and continents between Harvis and the event that letters and progress reports failed to close. Too much was happening overseas. Distance and time had worked other changes in his sensibilities. Something had been lost in translation from the English to the Persian words like home, country, father, mother, wife – and then son.

His man-child was standing on his feet, fully formed and laughing healthily. Harvis realized his umbilical cord to home had stretched but not snapped. The thought of his son, if not the touch, was a permanent part of him. Maybe these months away from Moreno was the required period of gestation for a man to get used to the idea of fatherhood.

He didn't notice Betty had entered the office.

'What's so amusing about that picture?' she asked.

Harvis sighed happily and put the photo down. 'Nothing,' he said, unwilling to share the warmth of his personal vision. It was like a return of his lost privacy. 'What's up?'

She spoke with harried efficiency. 'The ambassador has just picked up Mike Callahan at the airport. He'll want to see you the moment he arrives.'

'*The* Mike Callahan?'

'Incognito from Cairo.'

The Cairo Conference between Roosevelt, Churchill, and Chiang Kai-shek had begun. Harvis knew the President's bodyguard always travelled in secret when away from Roosevelt because his movements were considered important by the enemy. His business related only to the Commander-in-Chief.

'What's it all about?' Harvis detained her indiscreetly, knowing better, but this was unprecedented.

'You keep your secrets, I'll keep mine,' she said on her way out. 'But it's so big you won't believe it.'

Betty was privy to the ambassador's thoughts and coded cables. They were outside her relationship with Harvis. Her hint and the unannounced visit of Callahan were portents enough in the winds of war and diplomacy.

In a few minutes he would be receiving privileged information, some secret state manoeuvre, that was usually levels above his status. Harvis should have been excited. But his heart was elsewhere. The birth of his boy was no more something that had happened to his wife in a distant place. He was no longer disconnected.

Before a man becomes a father, he has to have been a son himself. And his thoughts about Jeff became mingled with his feelings about his own father. For one thing he swore he would talk his kid's ears off. When Harvis was a child, his father hadn't spoken much to him as if he were his mother's son. Later he didn't speak to his father because school interfered. Or so it seemed. Maybe his mind now was playing tricks with this matter of communication. Nevertheless, his memory was of a constant clash with his old man, particularly after a 'thing' when he was thirteen. He had no other word for it then.

On his last furlough they had come a bit closer; he had seen his father's first tears when he kissed his son farewell. Harvis was going overseas. His father was proud of his commission and his education, neither of which he had received. He had been called up near the end of the First World War and never left training camp. In the train station he had tried to carry his suitcase, but Peter wouldn't permit it.

They walked together ahead of his mother, a private goodbye, as the steam of the train swirled about their legs. When she caught up, there was a gush of tears. Harvis wore a reassuring smile.

After that he went blithely, eagerly, and unquestioningly off to the war abroad.

In Persia Harvis had begun to revise and soften towards his father, though the unspoken 'thing' still existed. Maybe he had reached adulthood. He was drafting words to put into a letter of reconciliation.

He determined his relationship with Jeff would be less barbaric. If fathers and sons had to fight, couldn't there be more love than hate in the timeless battle?

'I've got a kid to support!' he said aloud, as if Betty were still in the room.

He was really unprepared for the role of provider. Like being shot from a circus cannon, cracking the cozy insulation of the Army, and propelled into life-after-the-war. What would he wear? Harvis couldn't see himself out of uniform. He had always bought the best clothes.

He began to pace the office in self-centreing circles. There was a mystery about tomorrow in his mind. He was uncertain about teaching again in small town, USA. Harvis didn't consider himself a provincial anymore, a character in a Henry James story of narrow Americans abroad. Not after the city of Tehran and the society of diplomats. (Someday, he promised himself, he would reread Henry James in terms of the international theme.)

Harvis had prepared himself at the state college for a teaching job because his father, a depression-marked man, had said, 'Get on the government payroll. You can't lose, son.' His father was an insurance man, a habitual card gambler. 'Get security, son.' But the world had opened up to Harvis. Like one of the watermelons his mother grew in the backyard, breaking and spilling seeds. Moreno was a hick town, period.

Ambassador Gordell wanted him in the State Department; he thought of Harvis as a protégé. It was civil service and retirement benefits. And security, Dad.

There was no comparison between the San Joaquin Valley to the romantic capitals of the world. Gordell, of inherited wealth, was offering a lift to a social pinnacle. (He had once asked Harvis about his wife's 'style'.) Snobbishly, Harvis was tempted by this bid to an upper-class club. Yet he hadn't accepted.

HARVIS: Diplomacy is duplicity, sir.

GORDELL: Artfulness and national interest.

HARVIS: National interest is egomania. The 'I am number one' syndrome.

GORDELL: That's patriotism.

HARVIS: Here are some patriots, sir. Hitler, Mussolini, Stalin, Churchill, Hirohito, Roosevelt, Chiang Kai-shek, de Gaulle.

GORDELL: What do you suggest?

HARVIS: Wait till they die and start over. With a United Nations such as they're talking about.

GORDELL: Back to diplomacy.

9

'Hey, soldier,' the man in the back seat said to the GI driver. 'Step on it, willya?'

'Yes sir,' the American private said.

He hit the horn of the Chevrolet, but the horse-drawn droshky in front of the car wouldn't budge. There was little room to manoeuvre on the busy thoroughfare jammed with modern and ancient vehicles of all varieties.

'The traffic in Tehran gets worse everyday,' Ambassador Gordell said in defence of his driver. 'Just like your nerves, Mike.'

'Is it showing?' Mike Callahan was worried.

'When I saw you in Casablanca, you could still manage to work up a smile,' Gordell reminded him. 'Where's the wise-cracking Mick I used to know?'

'It's getting to me, all right,' Callahan confessed. 'Anyway, I don't like to be too far from the Boss.'

'Cairo is just around the corner.'

The forty-eight-year-old man had been Roosevelt's shadow from the governor's mansion of New York to the White House. When Mike Callahan left the conference in Cairo, it was to be one of the few times he was away from the side of the President.

'Maybe he should get off the main drag,' Callahan pressed impatiently when the car was stalled again. 'This is like World Series time at Yankee Stadium.'

Gordell leaned forward and instructed the driver. 'Get on a side street.'

Before they had picked up Callahan, Gordell had told the driver not to hurry back to the embassy, to get stuck in the usual midday traffic tie-up so the ambassador could make time with the man who knew the Commander-in-Chief better than anyone alive these historic days. Information pouring into the coding room kept Gordell up to date on the proceedings of the Cairo Conference. The three Allies 'in harmony with those of the United Nations at war with Japan will continue to persevere in the serious and prolonged operations necessary to procure the unconditional surrender of Japan'.

The meeting was mainly on the Pacific and Asian theatre offensives to be determined by Roosevelt, Churchill, and

Chiang Kai-shek. Again, Stalin had claimed he was too busy with the Nazis to attend. Russia was not yet at war with Japan.

Unlike Casablanca, Ambassador Gordell had not been invited to this meeting. Lend-lease was not on the agenda. But the arrival of Mike Callahan was the next best thing. He was backstage, the one remaining with the star after the supporting cast had gone. Though he stood in the wings, the President's bodyguard did 'hear things'.

It was Callahan who told Gordell at Casablanca about the private meeting, some called it a confrontation, between General Charles de Gaulle and President Roosevelt when everyone around the conference table had been dismissed. The Frenchman had sought the American's backing, but Roosevelt was in favour of twin rule between him and Giraud of the Free French. De Gaulle wouldn't share power with anyone. Callahan was a lone witness, partially hidden behind a drape, forgotten by the mutually antagonistic men.

The President's bodyguard overheard the bitter words exchanged between the towering Frenchman and the American trapped in his chair because his legs would not carry him. As if to add insult the general paced around the man who couldn't walk. At an angry crescendo, Callahan removed the pistol from his holster, reflexing as any trained defender, though neither of the arguing giants was aware of it.

For the ambassador's contemplated memoirs it was the priceless material of a book. He pumped Callahan for more of the same that could be the real stuff of history. If de Gaulle ever became a force in postwar France, there was no doubt in Gordell's mind the events at Casablanca would affect his attitude towards the United States.

Callahan obliged with some 'inside dope' just to make conversation. It was not the time to reveal the reason for his visit to Tehran, not with the straining ears of the driver who was more interested in the conversation of the VIP's than the street traffic.

'The English bulldog is sure doing a lot of growling,' he said. 'But the Madame is the real pain in the ass!'

The generalissimo's wife was doing all the interpreting for him, Gordell learned, thus placing herself in the centre of negotiations. Her American education was paying off. The ambassador knew Churchill had to resent the interference of Madame Chiang and the major emphasis of her interests at the Cairo Conference over the European theatre. The defeat of Hitler was primary to the Prime Minister; Japan would be easier later, was his contention. Although President Roosevelt shared a similar broad view of the global war, he could not slight the legitimate demands of the generals, Chiang Kai-shek, Douglas MacArthur, 'Vinegar Joe' Stillwell, and Admiral Chester Nimitz.

'You should've seen the Boss before we put down at Cairo.' Callahan smiled. 'Just like a tourist from Podunk, Iowa.'

'What happened?'

Callahan told how the President had ordered his pilot to vary the pattern for a sight-seeing flight over the Egyptian monuments, the Suez Canal, the Sphinx, and the Nile.

'Did he say anything?'

'About the Pyramids he said, "Man's desire to be remembered is colossal".'

Ambassador Philip Gordell memorized it.

'So this is your Captain Peter Harvis.'

From the way the tough man's steel-grey eyes drilled into him, Harvis could tell he was being judged for an important job. It wasn't a military situation, but he tried to stand at attention while Mike Callahan walked into the ambassador's office.

It had to be a big deal because Gordell was levitating, Harvis thought. He saw the ambassador as a split character, the youthful acrobat of the tennis court and the aged world-weary career man behind the desk, thinking of retiring to his Pennsylvania farm. Now Gordell had brought his game persona inside. He seemed about to make a triumphant leap over an invisible net.

'Where were you before this deal, Captain Harvis?'

'Two years' intelligence evaluation in the Pentagon,' Harvis replied. 'Before that high school teacher.'

'Wanna bet you play top tennis?'

Callahan was almost behind him when he spoke sharply, and Harvis should have been startled by the sudden irrelevancy, but an athletic peripheral vision saved him.

'How could you tell, sir?'

'I know how the old Ivy League champ operates,' Callahan said. 'Do you let him beat you?'

'I don't think he'd like that,' Harvis said. He decided Gordell hadn't briefed him. Callahan, the supercop, didn't depend on hearsay or require profiles on people. He had X-ray eyes. 'But he has his good days.'

The ambassador, who was staying out of it, chuckled. 'A lot more than you think, Mike,' he boasted.

'What would you say he picked you because you must've made your college team?'

Harvis had expected his application to be turned down in Persia. The impulse had come to him one day while sharpening pencils in his Pentagon office. Other Americans in the battle for freedom were flying planes, driving tanks, and steering destroyers. It was not an urge to shoot a gun or to be shot at, but just to experience a foreign 'theatre'. Boredom had set in with his marriage and his work. If it was truly a war of liberation, then Harvis thought he should be among those liberated first. He had volunteered for overseas duty, but there were better qualified men for the Iranian post.

'I don't know about the ambassador's judgment,' he said. 'But I'd sure as hell thank my father for buying me tennis lessons he couldn't afford.'

Gordell released a suppressed laugh from across the room.

'It's true we own the doubles title of the diplomatic colony,' he intervened. 'But Pete's got other attributes besides a big serve. We need young men with his tact and perception in the State Department. But he won't let me recommend him.'

Callahan asked, 'Why not, Captain?'

'Because diplomats get you into wars, Mr Callahan.'

'You ain't kidding.' Callahan snorted like a man who'd been there. 'Okay, Phil. Your boy's quick on his feet, can't be surprised, and has an independent mind. Tell him.'

Gordell leaped lightly into action.

'Pete.' He pointed to the portrait on the wall, making a ceremonial moment of it. 'He, Franklin Delano Roosevelt, the thirty-second President of the United States, is coming here. So are Joseph Stalin and Winston Churchill.'

'Uncle Joe and a Certain Naval Person – as he likes to call himself,' Callahan added. 'The Big Three.'

'We hit the jackpot!' Gordell crowed an outcry he used for tennis put-aways. 'Coo-eee!'

Harvis realized why the ambassador was so buoyant. It was a supreme moment in his career, a last-minute windfall of recognition. Tehran was an obscure post where State had put Gordell out to pasture before the war. He had worked hard and had been complimented by both Shahs for his knowledge of the language, but there was little necessity for diplomacy. He was primarily a social guide for American business hustlers. Recent events had elevated the mission. Now the prospects were great, but Harvis didn't see how it benefited him.

'Pete,' Gordell said finally, 'you'll be in charge of security for the President while he's in Tehran. Under Callahan, of course.'

Callahan made it clear. 'From the airport to here and around the embassy. I'll expect detailed reports and pictures daily before I come back.'

Harvis breathed a low whistle of awe, his spine tingling, now in tune with the jubilant ambassador.

'What about the Persian Gulf Command?' he asked. 'I'll need help from the general.'

He had directed it at Gordell, and Callahan caught a dubious implication. 'What about him?'

Gordell minimized it. 'General Andrews and I are having a little jurisdictional friction. But we'll work it out—'

'There's no time for protocol. I'll take care of Tom-Tom,' Callahan said, familiar with such rivalries. 'He'll give us the troops. But I want the Presidential detail under one roof near me.'

Gordell couldn't contain himself. 'Roosevelt will be staying here, Pete. In this building!'

The opportunity expanded in Harvis. 'Historic!'

'About this embassy.' Callahan's tone brought them to earth. 'The Boss doesn't fear anything or anybody in the world but one thing: fire. With all the other security this place must be made absolutely fireproof. Even if you have to tear down walls.'

Harvis was reminded of the ambassador's story about the battleship-fortified swimming pool the bodyguard had constructed for the President's air-raid shelter in Casablanca. But the fire precautions mystified him.

Callahan saw his perplexity. 'Your President can't walk, Captain Harvis. He can't move by himself for one step without help. He's never without pain. He wears braces. How he hates those braces. How they hurt him. So we have to carry the Boss.'

Harvis didn't realize his Commander-in-Chief was a disabled giant. Callahan was aware that the average American hadn't heard the full story of Roosevelt's invalidism.

'He can operate in a wheelchair, Captain Harvis,' Callahan said. 'That's why I'll want doorways wide enough. I don't want tables or chairs to get in his way. You won't need only soldiers to protect the Boss but carpenters. You know me, Phil. If I have to put a new roof on this joint, I'll do it.'

'Everything will be in order, Mike,' the ambassador assured. 'We'll have just as many fire extinguishers around here as guns.'

Harvis asked, 'When are they coming?'

Callahan's eyes dug into him. 'Not "they" but when is "he" coming,' he instructed scathingly. 'The President of your United States, Captain Harvis. Number One, get it?'

Harvis nodded, realizing that Mike Callahan was a one-idea man, a total obsessive – and loving – protective force.

'When the time comes, you'll be told,' Callahan said. 'Let me see a map of the city, Captain. How about a bourbon and soda, Phil?'

Harvis went to a collection of maps in a closet used for the purpose, while Gordell bounded to the liquor cabinet. Callahan walked about the antique Persian rug.

'The wind gave us a rocky time coming in through the mountains. That ride could be too rough for the Boss. What about ships and trains in this country?'

Gordell handed him a drink. It was too early, but he poured himself a congratulatory scotch.

'I'll guide you over all the possibilities, Mike.'

'We'll have to move fast,' Callahan pointed out.

Harvis hung up a large map of the city of Tehran with the significant landmarks plainly marked. He was calmer now, beginning to feel the weight of his responsibility. Callahan lighted on a chair temporarily. Gordell hovered in happy anticipation.

'You landed here, Mr Callahan,' Harvis began. 'This is the Shah's palace.'

Callahan shot from his side chair. 'Those are the British and Russian embassies!'

They were opposite each other in the heart of the city.

'How far are they from here?' Callahan asked.

Harvis answered, 'About four miles.'

Callahan looked troubled. 'That's bad. The Limeys and the Russkies are cosy neighbours. But what about us? Say hello to our first big headache, gents.'

'What do you mean?' Gordell asked.

'It's a summit meeting. They're calling it the Tehran Conference. Code name, Eureka. For the first time in the war the Boss gets together with Churchill and Stalin. Eyeball to eyeball in the same ball park,' Callahan said, then made a joke: 'The world serious. So what's the big question? The first one, I mean. Which one of the Big Three travels those four miles? For one week *in the open.* Going to whose embassy to talk?'

He paused to let Gordell and Harvis absorb this. 'There's only one answer.' Callahan's face set arbitrarily, jerking a thumb towards the portrait of the President. 'The Boss is the Nazi number one target. That's how we operate, men.'

'The President will be our first consideration, of course,' Gordell said. 'But Ambassador Volodya Volkoff and Minister Sir Henry Bolt rate their chiefs just as highly. We'll have to work out some Allied co-operation.'

'You grab what you need to protect our interests.'

'Pete,' the ambassador said judicially, 'give him some background on our situation, while I freshen his drink.'

Harvis brought out another map and hung it up. It showed Iran and the neighbouring nations of India, Afghanistan, the USSR, Turkey, and Iraq. Red string was pinned inside Iran to indicate the occupied zones.

'When England and the Soviet Union occupied this territory, they made a tripartite treaty with Iran. That was two years ago,' he explained. 'We've been here – that is, the United States Army – less than a year to supply lend-lease to the Russians, under the protective command of the Persian and Iraq Force of the British Army. And, of course, the Russians have their own zone of influence.'

Harvis continued, expecting to be cut short momentarily by Callahan, who wandered about with his drink. The non-combat American Persian Gulf Service Command operated the port facilities at Khorramshahr and Bandar Shahpur, also Iran's railways and principal highways for truck convoys. But the United States was a political anomaly, being neither a hostile occupying force nor in the country by right of treaty. Meanwhile, American technicians had rebuilt the ports for Victory ships, added rolling stock and equipment to the railroad system, and improved the highways. American GI's worked in unbearable heat to deliver millions of tons of lend-lease goods and war matériel through the 'Persian corridor'.

'In effect the British and Russians are here to protect us,' Harvis concluded, pleased he was permitted to finish. Apparently, he had fascinated the stony-faced man.

'Okay, they carry the guns and we carry the goods.' Callahan assimilated the information. 'Sure, you co-operated with our Allies. But in our favour, see?'

They saw.

The phone beside the ambassador rang, and he picked it up. 'It's for you, Pete.' He handed it to him.

Harvis conversed, then hung up, his face ashen.

'It was Major Mirza's office. They say I can meet the prisoner,' he informed them. 'But I'm thinking —'

Gordell was struck by the same thought.

'Oh, my God,' he exclaimed. 'They came for the conference!'

Callahan demanded, 'What's all this about?'

The ambassador told him about the beginning and of the end of the German commando team.

'It looks like everybody is coming to the party,' Callahan commented grimly. 'You'd better get going, Captain Harvis. Keep in touch.'

Harvis heartily agreed, 'Of course, Mr Callahan.'

'Good luck, Pete,' Gordell smiled. 'Let's see your big serve!'

Betty was waiting for Harvis when he emerged from the meeting. She appeared owlish in her glasses, affecting innocence. He knew she'd be in the corridor.

'Salaam, Excellency,' she greeted. 'What happened?'

Harvis hadn't changed his pace towards the exit of the embassy, and she kept up with him.

'I saw you listening through the crack in the door,' he charged sanctimoniously. 'You know what they do to spies during wartime, Miss Mata Hari. I'll see that you pay the supreme penalty!'

'What a break this assignment is for you, Captain Harvis!'

'I'll be seeing you, wiseass.' He beamed happily in farewell as he went outside.

She called out in Persian, 'May heaven never take you from me!'

10

Order and coherence, Harvis thought, driving his jeep through the streets of Tehran to police headquarters. And high purpose. He had it for the first time since he arrived in Iran. A sudden focus. Ironically, the job came from a tough-guy civilian named Callahan. It was his first meeting with ungloved authority in the Army, the hard knowledge that failure had consequences.

Until now Harvis had to acknowledge the confusion inside him. From the moment he faced this strange land he was attacked from all directions, physically, mentally, spiritually, by new ideas, sights, sounds, and smells. His senses were bombarded, and he wandered in bewilderment. The new stimuli unmoored him.

It was a thrilling sight the first time he saw Tehran at the foot of the mountain range. An island in the sky. As the sun rose from behind mythic Mount Demavend, the city held poetic promise, as from a magic carpet. But after Gulistan Palace and its Peacock Throne of jewels, the rest was a cultural shock of conflicting East and West styles, a hybrid of 1943.

He had arrived with an Aladdin's lamp dream of Persia. I-ran all the way. But the fantasy flopped.

Yet the city had mystic power he couldn't place. Tehran intimidated him, like an oncoming thundering herd. Harvis had never been to a large American city like New York, coming from uncrowded California and ordered to Washington, D.C. He wasn't used to crowds; he feared this one.

Today everyone was out, except the Jews because it was Saturday. Tomorrow the Christian Armenian merchants would close up shop. Yesterday it was the Shiah Moslems, the official religion. Did the Zoroastrians observe a sabbath?

He played his singsong memory game of alphabetical tribes with the crowd: Arab, Azerbaijani, Bakhtiari, Baluchi, Gilani, Kurd, Lur, Mazanderani, Qashqai, and Turkoman. The great unhorsed corralled with city workers. Their colours blurred with the beat-up buses, tired donkey carts, mangy horse droshkies. No place like homogeneous.

And the foreigners. Exiled, lost, transferred, shipwrecked. Then march in armies of Russians, English, and American troops. Now drop off thousands of Polish refugees. All blessedly shitting up a city with an aboveground sewerage system called jubes that flowed along the sides of streets.

Burgeoning boomtown. The bustle for bread. The clamour for money. The locust buzz of the bazaar. The rial truth.

Fragments of language. Then all Babeling at once, five, six, or seven hundred thousand people. The regal rich and extreme poor. Poverty and degradation that had caused Harvis to vent daily outrage and pity and charity. But now he could turn down beggars. Misery was company. He didn't recognize rags. He didn't mind the smell of corruption. He had become calloused, Harvis thought suddenly. What happened to a crew-cut American type?

He had made a real effort to learn Persian, hiring a teacher and translating Omar Khayyam. He did well with the language, but it spoiled the poetry. He found the Arabic script a tiresome business. The characters didn't belong to a non-Arabic people, who were of Indo-European origins. Actually, the Persians looked down on the Arabs. Harvis sympathized with Reza Shah Pahlevi, the exiled father of the present Shah, who tried to reform the language of his country with Romanized letters but was defeated by the Moslem mullahs.

His work was writing reports on politics, people, and spies. What Harvis didn't see or read about was supplied by paid informers, friends, and Allies. The informers sold their information to anyone, the friends were ill informed, and the Allies were self-serving. Iran was not where the upper-echelon espionage action took place. It was a hotbed of small intrigue and rumour.

Harvis had come to trust only his own taste and touch in any situation. Betty thought he was too romantic and apt to fall into sentimental traps. While she considered the deposed Reza Shah a progressive tyrant, Harvis saw him as the commoner who became king. The man from the ranks whose bearing was more imperial than the divinely rightful one.

'You always give the devil his due,' Betty warned. 'You'll end up in a hell of a mess.'

To Harvis the politics of the country were chaotic. Iran was ruled by a twenty-two-year-old Shah, newly enthroned, under foreign military occupation, with armed tribes who didn't recognize the central government, a paralyzed majlis, rampant inflation, and hunger created by high prices and food unharvested through lack of transportation.

Harvis had met His Imperial Majesty at the traditional diplomatic reception in March, the Iranian New Year, *No Ruz*. Mohammed Reza Pahlevi, the handsome Shah, was about his own age, which made for instant, if momentary, rapport.

'He's been educated in Europe,' Harvis said, describing to Betty the glittering experience. 'And he declared a constitutional monarchy. It's a beginning.'

'They should start with a republic.'

'Ready or not?'

'You've got stars in your eyes because you've been to a real Persian palace and met a live king,' she said. 'It's all a fairy tale.'

Harvis couldn't deny he was dazzled. 'Anyway, I hope he rides out the storm.'

'He'll go down with the ship.'

Harvis was handicapped by a lack of knowledge about Iran. Betty organized his reading from her own historical perspective and economic determinism. He read about Alexander the Great, Genghis Khan, Tamerlane, and the Koran-carrying followers of Mohammed. Then the modern times Bible-bearing Kipling characters, the neighbourly czarist, then Communist caviar coveters, German scientist tomb diggers establishing Aryan brotherhood, French Catholic art tracers and poetasters, and American missionary medicine men.

'So it's all about old gold and oil,' Harvis observed.

Betty said, 'Together that makes black gold.'

Nature determined the country's destiny, and geography exposed it. Big-power greed and small-power weakness. England and Russia clashed historically over Persia, then jointly occupied it in both world wars. Now there was the German drive to the East. Today the Americans were on the ancient scene. Coming from California, Harvis understood the corruption of oil.

'We're here to stay,' Betty said, making an educated guess. American experts, following the armed forces, were already showing up in Tehran, checking into the embassy. 'The Russians are afraid of us. And the English are afraid of our shadow. It's our turn at the well.'

The ambassador gave Harvis time off for trips, permitting Farsai, the embassy interpreter, to accompany him. Farsai was also his teacher of Persian. They worked on the language as Harvis drove his jeep over vast solitudes in the Land of the Lion and the Sun. There were storied Shiraz, ancient Persepolis, and blue-beautiful Isfahan.

They passed nomadic tribes, camel caravans, and pilgrims to Mecca. Mostly it was mud hut villages getting water from qanats, the uniquely Iranian underground aqueducts. The ancient past resembled a burden like a heavy debt. Trodding narrow furrows of existence for ever. Regulated by the seasons into automatons, even like the roofless nomads. Moving on the same tight trails for centuries.

He saw poverty and pride, poetry and prayer. And hats, all varieties and colours and sizes. No Iranian went bareheaded. Each piece of headgear revealed the man's region and station in life.

An old shepherd had asked Harvis, 'Is there a moon in America?'

'Yes,' Harvis had assured him.

'*Allahu Akbar*,' the aged man had said. 'God is great.'

Harvis ate kebab from a stick, picked up fleeting fevers, broke flat bread, blew charcoal under a samovar, got diarrhoea, watched a child weave a carpet, and listened to a muezzin from a mosque. Once he refused an offer of opium, and Farsai thought he had been impolite.

'I read someplace the road into addiction is easy, the road out very hard, and the usefulness of an addict almost zero,' Harvis said. 'I'm a whisky man.'

'There is a saying,' Farsai replied. 'Alcohol makes a swine out of a gentleman, but opium makes a gentleman out of a swine.'

The idea grew on Harvis after these journeys that his role was more that of a civilian tourist than a soldier on a tour of duty. He was encouraged in this elegant notion by the traditional Iranian hospitality and friendship, flattered with the respect and undeserved privileges. (He washed his hands before eating, then ate only with the right hand; never took too much food, drank only boiled water, brought his own toilet paper, relieved himself only in secluded spots – never exposed his body in front of an Irani male because of their modesty.)

There was a curious aspect of the Persian politeness and welcome that Farsai clarified for him. Mere sightseeing was something the peasants couldn't comprehend. They were historically used to alien hordes coming to conquer who were preceded by such innocent travellers.

'They thought I was an American spy!' Harvis laughed, relating his adventures to Betty.

'Aren't you?'

'What do you mean by that?'

She replied enigmatically: 'Moses sent spies into the Promised Land.'

Her words bothered Harvis when he wrote his report for the ambassador. The peasants understood better the nature of his work as intelligence officer than the sophisticated young American. His tourism wasn't a free ride after all.

Harvis parked his jeep at the Tehran police headquarters and bounded into the building.

Waiting for him inside the door was Sergeant Mostaffa, Major Mirza's young aide, who was a pleasant pistachio splitter. He immediately offered tea to the American.

'No, thanks, Sergeant,' Harvis said, realizing something was wrong. 'Where is the Major?'

'He is not here, Captain Harvis,' the sergeant reported, then repeated the courtesy. 'Please have tea.'

'Where is he?'

'The zurkhaneh,' the sergeant said. 'Please go there.'

'You told me to come here on the phone.'

Sergeant Mostaffa smiled. 'I informed you the major would permit you to see the commando prisoner.'

'That's true, Sergeant,' Harvis said. 'Is he here?'

'Yes.'

'Take me to him.'

The sergeant sighed. 'I do not wish to disappoint you, Captain Harvis. But it is possible only in the presence of the major.'

It was Mirza's whims at work, Harvis thought. There would be no dashing back to the embassy with some sensational news for Mike Callahan to take back to President Roosevelt in Cairo. Gordell would be just as anxious to hear something. He doubted now if the Iranian commando was even in the building. But the reason for this delay would reveal itself, reasonable or not, after he saw the major.

'I'll go to the zurkhaneh,' Harvis told the relieved man.

He turned about and walked out, furious. Persians toyed with time and truth in a manner that was maddening to a direct and energetic American. They worried more about form than efficiency. Harvis was always caught short because of this concept.

Sergeant Mostaffa had followed him to the jeep. 'Please have some tea, Captain Harvis.'

'Keep it boiling, Sergeant Mostaffa,' Harvis said. 'I'll be back.'

He was learning, Harvis thought, as he drove off. That was the perfect Persian indefiniteness about time. When an Irani said 'now' he meant 'this very hour'. *Far-dah* (tomorrow) meant 'sometime in the future'. When you leave the American embassy, forget your wristwatch.

Mike Callahan would never understand.

11

Colonel Konrad Zenner had brought his own private means for the Iranian mission, mental and physical, special equipment for the psyche and the material parts of himself. His astonished men were introduced to them, as they took their ease about the Shiraz hill camp, like sportsmen on a hunting trip taking time out for lunch. They had travelled light on the British Lancaster, with only sidearms, knowing the underground would well provide. But their leader had carried two extra items, a canvas bag and a custom black leather case. They had no idea as to the contents, but now the mystery was revealed.

Yorck sat at his post in the radio tent, nibbling at food, but turned so he could observe the curious activity of the colonel through the open tent door. Sitting on the ground, Reza and Sepp paid little attention to their meal, fascinated with their chief. All they knew about the personality of their commander, besides his worthy war record, was limited to the necessities of a training camp; he didn't sleep in their barracks. The rigours of the course had been unrelieved by nighttime companionship. They had not volunteered for a furlough. Now they were viewing a unique aspect of Zenner, far from their knowledge of military ritual and rather bizarre.

First of all, he sat apart from them, which they recognized as not uncomradely, but a part of his unusual system of living. Then he didn't share their rations. Their fifth-column friends had left ample and varied delicacies, really a German picnic. It was a feastlike contrast with the soldierly regimen they had left. But Colonel Zenner had his own diet of nuts, dried fruits, and grains, which seemed like meagre and inadequate sustenance for such a huge and powerful man. He preferred water to the wine they had found waiting for them. The good German hosts had also supplied a treat – American cigarettes. Their leader didn't smoke.

The rite had begun with the cleaning of a blanket, shaking it out, making it absolutely lint-free. After spreading it on the ground, Colonel Zenner had stripped to the waist, neatly stacking his shirt and field jacket, leaving only Hitler's precious medal on his bare body. There was sunshine, but it was not a warm day. When he sat down to eat on the blanket, it was a cross-legged position. Except for the marring scar on his face, he was a perfect figure of a strong-shouldered man, appearing like a giant bronzed Buddha.

He was six feet five. He had his men's respect. But now he seemed to grow proportionately, looming awesomely, as if he were adding powers to their mission that were magical. It fortified their fealty to Colonel Konrad Zenner.

His ceremony of eating had a timeless concentration and unconcern for anything or anyone about him. Yorck, Sepp, and Reza might have been on another planet. After that he opened his leather case which contained the separate parts of a special rifle. He cleaned them. Then he put the weapon together, tested the mechanism, broke it apart again, and returned it to the fitted compartments of the case. The meticulousness was not an example to his men; they cared for their weapons. It was his own observance of perfectibility.

It was time now for his breathing exercises. They were a deep intaking and expelling of air, as though he were drawing strength from the atmosphere and the sun to supplement his other nourishment. It included torso bending, forehead to the blanket, like bowing to an unseen God, though his only homage was to Hitler. The preparation, however, was towards single thoughts or the rejection of all thinking. The book in his father's library had inspired these ideas ten years before, attracting him first by the picture of a fierce Samurai warrior, long before the Japanese became war allies. Goebbels hadn't yet fully rationalized these inferior, coloured Asian friends. It was Zenner's only discomfort with the method.

His Nazi education had been a deliberate repudiation of the past. These forms the colonel practised were an incomparable aid to his control of mind and emotions. It had become a game. Thus, he could handle the loss of Wolf Pack Number Two with clarity and economy. It was a blow, but far from a fatal one. Their target had been Tehran. He would still infiltrate the city when the time came. The colonel didn't have to be there to describe their deaths exactly. They died bravely and even nobly. The Iranian guide was now the problem of the underground.

Eliminating them from his memory should have brought a pleasant nirvana of nothingness. The repression was incomplete because the days beyond yesterday were stubbornly unyielding. His blue eyes glowed fiercely but couldn't burn away his mother's last words as she left her home for the concentration camp with her Bible.

'I will pray for you, my son.'

Konrad Zenner was fifteen in 1933.

He was oversized for his age, a good athlete, whose idol was Max Schmeling. He dreamed of making the boxing team of his country for the 1936 Olympic Games to be held in Germany. Another ambition was to emulate the world-ranked tennis player Baron von Cramm. His father frowned on his interest in sports and the movies. Herr Zenner wanted his son to follow him into the legal profession. Konrad was more anxious to develop his muscles than his brains.

It was a time of political turmoil. Young people recognize crises; negation is not in their nature. Konrad Zenner found a yes to life in the Hitler Youth. He became a Teutonic Knight gloriously engaged in a crusade against the evil spirits that were polluting his country and the gathering enemies in the outside world who would destroy Germany.

There were plainly wrongs that had to be righted that any young person could perceive, as Konrad and his group marched and sang, blew trumpets and beat drums, hiking and camping among beautiful rivers, forests, and hills. They preferred primitivism to the despicable commercial city.

Konrad had listened to the endless debates of his father and his friends around the house, concerned with the economic and social chaos that stifled and bled Germany. It confused him, for the young yearn for structure and hope and a goal. Recruited by his best friend, the teen-aged Zenner found guidance in the Hitler Youth, which was led by youth.

Zenner and his pal took an oath to restore their country's fallen honour after Versailles and thereby achieved identity and national pride. The models of the Reichstag, the Kremlin, the Vatican, and the White House were alien. The Weimar Republic was Jewish, Russian Communism was Jewish, the religion of Christianity was Jewish, and American democracy was Jewish. Plutocracy was Jewish. Poverty was Jewish. It was as simple as that, Hitler repeated again and again. Also they were linked in an international Jewish conspiracy against the Fatherland. One idea was sufficient if shouted often enough. Germany! Germany! Germany!

It was this purity of impulse and collective purpose that his father said was a perversion of patriotism. It was a lot of fun and often a public-spirited substitution for studying. Because they made a cult of muscle over brain, his old man called them a bunch of 'noble savages'. Konrad's mother was concerned because he stopped going to church. She thought Satan was loose in the land, having no doubt what to render unto Caeser and what to God. But her pastor had taken a personal oath of allegiance to the Führer because 'National Socialism was God's will'.

In Konrad's arsenal of arguments to influence his folks was a new movie, *Hitlerjunge Quex*. It was one of the first films made by Reichsführer of Propaganda Joseph Goebbels after the Nazis came to power, who had said, 'No great goal is attained without pain, sweat, sacrifice, or spilled blood.' His theme was dramatized with unlimited money and talent for the screen. All the prestige of a dominant political party was mobilized behind the picture. Hitler attended the opening in Munich. The newspapers advertised it as 'a film on the spirit of sacrifice of German youth'.

After Konrad saw it with friends at the Ufa-Palast Astoria, he insisted his parents attend the theatre the following night. The posters in the lobby announced what to expect. 'The Hitler Youth are marching.... Thousands of luminous flags are waving over Germany, blood-red flags.... Young people by the hundreds of thousands are marching in limitless columns, rediscovering their energies, they follow this flag that they know well and this idea guides them: to unite with the Führer who has recruited them.... Proud and conscious of moulding the Germany of today ... of being tomorrow's Germany.'

The film told the story of a true incident of a young boy working for the Nazis who was murdered by the Communists in 1932. Dr Goebbels made a moving speech over the boy's open grave at the time, so he had pushed the production forward. The scenario was based on a novel published on the subject. For the first time in the history of the cinema a film was addressed directly to young people like Konrad Zenner.

On the screen the heroic boy's name was Heini Volker, nicknamed Quex, quicksilver. He was fifteen, the same age as Konrad. And like himself, Heini had joined the Hitler Youth in opposition to his parents. To complete the empathy, he resembled the star of the film, so blond, so Germanic.

It was unremittingly realistic in the best German film tradition, technically and esthetically, strongly political and unpoetic. The background was Berlin with its grey working-class neighbourhoods, cafés where people relaxed over a warm beer, dark squares, and occasional wandering carnivals. It was not the way his family lived, but Konrad knew the milieu.

The hero's parents were Reds, who made their son join the Communist youth movement. His father, a workingman of the people, beat Heini and forced him to sing 'The Internationale'. Frau Volker, torn between husband and son, chose suicide. The dramatic scene brought tears to Konrad's eyes and fears of a similar climax in his own household. Realizing the error of his thinking, Herr Volker was moved to learn he was a German before a Communist. In the same fashion Konrad hoped for his father's patriotic conversion.

In order to gain acceptance into the Hitler Youth, Heini had to become an informer to show his honest intentions. He then tipped off the Nazis that the Communists, his ex-friends, planned to attack their headquarters. After that he denounced the Reds to the police, thereby earning the right to wear the uniform of the Hitler Youth. Konrad and his companions cheered this sequence of the film.

It was while distributing anti-Communist material on the 'Famine and Misery in Soviet Russia' that Heini was assassinated by drunken Bolsheviks. They tracked him down like an animal for the kill in a deserted square at night. He died singing the opening words to the hymn of the Hitler Youth which dissolved into a marching crowd, picking up the song and filling the screen with flying flags.

Heini was the martyr of a new religion.

Even now, sitting on a blanket under the sun of Iran, the film had the power to stir Colonel Konrad Zenner. It took no effort to evoke a vision of the time ten years earlier when he had waited up for his parents to come home from the movie theatre. The motion picture marked the beginning of an undeclared war.

His father said *Quex* was a Machiavellian masterpiece of film art created to condition boys to die in the future war plotted by Hitler and his gang. Goebbels was a genius, a damned one. His mother thought *Quex* diabolically taught hate. She didn't believe Frau Volker's suicide because no good German woman could reach the kind of extremity that would force her voluntarily to abandon her home, menfolk, and God.

Konrad was disappointed in their responses, but it was to be expected from the older generation, he told them. They just didn't understand the new Germany. They never would.

In the days that followed his parents fought a losing battle for the soul of their son against the state. Zenner thought his boy had been poisoned, as from a political disease. His wife said her Konrad was possessed. He was the innocent victim of the Satanic tyranny of Adolf Hitler. There was the devil preaching from the pulpits of the screen, radio, and press.

After a long time his parents gave up resistance; they even had reason to fear his fanaticism. Frau Zenner became more devout. Dr Stefan Zenner retired behind the closed door of his study to write legal briefs. He was also secretly engaged in a book on German jurisprudence under Nazi rule. His son stumbled on it, having accidentally read the theme: '... they were criminals who had perverted German law and should be so judged by the German people.' Konrad said nothing at first but used it in their final dispute.

They went through the routine forms of family life. But young Konrad Zenner had been permanently cast in a heroic mould by the leader of his country. Of course, there was some sacrifice involved, a price to pay. There was no grey area of compromise; it was all black or white. He had handed himself over to Hitler, who demanded all or nothing.

Then the war his father envisioned exploded, and there was no time for filial sentiment; now he was fighting for his life. A soldier's body becomes military inventory, no longer his own property.

When SS Captain Konrad Zenner came home from the despairing trauma of defeat at Stalingrad and saw the fugitive Jew in his home, what truly drove him berserk was not the ragged racial enemy, but the two longtime haters of Hitlerism, his father and mother. Their incarceration was no accident.

'I will pray for you, my son.'

And now the colonel inhaled a great draught of Persian air, expanding his huge chest, feeling larger than life, godlike. He held his breath for a suspended moment of blankness, then released it with a sound like Thor, blowing his mother's words out of his mind. It takes less to exorcise a saint, he thought, than a devil.

Zenner would never hear her voice in his head again.

Why had Mirza deliberately diverted him to this place?

Harvis sat with a handful of other spectators in what seemed like a gymnasium. It was in a basement. Below him, in a small arena like a cockpit, Major Ali Mirza performed exercises. He was among a dozen athletes dressed only in striped knee pants.

This was a zurkhaneh, a 'House of Strength'.

A man sang a song and beat a drum to maintain the rhythm of the exercising men. The *Shah Namah* was an epic poem written in the tenth century by Firdausi. It told of ancient heroes, an appropriate inspiration for these athletes.

Was he here for the vanity of Mirza, a forty-year-old man doing difficult feats, or the education of an American? Was he witnessing a sport club or a secret society? It was a land of split decisions, Harvis thought.

There was still enough time to bring the information about the captive commando to Mike Callahan before he took off for Cairo in the Air Transport Command C-54 standing at Mehrabad airport. Harvis had no idea how long Mirza would perform. Or if having Harvis see the prisoner was in his plans.

Mirza did whirling dances. Then he wrestled another man. All trained with heavy clubs, wooden shields, steel bows, and chains that require strong bodies. Pre-Islamic warriors must have used similar weapons, Harvis surmised. There was an intensity about the exercises that suggested ritual.

Despite his anxieties and plotted entrapment, Harvis was moved by what he witnessed in the arena. His emotions somersaulted with the feats in the pit and the song of heroes and the beats of the drum.

Stirred by the total theatre of sound and strength, Harvis was encased in a steamy sweat of excitement. He sensed there was a message from the spirit of Persia that Mirza wanted him to receive. Perhaps it was more important for the Persian to have the American in the zurkhaneh than meeting a prisoner in the jail.

Another thought, less profound, pierced him. Mirza was simply showing what he could do to anyone messing around with his daughter, Faraj. Break him into bits, that's what.

Had he found out about them?

It was with her father's permission that Faraj had come to

his apartment for parachute nylon Harvis had come by for trading purposes. It was a highly unusual thing for Mirza to do. One could not pick up an ordinary girl or date one without a formal introduction. Women were kept in the back of the house. Most social life was for men only. They didn't walk with their wives. The rules about Iranian girls were strict, deriving from the Moslem religion.

Mirza knew his beautiful daughter was crazy about American things. All her romantic notions were inspired by Hollywood stars. Captain Peter Harvis had come to Iran out of the same stamp that created Errol Flynn, Robert Taylor, and Tyrone Power. It was inevitable they would be attracted to each other.

What's your game, Ali?

There was so much left unsaid in this country, Peter thought. Glances told stories. Gestures were sagas. He was always committing himself too soon, orally and facially. He would have to guard himself against that strong man in the arena. When it was over and they came up to daylight, Harvis greeted Mirza with genial readiness.

'Major Ali Mirza, you are a bull in the pit, a lion in battle, a wise owl in counsel, a fox in the marketplace, a dove in religious practices, and an eagle who has been many places.'

Mirza loved the Persian style of eloquence and made the typical response of modesty.

'I do not deserve such praises.'

'So I take it back, and let's get your ass back to the jail to see the prisoner!'

'Of course, it is our duty.'

Then he started in the opposite direction.

'Ali!' Harvis was flabbergasted.

'We must go to the bazaar.'

'I have to bring back a report on this deal to the embassy,' Harvis pleaded. 'You're going the wrong way.'

'It is not the right way,' Mirza admitted. 'Only the best way.'

'Sometimes you don't make sense.'

'You have not been in my country long enough to know.' Mirza smiled and walked away.

After a moment Harvis sighed and walked after him, thinking of his daughter, Faraj. She had come to his embassy office the day before yesterday.

Harvis was in his favourite position, feet on his desk, reading an interesting State Department analysis on the Middle East, when he heard tapping on his office door. He recognized the touch and bounded from his desk.

'Faraj!' he called out before opening the door. She had been in the back of his mind.

She was eighteen, small, olive-skinned, with huge brown eyes and jet-black hair. Faraj was the kind of prize a Shah stole and Persian poets celebrated. She had one flaw in his eyes, a major one: She was the daughter of his friend Major Ali Mirza, and he was a powerful papa.

'Doll!'

It was an apt description. She smiled at his American exuberance and waited to be invited inside.

'Hello, Peter.'

Her voice was soft, almost vague, unlike American women. They were self-effacing here, without the egos of girls he had known. Often Harvis had to ask her to repeat words.

He suddenly remembered form. 'Please, come in, beautiful.'

'Thank you,' she said.

He closed the door, saying, 'This is my lucky day. What a fantastic surprise!' He took her purse and began to remove her coat, but she resisted.

'I cannot stay,' Faraj told him.

He tried to embrace her.

She shied away. 'It is not nice here.'

'It's my private office.'

'I have seen Betty Grable, Lana Turner, and Ginger Rogers in offices,' she said. 'But I am not yet an American girl.'

He protested, 'I haven't seen you in weeks.'

She settled into a chair. 'It is better in your apartment. That is not a public place.'

He tried to force a date. 'When?'

He had only seen her five times since they had met six months earlier. She appeared and departed like a genie out of *The Thousand and One Nights.* Their meetings were solely her decision. Pursuit by him was socially impermissible and culturally unthinkable. Major Ali Mirza had invited Harvis to meet his deeply religious wife and their three daughters so they could see an American close up. Yankee exotica. Just once.

'Answer me, Faraj!' he appealed.

She smiled a promise. 'Soon.'

'In this country that's something between ten minutes and ten years!'

'You are in my mind always,' she murmured distantly.

'Okay, how about a meeting of the minds at noon today?' he proposed warmly. 'There's a new Cary Grant picture. Or how about Henry Fonda in *The Ox-Bow Incident*?'

Faraj loved American movies. They would rendezvous in a theatre for some opening scenes, then go to his apartment. Thus, her time was accounted for at home.

'I have a fitting for a lady,' she explained. 'That is why I can come here.'

'Thank you!'

She was learning dress design and foreign languages so she could read the international fashion magazines. Harvis got her all the pertinent American publications. She was a talented artist. Her exterior was usually chicly European or smartly American. But never without a decorative amulet to ward off the evil eye.

'What about tomorrow?'

She sighed pensively. 'Sometime soon —'

His image of her was that of a bird in flight.

'One of these days,' he said with fervour, 'I'm going to get a cage big enough to trap you for ever!'

Her face clouded, and Harvis knew he had said something wrong. Her large eyes searched him for sincerity. Her seismical sensitivity stemmed from the inferiority of the female in their society.

'You should not say such words,' she admonished.

Anything could upset the delicate balance of their friendship. But Harvis enjoyed the insecurity like a crap game.

'I'm sorry,' he said. 'But what offended you?'

She spoke up sharply. 'Moslem women are born in a cage.'

She became a changeling on the subject of women's rights. A woman's place was in the home or field, dumb and obedient.

'Now I'm really sorry,' he said.

'We are the slaves of men!'

She had lectured Harvis at length about it because Iranian men didn't listen. 'You know I don't consider you a second-class citizen,' he told her. 'In my book you're number one!'

'That is why I am going to the United States.'

She had secret plans to leave, and Harvis had co-operated. His influence at the embassy was important. It had made him uncomfortable in the presence of her father. But there was nothing he could deny this independent spirit. He was literally under her spell.

She was sunny again. 'Do you have the nylon?'

'It's been waiting for you.'

Harvis didn't prefer the suffragette part of her. Happily, he went to the closet and brought out a package of parachute nylon that he had wangled again. The price was rising. Faraj used it for her sewing, though there was enough cloth in the country. It had some fashion value as an American product. Mostly, it was her way of maintaining contact with Harvis that satisfied her folks.

'Thank you, Alexander,' she said graciously.

The reference was their joke. The men of Iran hated Alexander the Great who had conquered Persia in 331 BC, smashed their empire, and burned Persepolis. The women honoured him because he took Persian wives, treating them as equals, and commanded his men to marry them.

'I'll have tea brought in,' he suggested.

'After the lady I must go to class,' she demurred.

'Please don't go —'

She was firm. 'I must.'

He knew when to pull back. Love would never interfere with her studies, nor parents with her goal. It was a rare stance for a female in a country where marriage was arranged and the family supreme. Yet she was so fragile.

'Just one kiss,' he begged piteously.

Faraj was tempted, sent a fleeting glance at the door, then showed discipline and left the office.

He was rooted in a magic circle. The effect she had on him was simple bewitchment. He stood staring at the closed door, wondering if he'd ever see her again.

He went back to his desk but couldn't resume reading. Her perfume clung to him. . . .

Her scent enveloped him as it had the first time in bed when he was drenched in her fragrance. The entwining and contrasting skins. The full lips of love. And the gasping ecstatic end of maidenhood, for she hadn't told him it was the first time.

Meeting in his place had been an accident, a natural one. It was later, for he was ignorantly new in the country, that Harvis understood the value of virginity in Iran. It was part of the marriage contract.

He had received a gift from the gods. Or a stolen jewel from the Peacock Throne.

But why me?

Because Faraj was in love with America.

Harvis followed Major Mirza into the bazaar. He had been there often and liked it, despite the teeming people. This was a crowd he understood. There was nothing elusive about the marketplace. Among the stalls and the small stores in the long serpentine building it was the changeless East. There was no language barrier. Money was the linguist of all time. A bargain was a bargain was a bargain.

'Ali, I give up.' Harvis talked as they strolled. He was giving up hope of seeing the prisoner, but he couldn't go back to the embassy empty-handed. 'Me, time, and the Persian can't make it. It's like you're working on another system.'

'We have hearts, not clockwork.'

'That's beautiful,' Harvis said. 'But next time you say be somewhere at a certain time, I won't believe you.'

'Now you are speaking of truth.'

'I'm not saying you're a liar,' Harvis surmised. 'It just comes to me we're operating on different blood counts.'

Harvis was familiar with the bazaar, but it was a fresh experience with the Iranian police major along the crowded passages under the lofty vaulted brick and mud roofs. Everyone knew and respected Mirza, some showing fear of the man.

The packed place always reminded Harvis of a Christmas rush in a department store at home. But to his Iranian friend it was the throbbing pulse of the city. The American visualized a hydra-headed-multi-armed money beast. Mirza thought of the bazaar as a sensitive political body.

'Sometimes you should not tell the truth if it hurts,' Mirza continued the discussion. 'In that way lying becomes a kindness.'

'I'm sure you have a poem to cover that philosophy,' Harvis parried. It was a testing game Mirza never failed, and the American marvelled at it. 'You have five seconds.'

Mirza welcomed the challenge.

'It will be from Saadi, my second favourite poet,' he said, then quoted: ' "Words that beguile thee / But thy heart make glad / Outvalue truth / Which makes thy temper sad." '

'That explains why you won't let me see the prisoner. You're torturing him like Boris and Sam, and you don't want to hurt my feelings.'

Mirza wagged his head. 'He is like the Germans. He will not talk. His mind must be prepared.'

Harvis had forced the issue without result. 'I'll crack first,' he said, thinking of Callahan. He would want all the information he could get on the commandos before leaving Tehran. He could hear the prodding voice reminding him who was Number One.

It seemed the prisoner was the least of Mirza's concerns. Harvis counted the artisans, merchants, labourers, beggars, and shoppers, who nodded to Mirza, greeted him, whispered messages, or delivered notes. The time was of social ferment. A twenty-two-year-old Shah. Rising prices. Not enough goods. The big war. The occupation. The threat of strikes. Even revolution.

'I smell trouble,' Mirza reported.

He made comments along the way, a priceless reading of Iran for the young American. They were wise people in the bazaar because the wares on their walls brought news from everywhere in the country and the world. It was being inside Persia for the first time, Harvis thought. Mirza was more than a guide. The association with the major meant acceptance beyond the last line of reserve towards a foreigner.

The complaints of camels, mules, and donkeys mingled with the yells, curses, conversations, and appeals of people. The rattling and pounding of tin, copper, and nails. The tearing of cloth. The thumping of bales and carpets. The shuffling of thousands of feet. This was simply the tremendous din of commerce, Harvis thought, deafening. Then he realized there were messages of temper and mood for Mirza in the noise. The bazaar was his listening post.

Along with the deep hum of voices an odour permeated the narrow bazaar. Spices, leather, dung, fruits, and vegetables, human perspiration, woodsmoke, garlic, animal sweat, dirty alleys, filthy gutters, and other indefinable smells clung to Harvis. Mirza sniffed these scents as winds of change. He caught rumours on the wing. And the beginnings of gossip. News travelled fast in the bazaar and into the city like a prairie fire.

They stopped at a store in the carpet section.

A bearded dealer left the rug he was repairing to greet them. 'Major Mirza, my old and honourable friend! So you have brought your illustrious American friend. I have the rug your generous heart desires. It was not easy to find. But I have it!'

The dealer disappeared into the rear of the store.

'What is all this, Ali?' Harvis demanded.

'The big nations have invaded my little country for centuries. For what reason? Carpets!' he said obliquely. 'My country is a carpet for the armies of the world!'

'Come on, Ali—'

'A present for the birthday of your son,' Mirza said, then remembered: 'And your faithful wife in the United States.'

The dealer brought in the rug.

'A most precious one, monsieur.' He forced it into the foreigner's hands. 'Only as a special favour for Major Mirza.'

The size was barely manageable. 'I can't accept this,' Harvis said lamely.

Mirza showed rare irritation.

'Captain Harvis, do you sincerely wish to learn about this country? Then you will keep this carpet and study it,' he said firmly. 'Our lives are woven into them.'

Mirza marched off.

Harvis was momentarily stranded. He had no choice but to stagger after his friend, struggling with the rug.

The major had gone into a teahouse, and Harvis took his place beside him on the bench. It was late afternoon, and both men required the interlude of this Persian pastime. Mirza had slipped into sightless contemplation. The American resigned himself, hunched over, wordless.

It was plain that Mirza had his own unique approach to the prisoner that excluded Harvis. The American's urgent schedule was meaningless. He was convinced no amount of GI enterprise or official necessity would move this tranquil man. Even if he broke security and told of the coming conference to decide the course of the Big War. It wasn't the Persian's conflict. Roosevelt, Churchill, Stalin? Mirza recognized the Shah of Iran. A personal appeal had already failed. He was simply no match for this Persian potentate.

What was Mirza up to? Did it relate to Faraj? First the threat of the zurkhaneh, then the bribe of the rug, and now the truth serum of tea. As he sat like a Sphinx-Buddha, the major's silence was unsettling.

One of them had to speak first, Harvis thought, overcome with a form of unbearable blame. A girl of Faraj's class was untouchable. In a country of no incorruptibles he had committed an unpardonable offence. Yet if there was a fault, it was a shared one – if truth was a defence.

He did have sexual scruples. He was not a soldier-rapist. If Faraj had offered the slightest resistance, a hint of virginity,

Harvis would have retreated. In Iran at age twenty-five he was considered an old roué.

She had told him about the relatives and representatives of suitors who were coming to her house. There was one from an important family in the government which would make an advantageous alliance for her father. Traditionally Mirza could force such a marriage. But they were allowing her to choose.

'Say, Ali?' Harvis began.

Mirza came to attention. 'Yes?'

Harvis lost his nerve. To hell with this American lay-it-on-the-line shit, he thought. Let the major do what he must in the best circuitous route of the Persian style.

Mirza urged. 'Please tell me what you are thinking.'

'I'm thinking how simple life would be if the prisoner got the firing squad last night so I wouldn't have to think about what Mirza, Gordell, and Callahan were thinking about him.'

Mirza chuckled and pointed behind Harvis.

Sergeant Mostaffa had entered with the prisoner in custody. The young Iranian was sleeplessly wild-eyed and bewildered. The sergeant delivered him, released the handcuffs, then left the chaikhana with them. He said nothing, only winked broadly at the astonished American.

Mirza was a perfect host.

'Sit down,' he told the prisoner. 'This is an American, Captain Peter Harvis.'

The prisoner half smiled, then warily took a place on the bench, not exactly where the major indicated, but closer to the foreigner.

'Thanks, your Excellency,' he whispered.

Like the prisoner, Harvis was fascinated with Mirza's performance. He expected this etiquette to explode in some unpredictable but policelike fashion. But the major was his stolidly gracious self as he poured tea for them.

'This nameless one lived in Berlin without tea because of the war,' he informed Harvis. 'The lack of it froze his tongue. Drinking tea in his native land will warm the words so they will flow like a river.'

The prisoner took his tea, closed his eyes, and sighed. They observed him like an experiment, watching the national drink work its wonders.

Finally the prisoner spoke. 'My name is Nadiri.'

'Aha!' Mirza exclaimed like a proved scientist. He nudged Harvis. 'See!'

Harvis gave him a congratulatory slap on the back.

'It was not the tea,' Nadiri said diffidently.

Mirza glowered. 'What do you mean it was not the tea?'

'I heard the Germans were put against the wall,' Nadiri said bleakly. 'I do not want to die.'

'Why did you join them?' Harvis asked.

'I was a student. Homesick,' Nadiri said, looking at Mirza, who was no longer friendly. 'There was no other way for me to get out of Berlin. The air raids. People dying. The house I live in burned to the ground. I did not want to die in a strange land.'

He finished his tea and waited politely for more. It was not a moment for cordiality.

Mirza ridiculed him. 'You were afraid in Germany, and now you are afraid in Tehran. What kind of man are you?'

'Who wants to be buried in his own country in an unmarked grave?' Nadiri appealed pathetically. 'My father and mother must know of me. I must have their prayers.'

The sentiment defused the major.

'The Germans required a Persian guide.' Mirza made it unnecessarily clear to the American, now pouring tea for the prisoner. 'So he guided them to the Russians!'

The Iranians burst into laughter like discovered allies in an ethnic joke on the alien in their midst.

'How many were you?' Harvis interjected, clinging to his skepticism. 'I mean altogether, Germans and guides.'

Nadiri took a sip of tea as if to ease his memory. 'Twenty-two. There was a guide for each team of six in the English airplane. A White Russian born in Azerbaijan. A German who studied here. And an Iranian —'

Mirza broke in. 'Another one! What is his name?'

'Reza. He would tell me no more. We did not ask questions because it was against orders. I did not want to know more. The Germans took a blood oath of silence.'

Harvis had seen it borne out in action. 'Who was the officer in charge?' he asked, thinking Nadiri was either a lucky naïf or a shrewd terrorist.

Nadiri tasted his tea, then answered, 'Colonel Konrad Zenner. Reza and two men stayed with him. I believe they would be jumping from the British Lancaster after the rest.'

There was a pause.

Nadiri said, 'That is everything I know.'

Mirza looked hard at him. 'Everything?'

Nadiri returned the gaze directly and nodded.

'Go home,' Mirza told him.

Without a second glance, Nadiri jumped from the bench and sprinted out of the place.

It was all too quick for Harvis. 'Hey?'

Mirza asked him, 'Did you have more questions?'

Harvis shook his head slowly, waiting for an explanation he knew would not be forthcoming.

'It was much better here, do you think, Peter?'

'Jails stink.' Harvis sighed. 'You have style, Ali.'

Mirza seemed content with himself, as if he had accomplished much. 'Have more tea, please.'

He must have missed something between the two Iranians, Harvis thought. Or had he? Was there some form of communication he would never receive? Boris and Sam would have shot Nadiri at midnight with the others. With few, if any, questions asked. Wiping out an innocent man. Or was he? Harvis was off-balance again. For a little while during the day with Mirza he thought he had had it made, integrated. He was still an outsider.

'You know what you look like to me?'

Mirza was curious. 'Tell me.'

'A Moslem dome of intricate design in many-coloured tiles. A perfect example of Persian art.'

Mirza sucked tea through the cube of sugar in his teeth; then he said, 'I am unworthy of your compliments.'

13

The embassy was closed when Harvis returned from the bazaar. The MP guard let him inside. Betty was waiting for him, dressed in a fur coat, chatting with the interior guard in the lobby. She was irritated.

'What happened to you?'

'I'll tell you at dinner,' Harvis said, signing the guard's register. 'Where's everybody?'

'Mr Callahan is gone,' she said. 'The ambassador is in there. You'd better have a good story.'

It was a warning.

He started forward, then stopped, feeling unarmed. 'Brief me.'

Callahan had gone on a flying tour of the Persian Gulf for possible alternate entry points for President Roosevelt, she said quickly. He was going on to Cairo. The big news was the arrival of the other security chiefs, Comrade Goria for Stalin and General May, Churchill's man. These men with the three ambassadors, Gordell, Volkoff, and Sir Henry, had met for lunch in a preliminary discussion of defence matters for the Tehran Conference. No date had been set when it would begin. It depended on the Cairo talks. Within a week probably with twenty-four hours notice. Events were in motion.

Harvis kissed her on the cheek, took a deep breath, and strode into the ambassador's office.

Betty sat down to wait.

'Where the hell have you been?'

Betty had left out the important part, Harvis thought. The morning euphoria of the ambassador had vanished, replaced by a barely controlled rage. His casual elegance was in disarray. Gordell had begun the day boozing with hard-drinking Mike Callahan and was still at it. That was not his style.

'Major Mirza strung me out, sir. But —'

Harvis couldn't insert the justification because the ambassador seemed implacably determined to trample him.

'You hung up Callahan. You – and especially I – can't be caught displeasing that man,' Gordell said with unusual asperity. 'The stakes are too high. The highest!'

Harvis made up his mind to wait it out.

'He has that man's ear.' Gordell jerked his chin towards the photograph of the President. 'Something I never had. But it's coming. Right into this room.'

Harvis stood nailed in place. Ordinarily, Gordell, always considerate, never condescending, would have indicated a chair. But the desk between them was a sudden gulf. Behind it paced a man exposing a ruthless self-preservation.

'We met with the Russians, and Callahan got their version of the Nazi story. But he didn't want to leave town without your report on the prisoner. He had me check Major Mirza's office. I even sent to the zurkhaneth.' Gordell took a breath accusingly. 'Where did you go from there?'

'I did get to see the prisoner, sir,' Harvis replied without answering directly. The bazaar and the rug were better left out. 'But the major made a hide-and-go-seek game out of it. A surprise party. But I do have the whole story.'

'Okay —'

Harvis related the incident with Nadiri. He didn't hurry the important information, letting the ambassador's irascibility dissipate. He could see appreciation, then shocked concern, but still annoyance.

'I wish I could have laid this bombshell in Callahan's lap,' Gordell lamented. 'He goes straight to FDR.'

'I couldn't get away, sir. You know how they are —'

He hated to shift the blame to Persian psychology because it was a half-truth. He had lingered with Mirza, unwilling to dash off boorishly with the sensational news. It was a scene the Iranian major had savoured like a good story with an unexpected ending. He was his own best audience. But Harvis wasn't fooling the ambassador.

'Yes, I know them well. Also, I know how goddamn *simpático* you can be. Forget tender sensibilities until this Big Three thing is over and done with,' Gordell instructed harshly. 'I have a big investment in this Tehran Conference. It must pay off for me, Pete. I can't afford anything but your best efforts.'

'I'll give it all I've got, sir.'

'Look, Pete,' Gordell said in relenting tones, 'I'm really not ready for retirement. The word makes me sick. It's like a form of death. I feel too young to die.'

Harvis smiled his support. He considered his doubles partner a remarkable man even off the tennis court. Gordell was a little older-appearing among young people, but younger-looking with his contemporaries. It was his spirit and self-possession – the unworried way of the wealthy, of course.

'The State Department invited me to Casablanca. But not to the Cairo Conference. They love me, they love me not. But Tehran is my own backyard. I intend to make the most of it,' Gordell vowed to himself. 'They can't stop me from talking whether they listen to me or not.'

'I'll help all I can, sir.'

'They misjudge the important people. As if there were static conditions with no possibility for change, up or down, good or bad.' Gordell moved from behind the rampart of his desk. 'They did it to General de Gaulle in Casablanca. They're doing it now with General Chaing Kai-shek in Cairo. Underestimating one, overestimating the other. Let's hope they analyze Stalin correctly here.'

Harvis was itching to be with Betty.

'Some say history makes man. The other theory is man makes history. But there's no doubt history goes on even when wars stop.' Gordell closed the gap between them. 'Think about it in relation to the big shots who lead historic conferences, Pete.'

'I will, sir.'

Gordell offered his hand. 'Remember, first things first.'

Harvis shook hands. 'Good night, Mr Ambassador.'

He went out thinking: So Gordell was a man who didn't have everything, after all. He had discerned it in the crack of his cultured voice and the smooth face, revealing age truly when it was furious with desperation, when it was afraid of Callahan, the man with a gun who helped a President walk.

'All of a sudden it's a big deal,' Harvis told Betty, as they signed out of the embassy and went into the Tehran night. It was his only comment on the session. She didn't expect more.

'The biggest,' Betty agreed. 'We'll be making history. But not together.'

'What do you mean?'

'I'm moving in with the ambassador.'

'What for?'

'He sees a book in all this. It's the diplomat's dream – which sounds like a good title,' she said. 'He wants me to catch whatever gems of statesmanship drop.'

They went to the Ararat, a restaurant run by an Armenian, named Hagop, who claimed to have a cousin in Moreno. Harvis always tried some of the Armenian he had learned from a schoolmate. *'Inch-pa-sess?'* *'Chad Lov.'* Hagop invariably repeated the words in English like it was a big joke. 'What's doing?' 'Okay.' Harvis would get an extra helping of food, but it obliged him to leave a larger tip.

Harvis recounted his day with Mirza. 'Here I was with this big conference story and dying to tell him.'

'Why?'

'It's his work.'

'Iranians will be the last to find out,' Betty said. 'We've borrowed their country for the duration.'

'I'm going to miss that guy.'

'When?'

'We have to leave sometime,' Harvis said. 'I mean us soldiers. You're permanent party.'

'If Major Mirza thought you weren't here to stay, he wouldn't be treating you so royally,' she said. 'He's a typical Middle Eastern opportunist.'

Betty always carped about his friends. She disliked Skeene because he was too cool; he hardly noticed her. On the occasions he invited them for a swim in the pool of the park-like British legation, the Englishman would act properly aloof. And she didn't care for Artukin because the Russian lacked all reserve. She was certain he invited them to dinner only to make a proletarian pass at her. Now she was undermining his relationship with Mirza and Harvis didn't like it. His grasp on the man's personality was tenuous enough.

'Stop casting as-persians,' he said.

'The old imperialists are finished. We're the new-style rulers of the world,' she claimed expertly. 'Foreigners have been here for centuries, one way or another. The Persians take what they need from each of them without losing their identity. We're just the latest model.' She patted his face. 'You're just a Yankee guinea pig. But handsome!'

'Mirza is my friend,' he said.

'Overfriendly,' she persisted. 'The man whose place you took got a cool reception from your shrewd Major Mirza.'

'Maybe he was too old for his daughters.' Harvis grinned, watching her face fall. 'Eighteen, sixteen, fourteen. Three beauties!'

'So that's it!' Betty's infallibility was shaken. 'But you're a married man!'

'Look who's talking!' Harvis laughed. 'The legal quota here is four wives. He was showing me around this Persian garden, and there were his girls – three flowers.'

'You're such a dreamer, darling,' she said. 'Polygamy is for the lucky Moslem male. You're just a pathetic monogamous American.'

'Why didn't they discover America?'

'Don't forget the Mormons.'

Harvis drove Betty to the ambassador's house, thinking the dubious drift of his life in the Army was about to end. The future held some promise in Persia! he was playing a part in the war.

Betty asked, 'What are you thinking about?'

'The conference, what else?'

'It seems sex can be secondary,' she said reflectively.

'First things first, baby.'

'It's kind of thrilling when you think of it. Roosevelt, Stalin, Churchill,' she said. 'The descent of the gods from Olympus.'

'The Big Three and us make five.'

It was an amusing notion.

14

Harvis didn't mind being home alone that night. He had discovered some appeal in isolation since he had left American soil. It was part of the self-sufficiency he had achieved away from the pampering of his wife and mother. One luxury was the restored premarital bliss of reading in bed. He had begun to hoard privacy.

Under the lamp of his bedstand there was a stack of new armed forces books, magazines, State Department publications, and letters. He began with the letter from his brother-in-law because Harold had never written to him before. He was a navigator of a low-flying bomber in the Pacific war. It had taken two months for the sweat-stained V-mail letter with the San Francisco APO number to reach Tehran from the censored island in the Pacific.

'I just came off another milk run and I'm sitting in my tent listening to the rains come down. Which means my suntan will never get dry. The jungle rot in my ear itches like crazy. I feel like a sad sack sweating it out. Instead of griping to my buddies, I figure it's about time I wrote you. Oh, I forgot. The turkeys for the holidays came early, but they were rotten because of a snafu in the refrigeration. God bless America.

'When you get this, you'll be the father of a one-year-old like I am. Only I didn't get to see my daughter when she was born, but they gave you a furlough just to look at your son through a hospital window. That's the difference between a sergeant and a captain, you big shit. But I hear the cousins love each other. When it's all over, it'll be fun taking our kids someplace, huh? While they play, we'll shoot the crap about how I got the Japs and you got the girls, you lucky bastard. Banzai.'

Harvis chuckled. The war was hard and dangerous for Harold. It was safe and soft for him, a spectator sport. They were two random markers in the gambling of the gods.

He opened his wife's letter. 'My dearest,' she wrote. 'I have terrible news....'

Her sister had received the dreaded telegram from the War Department. Harold had been shot down in the Pacific Ocean. Lost without a trace.

Harvis turned over and wept into his pillow.

And then he wished for his wife, first for mutual consolation, then for sex, as if to assert life over death, now reminded of his mortality. To embrace her would make him feel more alive, locked together against death, creating life. The ecstacy and the orgasm, the forgetting gush, was a victory over death.

But he was alone with death.

I must die, too, he thought.

He jumped from the 'death' bed, leaving the letter. Then Harvis went about his three-room apartment, turning on all the lights because death lurked in shadows to snatch unsuspecting people. He poured himself a vodka as one would at a wake. Not for mourning, but to celebrate life.

As he downed half the cup, Harvis heard a tapping on his apartment door. Recognizing the sound, he left the vodka and hastily put on a bathrobe over his naked body. He noticed it was after midnight.

He opened the door, and Faraj stepped inside breathlessly, then smilingly stood with her back against the door, calming herself, enjoying the surprise on his face with girlish delight. She had never done this before.

Harvis stared at her as though she were a materialization of his emotions. She was the yearned-for partner in grief and desire.

'I was doing a fitting for a lady who must have a new dress to meet the empress at the palace for breakfast.' Her soft voice was hardly audible. 'Please excuse me.'

He thought his blood would boil over and his heart pound through his breast. Maybe it was the stiff drink, but he could feel his sorrow dissolve. Not to frighten her away, Harvis tried to appear undisturbed. But his glistening eyes were giving him away.

He asked cannily, 'How did you get here?'

Looking into his eyes, she faltered. 'A friend with a car.' Faraj had sudden misgivings. 'It is with my father's permission.'

She had never appeared so enchanting and beautiful, he thought. As he reached out to lead her away from the door, his hand shook. 'Come in and —'

She retreated to the door.

'I'm not here for that.'

Her resistance angered him. 'What is "that"?'

'What is in your eyes.' She touched the amulet pinned to her dress. 'They shine like a demon.'

'It's not the evil eye,' he said, showing his first impatience with her superstitions. 'Love is like a demon. A friendly one.'

'I'm not here for that,' she repeated. 'I came to ask you something. It would be better another time.'

She turned to leave, taking the doorknob. Harvis put his arm out and leaned on the door. He had an urge to seize her. It was a form of violence he had never felt before. She whirled back, almost into his arms. He saw fright in her eyes, as if she had entered the lair of a beast.

'You want something and I need something. Maybe we can trade like a bargain in the bazaar,' he urged gruffly.

She shook her head, shivering now. 'I am sorry. I am to blame for coming.'

He leaned to kiss her, but Faraj jerked her mouth away. His hot breath burned her cheek. Harvis made a last attempt at lecherous cunning. 'What did you come for?'

'I have a friend who wants to go to America with me.' Her small voice was vague. 'Perhaps you would help —'

'Who is it?'

'He is waiting outside. I will get him.'

She made another move to leave, but Harvis was between her and the door now. He thought of locking it.

'Why is he doing it this way?' he asked. 'All he had to do is —'

She cut in. 'It is hard the official way without help. He wants to bribe you. He is very rich.'

'Persian style,' Harvis said. 'Using a woman is part of the game, too.'

'I could not refuse him.'

Men were pushing her around tonight, he thought.

'I don't take money. I can't make that kind of promise,' he said. 'And I want you, Faraj.'

'Another time,' she said evasively. 'He is waiting.'

'He won't care how long it takes or what you'll do to get him a visa.'

She shook her head, backing away from him.

In a paroxysm of passion, Harvis made a brutal grab and then swept Faraj up towards the bedroom. She didn't struggle. There was the trembling submission of centuries in her blood, as the property of dominating men and the prize of conquerors. Harvis dropped her on the bed, then pinned her with one leg, while pulling up her dress, and tearing off her silk underwear. He was undetered by her limp silence.

As he twisted to strip himself of the bathrobe, Faraj turned and bounded away from the bed, fleeing the apartment. She didn't make a sound.

Harvis was back in the bed he had left, crying again. Not out of fury, frustration, repentance, or shame. It was that he was still not alone. The letter was on the pillow. Death had not gone.

15

It was still dark in the Bakhtiari territory of Iran as the five men of the German commando mission, Wolf Pack Number Three, moved quietly towards their objective. Their radioman had stayed behind in their hideout at the abandoned caravan-serai.

They stopped silently at the edge of a camp where a dozen tribesmen slept, the deep sleep of hardworking riders on a long trek. Their horses were tethered nearby, saddles on the ground. The herd of sheep they were transporting stood quietly, though some bleated for the oncoming dawn.

The commandos observed this scene of pastoral innocence, of people and animals resting in their natural habitat in an ancient corner of the world. The Germans communicated by hand-signals as they made ready to end the unknowing neutrality of these inert men. Then with practised stealth and brutal eagerness for their first action, the Nazis pounced on the sleepers with knives. They had guns, but shooting might have attracted others they didn't know about.

The slaughter of the innocents didn't take long because of the throat-cutting and back-stabbing efficiency of these well-trained Germans, while the moon glinted off their sharp strokes. Most of the tribesmen died without waking, but those with enough life left to resist were dispatched a little later. The Nazis said nothing even when there was none alive to hear.

Then they moved among their victims in the moonlight and stripped them of their distinctive tribal garb, each of the five men selecting what might fit him best. They collected one special set of garments to take back.

The murdering commandos saddled up and mounted the horses, taking along an extra one. Leaving behind the butchered bodies, the Nazi team rode off into the night. The sheep bleated farewell.

Once again the tribesmen's camp was tranquil.

At daybreak a light German Storch observation plane circled above the crumbling caravanserai, bypassed by history. It carried a German pilot and Colonel Konrad Zenner, the passenger capacity. The Royal Air Force insignia on it was freshly painted. In a few moments they found a landing area, and the plane put down. As the two men jumped on the ground, the radioman came running from his station in the ancient caravanserai to greet them. The colonel carried his leather gun case.

It was a perfect rendezvous because the masquerading commandos on horseback came riding into view, leading the unmounted horse. From a distance the five men appeared no different from the tribesmen they had slain. When they arrived, Colonel Zenner signalled there was no time to dismount; they had a rigid schedule to maintain.

The horse was for Zenner, and so were the extra tribal clothes. They were too small for the big man and caused some amusement as he tried them on. But he managed a makeshift camouflage, then mounted and led his men away. The pilot and radioman went into the caravanserai to wait for the outcome of the next raid. It was good weather for war.

One hour later Colonel Zenner and his men were in the woods of hill country along the tracks of the Iranian State Railway. The Nazis were on foot, their horses hobbled among the trees they would use for cover. Positioned for shooting at a moving object, the colonel had his men spread out at twenty-yard intervals. Although he carried a sidearm, Zenner had not yet opened his black leather case. It was a weapon designed for special circumstances. There was no likelihood that Wolf Pack Number Three would require their leader's sharp-shooting talents.

There was the approaching sound of a freight train. Colonel Zenner noted the time as it began a grinding pull on the upgrade he had selected for the attack. En route to Tehran, it was only a few minutes off schedule. From the head of the column, Zenner made a signal that was passed down the line, alerting his men and their rifles.

From the underground intelligence group, Zenner knew the crew consisted of one Iranian, the brakeman. The rest would be Americans, a sergeant-engineer, a sergeant-conductor, and a corporal-fireman. There was also an MP guard, a private, armed with a carbine.

Coupled to the boxcars and tankers would be a recreation car that showed films, a rolling chapel, and a caboose with two Red Cross women, the colonel had been informed. The amenities were for the American soldiers at the station stops and maintenance crews in isolated camps that extended from

Bandar Shahpur on the Persian Gulf to Bandar Shah at the Caspian Sea.

The colonel's main interest was in the load of war matériel being transported for the armies of the Soviet Union. They were delivering tanks, jeeps, trucks, gasoline, guns, ammunition, food, clothing, and medicines.

This was the lend-lease Hitler had chosen him to smash, Zenner thought. He would always remember the meeting with the Führer, who was petting his dog ('my only true friend'), that began with pleasant words, then crescendoed into a livid tirade against his hated adversary, Roosevelt. He had stood hypnotically while Hitler ranted on about how Churchill had praised him in 1938, that Stalin had made a pact with him in 1939, but Roosevelt had been his uncompromising foe from the beginning. Aid to Britain, supplies to Russia, then came the American Army.

Now the trust placed in him by the mesmerizing man inspired Zenner to open the leather case and assemble his rifle. There was no calculating how many man-hours of American industry he and his disguised commandoes could destroy in a matter of minutes. His men were capable enough, but now he altered the operational plan to enlarge his own role in the raid. Like a Teutonic Knight, the colonel decided to pit himself against this massive collection of capitalistic output inside the belly of a steel beast of burden. Let Wolf Pack Number Three observe their leader in action, he thought, loading his rifle.

The Iranian State Railway had been completed by the 'Old King', Reza Shah Pahlevi, out of his own treasury in 1938. Not using foreign capital was a source of national pride for a country historically dominated by big powers. It had been considered an impossible feat. A single track ran almost nine hundred miles, crossing deserts and climbing mountains, went through a hundred and twenty-five tunnels, and over hundreds of bridges. In 1942 the Persian Gulf Command of the United States Army took over the railway, declaring it scenically spectacular but inadequate for the twenty-four-hour schedule and tremendous hauling demands of wartime.

The long freight train was now lumbering up an incline in wooded hill country, temporarily slowed to a crawl by the excess weight in the bulging boxcars. The Iranian member of the crew swore in English, and the Americans swore in Persian because they were losing time as the locomotive laboured and roared. These experienced railroaders had pride of performance, being former union men whose jobs were waiting for them back home. The Iranian railroadman was no less dedicated to delivering goods according to timetables, train orders, and signals. Not to be outdone by bomber crews, their engine was named Casey Jones. The old folk song had timely reference to drafted men in a war.

Over the straining sound of the train, as Casey Jones exerted brute strength and pulling power, the crew couldn't hear the gunshot. But before their horrified eyes they saw the engineer fall dead from a bullet that smashed his skull, blasting him out of his seat at the controls.

For an instant the four men went rigid in a moment of aghast shock. Then the MP went to investigate, while the fireman and the brakeman moved the engineer with the burst brain to one side, and the conductor took his place.

Looking back from the wide window of the cab, the MP saw nothing to aim his carbine at, as the train travelled slowly through the woods. Whoever it was had to be behind him now. For a better view, unheedingly, the MP went down the iron steps of the tender and held to the handrail, leaning out recklessly for a wider rear angle. He saw only trees, tankers, freight cars, and the caboose with the Red Cross women and the chaplain.

Then a line of five tribesmen stepped forward from the trees in a simultaneous gesture, resting rifles disdainfully across their arms. A sixth tribesman, a giant on a rearing horse, emerged and raised his rifle in a scornful greeting.

The MP and the crew simply gaped at this taunting game of bravado as the train passed by, as if in review. Urged on by the crew, the MP got off a wild shot at the horseman, the most outstanding target, who seemed like the leader. They took quick cover behind the trees. But they were in no danger because the MP was unstable on the steps and had never fired his carbine before, duty having always been as a 'scarecrow' against petty thieves around the railroad. This was different.

The young private had the unnerving realization that any of the tribesmen could have shot him, like figures in a shooting gallery returning fire. He had rashly exposed himself on the iron steps. The MP climbed to the safety of the cab, then stood behind the conductor at the controls and peered out, cautiously. Meanwhile, the crew prayed for the struggling

Casey Jones to make it over the crest and away from the trees.

The MP and the conductor were perfectly framed in the wide windows of the engine cab. The conductor had the throttle to the last notch of the steaming behemoth they affectionately called their iron horse. The jittery MP swept his eyes behind them, knowing it was the massive horseman he had to fear. It was all either a baffling manoeuvre or a single-chance encounter. The Iranian said shooting at trains was not uncommon. But not with such deadly accuracy.

This time the huge tribesman appeared far ahead of the creeping eight-wheeler, riding out of the trees. He calmly dismounted, then used his horse as a shield while firing his rifle. As the MP came opposite him, he shot the American soldier in the forehead. He sank to the bloody floor of the cab. In the same rapid movement, the marksman got off a second shot that struck the conductor, splintering his temple.

By now the heavy-duty freight train had completed the climb and was on a short level roadbed, travelling on its own momentum towards a downhill stretch; then the track curved around a bend. In a few moments it would be a highballing runaway. Like the song, Casey Jones was heading for a wreck.

The Iranian brakeman moved the body of the conductor in order to free the controls for the fireman. The American was in no hurry to show himself in the windowseat in which his good friends had died. Both men offered no part of themselves to the awesomely sized, daredevil, sharpshooting tribesman.

The freight train picked up speed on the long downward slope pushed now by the heavy load. They had to stop it or jump for their lives. To hit the bend with this velocity meant certain derailment.

They were beyond the trees, and the fireman went to the controls because they could still save the train with the air brakes. The dead MP lay at his feet. It was then he saw the enormous tribesman, riding hard and pulling alongside the engine, as if escorting it to disaster. He fired his rifle full in the face of the frozen fireman, who fell back into the cab. The Iranian now elected to leap from the other side to the speeding ground, choosing his own way to die.

The released train outran the horse, and the rider reined his sweating animal to a halt, having made certain the controls were unattended.

He tore the turban from his head and watched with hard-breathing satisfaction as the charging carrier of enemy matériel met the bend with tremendous impact. The train left the tracks, taking its precious cargo over a ledge to destruction.

Colonel Konrad Zenner had no more idea of the meaning of 'Casey Jones' painted on the American locomotive than the 'A for Alfie' on the British Lancaster. A swastika was all that decorated German machines on the ground or in the air. They were fighting for Adolf Hitler.

16

Iran was earthquake country, and it seemed to Captain Peter Harvis that the freight train wrecked by the German commandos had the scale of a huge trembler to the island of Allied occupation in Tehran.

Harvis could feel the repurcussions of the astounding raid as he stood before the ambassador's desk. It was three hours after the attack. Gordell informed Harvis that the Allied ambassadors and their general officers were already en route to the American embassy for a hastily called meeting on the grave matter. The coded word of the Nazi commando success had been transmitted to their superiors, and the return message was plain: Extraordinary provisions must be made for the security of the Tehran Conference and the protection of the Big Three.

Ambassador Gordell's instructions came from Cairo.

'Pete,' he said, 'Mike Callahan wants a preliminary survey of the route the President will take from Mehrabad Airport to the embassy right away.'

Betty came into the office.

'General Andrews is here,' she announced.

Gordell grimaced his undisguised dislike for the transportation chief. 'He's off schedule. Tell him I'll be in the conference room precisely on the timetable.' He always referred to him derisively in railroad terminology. 'Derail him to a siding.'

'He wants to talk with you before the meeting.'

'Okay, signal him through.' Gordell dismissed Harvis with a wave of the hand. 'As far as you're concerned, the Tehran Conference has just begun.'

'Yes, sir.'

As both Betty and Harvis started out, General Tom Andrews entered unceremoniously. The commanding general of the Persian Gulf Command was a broad, brusque man of fifty. He was accompanied by a husky young black lieutenant. Betty sent a hidden gesture of helplessness towards the ambassador and disappeared. Harvis was required to be courteous.

'Good morning, General Andrews.'

'I was looking for you, Captain Harvis.'

'At your service, sir.'

'When are you starting your Presidential detail?'

'I was just leaving.'

'That's getting on the track,' the general approved. 'This is Lieutenant George Keyes.'

'I've seen him around the officers' club.'

The black officer was about Harvis' age, twenty-five. 'We'll be seeing more of each other now, Captain.'

'He's your partner,' the general said. 'Now highball it out of here.'

Harvis vacillated, sending an uneasy glance to the ambassador. Gordell rose from behind his desk and moved towards them, as if to project his authority. It threw Lieutenant Keyes off-balance.

General Andrews said sharply, 'Godammit, I said get going, men!'

Lieutenant Keyes wheeled and went out the open door, Harvis hard behind him. The general closed the door and smiled a delayed greeting back at the ambassador.

'Good morning, Phil!'

Gordell had been gathering fury.

'What was that all about!'

They despised each other. Because General Andrews was committed to schedules and quantities of goods delivered for the lend-lease programme, he was for ever at war with the Russians, the English, and the Iranians for transportation problems and matériel piled up at depots. He had no patience with diplomacy, and the ambassador often found himself smoothing out relations with their Allies. He described the general as a 'runaway boxcar in a china shop'. To Andrews, Gordell was a 'pinko-cookie pusher'.

'I don't have to tell you what those Nazi bastards did to my train,' the general fumed. 'You won't believe how much time and tonnage they set us back.'

'I'm aware it's a calamity of tremendous proportions,' Gordell protested. 'But you still can't give orders in my embassy to my people like it was one of your train stations!'

'I'm supplying the troops for the President, so your Captain Harvis is under my command.'

'Technically!'

'Take it easy, Phil.' The general grinned. 'Look out your window and you'll see I doubled the guard around this place. So I gave one more man to the captain. Don't tell me your friend Mike Callahan wouldn't want that.'

'Of course, there's no objection to extra precautions,' Gordell admitted. 'I was going to request them when you got here.'

'I knew you would,' General Andrews said. 'So we got rid of some red tape and all this protocol crap.'

Betty came in again to announce, 'Ambassador Volkoff, Sir Henry, and their people are here.'

'We'll be right out!' Gordell shot back sharply.

She gave him a quizzical look and left the office.

If he were to preside at the emergency meeting, Gordell would have to regain his diplomatic equanimity. The general's points were as indisputable as his style was gross. There were some bulls a subtle matador never penetrated.

'Look, Tom,' he said, reasserting his arena, 'that conference room is still my embassy. I'll have to insist on the right-of-way.'

'Sure, Phil.' General Andrews bent a little. 'I'll keep my trap shut in there. Economics, politics, international law, and diplomacy – that's not my gauge of track. I'm in this country for one thing only – deliver the goods to Russia.'

'That's why you do it so well,' Gordell said truthfully, then launched one last banderilla. 'You have a one-track mind.'

'I like that!'

As they left the office, General Andrews continued laughing louder than the quip deserved, the ambassador thought. More sly than crude. It convinced him the general had taken advantage of the critical occasion to place his man on the vital embassy detail where Mike Callahan had given Gordell priority. By custom they would be the equally sharing hosts to the American delegation coming to Tehran. But Gordell had just lost an early round of infighting. As they walked down the corridor, the ambassador seemed somehow in the presence of the General George S. Patton of Casablanca days. Gordell felt persecuted.

Captain Peter Harvis was hardly civil to the partner forced upon him by General Tom Andrews, as they drove away from the embassy in the jeep. Because he was junior in rank, Lieutenant George Keyes did the driving. For the first part of the ride, Harvis played the role of senior officer with a clipboard in his lap. He hoped, however, the black man didn't interpret his attitude as bigotry. Like Gordell, he hated the general.

Then, as they travelled the streets of Tehran, Harvis learned Keyes was intelligent, a hard-worker, with a sharp eye for detail. And he had anticipated his role by bringing along a camera. The foresight impressed Harvis. But it was all nothing compared to the fact that Keyes had recently been commissioned by the general for bringing a runaway train with burned-out brakes to a safe stop. The lieutenant had taken over after the engineer had panicked and leaped from the train.

Harvis wailed. 'You're a genuine hero, for chrissake!'

Keyes was another one like Boris and Sam whose accomplishments in the war made his own work seem like malingering.

'I had to,' Keyes said modestly. 'If I didn't, old Tom-Tom would slap a court-martial on me.'

Keyes related the thankless existence in the delivery system of the Persian Gulf Command, around the clock, regardless of weather, wearing out trucks, trains, and men. General Tom Andrews was a tough taskmaster, quick to punish or reward, but the right man for the job. The lieutenant idolized him.

'This deal is a featherbed,' he admitted privately. 'But it's sure important to Tom-Tom.'

'It means a lot to my boss, too.' Harvis was equally candid. 'But opposites don't attract.'

'Yeah, I was the troop in a beachhead.'

'Like a Marine parachute drop.' Harvis was now grateful for this companionship. 'I don't mind. Just so long as it stays exactly like it is.'

'I get it. You're in charge.' Keyes was reassuring. 'But he almost brought down a major to outrank you.'

'The ambassador would have shot that down right away.'

In his turn Harvis satisfied the black man's questions about the workings of the American embassy. He recounted Gordell's breakfast briefing session, fascinating Keyes as if they were whispered secrets of state. The communiqués out of Cairo indicated the talks between Roosevelt, Churchill, and Chiang Kai-shek were arriving at decisions. Japan would be stripped of all the conquests that country had made since 1894. China would be given Manchuria and Formosa. Korea would regain its independence. Though not yet in the Pacific War, the Soviet Union would obtain the Kurile Island chain and the southern half of Sakhalin. The United States would acquire the Japanese mandated islands of the Central Pacific.

The capitals of the world were already speculating beyond Cairo, towards the inevitable meeting of the Big Three. Would it take place in Tehran, so near Cairo? Everyone knew the agenda: the second front. Would Stalin get it? Where would the landing take place? At Churchill's politically strategic point? Or Roosevelt's?

After time off for a quick lunch at the officers' club, Harvis and Keyes continued with their jeep through the crowded streets of the city, taking pictures and notes. The lieutenant was an excellent photographer. The British and Russian embassies were approximately four miles from the landing field. Another four miles beyond them was the American embassy. Thus Churchill and Stalin would reach their destinations first as the planned parade progressed, while Roosevelt had twice as far to ride in the open car before the end of the ceremonial drive.

'Double jeopardy!' Callahan had warned Harvis. 'Don't forget who's Number One!'

They intended to record every building and each corner of the boulevards for possible snipers' nests and commando access angles for attack. Then they would estimate the required number of American MP's to be stationed at each exposure point, as well as the soldiers riding in armed vehicles preceding and behind the President's car. Harvis and Keyes noted teams of British, Russian, and Iranian security men making similar tours of Tehran. Altogether there would be a formidable protective force around the Big Three, intensely alert to the threat of Colonel Konrad Zenner and his commandos.

'The general thinks they ought to call off the Tehran Conference till they clean out those guys,' Keyes said. 'It hasn't been officially announced yet anyway.'

Harvis groaned. 'It has to be the world's worst-kept secret.'

'Do you think that's why they came?' Keyes asked. 'Could there be a leak?'

'Of course!'

'Wanna bet there's a spy in Roosevelt's cane?'

Harvis topped him. 'How about Churchill's martini?'

'Stalin's pipe?'

'Hitler's moustache?'

'And a double agent up each other's ass!'

They roared with laughter.

It was a nice humour to end the day, Harvis thought, as Keyes brought them back to the embassy. They had completed yet another circuit to Mehrabad Airport and return. He stepped out of the jeep, pleased with their relationship and the results of their efforts.

'See you in the morning, George.'

'How about one more go-around, Pete?' Keyes had waited until the last reluctant moment.

'You're kidding!' Harvis exclaimed. 'I've got a meeting.'

'It's the general's orders,' the lieutenant said inflexibly. 'I have to put in a full day and make out a worksheet. It's only four thirty.'

'You mean he wants you to spy on this deal?'

'He says you guys are a bunch of sissy fuckoffs,' Keyes maintained. 'I can't go back now, and I can't find a way to stall around.'

'Now that is a very big crock of shit!'

Harvis returned to his seat in the jeep, thinking the marines had landed and were mopping up.

He was late to the meeting in the Tehran police headquarters. And as he walked into the office, Captain Harvis realized they had formed a silent frieze while waiting for him, like figures on the ancient tombs of Iran. Then his friends came to life, Major Mirza using his beads, Major Skeene his knuckles, and Colonel Artukin his nervous chuckle of greeting.

Their tension was connected to a middle-aged tribal khan and his armed bodyguard, sitting sternly away from the others. The only seat available to Harvis was opposite them, as if in the enemy camp. The khan snorted his annoyance with the American's tardiness, and his bodyguard, sullenly alert to every movement, tracked the latecomer to his place.

Behind his desk, Mirza was between the three Allied soldiers and his two countrymen, an uneasy position of political crossfire. As he began the introductions, Sergeant Mostaffa started to pass out glasses of tea from the samovar. The major's moustache perspired as he extolled and complimented the frozen-faced khan, as the leader of a tribal subdivision of the numerous Bakhtiari tribe, who was a greatly respected voice and a powerful figure in the Bakhtiari council.

Like addressing a totem pole, Harvis thought. He knew the Bakhtiari were mostly nomadic, but could muster a large military force in favour of – or against – the central government as history demanded. The troops of the Shah could never reach these fiercely independent mountain people, protected by nature in their inaccessible and impassable gorges. His friend Mirza was treading a diplomatic tightrope.

It was a terrible tragedy this murder and robbery of the people of the khan's tribe, Mirza said. He had brought these foreigners together to help him understand what had happened, but they would never alleviate the loss of the khan's men.

The Englishman, the Russian, and the American each made a speech following Mirza. They informed the khan, who sat like a stone wall of disdain, about the investigating team that had arrived soon after the daybreak attack on the train. The Iranian brakeman had miraculously survived his leap from the wreckage. From his testimony and the evidence in the woods, it was clearly the precision work of a German commando team wearing the clothes and riding the horses of the khan's murdered people.

They explained that Colonel Konrad Zenner had cleverly used this method to hurt the Allied war effort and at the same time to sow discord in Iran and distrust among the Allies. And despite the vast loss of matériel and the smashed freight train, they made offers of compensation to the khan. Americans, too, had perished in the crash. It was a regretful incident.

There was silence before the khan spoke, as if he considered their words. Then he responded in sorrow and fury.

'Who are these dogs and sons of dogs who kill my young men in the dark? Who are these black-hearted bastard spawn of dishonoured mothers, who steal the clothes and horses from sleeping warriors and leave them dead for the hyenas and jackals? Germans, you say, who dropped from the sky for this purpose.' The khan shook his head. 'It is beyond my belief and the women of these murdered men who wail and tear their hair and the tears of their children, who lost brave sons, fathers, and providers. Who will feed the families of these fallen young lions? Even as they are buried facing Mecca, I will make a vow on the Koran to avenge the death of these heroes of my people. We will not dishonour their memory and accept blood money. We will take blood for blood!'

Then the wrathful khan strode from the room. His bodyguard followed him out.

They left heavy silence.

Harvis had never felt more like a trespasser in Persia as he listened to the speech of the outraged khan. Embroiled bystanders in a war they never made. They were unbridgeable worlds and centuries apart. Time and the Iranians? One had to think in terms of epochs.

Artukin gave his odd laugh. 'What did he mean "blood for blood"?'

'He will attack the trains and truck convoys that pass through his tribal territory,' Mirza explained.

'That is the lifeblood of all my people!'

'Perhaps he will be more understanding after the funeral tomorrow,' Mirza suggested. 'He is in mourning now.'

Skeene offered, 'It would be best to hang those Nazis where he could see them for proof.'

'Why did the khan turn the money down?' Harvis asked. Payment was an old and honourable custom.

'There is political advantage,' Mirza explained. 'Before the father of the Shah came to power, the Bakhtiari plotted to rule Iran. Reza Shah defeated their plans. Now they see an opportunity with a young Shah on the throne. Because he works with the Allies, they will blame him for the death of their sons. To take money would mean to forget it. Now it will be a battle cry.'

Harvis glimpsed a fleeting look of atavistic contempt on Mirza's face for the politically sanctioned soldiers who had caused this imperial impotence.

Then Mirza informed them of the intelligence he had received on the Iranian still with Colonel Zenner, Reza. 'He is the son of the khan of the Qashqai. He was a student in Switzerland when the war began, a smart one. The khan sent him to Germany to make an alliance for guns and matériel.'

'Why?' Harvis asked.

'The Qashqai are like the Bakhtiari. They, too, have always intrigued to gain the throne of Iran,' Mirza said. 'He needs weapons to march on the palace because he believes the government is weak. Our Shah has many worries.'

'How many soldiers do they have?' Artukin asked.

Mirza shrugged. 'They have a population of five hundred thousand in the region of Isfahan and Shiraz.'

'In the British zone,' Skeene pointed out.

Artukin reminded, 'We have the Kurds and Azerbaijani.'

Who don't even speak Persian, Harvis thought. Unlike the tribes, they didn't have designs on the throne, only their independence. Historically, both the Russians and the British had used the minority groups for their political ambitions.

'Bubble, bubble, tribal trouble,' Harvis sang out.

'The Germans know what they are doing. This Colonel Zenner must be stopped. If they cause conflict in my country and win the war, His Imperial Majesty will be forced to leave Iran,' Mirza explained. He loved the exiled Shah, the 'Old King', and never failed to salute his statue in Tehran. Now he had transferred his loyalty to Reza Shah's son, the yearling in the palace, for whom he held a fiercely protective attitude.

Then the major reaffirmed his allegiance to the foreigners in the room, though he resented the extraterritorial rights of the occupation that limited his police powers over transgressing soldiers and nationals.

'I will aid the security of this great conference that is coming to Tehran,' he asserted. 'We are carefully watching Nadiri, the commando who was with the Germans.' He smiled at Harvis. 'He did not tell us all he knows. I have discovered the German underground owes him money for his services as a guide.'

So his instincts had been correct, Harvis thought with gratification. He would have to stop thinking of these people as enigmas. Mirza's pretense of believing his countryman had been playacting. He had let Nadiri 'escape' from the teahouse. The Iranian had not been homesick or a collaborator, but simply hungry and in desperate need of money.

'Well, there it is,' Harvis began to summarize, receiving instant attention. If nothing else, they had a genuine respect for his analyses and talent for synthesis. 'Sabotage the Middle Eastern supply line of the Russians, disrupt the Iranian government, and assassinate the Big Three.'

'That is Zenner's specialty,' Artukin sneered. The Allies had pooled their information from the various G2's about the commando leader in Iran. 'Murder in the night and a stab in the back for Heinrich Himmler and then for Adolf Hitler.'

'His personal representative to the Tehran Conference,' Skeene muttered a droll aside.

'If you operate on the premise that the Führer is losing the war, then he needs one masterstroke,' Harvis reasoned. 'A desperate act of Nazi-type diplomacy. Like this commando mission.'

'They are rats from a sinking ship!' Artukin scorned.

Harvis went on: 'Kidnap – or kill – all or any of the Big Three. Then bargain for better peace terms. Think of Roosevelt, Churchill, or Stalin in a Berlin bunker with Hitler's Luger at their heads.'

As they jointly considered this highly dramatic possibility,

Harvis picked up his notebook and rose to leave. Skeene tugged at his sleeve, astonished. 'Where are you going?'

'To the office,' Harvis replied firmly.

'Are you crazy?' Artukin exploded. 'It is closed!'

'I have a table for us at the Moulin Rouge,' Mirza exclaimed in dismay. 'It is my party. You must come!'

Each month they chose another nightclub or restaurant for their meetings. Prior to the announcement of the conference and the commando drop, their intelligence discussions had been trivia, excuses for entertainment and camaraderie.

'I have reports to make on this stuff,' Harvis maintained diligently. 'You guys must have heard of Mike Callahan.'

Artukin ran a finger across his throat. 'I have Comrade Goria.'

'We've all got guns at our heads,' Skeene argued. 'Haven't you ever heard of warrior's relaxation?'

'How could he?' Artukin taunted. 'Petroushka has never been to war.'

Stung, Harvis capitulated. 'Okay....'

17

Colonel Konrad Zenner stood outside the radio tent door at his Shiraz hill camp, lighting up the interior with a flashlight. It was ten o'clock at night. The beam shone on Reza, wearing the headset, as he sat before the receiver, nodding respectfully to the words being broadcast into his ears. The Iranian smiled up at Zenner as if receiving good news. They were instructions from the khan of the Qashqai to his son.

Yorck and Sepp were close enough to the colonel to observe his reactions. Their leader reflected satisfaction with the incoming information, and taking their cue from him, the pair grinned in unison. They resembled two Doberman pinschers straining at the leash. The radio conversations between the Iranians were supposed to set them into motion. That morning Wolf Pack Number Three under the leadership of Colonel Zenner had destroyed an enemy freight train. Now they craved action.

Then Reza removed the headset and left the tent. The three Germans crowded around him.

'My father has received everything that has been promised.' He smiled. 'The guns, the gold, the equipment. He thanks you for the presents to my mother.'

'It's only the beginning,' Zenner told him. 'A down payment. In Berlin they're encouraged by what we have already done. They're giving us unlimited backing.'

'My father heard about the train,' Reza reported. 'He said it was a big thing.'

Yorck flexed his muscles. 'Watch what we can do, eh, Sepp?'

'We'll show them!' Sepp playfully punched his partner.

Reza spoke with pride. 'My father respects power.'

'He's a man to admire,' Zenner declared emphatically. 'The khan can have anything he wants. There's no limit.'

'That's what he would like to hear.' Reza had the finesse of a skilled negotiator. 'He's already beginning another list. He asked if you could leave the airplane with him on the mountain when you are finished with it.'

The colonel's response was quick. 'It's his. But the pilot will have to go back to Germany.'

'I'm a flier,' Reza said audaciously. 'The Qashqai Air Force.'

'Anything more?' Zenner offered zealously.

'That's all for the time being,' Reza said, satisfied with himself. 'Now I'll keep my part of the bargain.'

They selected handguns, which they hid under their shirts. Then Reza showed the way out of the camp, down the hill. It was a clear night. The lights of the city of Shiraz, their destination, sparkled distantly below them.

As they walked in single file, the four men appeared like three foreign tourists with an Iranian guide. It was not an uncommon sight for the city of poets that had received such alien visitors for centuries.

Having wonderful time. Wish you were here. Captain Peter Harvis wrote a mental postcard to whom it may concern. Am in the Moulin Rouge nightclub. The belly dancer is sensational!

Once again he was into the role of civilian guest to an international party of rich, romantic, and very important people. The official greeting he had received from the United States government signed by the President wasn't a draft notice but really an invitation to a costume ball in Tehran, Iran (Persia). All expenses paid.

He wasn't the only American at the party. The nightclub was jammed with wealthy Iranians, Middle Eastern royalty, oil-rich sheiks, Allied military brass, and fortunate foreigners. Among them Harvis noticed two American officers with local businessman at different tables. Betty had pointed them out once as the 'Colonel for Coca-Cola' and the 'Colonel for Pepsi-Cola'. They travelled with the troops, competing for cultural bridgeheads.

There was a happy party of GI's, probably blowing black-market money on some Polish refugee girls who couldn't speak English. The soldiers sat close enough to touch the belly dancer and tried to catch the flying gold rings attached to her skirt. But she was a marvellously moving target.

Another American had gone out of his way to greet Harvis. They had met before at the Fourth of July celebration at the embassy. Ebenezer Foster Waite was an old resident of Tehran, an elegant fifty-year-old man, who was a poet and lawyer. He sat with an outlandishly attired young man of twenty, with a mass of curling black hair shiny with brilliantine. They took no notice of the belly dancer.

In his first days as intelligence officer Harvis had gone over a list of Americans in Iran with Betty. She had described Waite as 'a lousy American right-wing fascist who gave poetry a bad name'. She liked to label people. He's no closet queen, Harvis observed. But Betty had not told him Waite was a homosexual. Maybe it was insignificant to her, but the couple leaning across the table to each other repelled him.

He saw other of his countrymen wearing Betty's invisible name tags: 'The Chicago goodwill dope dealer', 'the Biloxi missionary phony', 'the Philadelphia society whore', 'the Los Angeles geologist bail jumper', 'the New York radio star child rapist', and 'the Boston DAR lesbian'.

Harvis had learned the rest of the world was a haven for Americans who must feel superior to 'natives'. He had seen them browbeat servants they could never hope to employ in the States. They complained about the people, discovering new inadequacies daily: Villagers were illiterate, uneducated, worthless. Carpet workers were cheats; watch out for dyes and ties. Servants were not dependable, untrustworthy, opium users. Landlords were knaves. Government officials were corrupt. The bureaucracy was confusing, and you had to 'know somebody' to get anything done. The roads were bad because the road workers were lazy. Soldiers were stupid.

They knew little of the language and nothing of the culture. It was a 'backward' country. There were self-sacrificing teachers, missionaries, serious scholars, and philosophical expatriates, but mostly it was those who couldn't make it back home.

'Peter, you are not drinking!' Mirza insisted.

Tonight it was the Iranian major's treat. Until he had met him, Harvis hadn't known there was a special Persian pleasure in playing host. Mirza loved to entertain. While his friends got drunk on vodka, he sipped Shiraz wine soberly, in order not to miss a nuance of the night, especially the belly dancer.

'The ease of my guests is my delight,' he always said.

More than usual the police major seemed made of mystery and mercury, Harvis thought, being himself more drunk than usual. Each time he saw the man Faraj appeared like a double vision. Harvis decided the father was unaware of his daughter's secret life and ambitions. He was reminded of the unproud episode of her midnight visit. 'No harm, no foul?' Faraj and he had learned something about him. He could be a tough guy. But the total knowledge was recondite. Death and tragedy. He didn't want to dwell on the first anymore. But sex seemed to enhance the second. Getting laid was part of the desire to live. Anyway, since she needed him, Faraj would pretend it had never occurred, like a Persian. He intended to act the same way. These people knew about life.

'Bravo!' Artukin shouted at the belly dancer.

There was a man who understood it all, Harvis thought. His Russian friend was going vodka-wild with desire for the performer and her fluid undulations. Mirza had already sent a message backstage in his behalf. All varieties of women provoked passion in the broad breast of Colonel Boris Artukin, fulfilling his fantasies from the terrible Russian trenches.

Although he followed the movements of the belly dancer with a fixed smile, Skeene was unmoved by her, Harvis knew. The sensitive Englishman's eyes were really turned inward, contemplating sensations yet to come. He was waiting for a man to bring him hemp, which he had smoked since his escape from the Germans. Harvis thought he would always be a prisoner of war.

He had once confided to Harvis, 'Hemp helped me to understand the sanity of *Alice in Wonderland*.'

Another time he had shamed the young American into trying it. Harvis was too resistant for the effect. He had acted the clown. He wanted the Englishman to ask him again, but Harvis realized he'd been given his first and last glimpse of the world Sam Skeene walked.

He explained himself one day with rare revelation. 'Every friend I made in the Army died, so I don't like to make new ones.'

Harvis had seen him with a woman only once when Skeene had invited Betty and him to the British legation pool for a swim. She was an English nurse. He never talked about his family in England. He never discussed sex. Perhaps he was hurt....

'Bravo!' Artukin called out again at the belly dancer and nudged Harvis. He joined in with a shrill whistle of appreciation. The audience inspired her to wilder movements. It seemed through his vodka vision that the separate parts of her ample anatomy had their own erotic rhythms. The bells on her body and the accompanying music made sounds of rampant sex.

As a Westerner, Harvis realized Mirza's reactions were different from those of his guests. There was a unique dialogue between the belly dancer and the major. It was a pantomime of gestures, most of which Harvis didn't get, involving the tease, the acceptance, and the consummation of copulation.

She finished to frenzied applause and disappeared backstage. The band played Iranian improvisations on strings and drum, called the kemanche, santour, ney, and tar, as accompaniment to a male singer. It was subtle, surprising, and intense music Harvis wasn't sure he would ever understand, the Dastgah.

The waiter brought another bottle of wine for Major Mirza, but Harvis wouldn't let him open it. 'Give us a poem first,' he demanded of Mirza, who could quote whole passages from the Koran or any of the Persian classics in poetry and prose. 'How about one for pouring wine?'

The major was happy to oblige. 'It shall be from Hafiz.'

He gave the waiter money to pay the musicians for the appropriate 'Hafiz mode', reminding Harvis that music and poetry had a natural relationship in Iran. He'd recite anything but Omar Khayyam, Harvis thought. Mirza had influenced him to drop Khayyam for study, claiming the American could get closer to the heart of Iran through Hafiz, the fourteenth-century poet, philosopher, and epigrammist.

The band began, and Mirza stood up to pour the wine. The moment between him and the musicians passed unnoticed amid the gaiety of nightclub babel. They were just another party in the crowded room. Then Mirza quoted:

Then drink! For now the winemaker's heel
Stamps on the night's grapes! See, through the shattered peel
The crimson juice pours out and fills the bowl
Dawn will soon die – drink, while this wine is real!

Mirza made a slight bow, and his friends raised their glasses to him, shouting 'Bravo!' All eyes in the Moulin Rouge turned to their table. Mirza sat down, shyly, suddenly embarrassed.

What men! Harvis idealized drunkenly, measuring himself. The one who could accept the challenge of poetry, wrestling, or battle. The all-time womanizing war hero. The deeply wounded addict who had made a dangerous getaway against impossible odds. They all had been under fire. They had slain enemies. Boris and Sam considered him a kid brother. To Mirza he was like a young nephew. Why not? He was lucky to be tolerated. He was in the company of giants!

'Fellas, I've got a great idea!' Harvis said thickly.

At that moment a man came and whispered to Artukin. The big Russian jumped up, threw a kiss to the table, and left for the dressing room of the belly dancer.

Harvis gained momentum. 'Sam, there you are in Tehran with your Indian Army signalmen in a radio van tracking down underground wireless networks. Real busy —'

'*Very* busy!' Skeene was high, but it was not the high he was seeking. What he required was hard to obtain; it wasn't grown in Iran. 'Very frustrated, too!'

'And Boris is out all day on the streets of this city with his squad of Russian mujiks sweeping the area for German spies. Right?' Harvis demanded.

'Wrong!' Skeene said. 'He hasn't caught a thing!'

'Meanwhile, Ali here is operating twenty-four hours defending his country. Okay. What about me? Well, I've decided to help out the cause by looking for Colonel Zenner.'

Skeene said, 'Single-handed, of course!'

'Why not?' Harvis grinned. 'One on one. *Mano a mano*.'

Skeene realized he was not joking.

'Have another drink and drown the bloody thought,' he suggested. 'Do you know what they call him?'

'Sure, the most dangerous man in Europe.'

Mirza put in paternally, 'Peter, we have a saying – do not place your feet beyond your carpet.'

'How does that apply?'

Skeene said, 'English translation: Have you ever fired a gun at a man, old chap?'

A brown-skinned man in a turban materialized at the table out of the nightclub fog. He carried a briefcase. 'Major Skeene?'

Skeene stood up, with a broad smile of relief. 'Pleasant dreams, Petroushka,' he said, turning away.

Harvis lashed out in retaliation. 'Fuck you, Major Sneer!'

Skeene halted in his tracks.

'If you see your asshole buddy, fuck Colonel Leer, too!'

Skeene appeared puzzled, then went off with the Indian. The Englishman had his hemp.

Harvis drank the last of the vodka, ignoring Mirza. He had taken a hard blow to his gathering ego. Plummeting from some Mount Demavend into an Iranian abyss, then coming face to face with an old man exactly like the one he had met in a village. The man was a sayyid, who had made the journey to Mecca, a haji with a green waistband. When Harvis had offered his hand, the old man refused it as unclean.

'That's me around here,' he submitted to the world at large. 'An untouchable infidel!'

'I will drive you home,' Mirza said placatingly.

'I can take care of myself tonight. And from now on, you hear, Major Mirza?'

'Of course.'

'I want to pay my end of the bill.'

'But you are my guest,' Mirza protested patiently. 'Please —'

'I won't be needing a Persian guide anymore.' Harvis began to fumble for his wallet. 'I know enough to get around.'

They hadn't seen Ebenezer Foster Waite come to the table. He was accompanied by the manager of the Moulin Rouge.

'If you're arguing about the cheque,' Waite said, 'I've settled it.'

The manager grinned at Mirza. 'Monsieur Waite has become your generous host,' he said and went away.

Mirza looked at Harvis.

'Why not?' Harvis said. He had no real desire to go home.

The tall, imposing American intrigued him. Waite's twenties avant-garde poetry was in every college lit course.

There was a singer onstage now. 'She is my favourite,' Mirza said, meaning he would prefer to stay.

Waite sat down. 'Thank you, gentlemen.'

He must have left the States because of a sex problem, it struck Harvis irrelevantly. Betty insisted Waite was paranoid on pet economic theories. Influenced by a college professor who had made a big case about Waite's rejection of American materialism, Harvis considered him a principled poet, despite his politics. It was his flaunted homosexuality that he found offensive. But though she hated his ideas and thought his poetry obscure, Betty didn't think what people did in bed should be used against them.

Waite turned to Harvis for sanction. 'May I?'

Harvis shrugged. The night was getting queerer. The liquor weighed heavily on his lids. He had trouble keeping his chin up.

Waite beckoned. 'His name is Mario, an Italian.'

Mario table-hopped in a moment. At close range, Harvis thought the fruit was a wet-lipped, dreamy-eyed piece of Roman sculpture. Waite introduced them.

The waiter brought a bowl of iced fruits. Mirza and Waite ordered liqueurs. Mario took a bunch of grapes. Just like a fag, Harvis thought. He settled for ice water, showing great restraint. He was determined to remain alert because Waite was after something: he anticipated some stylish sleight of hand. But first there was the customary teshrifat, some social sparring.

'On the first day I came to this country – twenty years ago –

I learned a bribe doesn't necessarily produce what one expects,' Waite said. 'It was this charming unpredictableness that convinced me to stay. And I don't have a single regret.'

Perfect for Mirza, Harvis thought. This had to be the voice and manner of the New England Brahmins. The old rich.

'The poetic temperament at work,' Harvis mumbled vaguely.

Waite archly ignored Harvis, leaning towards Mirza. Harvis wondered how he had offended him. Mario simply smiled at each one in turn and plucked grapes. An empty-headed fairy, Harvis decided. His brains were in his ass.

'You understand my country,' Mirza complimented. 'I have received great enjoyment when you recite Firdausi's poems on the radio.'

'You're very kind,' Waite told him. 'It should please you to know I was the first American to translate Hafiz for the United States.'

Mirza glowed. 'That was a noble enterprise.'

'It was a noble failure,' Waite said, then recognizing Harvis, as if fixing the blame. 'I was casting pearls before swine, Captain.'

Bad manners shocked Mirza. 'Mr Waite—'

'That's okay, Ali,' Harvis said foggily. 'We come from a country where there's free speech.'

'Free for niggers, kikes, wops, and greasers,' Waite said. 'Not for queers, fags fruits, and fairies.'

Mario giggled. 'Neezie,' he chided.

Harvis felt transparent. And guilty, as if he had uttered the words in his mind. He must have looked them.

'To know Hafiz is to know my country,' Mirza said, bringing back the subject, divertingly. 'We do not think of you as a foreigner.'

'Some say I'm more Persian than the Persians!'

'Others say you're less American than the Americans,' Harvis rallied. 'How about getting to the point?'

Waite looked straight at Mirza. 'Mario is a poet, too,' he said, his tone shifting, 'He wants to remain in this country, Major Mirza. But he's an Italian.'

'An enemy alien.' Mirza got down to business. 'Why was he not deported with the Germans?'

Mario had dropped the silly grin and was following each word greedily, Harvis noted. He looked less effeminate, more like a tough hustler.

'There is an unfortunate mixup in the papers,' Waite explained. 'Mario was brought here before the illegal occupation of Iran by the so-called democratic forces.'

Harvis didn't rise to this. Waite never hid his views from the embassy, and he wasn't addressing him now. Harvis was more curious about Mirza's reactions.

'I do not wish to discuss politics,' Mirza replied.

'You must agree this is not your war, Major Mirza.'

'The Shah's will is my will,' Mirza said, with touchy nationalism. 'That is all.'

Harvis saw Mirza's embarrassment. These were taboo subjects between them. Their dialogue was sobering Harvis.

'I can't believe you *really* co-operate with these foreign soldiers, Major Mirza,' Waite went on relentlessly. 'No true Iranian should.'

This is it, Harvis thought.

'I believe in Iran for the Iranians, Mr Waite,' Mirza said with quiet conviction. 'Because of that I work hard and *sincerely* with them – so that they will leave sooner.'

'Fair enough,' Harvis said out loud.

Mirza and Harvis made a simultaneous move to leave.

'Hold on,' Waite said. 'I have a proposal. It will interest you, too, Captain Harvis.'

He was an international lawyer who represented business interests from all over the world, Waite said. He had clients on both sides of the war, among them deported members of the German community in Iran who left their affairs in his charge. One of them had brought Mario from Italy to work in his firm. This 'certain person' was out of the country now. But he had imperative reasons for slipping back. It would be illegal entry. And Waite wanted Mirza to arrest him at the proper time.

'This "certain person" is so important he is worth a visa for Mario?' Mirza said, looking at him.

Mario smiled appealingly in return.

The 'affairs' left in Waite's charge must be Mario, Harvis thought. It was a homo triangle. Waite was getting rid of a rival. The German had to be in the underground. It was the only value in the transaction.

'The capture of this "certain person" should be worth a permanent residency for Mario,' Waite bargained. 'Is it a deal?'

Mario beamed winningly.

'It is unpredictable,' Mirza said.

Mario hissed something in Italian, knocked over a glass of water, and left the table. Waite's poise cracked. With a look of lovelorn distress, he chased after Mario. They left the Moulin Rouge together.

Mirza and Harvis made tacit communication. The major then got up and left the nightclub.

19

'This is the tomb of Hafiz.'

From the moment they had flown over the borders of Iran in the British Lancaster, Reza had maintained a constant stream of information about his country. He had pointed out the famous landmarks from the air. Now he was continuing on the ground, walking the historic streets of Shiraz. It was past midnight, and the burial place of the poet was hardly visible.

'The other great poet buried here is Saadi.' Reza knew they were uninterested and tired after the two-hour hike from the hills, but he didn't mind talking to himself about the land he loved. 'Shiraz is where my people go to town.'

Yorck and Sepp mumbled nothings.

Colonel Zenner said, 'It won't be long before the Qashqai own it.'

A half hour later they were brought by Reza to a house with a garden. The occupants were asleep.

They spread out quietly, checking the grounds. Zenner found a Chevrolet station wagon in the garage. It had a full tank of gasoline, reserve tins filled also, ready for travel.

Then Reza went to the front of the house, while the Germans waited in the shadows. He pounded on the door. In a few moments the lights in the house went on.

A young man's voice came through the door. 'Who is there?'

Reza replied. 'I have a message for Professor Rudolph Berger.'

'He isn't home.'

'It is important,' Reza said. 'Who are you?'

'Kasim, his son-in-law. Slip it under the door.'

'Is the wife of the professor there?'

'Yes,' Mrs Berger called out. 'My husband is away.'

'I must have you sign it,' Reza insisted.

There was a moment of hesitation or consultation. Then the door was unlatched and opened.

The four commandos burst into the front room of the house. Yorck and Sepp pounced on Kasim, a slight young Persian. Reza locked the door. Colonel Zenner faced two women in nightgowns, mother and daughter, who stood in mute shock. Mrs Berger was an attractive Persian woman of forty-five.

Anna was a beautiful young woman, eighteen years old and just recovering from childbirth. There was silence while they assessed each other.

A baby began to cry.

Zenner commanded, 'Take him to the garage and ask questions.'

Yorck clasped a hand over Kasim's mouth and held the top of him while Sepp picked up his legs. They carried the squirming man out through the back of the house.

Zenner nodded to Reza. 'Search the house.'

Reza left the room. It was filled with books and Persian artifacts. The women moved together, eyes dilated, as if observing a nightmare that took them out of bed.

The baby still cried.

Anna pleaded finally. 'My baby —'

'What is it?' Zenner asked.

'A boy.'

'It's good for him,' Zenner said. 'Sit down.'

The women obeyed, holding hands on the couch, trembling. This evil visitation was beyond all comprehension.

The baby stopped crying.

'Frau Berger,' Zenner said, 'your husband is the greatest living authority on Persian culture. A famous archaeologist. Where is he?'

'The occupation. Then Iran declared war. Germans were ordered to the embassy in Tehran.' Mrs Berger spoke numbly. 'He went there. We pray he is safe in Berlin.'

'Not all Germans came home,' Zenner said. 'Some are in the camps of the English and the filthy Bolsheviks. Some stayed behind in the cause of the Fatherland.'

'He is too old to fight,' Mrs Berger said.

Anna added, 'My father would not hurt anyone.'

'The records are in Berlin,' Zenner said. 'The professor did not report to the German embassy.'

'What do you want of him?'

'I need him, Frau Berger. Where is he hiding?'

'If Papa is still here, he would send word,' Anna confirmed. 'He would not let us worry.'

Yorck and Sepp came into the room. Their report was a grin and a shrug. It was enough for the colonel.

Anna sprang forward. 'Where is Kasim?'

Sepp ogled her full-bodied beauty. 'He's waiting out there.'

'He wants to take you for a ride,' Yorck teased.

She tried to run by them. The young SS men made an amusing game out of blocking the scantily clad girl. They found her mounting hysteria hilarious.

'Kasim!' she screamed.

They pushed her to the couch beside her mother. The colonel considered the byplay part of the intimidation.

'Well?' he asked Mrs Berger.

She shook her head.

Reza returned with a big basket of packed food, a filled thermos jug, and car keys.

'Look what I found!'

Zenner ordered Mrs Berger. 'Get up!'

The Persian woman rose to stand straight. Anna cringed on the couch, whimpering her husband's name.

Zenner indicated the food basket. 'Where is the professor waiting for this feast?'

'It is not for him,' Mrs Berger asserted valiantly. 'We are going on a picnic with friends.'

'Take them away,' Zenner said to Yorck and Sepp. 'Come back with the truth.'

The women were appalled as the two coveting men started for them. Mrs Berger tried to envelop her daughter protectively. Anna broke away to confront her tormentors.

'Leave her alone, do you hear? Take me, but leave her alone.' She advanced on the colonel. 'Haven't you any pity? She's my mother. Haven't you ever had a mother, you animal?'

Zenner's blood drained in a sick rage. Looking at him, his men backed off, as if to make space for his violence. The colonel gripped the girl by the shoulders in his powerful hands and pressed her painfully quiet.

'You half-breed bitch! You mongrel mix-blood! How dare you speak of my mother!'

He flung her to Sepp. Then he slapped Mrs Berger, knocking her to the floor.

'Filth! You'll get what good wives deserve for helping their husbands!' Zenner shouted. 'Get them out of my sight!'

Yorck took Mrs Berger, while Sepp held Anna. Mother and daughter resisted, screamed, and pleaded. The Nazis stripped them, then carried the struggling women into the bedrooms.

The baby started to cry again.

It was a scene Reza was unprepared for and had no desire to witness. Revolted, he said nothing.

'Let's go,' Zenner said to him. 'You'll have to take me to the pickup point.' Then appeasingly, having noted Reza's repugnance: 'Your Storch.'

'It's a beautiful plane,' Reza said sullenly. 'I can't wait to fly it.'

'You can fly me to see your father.'

They went out the rear door to the garage, shutting out the baby's cries and the wailing women. Reza halted with a rankling issue to resolve.

'Something is bothering me. Why did you call that woman filth? She's Iranian, like me.'

'We Germans have Japanese allies, too,' Zenner told him without cant. 'The allies of the dirty Russians are English lords. We don't have to like our allies.'

'We don't say allies, we say friends.'

'Friends are for a long time,' Zenner said uncompromisingly. 'This war won't last that long.'

'We live and learn,' Reza remarked bitterly.

'Just live, Reza,' Zenner advised in a vague threat. 'Learning can get you killed.'

They found Kasim dead in the back of the station wagon. He had been strangled by either Yorck or Sepp. Both were capable of it. Zenner took a moment to consider the awkwardness.

'We'll drop him off,' he decided.

Reza had the keys and took the wheel of the station wagon. The colonel sat beside him. Behind them, Kasim seemed asleep on the back seat. It was after midnight when they drove away from the Berger house.

'I want to show you the tomb of Saadi,' Reza requested. 'It is a beautiful garden.'

Zenner showed indulgence. 'We have plenty of time.'

20

It was after midnight when Captain Peter Harvis left the Moulin Rouge. There was a wintry chill in the streets of Tehran, but he wore the weatherproofing of vodka.

He drove to the embassy to file the report he should have written before the party in the nightclub, though it didn't seem possible after the amounts of liquor and emotion Harvis had swallowed. Waite, Mario, Mirza, Skeene, and Artukin were still jostling him in the jeep like unruly passengers. Only the extraterritorial refuge of his office would shake them.

'Working on the "monster", Captain?' The MP guard used the staff's code name for the conference preparations.

Harvis signed in. 'Yeah, the one with three heads.'

'Looks like you got two of them.' The guard grinned. 'There's some coffee brewing.'

He carried the coffee cup from the embassy kitchen to his office and drank it before he sat down at the typewriter on his desk. Then he removed his cap and coat to work. It was impossible to isolate his report from the high events in the nightclub. Major Sam Skeene's demeaning insults clung to him like the tenacity of truth. The embittered Englishman meant if you're a soldier, do what soldiers do. Fuck, rape, torture, kill. A uniform is not a camouflage. Harvis should be court-martialed for not impersonating an officer of an army at war.

His territory included the small arsenal in the basement of the embassy building. Harvis took the keys out of his desk drawer and went down the stairs to open the armoury. It contained a rifle rack, handguns, ammunition, and a narrow target range.

Cosy, he thought. Like the Mole's burrow or Ratty's place in *The Wind in the Willows*, his favourite book as a child.

He selected a carbine, his mind going back to his experience with weapons. Not to Camp Kohler in Sacramento, where he had done his Army basic training, but to the time before the war, when he was eleven years old in Moreno, during a hot summer in the San Joaquin Valley. His family had lived on the outskirts of town, near an old wooden speedway used only by bike-riding kids, who inevitably came home with painful slivers.

He owned a single-shot twenty-two. Barefoot in the heat, dressed in overalls, he used to go hunting with his collie dog, Shep. He went after quail and rabbits and birds, missing most of the time. (Later, he had done much better on the Army rifle range.) And when he picked grapes on the old American's ranch during the summer for school money, he always had his rifle for snakes. He never saw one, though it awed the other working children in the vineyard. (And then swimming in the ditch to wash off sweat and dust.)

Once he came across a cat under a tree. He was a dog-loving cat-hater, naturally. He aimed his rifle, expecting the scaredy-cat to flee. This one didn't move and looked directly into his eyes. He pulled the trigger and shot the cat in the head. It didn't make a sound. Just died under the tree.

He never used the twenty-two again.

'Good idea, Pete.'

The ambassador had entered the armoury. He appeared tired and troubled, lost in his own domain. Harvis felt caught in an embarrassing act, his privacy violated.

'I figured I'd brush up, sir.'

'With a man like Colonel Konrad Zenner loose, anything can happen,' Gordell concurred.

The upper echelons were conferring at any hour until the arrival of the Big Three. Harvis should have welcomed the infrequent familiarity of this midnight communion. But now he resented the intrusion because the precious solitude had transported him home.

'After the calling card the colonel left at the ruined train this morning, I suspect we'll be hearing more from his commandos very soon.'

'Why, sir?'

'A hunch.'

'Hunch?'

'It's the witching hour, Pete. Systems and regulations are nine-to-five stuff,' Gordell pointed out. 'I figure the Nazis will operate on my famous rule of three theory.'

'What's that?'

'I got that from Charlie Chaplin's rules of comedy. You prepare a joke in three stages. It applies to anything.'

Harvis laughed. Instead of going home, the lonely man had come here because his wife was in the States. He was amused, but Gordell was still an uninvited guest. He began an elaborate inspection of the carbine to discourage further conversation.

'If you consider that funny, you should hear my theory of the momentum of mediocrity.'

Harvis smiled abstractedly.

Gordell didn't require encouragement. 'That applies particularly to American politicians who succeed by a consistent accumulation of mistakes. A stupid man could become President because we always give losers a second chance. Probably because our nation was first populated by losers.' He laughed. 'That's what happened to my career, Pete. Too cautious. I never made errors. People hate perfection.'

It occurred to Harvis that silence might be rudeness. 'What happened at the meeting, sir?'

'It broke up early because of me and General Andrews.' Gordell smiled. 'We were making life miserable for Volkoff and Sir Henry, asking what they were doing about the German commandos. The general was his most obnoxious, demanding more troops for our shipments. But we're all on edge. It's touch and go about the Tehran Conference, you know.'

'They might call it off?'

'After all, Roosevelt and Churchill could remain in Cairo and have Stalin come here,' the ambassador said. 'For selfish reasons I would hate to see it happen. But if our President's life were in danger, well —'

Bullshit, Harvis thought.

It was the only time in their association Harvis had reason to doubt Gordell's sincerity. He had a once-in-a-lifetime opportunity to play a role among the most important statesmen in the world. If Colonel Konrad Zenner had the American embassy under siege, Gordell would have FDR expediently dropped by parachute to promote himself.

'It wouldn't be the first attempt on President Roosevelt's life, you know,' Gordell said.

Harvis regretted his first response. He made a show of counting the ammo. There was no stopping the ambassador from rambling on.

'Imagine for a moment what one man with a fixed idea in his warped mind, the nut loose in the perfect machine, can do with a rapid-firing rifle. A sharpshooter like Colonel Zenner for instance.' Gordell was caught up in a vision of violence. 'Pete, our end of the defences must be perfect!'

Harvis nodded affirmatively, though Gordell wasn't looking at him. He was really talking to himself.

'If the worst took place, what would happen to *me*?'

He would die, and you would live, Harvis thought uncharitably. The ambassador suddenly appeared older than his age, a candidate for the retirement he disclaimed. ('I'm not ready for the rocking chair yet, Pete.') Harvis saw him visibly shiver. The armoury was like a cold storage, but he thought Gordell was contemplating his own aging.

Gordell broke out of it. 'Pete, did you get your report off to Callahan?'

It was probably why he returned from the meeting, Harvis thought. 'Not yet, sir,' he said, sighting his carbine. 'I thought I'd try a few rounds first.'

'Of course,' Gordell said. 'I'll watch, if you don't mind.'

Harvis didn't like critical people peering over his shoulder. There were earplugs on the counter, but he perversely didn't suggest them. He took aim and squeezed off some thunderous shots. He was disgusted with the results, particularly with a spectator.

'I stink!'

He turned to find the ambassador gone. Spying on me, he thought. Just like General Tom-Tom.

21

Colonel Konrad Zenner watched Wolf Pack Number Four work. Looking down from the mountainside above the highway, he could see the five men performing the methods he had taught them. They had begun mining the mountain road at sunrise and would be finished in exactly two hours, he noted. It was the kind of speed and expertise he expected from graduates of his school of death and destruction to the foes of the Third Reich.

When the young team of Nazis climbed up to the observation point, the colonel congratulated them. They attached the wires from the explosives to the detonator like activized reins. After that there was nothing to do but wait for the American truck convoy. The terrain was perfect for Colonel Zenner's purpose. It was a barren mountain, unlike lush Germany, rocky and treeless. 'No birds,' Zenner commented critically to his men.

They heard the American trucks making the tortuous climb up the mountain road in low gear before they came into sight. Zenner's calculations jibed with the information signalled to him from friends in Khorramshar as to time. His intelligence would be no less detailed than before; he had broadcast the quantities to Berlin. He anticipated one hundred trucks loaded with war matériel for Russia. There would be a jeep in the lead with an American corporal driving, plus his lieutenant. On the rear seat would be a Russian captain, whose duty it was to follow the lend-lease from the American ships through Iran, across the Soviet border. The fourth passenger in the jeep would be an English lieutenant hitching a ride north.

The colonel had selected a narrow, sharp, twisting, and steep section of the highway, ideal for easy landslides and long drops of the mountainside, thus making nature an ally. The sound grew louder as the truck convoy inched upwards. Now Zenner took over the detonator; there was a matter of precise timing necessary. He let the lead jeep go by and then he pushed down.

The German commandos observed the outcome of their handiwork, the organized chaos. It seemed from above as though the highway were a dying dragon, heaving and spewing fire. Trucks toppled off the road, and ammo carriers blew up.

Men ran, shouted, and died. Others wandered in bewilderment with no enemy in sight.

Colonel Zenner and his men were happy with this havoc. Then they headed downward towards the jeep Zenner had deliberately isolated. The plan was to create a landslide between the men in the Allied jeep and the convoy behind them. The manoeuvre had succeeded beautifully, Zenner commended his team.

The four men in the jeep could hear the voices and the explosions, but they were helpless unless they could scale the huge mound of rocks and dirt blocking the road. They abandoned the jeep to make the attempt.

As they left, the Nazis came to the jeep. Then Colonel Zenner and his men opened fire on the backs of the unsuspecting quartet who were scrambling over the landslide.

The Englishman fell first. The two Americans and the Russian whirled to face the surprise attack with their handguns. They were cut down by bursts from automatic rifles and died in the dirt without returning fire.

The panicked survivors of the convoy could hear the shots above the burning wreckage. They knew it involved their cut-off officers in a gun battle, but the road between them was insurmountable.

'No witnesses,' Zenner reminded his team.

To make certain they emptied their clips into the bodies of the four prone men. They jolted lifelike as the bullets struck. Then the SS men reloaded.

The American jeep was a prize of war, and the Germans drove off in it. His men proved again they were apt pupils because Zenner had taught them to use the enemy's resources. An hour later the Nazis, singing songs of war, returned to the forgotten old fort the team used as a hideout. The radioman and the pilot of the Storch lightplane were waiting.

Proud and respectful, Wolf Pack Number Four waved farewell as Colonel Konrad Zenner boarded the plane and flew away.

22

It came to Harvis as he stood under the downpour of his morning shower that someone was pounding on his apartment door. He turned off the water and hastened to respond, grabbing up his bathrobe en route. Being roused by a messenger in this fashion was to be expected. These days there was a rumour a minute in the bazaars, teahouses, and ministries. The winter air crackled politically like a lit fuse.

'Who is it?'

'It's me, Pete.'

'For chrissake, George,' Harvis complained, letting in Lieutenant Keyes. They were to meet at the embassy in an hour. 'Are you some kind of nutty early bird after the worm? Did it ever occur to you that General Andrews was really Simon Legree?'

The black man mumbled miserably, 'I'm sorry. Real sorry.'

He began to wander about the room unevenly.

'You're drunk!' Harvis crowed, delighted to find a flaw in the proper fellow. Momentarily, it was a weakness in the general's man he could exploit. But he seemed in such utter distress. 'Hey, what is it?'

Keyes wagged his head in forlorn grief.

'How do you like those bastards knocking off a whole goddamn truck convoy?'

'What do you mean?'

'I thought they knew everything at the embassy.'

'I haven't been there yet.'

'You can bet old Tom-Tom is there burning the ambassador's ass right now.' Keyes fought back tears. 'He's plumb out of his mind.'

'Sounds like Colonel Zenner and his boys did the dirty again.'

'They got a lot of my buddies.'

The lieutenant sat down and began to sob gently.

It was a staggering second strike by the Nazi commandos, and his first impulse was towards the embassy and the ambassador's morning briefing, but Harvis had Keyes to console.

'I'm sorry,' he said. 'I'll get you some coffee.'

Keyes gestured him aside. 'I'll do it myself.'

Harvis went into the bedroom, leaving the black man alone

with his sorrow. Just now he wasn't the stocky digest version of his idol, General Tom Andrews, but a broken-hearted kid, Harvis thought, putting on his clothes. They had parted badly yesterday. With firm efficiency, the lieutenant had made them operate on the general's timetable. Harvis was pressed between them in a lockstep just as the ambassador had crowded him in the haven of the armoury last night. He had vowed resistance.

Harvis found him drinking coffee in the kitchen. Keyes had himself under control, unclouded now, but embarrassed. He had poured a cup for Harvis.

'I'm sorry,' Keyes said again. 'I'm not used to drinking liquor before breakfast.'

'Who is?'

'I'm not used to drinking period.'

'Forget it.'

'I'd give anything to be with those Limeys and Russkies going after those lousy Germans right now.'

'That's their work around here.'

'I heard they cancelled all leaves. Covering the whole country,' Keyes told him. 'I'm just a jerk shipping clerk.'

'And that's our work,' Harvis said. 'Funny thing. Thinking about Colonel Zenner woke me up this morning. I'll bet it was about the same time he was hitting the convoy.'

'That's crazy.'

'It's probably because I was talking about him with the ambassador last night.' Harvis could see now he had been infected by Gordell's rampant fears for the assassination of Roosevelt. 'I've been getting intelligence on this Zenner fellow. He's not someone to be underestimated.'

'The man who gets him will be a real hero around here.'

Harvis aped a gunfighter's stance.

'Ah'm considerin' the assignment, podner. What's the reward?'

Keyes could smile now. 'I'm ready to work the parade route.' He tested himself on his feet. 'I think —'

'Take it easy.'

'Maybe you'd better drive today.'

'Sure.'

It signalled a shift in their relationship, Harvis thought. He intended to handle the jeep in the manner he would take over the whole deal, perfectly. The direction would come from him. The general could shove his worksheets from now on.

'What would Tom-Tom do if he saw you now?' Harvis asked, as they started out of the apartment.

'Clobber me with a court-martial.'

'I've got a name for those streets we're checking and trekking out,' Harvis said. 'Nightmare Alley.'

Lieutenant Keyes pressed his fingers to his temples. 'That's all the way it is....'

It was late in the afternoon when Captain Peter Harvis showed up at the Tehran police headquarters, having put his hung-over partner to bed. The call from Major Ali Mirza had been imperative. Harvis and his friends were an informally organized unit created for the convenience of their ambassadors, a conduit to each other outside ordinary channels. The four-man group had no name, meeting at their own discretion, provided it didn't interfere with their regular work. So they had no idea what Mirza's emergency was all about.

Sergeant Mostaffa offered tea. But it was the time of day when Harvis preferred a cocktail. He was tired and hungry after working with the mourning Lieutenant Keyes, who had been disconsolate. Keyes had been too upset to eat or focus his camera. He still carried unprocessed film taken of friends killed in the commando raid on the truck convoy.

Colonel Boris Artukin and Major Sam Skeene were there, but Mirza would be delayed, according to his aide. Harvis had entered with the usual banter but found his friends in no mood for humour. They grunted greetings. He had a prepared apology on his lips for being an oversensitive bore at the Moulin Rouge last night but relievedly realized it was trivial in this atmosphere.

At any other time Boris would have buttonholed him at the door about his sexual adventure with the voluptuous belly dancer, going into pubic detail. Now the usually restless Russian sat brooding into space. The Englishman was reversing his role by being outside his shell of detachment for once. It was his custom to sink into a chair and rub knuckles under a thoughtful nose. Skeene was on his feet, pacing out his problems.

They had been on the investigating team of Allies flown to the scene of the convoy destroyed by the SS Colonel K. Zenner and his men. Harvis was filled in by them on the Allied dilemma. By treaty it was the duty of the occupying powers, Great Britain and the Soviet Union, to defend Iran from outside attack. Now the pressure had been brought on every unit in both armies to seek out and destroy the Nazi commandos. The deadline was the approaching Tehran Conference.

The combined forces of the Allies were overwhelming against the tiny band of the enemy. But the commandos were masters of camouflage who could not be spotted by the reconnaissance planes looking for them. Iran's mountainous terrain was perfect for their lightning hit-and-run tactics. There were innumerable tribal retreats from which to launch guerrilla warfare. They were in contact by shortwave radio and supplied by airplane drops and friendly tribesmen.

Major Skeene commanded a company of Sikh Indian Army signal corpsmen. They used radio vans equipped with listening devices for illegal broadcasters, monitoring all Tehran. So far they had triangulated one suspect. He turned out to be a Swiss who claimed he was a ham operator.

Colonel Artukin searched out the underground with squads of soldiers, constantly combing the city for illegal Germans and other pro-Nazis. He had picked up some insignificant individuals. But he was getting no closer to the hard core of the network they knew existed somewhere in Iran.

'Some guy, this Colonel Konrad Zenner.' Harvis offered grudging respect. 'He's got brains and brawn. Lucky for our side there's only one of him.'

'I suppose we have to give the Kraut credit for superb planning and brilliant execution,' Skeene said. 'A foxy fellow, I must agree.'

Artukin would concede nothing. 'When we skin the fox, there will be a swine to kill. The cockroaches with him we will squash to nothing!'

Then there was the propaganda triumph, Harvis thought. Equal to the sabotage. It was tactless to bring up, but everyone in Iran thought these attacks on the train and trucks were secretly organized by the Russians and the English to justify their occupation of the country. In their history of intrigue it was not a farfetched plot for the Persians. Whoever heard of a popular occupation? One of these days, Harvis promised himself, he'd do this country without a uniform.

'Ambassador Gordell and General Andrews figure their main mission is the conference,' Harvis said. 'We're doubling the troops. I suppose your people will be beefing things up around here, too. If you can't find them in the provinces, secure the city.'

'That's a proper American viewpoint,' Skeene said testily. 'But our mission here is military. We can't just sit still.'

'You do not understand, Americansky,' Artukin echoed. 'We must hit them before they hit us again!'

'What do we Yanks know?' Harvis struck back sarcastically. 'It's only our matériel and our men the Nazis are wasting out there!'

'Of course,' Artukin acknowledged apologetically.

'We are appreciative,' Skeene conciliated. 'I'm sorry.'

The nationalism was a new note among them, Harvis thought. He had just come off the streets sweating out the problem of Roosevelt's appearance. It was not a complicated business, his assignment with the help of Lieutenant George Keyes. A matter of manpower in the proper places. But he was haunted by the ambassador's King Lear-like lostness and midnight soliloquy in the embassy armoury on assassination. Among Gordell's capricious propositions his presentiment about Colonel Zenner had the knell of probability. One man, one rifle. How would he get through? A clue was the disguise he used in the train raid. That was the flaw in the Allied defence system, the Achilles' heel, the deliberate dot in the perfect Oriental vase.

He could hear Mike Callahan's bulldog bark at his heels. 'The President is Number One! America first, see!' and Captain Peter Harvis saw.

Skeene was surely being whipped by the arrival of Churchill. The coming of Stalin must have Artukin in a squeeze. Harvis had personal differences with them, but politics never entered into it. That included Mirza's tender presence in the quartet.

'The major's jeep is here,' Sergeant Mostaffa announced, hearing it. Then he served another round of tea.

Harvis continued to assess his associates. They never pulled rank. It merely indicated the importance each country placed on the post. Their wartime relationship was a unique one, possible only by submerging his democracy, Sam's conservatism, Boris' Marxism, and Ali's monarchism. Or variations of the same. Their meetings had been consciously social affairs in which they learned more about each other as men than systems.

He was in Iran on behalf of the Big War like all recent American soldiers. But Harvis was acutely aware of the parallel little wars that entangled his three partners. The Caspian Sea fisheries, the Persian Gulf oil concessions, the endless separatist movements among the Kurds and Azerbaijani. These conflicts long preceded this war and would continue after it was over, Harvis had learned. Yet none of this surfaced in their conversations.

Skeene and Artukin were war-weary men who had fought beyond ideology to simple personal survival. Harvis was willing enough to argue for his country. Though he had learned so much more about the United States outside it, he was undergoing a process of self-reeducation. Like Columbus, looking for India and discovering America. And Mirza's form of patriotism was patience in the Persian style; these armies too shall pass.

Harvis' inner barometer recorded subtle chills in the air between them. If the Tehran Conference was to change the political climate of the world, he thought, then the declining weather in the room was a forecast of storms to come.

The temperature took a further drop when Major Ali Mirza entered his office. He went briskly to his desk, without the typical formalities. He even waved off his habitual tea from Sergeant Mostaffa, who gaped in disbelief.

'Last night I observed the house of Ebenezer Foster Waite, the American lawyer.' Mirza took photographs from an envelope and put them facedown on his desk. 'A woman in a black chador came out of the house with the Italian friend of Mr Waite. They kissed farewell. She drove away in a white Mercedes. I could not see her face.'

It wasn't a male triangle after all, Harvis thought. Mario was a switch-hitter, a bisexual prostitute.

Mirza continued: 'The white Mercedes is the same one that picked up Nadiri, our Iranian commando. We lost it before. This time I followed it to Isfahan. I could not investigate more alone. I believe the German underground control centre is in a pension in the Yahudieh, the Jewish quarter.'

Harvis grew angry. It wasn't entirely unexpected, but the report rasped his spine. A face covering like a chador masked the identity of a woman, a typical dress for the Moslem female. But Waite was an American caught with his pants down dealing with the enemy. Harvis coloured, feeling a curious sense of shame, as though a countryman couldn't be guilty of treason.

'That's why Tehran is quiet,' Skeene said. 'They've been operating outside the city.'

'We should go there!' Artukin clamoured.

Skeene concurred. 'Immediately!'

What bloodthirsty bastards! Harvis smiled to himself. If there was anything they would drop sex and dope for, it was to kill Germans. It was impossible to imagine them in the peacetime occupations of engineer and collective farm manager. They were professional killers. Torturers as well.

Mirza picked up the photos. 'This is the wife of Professor Rudolph Berger and his daughter, Anna.' His hands shook as he turned them up on his desk for them to see. 'He is the illegal German who has not left Iran.'

The pictures had been taken by the Shiraz police and showed the bodies of the two women in their bedrooms, stripped and beaten to death. Harvis had read the professor's books in the embassy library. Now he felt ill, as if the murdered mother and daughter were friends.

Skeene leaned forward to look at the pictures, then fell back in his seat, gripping his knuckles tightly. Artukin smiled curiously, then turned away and let the tears fall. Mirza made his beads click. Sergeant Mostaffa began to serve tea to wash away the horror.

Finally Mirza asked, 'Why do you cry, Colonel Artukin?'

The Russian looked at him and blinked in disbelief. 'The Fascists murdered my whole family this way, Major Mirza. Why do you ask such a stupid question?'

Mirza tried to maintain control. 'The husband of the daughter cannot be found. His name is Kasim. Could he be in a Russian prison camp?'

Artukin rose to tower over Mirza.

Alarmed, Sergeant Mostaffa moved to his chief, hand on his sidearm. But for the shuffle of feet, the office was quiet. The Russian's voice reverberated.

'Major Mirza, do you say this is the work of my men?'

Mirza's lips quivered. 'The Russians hunt Germans.'

'We will chase the Fascists to hell!' Artukin bellowed. 'But we would not do this!' He pointed to the pictures, then to the Englishman. 'Shiraz is in the British zone!'

Skeene jerked as if slapped.

'That would be unthinkable for an Englishman!' he retorted hotly. 'We are a civilized people!'

Mirza rocked with indignation.

'Our women have been molested and insulted!' He stood up and pounded his desk. 'Raped and robbed!'

He's thinking of me, Harvis thought wildly. There were incidents with American troops in the streets, clubs, whorehouses – and in his own apartment. Despite his guilt, Harvis didn't think that was the true issue in the room. It was the restraint that had broken down among them, the Allies.

'Major Mirza, I believe you must be speaking about the American GI's,' Skeene prompted venomously.

'All foreigners are to blame!' Mirza declared impartially.

Skeene persisted. 'What do you say to that, Captain Harvis?'

As the attack shifted to him, Harvis had the unprecedented knowledge that his was the only cool head in the room. Artukin was a raging mujik, Mirza a suspicious peasant, and Skeene a vicious snob. He got lightly to his feet as in his varsity tennis days.

'I can hear Colonel Zenner laughing,' Harvis said evenly. 'He never leaves witnesses. He loves to see the enemy at each other's throats. Ali, are you going down to investigate this?'

Mirza said stiffly, 'It is my duty to report on this matter to the Shah.'

'I'd like to be in on it.'

'I will fly there in the morning.' Mirza was inhospitable. 'I will be at the Shiraz police headquarters.'

Harvis realized he was already late for Betty. 'Chow time, gentlemen. I'll be seeing you guys.'

'Oh, Peter.' Skeene stopped him. 'I've reconsidered your idea. I think it's a good one now.'

'What was that?'

'The one you thought of at our party last night,' Skeene half smiled. 'About going after this laughing colonel. You know, one on one. *Mano a mano.*'

So they hadn't forgotten, Harvis thought frigidly. 'I was drunk last night,' he said. 'You knew that.'

Skeene said blandly, 'I like you better that way.'

Harvis left the room. There were no farewells.

Then he stood outside the office in the corridor, as if to thaw out. The early breeze he had detected inside had turned to frost and then became an arctic zone of politics. When his blood warmed, Harvis left the police headquarters. It was a chilly day outside, too.

23

Colonel Konrad Zenner and his men arrived at Persepolis in the lowering afternoon. With two successful operations behind them, the four commandos travelled in a vaulting mood of victory. It was a time of exultation over the Iranian underground apparatus all the way to Berlin. These were all tributes to the colonel's detailed order of battle.

Because it was his home territory, Reza drove the captured station wagon, taking along the food basket that had been prepared for Professor Rudolph Berger by his wife. Zenner sat up front with him, Sepp and Yorck in the back. Their radio and other equipment filled every inch in the vehicle; what didn't fit was buried in the hills of Shiraz.

They rode into the ancient ruins of the capital of Iran built by Darius twenty-five hundred years before, then burned by Alexander the Great. Persepolis rested against a mountain on a terrace that overlooked the plain of Marvdasht. Despite its familiarity to Reza, he was always awed by the colossal visual history of his people. The remains of royal palaces, the lonely columns, the toppled stone figures, the beautiful bas-reliefs, the tremendous platform, and the massive stairway.

'We call it Takht-e-Jamshid.' Reza indicated the grandeur to the Germans. 'The throne of Jamshid.'

Yorck and Sepp were impressed. But the colonel wasn't listening, eyes darting, searching. Then he saw Professor Rudolph Berger a short distance away, standing at the top of the stairway of the Apadana, the grand audience hall of Darius I.

'That way,' he directed Reza.

The professor was a small man, who had spent most of his sixty years outdoors. His tanned face made a short beard and the hair from under his sun helmet seem whiter. Silhouetted against the roofless background, Berger presented a tiny figure at the head of the great stairway. The walls of the stairway were decorated by bas-reliefs of the Persian Empire's subject peoples coming to the king's New Year reception. As they left the station wagon and climbed towards him, the professor appeared like an old vizier of the court waiting to meet visitors bringing tribute.

Colonel Zenner introduced himself, indicating the vehicle. 'I was looking for you, Professor Berger,' he said. 'It was ready for you. So I saved your family the inconvenience. We will need it.'

'For what purpose, Colonel Zenner?'

'I will explain later.'

The professor's eyes regarded the men as they formed around him, blocking out protest. 'He is a Qashqai,' Berger said, nodding to Reza. 'But I don't know you Germans.'

'We're paratroopers,' Zenner said. 'We came from the Fatherland. Do you understand?'

'You dropped from the sky to do what?' Berger asked. 'I'm not so deep in my digging I don't know where the front is.'

'This is a commando mission,' Zenner said. 'On direct orders from the Führer. We need you.'

Berger shook his head. 'I'm an insignificant bookworm. I'm only good for old things,' he said, spreading his hands to encompass Persepolis. 'This is all I know about.'

'Exactly, Professor. You know the paths of the mountain tribes, the places the pilgrims walk, all the ancient roads, even the silk trade route,' Zenner said. 'Your knowledge is necessary in the service of the Fatherland.'

The professor's reply was interrupted by a sound like distant thunder. Then it became a mingled din of shouts and hoof-beats and rifleshots. Eleven tribal horsemen, trailing one rider-less mount, came charging towards the great stairway.

Reza waved to them.

They rode up the stone steps as their ancestors had done centuries before. Reza caught the horse they had brought for him and mounted it in a single magnificent movement.

The dozen horsemen performed an exhibition ride on the platform in a circling dash of a hundred yards, with Reza in the lead, then came to a rearing halt before their amazed audience. Reza said farewell. Then they took their horses carefully down the stairway, and the Qashqai spurred them away, with more shouts and gunfire.

'My guide is gone,' Zenner said to the professor. 'But you know Persia better than the Persians.'

'When I was so stupidly declared an illegal, I didn't go back to my home in Shiraz,' Berger confessed. 'I couldn't accept the political nonsense of being deported because I have so much unfinished work in this country.'

'It's good you didn't go back to Berlin.'

'The truth is history in my home,' Berger said.

'And what now, Professor?'

Yorck and Sepp shifted menacingly.

Berger temporized. 'But it can be said the lesson of history is that one cannot hide from it.'

Zenner interposed sharply. 'Enough of that, Professor.'

'Commandos should have explosives.'

'Yes, why do you ask?'

'I will help with your work,' Berger bargained, 'if you will help with mine.'

'What is that?'

'I have found a storehouse under the private palace of Darius. The door cannot be opened without gunpowder.'

Zenner nodded towards Sepp. 'He's the expert.'

'Then it is agreed.' Berger was pleased. 'How lucky for me!'

'Where is your camp?'

'By the palace.'

'We'll move there.'

They started down the great stairway.

'War and art,' Berger philosophized. 'An interesting combination.'

'*Deutschland über alles*,' the colonel countered.

24

Major Sam Skeene had scored a direct hit on his façade of conceit, fracturing it, Harvis thought soon after he had left Mirza's office. By the time he had picked up Betty Lanteri at the American embassy and brought her to the Armenian's restaurant the wound had opened varieties of misgivings.

What had made him offer to check out the incident in Shiraz? How would it change matters if Colonel Konrad Zenner had murdered the innocent Iranians? Or had not? Why should he get the Russians and the English off the hook? He had his own problems with a stretch of boulevard from the airport to the embassy.

Did something beautiful die in Mirza's office? He hoped not. Hope. In the year 1943 it was the Allies who carried the flimsy throne of hope on their shoulders. Harvis had done what he could to keep it from crashing in Mirza's office.

Through his thoughts Betty chatted gaily about her work with the ambassador on his book. She couldn't wait to finish eating and get to Gordell's house.

'The public figure and the private man are like day and night, and I won't say Jekyll and Hyde,' Betty told him. 'But I have opened a Pandora's box of diplomacy.'

Harvis was surprised to learn it was not the dull chore Betty had envisioned. She had worked for the ambassador for two years with no inkling of the profound and seething frustration he felt in the foreign service of his country. Now Gordell was planning to leave the State Department with a bombshell of a book.

'It's his last hurrah,' she gossiped, delighted to be in on a broadside against the establishment. 'And parting shot!'

Despite himself, Harvis grew interested as Betty related Philip Gordell's childhood dreams of becoming a diplomat. His wealthy father, who wanted him in the clothing business, opposed the idea. Then he relented and made a big campaign contribution to a needy Presidential candidate, who won. Gordell got the post, but he was a marked man, especially when the President left office.

Gordell should have quit after watching lesser men go up the ladder. But even in minor assignments there was the opportunity to suggest policy in the national interest. Spain, for example. He was opposed by two powerful factions in the State Department, the isolationists and the 'wrong war' people.

The theme of Gordell's book was to be that diplomacy and economy were two sides of the same coin. One without the other was disaster. And that there was a tragic contradiction between long-range policy and short-term Presidential politics. The ambassador claimed there would be no need for a Tehran Conference if his formulas had been followed.

'It'll be a diplomatic daisy chain,' Betty said.

Harvis was in no mood for debate, but he asked, 'Are you talking about Roosevelt, Churchill, and Stalin?'

'Strange bedfellows,' she said. 'I wonder who'll do what to whom?'

She counted on their mutual distaste of pomp. But now her irreverence annoyed him. The shouting match in the police station was still in his ears. It seemed Betty was adding to their din of doubts and distrust.

'What do you have against them?'

'The New Deal, the Boer War, and the Moscow Trials.'

It was meant to amuse, but Harvis didn't smile. His idols were literary, but he believed Roosevelt was to be a giant among politicians. Until the war, Harvis had been more interested in books than civic matters. Like any young sophisticate, he had snickered at the President's fireside chats, likening them to radio commercials selling soap. Now he was convinced Roosevelt had presided over the greatest social advance in American history. The people of the world looked to FDR as the symbol of democracy and freedom.

Betty was ambivalent towards Roosevelt. She loved him as a great leader and hated him for being a political charlatan, a manipulator of the American people. She would call him a wealthy stopgap out to save the rich, then remembered he was called a traitor to his class.

They both agreed the First Lady was to be cherished.

'Number One saved my family, so that ain't funny. But two and three are,' he said. 'Those guys coming here are all we've got. Unless you prefer the other big three, Hitler, Mussolini, and Hirohito.'

'That's not the choice,' she argued. 'Don't fall for "the leader" principle. Anyway, big shots come and go but the three vee's go on for ever.'

'What's that?'

'Revolution, poverty, evil.'

'Is that the ambassador's?'

'No,' she said.

'But it will be,' Harvis said. 'You're sure sold.'

'It was his stand on the Spanish Civil War. It took guts. A boy in my neighbourhood died there. If our country didn't do the dirty to the Spaniards, there wouldn't have been a world war,' Betty said. 'If there ever was a man who could say, "I told you so!" it's Ambassador Philip Gordell.'

Betty was going with the ambassador to the preconference preparations, hoarding letters and cables, jotting down notes and ideas, photographing scenes and people. Gordell would be in the heart of the historic event with Betty as a shadow.

'You should hear him and Ambassador Volkoff and Sir Henry have a go at each other,' Betty said. 'Their meetings almost break up every time.'

Harvis thought of Mirza's office. 'Yeah, it's every man for himself.'

'The Ambassador doesn't favour that concept,' Betty said. 'The last part of his book will be the prevention of the next war.'

'Already!'

'The world had better listen this time.'

'I'm not.'

'Don't you wonder about the postwar world?'

'I've been doing a lot of that,' he divulged. 'Wondering what to tell my son when he asks, "What did you do in the war, Daddy?"'

'What will you say?'

'Son, I was shacked up with a beautiful woman in a Persian garden, quoting Omar Khayyam, listening to musical nightingales, having the time of my life.'

'So you're back to the rear-echelon guilt and frontline fantasy,' she gibed mockingly. 'Here comes Captain Peter Harvis mowing down the enemy. Bucking for a Medal of Honour. Maybe you could sell your story to the movies.'

'Would you call Colonel Zenner and his high-flying commandos a Hollywood USO unit?'

'To be sure, the war has come to Mohammed,' Betty amended. 'But that's no reason for you to take up rifle practice.'

'They say practice makes perfect.'

She was contemptuous. 'Does it develop the killer instinct? Or is it the death wish? What is there about men that makes them have to prove themselves with a gun? Making it in bed is enough.'

Harvis inhaled and released his breath, deflating himself. 'You're so fucking right. How about it?'

'I'm already late for the ambassador.'

Harvis recognized a strange stab of jealousy.

'I need you.' He regretted the statement, knowing it was the wrong appeal. She was for mutual desire and sexual equality. 'Forget it.'

She smiled. 'I'll call you about midnight.'

'I won't be home,' he said suddenly. 'I'll be driving to Shiraz.'

'What for?'

'Security stuff,' he said.

It was an automatic shutoff. They never probed official business.

'That's over five hundred miles,' she said with concern. 'You'll be driving ten or twelve hours in the dark on the worst roads in the world.'

'Tough shit.'

Harvis drove Betty to the ambassador's house. They were quiet en route, as if spoken out. After a while she was the first to speak. He liked the urgency in her voice.

'Don't go to Shiraz,' she implored.

'Why not?'

'Callahan might wire any minute.'

'I'll be doing my duty.'

'Nothing over and beyond?'

'What are you thinking?'

'I'm thinking what the hell is he thinking with this absurd gun business,' she challenged. 'It's non-American around here. We're not gun bearers.'

'Boris and Sam never let me forget the Russians and the English are the "armed" forces,' Harvis said. 'We're just the delivery boys.'

'That's how the treaties read.'

'The bitch goddess of war doesn't respect them.'

Harvis stopped the jeep at their destination. Betty started to get out, then sat back in the seat, staring at him.

'Don't tell me, darling,' she said. 'You're thinking you want to kill that son of a bitch Colonel Zenner?'

'What gave you that dumb idea?'

'From the way you talk and what you wrote about him in

your report to Callahan,' she said. 'It had your best literary style.'

The commando leader had loomed larger than life when Harvis had put him on paper. He had been astonished to read in the intelligence report that Zenner was twenty-five, his own age. The German was an SS man engaged in a gory business, but he had been places and done things. Even the wrong road was adventurous.

'There's a Grand Canyon between the word and the deed,' he said.

Betty smiled. 'I'm counting on that. Watch out for stray camels.'

She kissed him on the cheek. He looked down at the steering wheel, unfeelingly.

'May your favour never grow less,' she said in Persian and went into the house.

Harvis didn't make the traditional reply, as he started up the jeep. He didn't fancy word games tonight.

25

Colonel Konrad Zenner emerged from the radio tent into the centuried silence of Persepolis at night. There was absolute blackness because clouds concealed the moon and stars. The ancient columns were dark sentinels for the German camp. He couldn't make out the hulk of the station wagon, twenty yards away, hidden in nocturnal obscurity beside the excavation. Yorck and Sepp were in their sleeping bags. Zenner's attention was focused on the dull glow of a lamp inside the tent of Professor Berger.

He moved with muffled commando tread across the distance and stopped at the tent door. There was a crack of light through the flap, and Zenner peered inside. The professor was writing with his back to the entrance. He sat on a campstool, elbows on a folding table, working under an oil lamp.

Folding back the flap with a satin touch, the colonel slipped silently inside the dim tent, then stood like an eavesdropper. It was an exercise in stealth the professor chose to ignore or was too intent to notice. There was a large leather briefcase at his feet, a sleeping bag in a shadowed corner, some digging tools, a camera hung on a tent pole, and his wife's food basket on the floor. It was unopened.

'*Achtung*!' Zenner said suddenly.

The professor ended his writing, then turned around sternly, removing his glasses.

'Why did you do that?'

'You reminded me of my father.'

'What would he do?'

'Chase me with a strap.'

'If I was your father, I would do the same,' the slight savant chided. 'Don't act like a child.'

The colonel, who had been stooping, straightened up and almost touched the canvas top. 'If you were my father, you'd be dead.'

'I'm sorry. The war?'

'Yes, the war.'

'Was it in the bombing?'

'He died in a concentration camp.'

'What a pity,' Berger retracted. 'I'm sorry I spoke that way. You thought of your father, and it just came out. How sad.'

'It wasn't sad.' Zenner's unemotional tone hadn't changed. 'I put him there.'

A gasp of abhorrence and disbelief escaped Professor Berger. He looked at the large man who seemed to fill the entire tent.

'Why did you tell me such a terrible thing?'

'You're of his generation. The "other Germany" they called themselves. They no longer exist,' the colonel gloated. 'There's one Reich, one Führer. You and I are together for one thing.'

The professor seemed punctured, as though he had underestimated a monstrosity. 'When I left Germany twenty-five years ago, it was to bury myself in the past.' He spoke with appeasing awkwardness. 'I have no interest in the politics of this century, Colonel Zenner. The past is everything to me.'

'Today is all that counts,' Zenner contradicted. 'I have no use for yesterday.'

The professor was like a wretched prisoner giving reassurance. 'I understand you, Colonel. Very well, indeed. But you must please try to understand me. I am finishing a book. My life's work,' he entreated. 'I will help you, but at night I must not be disturbed.' Berger put on his glasses with shaking hands and turned back to his writing. 'Good night, Colonel.'

The colonel's gaze caught the title page. 'Why do you call it *The Undying Flame*, Professor Berger?'

Berger spoke without turning around, his pen poised. 'Once they worshipped fire in this country. Then the flame was put out. I'm writing about what is lost,' he said, pushing his glasses to his forehead, facing Zenner, intrigued by the man's curiosity.

'I only begin in this country. Then I tell about the lesson to be learned for the whole world.' He paused, gaining self-assurance and to judge the interest.

Zenner said, 'Tell me about the fire.'

'What does it mean to you?'

Colonel Zenner's eyes lit, reliving it, as though ignited. 'Our cause was born in fire. The torchlight marches, the Reichstag fire, the burning of the books.'

'My fire is different,' the professor hazarded, bolstered by his book. 'There is the flame of science. Like the Bunsen burner in a laboratory. The flame of nature reviving itself in a forest fire. The burning bush in the Bible is the flame of the spirit.' Then he chanced an opinion: 'The world must choose between the flames of destruction and creation.'

Zenner had begun his response before hearing Berger out. 'These are Hitler's ideas!' he exclaimed. 'We are burning the old and creating a new Germany!'

'Yes, yes,' Berger said with sudden scholarly abstraction. 'It reminds me.' He turned back to write it down. 'The Egyptian bird, the phoenix. It requires exploration.'

Zenner reached over and extracted the pen from him.

The professor whirled about in fear and fury. 'This is my magnum opus! I told you what it means to me! Twenty-five years of work!'

'My father took his book to finish in the camp.' Zenner's tone contained a threat. 'I told them to burn it.'

Berger sat back on the campstool, gripping himself. 'What do you want of me?'

'I don't want a sleepy man,' Zenner ordered. 'Put it all away.'

Berger obediently cleared the table, putting his pages into the briefcase. 'What are you hunting?' he asked resignedly. 'I should know.'

'I'm after big game.'

'In this country?'

'The biggest in the world.'

'Once where we are standing was the centre of the universe,' Berger informed him. 'What political lions could there be now?'

'You'll know in time,' Zenner said. 'My mission will change everything for the Führer. It will change the world.'

'You're a powerful man.' Berger spoke not in flattery, but defeat. 'There are many myths in history about people like you.'

'The past is your present,' Zenner derided. 'You can stop playing with broken rocks and old graves for a while. Do some work for the Führer and the Fatherland.'

He snatched up the bulging briefcase in a swift movement. Berger made a desperate attempt to prevent it, but Zenner held it well out of the little man's reach, placing the book in hostage. The professor was beside himself with anguish.

'Colonel Zenner, what are you doing to me? Is this some kind of torture?'

'When I hold this, I have you. My father would follow his book to the devil's door. You'll have it in the morning.'

What was left of the professor's dignity shrivelled to nothing.

He sank to the chair, staring at Zenner as if he were an invading vandal. He opened his mouth to protest, then realized it was a futile effort.

As the colonel looked down at the shrunken man, his blue eyes gleamed, and the scar on his face was fire red. He raised his arm above the archaeologist's head.

'Heil Hitler!'

Then he went out into the black night.

26

After Harvis dropped Betty at the ambassador's house, he drove away hating the man. A couple of miles later in the cooling night he asked himself: Why blame Gordell? All he desired was a talented collaborator on his book. Betty Lanteri was a perfect choice. Anything outside of writing she might offer would be a bonus no male could decently reject.

Of course they'd get laid, he thought. When Betty spoke of the project, she had the forward look of an acolyte and the fervour of partisanship. The rest was natural for her. He didn't have a chance against the urbane crusader Ambassador Philip Gordell – who had been like a father to him. It seemed incredible to be competing with an older man for the favour of a woman.

Betty was a barricade looking for a cause. Maybe he was a lost one. Or even a completed 'project', and she had to move on. She loved ideas. She had a stronger feeling for 'the people' than a single human being. Her own children would suffer while she was suffering for the children of the world.

Yet the pain of rejection lingered.

Was it love?

It struck Harvis he was thinking like an unmarried man. What about his wife? He couldn't remember her voice or describe her face without the aid of the photo he had in his wallet. She had become the author of letters from a fairyland across the sea. Even his vision of home was becoming blurred.

Was that unlove?

His wife was secure now and surrounded by affection. Harvis had been an only child (he was unexpected; his father had had mumps), and his parents would make a fuss over the grandchild.

Every letter from his mother told of the baby clothes she was sewing for Jeff. She loved his wife as the daughter she never had. They were a matched pair, both devoted to their men, really sacrificial lambs. His mother had begun work during the Depression to bring in extra money and, because of his old man's gambling debts, continued in the dress shop. His wife had dropped out of school to help Harvis finish college; they were married in his senior year. They were one of the few couples on campus.

Harvis had a snapshot of the two women together that revealed a startling resemblance he hadn't noticed before. The perspective of Persia was a new way of looking at things. It disturbed him that he had wed the image of his mother. Just like the one that married dear old Dad.

How do you leave a girl like that?

He desired Betty. And he wanted to write 'love' to his wife and mean it. He didn't intend to lose that loyalty.

So it was possible to keep two women mentally in separate but equal categories. One for the mother of his child, the other the woman in his bed. Distance was cool and lent no enchantment. Betty's presence was overwhelmingly warm.

The distinction between love and sex became tangled in his mind when he thought of Faraj. She was sensuality. And as different in bed as his wife and Betty were to each other. But the Persian girl was a will-o'-the-wisp.

The blonde, the brunette, the black. Were these the married, the profane, the sacred love he'd read about? The profundities of the fuck by which America the dutiful operated from 1943 on backward. Ecclesiastical jazz. It was really all about just getting laid, wasn't it?

A man and a woman approach as equals. Then join because of a not holy trinity of instinct, chemistry, and proximity. Sex was like thirst. It was a sign of growing up when guilt was eliminated. Of course, there was still the deceptive heart to consider. And, for chrissake, responsibility.

It would help if he divined (not told by her) that his wife went to bed with a man while he was away. Offsetting transgressions. Not all his friends were drafted. The horniest among them was a 4-F, Tom Ballard.

The were a partying crowd who played with each other short of infidelity. But war broke barriers. Harvis could visualize his wife in a car, enough whisky, and co-operative rape. It would be old Tom-cat whose eyes were too bad for the Army but good enough to see through any female defence.

Harvis remembered an historical footnote about the Romans who sent messengers ahead to warn their wives when they returned from the wars.

It inspired his own postwar joke:

'Did you go to bed with Tom?' he would ask his wife.

'No.'

'Dick?'

'No.'

'Harry?'

'No.'

'What's the matter?' Harvis would ask wisely. 'Ain't my friends good enough for you?'

Anyway it was a solution – if there was one – he could postpone....

Harvis drove into the motor pool behind the American embassy. A lone light in the yard lit up the darkness. He parked the jeep and began to check it out for a long trip, putting in oil, lashing on extra tins of gas and water. Sudden laughter broke out behind him and Harvis whirled about in fright.

'His Excellency Captain Peter Harvis!'

Harvis recognized Ashgar, a tall, handsome Iranian in his late twenties. He was the son of a rich man and spent most of his time on horses. Betty had dated him for a short period before Harvis came to Iran. It was Ashgar who had introduced her to hashish, the 'hilarious herb', as she called it. Betty said he was brilliant and erratic and had met him at the embassy where Ashgar came for American magazines.

'What do you want, Ashgar?' Harvis asked, still tense.

Ashgar laughed because everything to him was humorous.

'I am your servant to command!' he said. 'But you must call me Joe. Joe DiMaggio, Joe Louis, Joe Palooka, and Joe Blow!'

Harvis found that funny. 'You scared the shit out of me, Joe.'

'Please forgive me, Agha.'

'That's okay.'

Harvis feigned nonchalance, leaning against the jeep fender. Ashgar had begun to call Betty again. He must be thinking I stole his girl, Harvis thought, feeling cornered now.

'What a wonderful word is "okay"!' Ashgar kissed his fingers. 'American slang is okay, Pal!'

Ashgar made a dance turn and threw up his arms in extravagant gaiety. As his jacket opened, Harvis glimpsed the jewelled handle of a dagger in his belt.

Harvis was wary now. 'You're pretty high. Is there anything I can do for you?'

'Excuse me, please. What is high?'

'Up in the sky, like from drinking or something —'

'Hashish.'

'Sure.' Harvis wondered if his joy excluded jealousy. The weapon worried him. 'I have to go now, Ashgar —'

As Harvis moved, Ashgar danced in his path.

'I beg you to listen, Excellency. I wish to tell you how "high" I am. We can teach each other.'

During his polka of politeness, Ashgar's hand had gone to his belt. He's a smiler with a knife, Harvis thought. He went back to his position at the jeep. Ashgar took the typical stance for poetical expression:

Like wild winds the drafts have raised me up.
Have I been drinking soma?
The drafts have borne me up, as swift steeds a chariot.
Have I been drinking soma?
Frenzy had come upon me, as a cow to her dear calf.
Have I been drinking soma?
As the carpenter bends the seat of a chariot, I bend
  this frenzy round my heart.
Have I been drinking soma?
Not even as a mote in my eye do the five tribes count
  with me.
Have I been drinking soma?
The heavens above do not equal one half of me.
Have I been drinking soma?
In my glory I have passed beyond the sky and the
  great earth.
Have I been drinking soma?
I will pick up the earth, and put it here or put it there.
Have I been drinking soma?

'Beautiful!' Harvis exclaimed. The words had moved him, and he was captured by the charm of the man. And the sadness. Harvis, too, had dreamed of escaping the force of gravity, breaking the chains of earthbound people.

Then Ashgar was convulsed with laughter as a new thought possessed him. He made wings out of his arms and airplane sounds. 'I am Superman on Alamut!'

Now Harvis was following his flights of fancy.

'Where's that?' he asked, laughing along. 'Superman!'

'The "eagle's nest". You must know of the Assassins,' Ashgar said. 'I know American history.'

Harvis remembered and repeated like a lesson learned. 'About a thousand years ago they were a secret order of Moslem fanatics who used hashish before they went out to kill their enemies,' he said. 'They also killed the Christian Crusaders.'

Ashgar applauded the almost perfect answer. And then his

clapping became rhythmic as he began to sing and dance 'Deep in the Heart of Texas'.

Maybe the man was happily harmless, despite the dagger, but violence, Harvis thought, was in the wind. There seemed to be some inner torment the drug wasn't reaching. He watched the handsome Iranian whirl around and lose his balance, then caught him before he could hurt himself on the jeep.

Ashgar twisted out of his grasp, changing the tune. 'Off we go into the wild blue yonder,' he sang, but now the reeling man had a dagger in his hand. 'I do not mean disrespect.'

Harvis was alert. 'I understand —'

'It is not necessary for the gods to condescend.'

Harvis caught the dagger's glint.

'What do you mean gods? Respect? Condescension? Take it easy, Ashgar,' he said, recognizing a muddled young man like himself on some way station in between. 'We're just a couple of Joes here.'

'Perhaps I am being impolite. Please, excuse me —'

'Come inside with me for some coffee.'

Ashgar seemed about to weep. 'I went to school at the Sorbonne. Then to Cambridge. But Columbia was my dream. The war came.' He used the dagger as a pointer. 'You must help me to go to New York.'

They came to the American embassy every day, asking about migrating to the United States, complaining about the restrictiveness and lack of opportunity in their country. Like Ashgar, they used hashish intoxication to break out of the straightjacket of their society.

'Okay, Ashgar,' Harvis said. 'We'll have lunch tomorrow and talk about it.'

Ashgar began to laugh uncontrollably, tears falling now. 'The French word "*assassin*" derives from *hashshashin*,' he said. 'The leaders of the Assassins on Alamut promised paradise. Your country is paradise, do you understand?'

There was a Moslem yearning for Mecca. America was the new Mecca. Harvis had learned that from Faraj.

'The Americans are the new Christian Crusaders!' The idea sent Ashgar to new heights of hilarity.

Faraj! Harvis thought, seeing a murderous look of sanity in the mad laughter. It wasn't Betty but Faraj who brought Ashgar here. He was from the prominent family that made the offer of marriage to Major Mirza. The man in the car, who had forced Faraj to visit his apartment for a visa.

Harvis made a sudden run for the embassy. Ashgar tripped him like a ballet dancer, and Harvis toppled to the dirt. The Iranian stood over him with the raised dagger for an instant, then dived at Harvis. He rolled away. Ashgar fell on his face, sticking the dagger into the dirt, finished, still laughing.

Harvis got to his feet, shaken, torn between kicking the man who tried to kill him, or breaking into laughter himself. 'Get out of here —'

Ashgar sat up on his elbow, smiling. 'Please, I pray I have not offended you.' Then he called out.

Two men came running from the street. Harvis was startled to see Sergeant Mostaffa arrive behind them. He was eating pistachios.

'Forgive my rudeness, but I must leave,' Ashgar said as the two men picked him up. He giggled as they carried him out. 'Thank you for the honour of this visit.'

'The pleasure was mine,' Harvis returned sardonically, uncertain if Ashgar was mocking his own country's typical politeness or doing as he was trained. 'And drop dead.'

'Good night, Captain Harvis,' Sergeant Mostaffa said.

'What were you doing here?'

The sergeant shrugged. 'I was driving by, Captain Harvis.'

He left the yard.

Harvis heard a passenger car and a jeep drive away. He raced towards the disappearing sounds in the night, feeling genuine fear. It was not a reaction to Ashgar. But to the question of Sergeant Mostaffa. His appearance was no coincidence. Mirza's aide was there to see Harvis dead.

A guy could get killed in this war and not by the hands of the enemy, Harvis thought. He could fuck himself to death.

Inside the embassy armoury he issued himself a forty-five and a carbine, with enough ammo, reflecting if he had been armed, he might have shot Ashgar. It had been surreal, even though the Persian had been narcotically inept. Harvis had almost been the passport to paradise Moslems received by slaying an infidel. Ashgar would go to heaven. But if Harvis had shot him, there would have been hell to pay, he thought ironically.

He took the weapons to his office, then changed into a warm field jacket, trying hard not to think of Major Ali Mirza. He who works in mysterious ways his enemies to behead. It wasn't hard to figure out, Harvis thought. On second thought, it wasn't easy either. He must have known right away what his daughter was doing and condoned it. Now he wanted Harvis to quit. The hard way. The attack was at least a warning if it failed. But why didn't he order Faraj to stop?

Mirza knew his daughter desired nothing more than a trip to the United States. And Harvis had arranged the necessary documents. Meanwhile, she had earned enough money with her dress designs. A designing woman? Harvis was a willing tool, if it was that. But he wasn't prepared to die for the indiscretion.

Then Mirza permitted his daughter to continue with Harvis because he wanted her out of the country. To save himself the disgrace of a deflowered child. It was not unusual for Iranian fathers to throw straying girls out of a dishonoured house. In time Faraj's affair with the American would become bathhouse gossip; secrets had a short life in their closed society. Then there would be no more go-betweens at the house of Mirza offering sons in marriage. If passion in America was controlled by conscience, here it was economics.

He hadn't seen her, but Faraj had picked up the papers at the embassy while he was out with Lieutenant Keyes. So Harvis had served his purpose. Now his presence would be an embarrassment, a constant reminder that Major Mirza had somehow failed as a father. A girl who didn't value her virginity had no respect for her parents. The American must die.

He took the musette bag he kept for emergencies out of the closet. It had a first-aid kit and toilet articles. He left a note for Betty to explain his absence to Lieutenant Keyes. On his way out of the embassy Harvis selected a small volume from the library. It was about Shiraz, by Professor Rudolph Berger. They had most of the man's translated works on the shelves.

Driving his jeep on the journey to the south of Iran was not unfamiliar to Harvis. The difference was doing it in the dark and being accompanied by the ineffable sense of loss. He knew it related to Tehran and the qualities of friendship. It gave him an uncomfortable mixture of unsolvable relief and regret. But he liked driving; it set his brain free and generated ideas. He hoped he could resolve his mind before he met Major Ali Mirza in Shiraz. He was sorry now he had committed himself.

Then the road brought back a pleasant memory to which he clung lovingly. It was the time he rode with his father from San Francisco to Los Angeles in their 1926 Ford. About the same distance he would be travelling now.

Only California was greener.

27

In the morning the colonel entered the professor's tent unannounced to discover him clothed in a complete change of identity. It was as if Berger had slept off the dour seriousness of a bookworm, Zenner thought. He beamed with eager anticipation, refreshed, and even fey, making his small beard elfinlike. It was a startling transformation from the miserable little man he had left the night before.

'Good morning!' Berger welcomed cheerfully.

Zenner had come with the briefcase and a rolled map. He had expected the professor to make a show of embracing his precious manuscript like the return of a loved one, but Berger ignored it. The colonel looked at him askance.

'You said you didn't want a sleepy man,' Berger reminded him. 'But you are disappointed!'

Zenner said doubtfully, 'If you had a gun, you would have shot me in the back.'

'I dig all day and I write all night. You forced me to take a rest. I had a wonderful night!' The professor spoke like a recuperated person. 'I was acting like a child. Out here alone, living with the ghosts of Persepolis, I have forgotten how to behave with living people.'

He was a *Luftmensch* after all, Zenner thought, his suspicions allayed. The otherworldly, impractical dreamers, the contemptuous intellectuals Hitler hated. His parents had entertained them in their home.

'I don't have time for trouble between us,' he said.

'We're Germans before anything else,' Berger pronounced, '*Deutschland über alles.*'

'The Führer and the Fatherland.' Zenner was mollified. He spread the map on the table. 'By the time we finish with this Sepp will be ready to blast open your stone door.'

'I should be with him,' Berger said anxiously.

'He won't set the fuse without you,' Zenner said. 'How many hours is it to Isfahan?'

'It's a treasure house!'

'I asked a question, Professor Berger.'

'It is five hours to Isfahan,' Berger said. 'Zenner, it would be a golden find. We must be careful —'

'And from there to Tehran?'

'About the same time.'

'Mark a road on the map,' Zenner commanded. 'No highways. No common roads. Your camel tracks, please.'

Berger picked up a pencil and sat down before the map.

'When you have a map, you won't need me,' Berger began a careful line from Persepolis north. 'Are you getting rid of this old dog?'

'Maybe,' Zenner said. 'But I'll need the station wagon.'

'Take it,' the professor encouraged. 'I'll wait for a wandering tribe. Most of them are my friends.'

'I have radio contact,' Zenner said. 'Everything is ready.'

'For what?'

'Does an old dog ask his master?'

Berger halted his tracing.

'A favour, please,' he asked. 'A good place for us to part is here' – pointing to it on the map – 'Naqsh-e Rustam. You can leave me there. Only a few miles from here.'

'Why?'

'For my book,' Berger said. 'I will need your help there.'

'If we have time.'

They heard Yorck calling, 'Colonel Zenner!'

'He has Berlin!' Zenner started out of the tent. 'Sepp will let you pull the string after you're satisfied the treasure is safe.'

'Thank you, Zenner.'

The colonel went out, taking the map, hurrying.

The professor followed him. Sepp greeted him at the excavation, happy for the chance to work his trade. He was their explosives expert. They could see the colonel and Yorck in the radio tent, communicating with the outside.

Berger had discovered by his historic calculations a stairway leading down to a storage room under a palace. It had been buried under dirt and rubble after centuries of wind and earthquake. The professor had dug out the stairway with his helper, Hosein, and his son-in-law, Kasim. But penetrating the vault was impossible without the proper tools and manpower, neither of which was available to him. For this, at least, the appearance of the commandoes was a boon to the archaeologist.

Sepp's idea was to use hand grenades wedged into the rock with a pick. He thought that artfully placed explosions would shake down the walled-in doorway to the treasure room. Sitting on the bottom step, Berger watched as the short and strongly built SS man ingeniously created a chain device that would set off the grenades simultaneously. A pull on a rope extended from the vault up the stairway would do the job, Sepp stated confidently. He was delighted and proud to show off his handiwork to the professor.

Berger praised him warmly.

Sepp then gave him the rope to carry aboveground. He attached his end of it to the tripwire connected to the grenades. He stood for a long moment, as if taking a mental picture of his accomplishment and checking details.

Looking down the stairway at Sepp's back, the professor then made up his mind to pull the rope. The explosion collapsed the entire excavation. Sepp was completely buried.

The earth-shaking blast brought Colonel Zenner and Yorck breaking out of the radio tent. They saw Berger, waiting.

The dust of the explosion settled.

Zenner asked, 'Where's Sepp?'

The professor said something inaudible, pointing to the newly made rock pile. His meaning was clear.

The colonel was stunned.

Yorck recoiled, as if struck, then cried out and lunged at Berger. The berserk commando grabbed the professor by the throat. The small man flailed helplessly in the hands of the muscled young Nazi.

At the last moment, Zenner came to life and tore Yorck off, breaking his death grip. Berger dropped to the ground, gasping for breath.

'He did it!' Yorck wailed.

'Why do you think so?'

'He must be a Jew bastard!'

'No, he isn't. You know how I feel about that,' Zenner soothed. 'He's just an old fool.'

Yorck stumbled back and dropped to his knees on the burial mound to mourn his comrade, like a keening warrior.

The colonel helped Berger to his feet.

'You would rather be on the other side of that door than at the gates of heaven, isn't that so, Professor Berger?'

The professor massaged his bruised neck, unable to use his voice. He nodded, trying hard to appear sorry.

Zenner suddenly shouted, 'Get out of my sight!'

As Berger turned, the colonel shoved him towards the tent, as if to get him out of his range of violence.

Inside the tent, the scholar's melancholy countenance wreathed into wrinkles of smiles. He had an instant recovery from his throat injury. By way of celebration, he opened his wife's basket of food for the first time and selected a peach from her providence. He found he could swallow without the least discomfort.

28

Harvis heard his name and felt a gentle presure on his shoulder. It was Major Ali Mirza, awakening him from a sleep of bone-tired exhaustion after the long hard drive from Tehran. He had arrived at the Shiraz police headquarters about five o'clock that morning. Mirza had wired ahead, and the police captain had been most hospitable to the visiting American. He provided him with a room and a cot and some breakfast Harvis couldn't finish because he had fallen asleep.

He sat up, orienting himself. He had expected Mirza at six, according to the captain. His watch read nine thirty. It was trivial, but everything about his friend was questionable now. Betty had always maintained the major was meretricious.

'Why did you let me oversleep, Ali?' he asked.

Mirza offered a fond smile. 'I have just come,' he explained. 'You should have much rest after such a difficult journey.'

Somewhere on the road to Shiraz, Harvis had made the effort but failed to convince himself that Mirza was innocent in the near fatal incident at the embassy the night before. Although he had learned to live with the preposterous in Persia, the suspension of disbelief was impossible. It meant that Sergeant Mostaffa's midnight materialization was sheer chance. And Ashgar's try at stabbing him had some motivations unfathomable to a Westerner. It was difficult to distrust this benign and mustachioed presence, but one had to doubt the word of a potential enemy.

'What held you up?'

'I was called to the palace,' Mirza answered. 'I must fly back at once.'

Harvis rose and stretched, thinking: Something more important than this investigation came up. But he had to come for me, to hear what I would say in good old American bluntness. If Mirza hadn't plotted the attack, at least his sergeant had reported it. But if Harvis broached the bad business, it would lead to an accusation he couldn't prove. He still clung to their fragile attachment.

'You should've wired if you couldn't make it,' he said. 'I wouldn't mind.'

'Ah, but I would have missed Shiraz,' Mirza said. 'Even a small visit with a sweetheart is to be desired.'

There was nothing false about that sentiment, Harvis knew. He brought out Professor Berger's little book, reading, 'The home of Persian culture, the mother of Persian genius, the sanctuary of poetry and philosophy.'

Mirza matched him with a quote: '"Right through Shiraz the path goes/Of perfection/Anyone in Shiraz knows/Its direction." That is from Hafiz.'

They exchanged quick, searching glances, then laughed together. Like old buddies again, Harvis thought. Mirza seemed willing to forget. Why shouldn't I forgive? After all, I'm still alive.

The door opened, and the police captain entered with a leathery-skinned man in his seventies, aged and hardy. An orderly followed with tea. There were salaams and introductions. The man was Hosein, who had worked with Professor Berger for many years.

The police captain made a speech about the great esteem everyone held for the German scholar. They grieved for his family.

'We will punish the killers of our people,' Mirza solemnly declared, setting the policy. 'The professor is on our wanted list. He is an illegal foreigner in our country.'

'Yes, Major Mirza,' the police captain said, falling into line. He saluted and went out.

Harvis sat off to one side, an observer. Because Mirza was an uncompromising emissary of the Crown, Hosein had stiffened toward him. But Mirza was practising none of his usual inquisitorial style. There seemed to be other matters uppermost in his mind. He can't figure me out, Harvis thought.

Hosein told his story of the morning he had found the murdered family. He was coming early to accompany Kasim, the son-in-law, to deliver food to the professor. So he was the first to find the lifeless bodies of Mrs Berger and Anna. Kasim was gone. Anna's baby was unharmed, praise be to God. Just before entering the house, Hosein had encountered the killers as they drove away in the stolen station wagon, which the professor had only lately bought from an American missionary. There was enough early light to make out four men, all foreigners. He got a good look at one, a big man who leaned out of the window. Believing he had a gun, Hosein jumped for cover. He thought the man had a scar on his face.

'He is Colonel Zenner,' Mirza informed Hosein. 'They are German commandos.' Then he turned to Harvis. 'You were correct, Peter. It was not done by the Allies.'

'That makes me an expert on the subject, I guess,' Harvis said wryly. So he was confirmed, and Mirza was appeased. For some reason he didn't care anymore. 'But don't count on me again.'

'Why did you go there so early?' Mirza asked Hosein.

Hosein was circumspect. 'To bring the professor food.'

'Where were you taking the food?'

'As is my custom, where the professor digs.'

Mirza took a breath of patience. 'What place?'

'An old place.'

Mirza said tightly, 'Tell me where he is hiding.'

'In an old place.'

The old man was not about to contribute to the arrest of the professor, Harvis thought. Somehow he was on the side of loyal Hosein, though the information was important to Mirza.

A short, stubborn silence was broken when the captain looked into the room. 'Major Mirza, the airport is calling!'

Mirza gave Hosein a look of rebuke. 'I will deal with you later.' Then he left the office, nodding for Harvis to follow.

At the phone Mirza assured the airport he would be on time, invoking the authority of the Shah. 'Do you wish to fly with me?' he asked Harvis.

Harvis shook his head. His jeep could be transported back to Tehran, saving himself the hard return drive. He thought of the release from restraint and the hemmed-in feeling he had achieved away from the city. But mostly he was uncertain about Mirza's motives once more.

'I may never come back,' he said flippantly.

Mirza was grave. 'You have an appointment in Tehran.'

There was a familiar oracular ring about the words. But with a new ominous note.

'Whoever it is,' Harvis said jokingly. 'I'm not keeping it.'

'There are certain meetings we cannot deny.' Mirza spoke as if the American's fate were sealed. 'I will order the captain to put petrol in your jeep and give you every assistance.'

Harvis was used to Mirza's metaphysics. But the co-operation was unnecessary; he could easily service his jeep at any Allied camp.

'Thank you, Ali,' he said.

Outside the police captain was ready to take Mirza to the airport. He sounded his car horn.

Mirza ignored it, surprising and alarming Harvis, for when

the Shah called, the major moved automatically. But a truce was about to be shattered. The masks of Mirza, he thought, the quick-change artist. His Highness would have to wait because of an irate Iranian father.

'Do you have messages?' Mirza's eyes narrowed imperceptibly. 'For anyone?'

The confrontation had been inevitable, after all. The flash of Ashgar's knife crossed his mind, and Harvis braced himself. In this Persian match he had to admit nothing while the opponent exposed nothing. He was wise not to have flown back with him.

'Yes.' He was specious. 'Please tell Miss Lanteri at the embassy I'll be in touch with her.'

The captain hit the horn again.

Mirza was deaf to it, standing his ground expectantly, as if Harvis hadn't finished his instructions. There was silence between them. Then the American supplied the rest compulsively like a man fed up with a game.

'Oh, and tell Faraj I'll have more silk for her when I get back,' Harvis said with a forced smile.

Mirza returned a faint smile because the first mention of his daughter's name was a victory.

'I believe she should not accept more gifts from you,' he said. 'You have been kind enough.'

'Sure, it's up to you.'

'It is her decision.'

Harvis was bewildered. 'You mean you discussed this with her?'

'No.'

A flicker of violence contorted his face; then Mirza left the station abruptly, as if to suppress himself. He didn't say goodbye, a sure sign of his profound agitation. Harvis noted that he took out his worry beads.

He watched Mirza drive off, wondering how a father and daughter could have lived in the same house without mentioning the American captain, both being aware the other knew everything.

It was a matter of face.

By silence Mirza was sidestepping a head-on collision with his strong-willed offspring. And perhaps he was a loving parent secretly collaborating with Faraj's ambitions.

Maybe, Harvis thought, Mirza had plotted it all in the best Byzantine manner, the introduction, the seduction, and the abduction from Iran. Giving his talented daughter the opportunity to express herself in the only place possible, the United States. He couldn't encourage her at home; he had a position to uphold. He was a good Moslem.

When Faraj went away, Mirza would appear astonished, outraged, offer public condemnation, and receive all kinds of sympathy. He would blame the foreign occupation for the subversive ideas of women's equality and emancipation.

All at once Harvis felt sorry for Mirza, despite everything, because he loved the man. He had an errant daughter, a female maverick. What happened to his belief that family determined fate? He could make her conform. But it would not restore a maidenhead.

The speculations were dizzying, and Harvis felt himself lost in a Persian maze, yet relieved of the cat-and-mouse game with Mirza. The one clear message – drop Faraj at the peril of his life. Or Harvis would not be the first foreigner found facedown in a murky jube mysteriously murdered.

Mirza was not finished with him. Not by a long shot.

Hosein was still there when Harvis returned to the office. He had been brought in by the police captain and must wait to be dismissed by him. The old man glared at the American, an ally of Major Ali Mirza, the Shah's disciplinarian.

'Hi, Hosein!'

The proud man rejected his friendliness with a curt nod. It created an awkward interval Harvis filled by putting on his field jacket, as if to leave. He had no place to go. Only inside himself there remained the persistent tug in his gut that had made him run from Tehran. It was a form of flight, and Harvis had stopped off in Isfahan, the midway point, to rest and consider turning back. But the pull to Shiraz had been undeniable.

He buckled on his web belt and sidearm, thinking he was at least rid of the idea he had come in the interests of Allied unity. That noble balloon had been shot down in Mirza's office. He saw the breakup of their clubby foursome as merely a loss of naïveté.

Bullshit aside, he had come gunning for Colonel Zenner.

Okay, so he had purged himself to pretence, and Zenner had been here as he had predicted. Now what? Asking himself the question served to eliminate it. The commando chief was anywhere and everywhere. Did Harvis expect him to be hanging around for a cowboy shoot-out in the streets of Shiraz?

Clueless, he was suddenly drenched in self-disgust. He was a phony, at the very least chicken.

Hosein made a sound. Harvis became aware he was being uncivil. He was constrained to speak.

'Professor Berger is not on my wanted list. I have a lot of respect for him.' He showed him the book. 'I've read what he's written about this country. He loves the Persian people and is making a great contribution to your culture.'

The lines in Hosein's face formed pleasure. 'That is true,' he said. 'He is in great trouble. I must help him. I cannot go to the police. You understand, Captain Harvis?'

'I got it, Hosein.'

'You are American,' Hosein said. 'Not English. Not Russian. Not Iranian,' he distinguished. 'I am Zoroastrian.'

The moment he began, Harvis winced inwardly. He had encountered this preface before. The United States, unlike the others, was the great reservoir of faith, hope, charity, and wealth. Americans were good guys, the helping hand from across the sea, angels of mercy. In Hosein's mind the religion of pre-Islamic Persia was a benevolent bond between them.

'I know very little about Zoroastrianism except that you don't bury your dead,' Harvis said. 'You leave them in the open in some high place.'

'The birds take them away,' Hosein said. 'We worship nature: wind and fire, water and earth, and holy elements. A dead body cannot be buried as it will defile the earth. It cannot be burned, for it will defile the fire.'

'Is it true you worship fire?'

'Yes, because the flame comes from the sun. The sun brings light, like our Lord, Ahura-Mazda.' Hosein beamed. 'He fights Ahriman, the Lord of Darkness. It is the eternal struggle of good and evil. It is like your war against Hitler.' Then coming to his point: 'Why is this Colonel Zenner in Iran?'

Harvis wondered where the old man was heading, answering, 'It's part of the war, Hosein. He's one of Hitler's best soldiers.'

'The professor is not a soldier,' Hosein said.

'How does he feel about the war?'

'He says Germany is in the hands of people who hate other people, even their own Germans.'

Harvis was perplexed. 'I'm sure Zenner is not in Iran looking for anti-Nazis.'

'He has come for the professor's great knowledge,' Hosein said. 'The professor spoke his true feelings only to his own family. His work was not with other Germans. This country was a new life for him.'

'You could be right. Zenner uses guides. Berger would be the best,' Harvis said.

'Better than the Persians.'

'So Zenner and his boys show up with the station wagon without you and his son-in-law. What would the professor think?'

'He would not know about the fate of his family,' Hosein said reasonably. 'He will think they stole it. His family would not betray him. That is why they died.'

'The colonel would kill witnesses,' Harvis said. 'Their intelligence is good in this country. They have dossiers on each member of the German colony. Zenner would know where to find Professor Berger anywhere in Iran. By the way, where is he?'

'Takht-e-Jamshid,' Hosein replied unhesitatingly. 'It is not far. Captain Harvis, please take me there.'

It wasn't the kind of entreaty he anticipated.

'I'm sorry,' Harvis said. 'The German business in this situation is mixed up. The Iranian part is worse. It's really the job of the English and the Russians. I have to go back to work in Tehran.'

'You are an American!'

'Just because I am, I could be breaking all kinds of laws and treaties,' Harvis said, knowing the futility of explanations.

'You have a gun,' Hosein said. 'Are you afraid?'

Harvis became uneasy. 'That's not it.'

There was the cry of a baby outside the door, and Hosein opened it. And old woman came in carrying a baby. She complained it was hungry and that Hosein had kept her waiting.

'She is my wife,' Hosein said. 'This is the grandson of the professor.'

Harvis was suddenly overwhelmed with emotion for the orphaned child. Inexplicably, tears came.

'I have a baby like that,' he said.

Then Harvis held out his arms naturally, as if it were his paternal right, his own son. Cradled by him, the baby stopped crying and looked up into his eyes. Compassion and protectiveness made Harvis hold the baby closer. The holding was a yearning satisfied, no longer a deprivation Harvis had suffered. And the touching became a connection forever. He kissed the boy, and his heart went back to his own father who must have kissed his son this way and still did into manhood. Thus the inner rite of continuity took place, and Harvis became at last a father, feeling the pride and the wonder. He loved this baby, his son.

The old woman took the baby back.

'There is a saying,' Hosein said. 'A baby belongs to everybody.'

Harvis said, 'Let's go find Grandpa.'

29

Professor Rudolph Berger was like a man coming to visit old and beloved friends after a long absence.

Naqsh-e Rustam was about three miles from Persepolis, and he grew animated as they approached the quiet valley that was a sanctuary and burial ground of Darius the Great and his successors. Even before they reached the area, the professor began to talk from the back seat of the station wagon about the rock tombs they would see, like a lecturing guide.

Yorck drove, scowling all the way, holding his grudge against Berger. He was unconvinced by the colonel's Christian clearance of the professor. He had to have some Jewish blood; the beard proved it. And his brains. Colonel Zenner sat beside him, looking hard ahead, unbothered by the man's murderous mood. The ghost of Sepp still made a quartet.

The professor spoke his profundities at the backs of the heads of the two Nazi commandos. He went into the minute detail of the burial ceremony of Darius I, twenty-five centuries ago, like a witness and intimate of the Achaemenian king. The other tombs belonged to Xerxes, Artaxerxes, and Darius II. The four tombs were alike, hollowed out of a cliff of living rock, each in the shape of a cross, creating a site of infinite majesty in the lonely place.

Berger told them of the building that stood before the tombs, the Ka'ba Zardusht, the Cube of Zoroaster, that was a fire temple. Below and to the left of the tombs were Sassanian bas-reliefs, added one thousand years later by another house of Persian rulers.

Then Berger asked Yorck to drive around the bend of the cliffs to view the two open fire altars sculptered from rock, before stopping at the first tomb. Passing the tomb of Darius, the professor translated the famous inscription in a feat of memory.

'I am Darius, the great King, King of Kings, King of the land peopled by many races, a Persian, son of a Persian, and Aryan of Aryan descent. By the grace of Ahura-Mazda, these are the provinces I have conquered afar.'

It was midmorning when the three men stepped out into the necropolis. Berger surprisingly continued his speech, pacing the sacred ground in an act of mental flexing and defiance, like a freed man, no longer directing the words to them.

Fascinated by the performance, Zenner and Yorck stretched their legs and waited by the station wagon. Only now did they have a sense of the country they had invaded, of the awesome surroundings.

'I have governed them, and they have paid me tribute. What I have commanded they have done; the law which was mine was imposed on them.' Berger wandered about. It was an incantation, like a prayer, or communication with the ancient people he could plainly see about him.

'Media, Susiana, Parthia, Aria, Bactria, Sogdiana, Khwarezmia, Drangiana, Arachosia, Sattagydia, Gandhara, India, the land of the Amyrgioi Scythians, the Scythians with the pointed hats, Babylonia, Assyria, Arabia, Egypt, Armenia, Cappodocia, Sparda, Ionia, Skudra, the Scythian lands away from the sea, Africans, Ethiopians, Magians, and Karkians. Saith King Darius: Ahura-Mazda, when he saw the earth in commotion, gave it to me. He made me King. I am King by grace of Ahura-Mazda. If you think the lands dominated by Darius are few in number, then look upon the image of those who support my throne. Then you shall know them, and you shall learn that the lance of the Persian has ranged far afield; then you shall know that Persia has fought her enemies far afield.'

When the professor was out of earshot, Yorck said, 'Look at him talking to himself. He's crazy.'

Zenner said leniently, 'We have plenty of time.'

'I'm going to kill him,' Yorck threatened.

'Why?'

'You know why.'

'Sepp made a mistake. He used too much powder. I didn't teach him that way,' Zenner said severely. 'The old man didn't do it.'

'Why do you care so much about his book?'

'It was our deal.'

'Well, I don't want to help him.'

'All right, it's up to you,' Zenner said. 'We'll leave him here and go on.'

'He should die anyway,' Yorck said. 'You told us no witnesses.'

'He can't hurt us,' Zenner insisted. 'He could be stuck here for a long time.'

Yorck looked his chief in the eyes. 'I didn't think you had a soft spot.'

It bordered on insubordination, and Zenner was irritated.

'He's been a good German. Nobody in this country could make up a map like that,' he said, ending it. 'If I kill him, it won't be for the reasons we talked about.'

'All right,' Yorck decided, seeing Berger approach them. 'I'll work with him.'

Yorck turned away so the colonel wouldn't detect his crafty intentions, going to the station wagon for the equipment. The tall, athletic scion of Prussian aristocracy had found a brotherly rapport with the sturdy son of a German peasant in the noble cause of the Führer. Whether it was the professor's fault didn't matter anymore; Sepp had to be avenged, as one SS man to the memory of another.

'A nice place to be buried, eh, Zenner!' Berger chortled. 'A very exclusive cemetery.'

'Take your snapshots,' Zenner said brusquely. 'Let's be done with it.'

Berger got his camera from the station wagon. Yorck was ready with a narrow rope ladder that had an attached grappling iron. Their portable radio began to crackle. 'It's the Storch,' Zenner said, picking up the earphones. He waved them off. 'Make it fast.'

Just before they started out, Berger offered some fatherly advice to his young partner, clucking at the sidearm Yorck had put on as an unnecessary burden. 'There is nothing to shoot at.' He wagged a finger. 'It will get in your way when you climb.'

'That's my business,' Yorck grumbled cryptically.

The professor took them around the first of the four tombs, that of Darius II. There was a path that would lead them to the top of the cliff. It was a stony and steep ascent. Berger was happiest in pursuit of his work, spry and gay. The wiry man had the agility of a mountain goat.

Yorck wasn't prepared for the rugged climb. He had to stop and shift his load, resentfully.

Berger scolded, 'I told you to travel light.'

'I'll be lighter when I get rid of you!' the Nazi snarled.

'Please, no more choking,' the professor said with grim amusement. 'It still hurts.'

'I don't know why, but the colonel saved your life.'

'It would mean killing his father twice,' Berger said obscurely, sifting the thought for himself.

'What does that mean?'

'He's sorry.'

Yorck lost interest. 'You've got some hold on him, but not on me,' he insinuated. 'Sepp was my best friend.'

The sun had burned off the morning mist by the time they reached a crow's nest of rocks above the tomb. More than one hundred and twenty-five feet below, Colonel Zenner leaned on the station wagon and gazed up at them. He raised his rifle in recognition. The professor's tent, folded furniture, food basket, and briefcase were on the road. Seeing this sign of eviction caused Berger to chuckle wryly. Yorck snickered insolently.

'Don't worry, Yorck,' Berger comforted. 'I will be staying with friends.'

The irony irked him. 'You could die this minute for all I care,' Yorck snapped.

'Not so fast, young man. There is a little more to be done on my book.'

'I shit on your book, you runt!'

The professor dissembled shamelessly. 'Such language! You surprise me, coming from such a fine family. I can excuse you for what you did to me because of poor unfortunate Sepp. But you really don't like me.' He looked guilelessly hurt. 'You shouldn't have come. Why did you?'

Yorck growled. 'You'll see later.'

'I taught my daughter German. But very polite and correct. She dreams of going there after the war,' Berger mused. 'But nobody will understand her.'

Yorck flushed guiltily, and his hand went to the butt of his holstered gun.

The menacing move alarmed the professor. 'What is it?'

'Nothing.'

The young Nazi went to work wedging the grappling iron between huge rocks. It was not yet Yorck's time for malice. Colonel Zenner had been unsympathetic to Sepp because he had failed a lesson. Setting aside his hatred for the professor, Yorck had first to demonstrate his mettle to the man watching him on the road below.

The cruciform of the tomb measured seventy-five feet vertically and sixty feet horizontally. The door to the tomb was in the centre of the horizontal, which was a replica of a building of Persepolis. The tomb was high enough from the ground to make it inaccessible to ancient grave robbers. It was Professor Berger's approach to make a commando drop from above. Yorck threw the rope ladder over the cliff where it dangled before the tomb.

With the exact needs of an expert, Berger sought close-up photographs of the carvings in the upper part of the tomb. It showed the king beside a fire altar, sitting on a throne upheld by the subject nations and blessed by Ahura-Mazda.

Hanging the camera around his neck, Yorck went down the rope ladder just as he had practised it in training camp. He hung in midair, swaying, enjoying the sensation. He then waved down to Zenner receiving a signal in return. Thus suspended, Yorck began to work the camera on the carvings in front of him.

At the same time, the professor took out a pocket knife to slash the rope from the grappling iron. He was partially hidden from Zenner's view behind a boulder. Berger noted the colonel had brought out binoculars, apparently in search of him.

Yorck called up, 'How many shots do you want?'

'Use all the film,' Berger told him, working on the resisting rope. 'Take everything twice. Even the cracks in the wall are important to me. Don't hurry it, please.'

The rope was too tough for the professor's knife. Then Zenner's voice scaled the cliff, clearly.

'That's enough, Yorck. Come down!'

The commando started up at once.

Berger hacked desperately at the stubborn strand. Then he gave up and stepped out, just as Yorck's hands reached the top rung. The professor started down, blocking the young Nazi.

'Wait,' Berger said.

He removed the camera from Yorck's neck, stalling them momentarily by this idiosyncrasy. Then Berger stepped back, allowing him to continue upwards. When Yorck's head and shoulders loomed over the top of the ladder, the professor kicked the commando full in the face.

Yorck fell backwards screaming to his death.

Instantly, Berger wheeled about to the protection of the boulder, but it was not soon enough. Zenner's bullet hit him in the back. He was thrown against the boulder, facing the ladder. Another bullet struck him in the chest, felling him to the ground out of gunsight. But it was enough.

As though the colonel wanted to empty his clip, more bullets dug the earth and chipped the rocks around the slight scholar. As the blood oozed from his dying body, the professor clutched the camera with the pictures of his ancient friend the king.

30

Harvis was in the presence of death.

Hosein sat on the ground with Professor Rudolph Berger in his arms, gently rocking, weeping, and whispering to the dead man. Berger's bloody body was still warm when they had climbed the cliff in the noonday sun and found him. His fingers were rigid around the camera.

This giant in his field was a tiny man, Harvis thought.

They had found the professor's message on a paper bag from the food basket. He had placed it on the caved-in excavation at Persepolis, knowing Hosein would find it. He warned against following these deadly commandos; it might spoil his own plans. He said he would make his getaway at Naqsh-e Rustam or Pasargadae, Zenner's next camp. He had finished his book and was seeing this through as a soldier in the service of his country, Germany. Tell his family not to worry.

In the jeep from Shiraz to Persepolis, Hosein had told Harvis about the professor's book, *The Undying Flame*. He was an uneducated peasant who had grown literate in the employ of the famous archaeologist; he had even brought certain Iranian insights to the work. Harvis understood the importance of the professor's masterwork, this gathering of a lifetime of knowledge, and was able to share the profound shock with Hosein when they found the empty briefcase and the manuscript burning in the two open-air fire altars.

They had also seen the hanging rope ladder over the tomb, the broken body of the German SS man, the possessions of the professor on the road, the tracks of the station wagon, which had just left because they could still hear it, and finally the bloody corpse of Berger.

'We should take him back now,' Harvis offered.

'There is only his grandson,' Hosein said. 'I will leave him here.'

A Zoroastrian funeral, Harvis thought. He would be left for the birds. It somehow went against his grain.

'He would want to be with the kings,' Hosein said. 'And the kings would want him.'

Harvis nodded approval.

And then Hosein bowed his head and began a prayer. Harvis

realized he was an intruder. He left the rocks and started down the trail, picking up speed, and finally running to his jeep.

Zenner had a big enough lead already.

31

Colonel Konrad Zenner drove the station wagon through the village of Madar-e Suleiman on the outskirts of Pasargadae without stopping. The people in the single street, the few markets, the only chaikhana held no interest for him as he headed for a point selected by the professor. He continued across the valley where the ancient Persians camped, passing the tomb of Cyrus, ignoring the ruins, on his way to the citadel that overlooked Pasargadae.

He arrived in a few minutes. Then Zenner got out to unlimber and look about. It was what he had specified of the scholar – soundless emptiness, no animals, nor humans. Not even a bird. No birds?

It was an hour beyond noon, and he was hungry. He brought out his blanket, shaking it well, and spread it on the ground. He filled a wooden bowl with his special diet and placed it in the centre of the blanket. He poured water from a canteen into a cup.

Removing his shirt, he bared a broad expanse of tanned skin to the generous rays of the sun. Taking his cross-legged position, he began a deep breathing routine. In that way he wiped clean the slate of his mind. The deaths of men and the murder of them were blown from his memory out of his lips to the winds of Iran. It was as though the oxygen charged the light in his eyes. They dilated as he looked in the direction of Berlin, the source of his inspiration.

Only the bird thought remained in his mind.

At his first meeting with Hitler there were tears in the Führer's eyes for the death of his favourite canary. Zenner saw genuine mourning for the bird. He had loved that pet.

It was the day he had received his major assignment, and the colonel recalled it had begun with thoughts of birds. He had come to Berlin to meet Reichsminister of Propaganda Joseph Goebbels.

'Where are you taking me?'

SS Captain Konrad Zenner asked the military driver, who held the door of the black Mercedes open for him. He towered over the average-sized soldier. They were outside the Ministry Building on the Wilhelmstrasse in the heat of a day in July

1943.

'Sorry, Captain.' The driver was tight-lipped. 'Orders.'

The captain shrugged and entered the Mercedes, where his six feet five took up a good proportion of the back seat. He had been ordered to attend a meeting in Berlin for an unknown but very important assignment. Why not an unknown destination? That kind of security had the scent of a promotion.

Zenner leaned forward to the driver. 'Don't go fast. I mean drive very slowly.'

The driver turned to explain why he couldn't comply and found himself staring into the scar on the face of a twenty-five-year-old giant who liked his orders followed.

'So you want to see some real life after the front, eh? I'll drive by way of the Kurfürstendamn,' he offered. 'You'll see lots of people, plenty of girls.'

'That's not it,' Zenner explained. 'I want to see if there are birds in Berlin.'

The captain had come from the Kharkov front, where he had fought with the SS Leibstandarte Division that had recaptured the city from the Russians. He hadn't seen or heard a bird in the entire area, which he had accepted as a natural consequence of battle. Now, as they drove towards the suburbs, Zenner listened and looked for the birds of the city in which he had been born and reared because earlier that day the Allied air force had bombed Berlin in a heavy raid. He had a desperate desire to know if the birds had taken flight like the birds of Kharkov.

In a time when humans took sides, willingly or not, only the birds were permitted neutrality. Did some instinct tell them when to fly away? Like the forewarning alarms that sent the citizens of Berlin running into shelters and the tunnels of the subway. Or did the birds of Berlin remain to be maimed or to die like their co-inhabitants of the city?

Through the lowered windows of the Mercedes, Captain Zenner observed the Hitler Youth, boys and girls, clean up rubble, along with prisoners of war and concentration camps. Buildings were still burning. People were being removed from the debris of a gaping apartment house. He was indifferent to the dying and the wreckage, the sounds of the sirens, the weeping women, the calls of men for lost ones, and the cries of children.

If the birds leave Berlin, he thought, then it's all over.

By the time the driver had delivered Captain Zenner to the

villa of Joseph Goebbels at Wannsee, fifteen miles outside Berlin, near Postdam, he had learned enough to satisfy his anxiety. The birds had come back after the bombing to their old haunts. He had heard them discussing the sun and the day's foraging. Like everything else Germanic, Zenner thought, the birds of Berlin were superior....

Sitting at the citadel above Pasargadae, Colonel Zenner understood now why there were no birds. It was an ancient battleground. Among subject peoples one must expect inferior birds. That was his firm belief, he thought. He had been taught that way.

The noise was tremendous.

Harvis had heard the oncoming tumult. Then he was forced to halt on the road to Pasargadae because of a nomadic people on the move, a tribe of Qashqai. There were thousands of sheep crossing the road, among them goats, cows, dogs, camels loaded with tents and carpets, donkeys carrying household goods and chicken coops, horses and ponies and more donkeys transporting men, women, and children. Overhead crows and vultures circled for scraps and fallen animals. All in a haze of dust.

Harvis turned off the jeep's engine and settled down to witness a human activity thousands of years old. It was just before one o'clock, and he was midway from Persepolis. On the other side of the migrating multitude Colonel Zenner would be almost at Pasargadae. In pursuit, Harvis had no idea how fast the German was travelling or if he was gaining on him. He had been driving at full speed until the Qashqai came between.

The Iranian river of people and animals meandered and swirled around the jeep. Harvis was in a wash of bleats, baas, moos, whinnies, brays, and the tribesmen's friendly greetings to the foreigner, the *feranji*.

His jeep became an island on which Harvis was alone with his thoughts, forced to review himself. In the midst of the din and dust he laughed out loud but couldn't hear himself. He suddenly discovered ironic detachment and saw himself standing out in comic relief as some kind of GI Don Quixote. We who are about to die salute you! Something Greek instead of Roman would have been more apt in a land conquered by Alexander the Great, but it was the best he could do.

He was in his trusty jeep, his own white charger, on a noble quest against evil. Like Hamlet, his fictional favourite, who could have chosen to turn back on the 'unweeded garden' of Elsinore or could accept the brave obligation to fight his enemies. So to be, or not to be, a good guy was no longer the question.

It somehow had resolved itself in his ridiculously reckless plunge down the tomb trail, like a fighting mad kid. The murdered man. The burned book. The strangled family. The orphaned baby. Then, calmer as he drove, Harvis knew it wasn't boyish bravado or youthful impulse, but maturing coalescence on the cliff with the great archaeologist and the gentle good man, the Zoroastrian.

He might have gone the other way, unravelling. Instead, loose ends formed a neat knot; something had clicked.

The cold outrage remained. He wanted cigarettes when they met, so he could rub one out on the balls of Colonel Konrad Zenner, like a proper pupil of Major Sam Skeene. Before that, of course, he would punch out the German commando in the Gothic style of Colonel Boris Artukin, who wept for all families because he had lost his own to the Fascists. Both men had been trying to tell their young Yankee friend something. At least he had heard the message.

Harvis thought of Betty, Ambassador Gordell, and Major Ali Mirza, the other conditioners of his reflex to evil. It gave him an uneasy sense of having been manipulated. Was he an absurd victim programmed to stalk Zenner? Or be murdered by him, 'the most dangerous man in Europe'?

He could reverse himself and go back to Tehran. Simple. Who would know the difference?

Harvis was reminded of the time he had attended a bullfight in Tijuana with Hemingway's books as a guide. He had witnessed a cowardly performance similar to the one described in the book. Hemingway wrote, 'Why did the man insist on being a bullfighter?' He could have chosen any other work without dishonouring himself.

The truth came to Harvis that he had slipped into this position by self-deceptive stages. But it was still his own decision, probably his last will and testament.

I am of age, not under duress, dope, or drunk, he thought.

Betty would rather have him in bed with her, Gordell would want him at his post, guarding the arrival of President Roosevelt, and Mirza would prefer a living friend like Harvis over a dead intruder like Zenner, as foreigners went. They looked alike to the Iranian police major.

Would they mourn his death?

The woman would shed a tear and consider him a jerk, the ambassador would be puzzled and believe he had gone off his rocker, then send for another tennis partner, and the Persian would shrug Orientally and declare it was fate, all in the hands of Allah. 'Every man's destiny is fastened on his neck.'

War was a vacation from peace, and these were the ephemeral friends one met on holiday. When it was over, they'd go their separate ways around the world, having finished their wars. Meanwhile, Harvis had his own war going. Their opinion of him, favourable or not, was unimportant. It was the mirror of himself that mattered in this self-imposed test.

Going for broke.

Harvis became aware he was surrounded by silence. The Qashqai were gone.

He started the jeep. Persia was now a personal arena. He was riding off to meet another foreigner who was using this land, Zenner. Thousands of years ago they had defined the boundaries of good and evil in this country, recognizing the eternal struggle. Harvis was really at home here or anywhere.

Anyway, good guys always did the right thing. Harvis laughed. And laughed.

33

He maintained his position on the blanket like a figure carved in stone, his mind becalmed, scarcely breathing, his naked torso absorbing the sun. The solitude of the high citadel was a classic setting for meditation. Colonel Konrad Zenner might have been a hermit rejecting civilization.

The food before him was still untouched. Self-denial and restraint were part of his ritual of purification, void, and nullity. He was motionless in a place of eternal quiet.

He was at peace.

Then his head shook as from a mental click. It brought him back to his need for food. He began to eat the contents of the bowl, washing it down with water.

At Horcher's it had been lobster and champagne, he thought. Zenner had been to the exclusive Berlin restaurant only five days before as the guest of Joseph Goebbels. He didn't like the Reichsminister, but the colonel couldn't turn down the powerful man's invitation for a 'going away party'. The propaganda chief had also arranged for a motion-picture actress to take Zenner home with her afterwards.

Crystal, silver, orchids on the table, plush chairs, waiters in full dress. The best food in Europe because it was a winner-takes-all. No prices on the menu, Goebbels explained, because after you ate such food, you didn't mind the cost.

Top Nazi leaders, industrialists, diplomats, aristocrats, celebrities like Max Schmeling in paratroop uniform at a table of generals. It was Göring's favourite eating place, and Zenner saw how one of the founders of the Third Reich had developed his hippo proportions. And not a ration stamp in sight.

It was a foretaste, Goebbels had said, of his reception when Zenner returned a hero. All the important people in Horcher's would come to his table and introduce themselves. Even now one of the famous newspapermen in the room was asking who the handsome young colonel was sitting with the Reichsminister. But, of course, his mission was secret.

A sound shattered his daydream and sent Zenner back to his spartan existence. It was the receiver in the station wagon. He put on the earphones and said, 'Wolf Pack Number One, Wolf Pack Number One.'

He made ready to leave.

34

Yes, the villager of Madar-e Suleiman told the American officer, he had seen the station wagon pass through in the direction of Pasargadae. They were familiar with the vehicles of the *feranji*, English, French, German, Russian, American, who came to dig in the ruins outside their village.

Did his excellency wish to hire him? It was only a few tomans a day for an experienced man.

He was only on a holiday, Harvis told him.

From where he stood beside his jeep, he could see the tomb of Cyrus. Harvis had been here before and knew the story of the place, as he did all the fascinating history of Persia with an outsider's zeal that embarrassed most Iranians, who preferred bread to glory. When a peasant dug his earth it wasn't for history, but for a hungry present.

Pasargadae, 'the camp of the Persians', was where the first great sovereign of the dynasty, the true founder of the Persian Empire, Cyrus the Great, lived and was buried in 530 BC. The site was a valley denuded of trees and water by centuries of changing nature. It held the sparse ruins of three palaces. Persepolis, built fifty years later, was much more imposing as the empire grew stronger and richer, and inevitably eclipsed Pasargadae. History and the preservation of the past moved Harvis in ways he couldn't explain.

Somewhere in those timeless precincts SS Colonel Konrad Zenner, the German commando, was camped.

Harvis felt surefooted, on solid ground, no more alienated, uprooted, and lost in Iran. Was it because he 'knew the enemy', as the Army training manuals propagated? Recognized evil? No, it went deeper. Each mile from Persepolis had increased his separation from the Army. The need for independence was in the marrow of his bones.

By the time he reached Madar-e Suleiman Harvis was thinking of his experience as publishable, the setting, his moods. He was beginning to observe himself in movement as a writer, already shaping his material. His perceptions sharpened and he was more conscious of smells, distance, and danger. His timid ambitions surfaced, and Harvis knew what he'd be chancing for a living after the war – if he lived.

Harvis smiled to himself, thinking of Ernest Hemingway and

Humphrey Bogart. And his father.

When he had turned his back on Tehran in pursuit of Zenner, Harvis had abandoned the noncombat security of his Army commission. Now he was renouncing the future tenure of a schoolteacher back home in Moreno. Look, Dad, I'm gambling.

So what am I? How about war correspondent? These fellows without uniform were known to die in combat zones. It was still a war Harvis was in. Inescapably. War was an acceptance of danger and death. Stupid, I ain't. I must be fearless, for chrissake. And following phantom orders.

He drove to the tomb of Cyrus, crossing into the past of Persia, like a warrior entering the lists, joining the ghosts of lancers and bowmen. The tomb stood on six terraces of receding steps, altogether about fifty feet high. Its simplicity was imposing.

Harvis climbed the steps of the tomb, remembering that Alexander the Great had done the same thing. Cyrus had been buried in a golden sarcophagus that reclined on a gold couch amid his great treasures. After defeating the Persians, Alexander honoured the memory of Cyrus. When he returned from further conquests, he found the tomb had been looted. He executed the satrap who had stolen the valuables.

He looked for the Nazi on the flat plain that had once flourished with trees, gardens, and ponds, according to the ancient travellers of the time. It was a silent and calm midafternoon, yet the air seemed alive with history. There was an unfinished citadel about a mile away situated on a defensive height that dominated the valley. It seemed like a good place for a hideout if Colonel Zenner required one.

In between were the remains of three buildings, a gatehouse, the audience hall of Cyrus, and the residential palace, like monuments in a cemetery.

Farsai, the embassy interpreter, had travelled with him on the last visit. He took pictures of Harvis, mostly gag shots, to send home. Before the famous bas-relief of a figure with four wings, wearing a long Elamite garment, and crowned with an Egyptian-style tiara, Harvis had bowed as if receiving a blessing. For another shot he pushed against the one slender column left in the audience hall, pretending to topple this last remaining relic. On the tomb of Cyrus he assumed a conqueror's stance, mimicking Mussolini's chin. Now he was here with a carbine slung around his neck instead of a camera. The silly times are behind me, Harvis thought.

If the station wagon were parked in the area, he would have seen it, unless it was out of sight in the excavation or behind the mud-brick walls that enclosed the palaces from wandering herds.

Then he saw it coming from the citadel.

Harvis felt a thrust of fear in his heart. He unleashed his carbine and dropped to his stomach, breathing hard. From a mile away the station wagon seemed like an approaching express train.

The colonel wouldn't be looking for him, but Harvis knew his jeep, parked directly behind the tomb, would come into view when the road changed course. He made out the German commando now at the wheel, driving leisurely. Harvis found his mouth dry. And his palms wet as he placed the windshield of the station wagon in the sights of his carbine.

Zenner turned left and stopped less than a hundred yards away. Harvis couldn't tell if it was by design or suspicion. The Nazi jumped out behind the station wagon with his rifle. Harvis pulled the trigger when he should have squeezed it. The bullet hit the front side window through which he saw the commando and the sound of the shattering glass came back.

The colonel ducked down, using the station wagon as a shield. Harvis had to maintain the surprise attack and at least disable the machine. It was an easy target. He steadied with each shot and saw the tyres on the right side sink as he emptied and reloaded his clips.

Harvis was breaking up the station wagon, hoping fragments would penetrate the German hiding behind it. Zenner held his fire. Harvis flattened, making the smallest profile for the moment when the commando would return fire in some daring manoeuvre. Shooting downward from the tomb, he had the upper hand.

It had all been reflexive, and Harvis was rather proud of his responses. Then he realized that as the sun set, so did his advantage. Zenner was staying put, not taking any chances because he was simply waiting for nightfall. A duel in the dark. Harvis felt himself drenched in sweat.

He held his fire, fixing his eyes on the station wagon. Behind it was a creative killer, Hitler's favourite assassin, plotting a counter-attack. He had glimpsed the German and was astounded at his hugeness. He had unhorsed him, but now the commando chief seemed more dangerous on foot.

The son of a bitch is a time bomb, Harvis thought, trembling a little.

Alone and afraid, he desperately needed help. Reinforcements, the military called it. He thought of Artukin and Skeene, who would be in Isfahan by now on the raid against the underground network, following Mirza's tip. That was about two hundred and fifty miles from Pasargadae.

Harvis looked down on his jeep nearby, gripped by an urge to jump to the ground and drive off to his friends in Isfahan. But what if that pension in the Yahudieh turned out to be a false lead and they had gone? He needed allies to capture Zenner. He couldn't do it by himself, unless he shot him.

The distance between Harvis and his jeep was risky with a sharpshooter like Zenner. He had already made his reputation in Iran. There was enough daylight space in which he would expose himself for the Nazi marksman to get off some shots. Unless he was caught by surprise.

He gathered nerve for the goal of the jeep.

A sound from the sky, breaking the graveyard silence of Pasargadae, stopped him. Then he learned what Colonel Zenner was waiting for: that this was a rendezvous point.

A light plane approached on course towards the tomb like a guiding pylon. Decreasing speed, lowering altitude, preparing to land on a perfect field.

The British insignia didn't fool Harvis; the commando mission had been dropped in Iran from a Lancaster. Any doubt was dispelled by Zenner's frantic waving from behind the station wagon, warning the pilot away. It was the most he had shown of himself like a pinwheel target of arm signals.

Harvis dared not divide his attention.

The pilot made a lazy circle, waving a greeting below, misinterpreting the colonel. Harvis grinned. In the shadow of the tomb wall, he was invisible from the air. But he would have to announce himself soon.

The next time over it would be close enough to hit with a baseball bat, Harvis estimated. It's a bird, and I'm back in junior high with my twenty-two. Only you used to miss 'em, Peteboy. But those were ordinary blackbirds. How could he miss this enormous bird of ill omen?

Then it was directly over him banking in a tremendous roar, and when Harvis opened fire, he couldn't hear his own shots.

The plane pulled out of a bank and took a straight course in the direction of the citadel.

I scared the bird away, Harvis thought.

Then it struck the mountainside and exploded.

Harvis almost stood up to cheer. You killed the big blackbird, Peteboy! The adult part of him saw a pilot incinerated. He had never experienced such exultation.

It was all quiet again at Pasargadae, and we're back to two slices, Harvis thought, containing his jubilation. Now the Nazi had to retaliate, after the flames on the citadel. He fixed his eyes on the station wagon for a sudden sign of his enemy, finger on trigger, confident about his marksmanship, like a practised rifleman.

Harvis heard it first, then saw a white Mercedes coming from Madar-e Suleiman at full speed. It was a meeting ground and the car was on time, but they'll have to change their plans, Harvis thought, as the car headed for the station wagon.

The driver was a woman in a black chador, who fit the description of the one Mirza had followed from the house of Ebenezer Foster Waite. That meant the American lawyer was linked with the Nazis. The Fascist fag!

Beside her, Harvis recognized the Iranian commando, Nadiri, the poor fish on Mirza's reel. He was probably brought along to take over the station wagon Zenner expected to leave behind when he took the plane. But he had shot down their air force and crippled the armoured car, Harvis thought. I'm a goddamn one-man army!

The car paused behind the station wagon barricade long enough for Colonel Zenner to hop into the back, then it headed towards the citadel. To shoot in the speeding seconds the connection took seemed like a waste of ammo, but Harvis sent off a shot. If it hit the sedan, the bullet had no effect.

Harvis didn't mind the escape. He stood up, smiling, his bunched bones expanding. It was more than physical relief. The swift interval had seemed like a welcome truce.

Then Harvis blanched as he saw the white Mercedes make a skidding turnabout. He thought they were going to the burning plane. Now the car was weaving back towards the tomb at a fast rate. He aimed his carbine at the black chador in the windshield; but the car made a sharp left, and his shot went wide.

The tactic was to permit Zenner to take aim over the lowered side window. Harvis lurched back against the corner of the tomb, almost falling off. The shot from the veering vehicle was a near miss even from the impossible angle.

Pressing his back to the stone wall, Harvis heard the Mercedes circle for another run at him. He started for the jeep, then stopped; they would run him down in seconds. He saw the open entrance to the tomb and scurried inside. It was already night in the chamber.

Outside, the Mercedes came to a halt.

Harvis realized he had dropped the carbine in his panic on the steps of the tomb. He had his sidearm. He waited, forty-five in hand, none too securely. Zenner wouldn't try to enter, nor would he suicidally reveal himself. At the same time, Harvis was trapped in the tomb.

There were noises outside the doorway Harvis couldn't distinguish. What were the means the commando might employ to murder him? Attrition, for one. His only chance lay in time, the schedule Zenner was operating on. From the style of his successful raids he was a soldier of Germanic precision. Losing the plane must have disrupted his timetable. This speculation, Harvis thought with grim humour, was a form of prayer.

There was the outside sound of gunfire and smashed glass.

He guessed Zenner was revengefully putting his jeep out of commission. It was underneath the entrance, and they had set it on fire. The flames made patterns on the walls inside the tomb.

Standing beside the entrance with his back to the wall, Harvis could feel the rising heat. He expected the jeep to explode. He wet his lips. He felt hot and helpless.

A gust of smoke entered, and Harvis retreated, coughing. More smoke chased him to the rear of the dark chamber. He holstered his gun and cupped his hands over his mouth and nose. His breathing came hard, but Harvis wasn't ready to run out and be shot by the SS colonel.

Then the suffocating smoke forced his desperate body beyond fear. He lunged forward on his face to the bottom of the open entrance, hoping the twilight and the black smoke would screen his head.

There was fresh air.

He heard the German car driving away.

The war game was over, and Harvis stood up in the doorway to breathe deeply of freedom. But then he gave way to his knees and slumped to the floor. It was a happy exhaustion. He was glad to be alive in the ancient tomb of Cyrus the Great, despite the clinging smell of smoke.

Dumb luck, he thought. It was an easy matter to become superstitious in Persia.

35

Betty was organizing the ambassador's desk when Lieutenant George Keyes appeared in the office doorway.

'Come in, Lieutenant.'

'I hope I didn't hold you up, Miss Lanteri,' the lieutenant said. 'Calling you at quitting time.'

'That hour went out with the Big Three.'

'You have to be hungry.'

'When the ambassador comes back, I'll be going to a meeting with him,' she said. 'Diplomats eat while they talk. We scold children for that.'

'I know he's with General Andrews,' Keyes said. 'I wanted to see you before the general goes back to headquarters.'

'Why?'

'That's when I hand in my worksheet.'

Betty indicated a seat. 'I'll get us some drinks.'

Keyes took a chair. 'I never drink on duty.'

'It's seven o'clock in the evening.'

'My day ends when I hand in my worksheet,' he told her. 'Go ahead.'

She leaned on the desk. 'I never drink alone,' Betty said. 'What's so important about the worksheet?'

'Should I put Captain Harvis' name on it or not?'

'Why the multiple choice?'

'He covered for me. I'm ready to return the favour.'

'I told you this morning Pete was out of town on embassy security business. Tell it like it is, Lieutenant Keyes.'

'If I don't believe it, old Tom-Tom won't.'

'So what if he doesn't?'

'He's laying for this deal, Miss Lanteri,' Keyes said. 'He's court-martial happy.'

'Why are you skeptical?'

'What's more important than the Presidential security detail?'

'Maybe that's what it concerns.'

'Look, I'm trying to help him —'

'Therefore, I will tell you the truth.'

'Well?'

'We don't know where he is,' Betty confessed. 'The ambassador is furious. Captain Harvis has never let him down before.

It was the wrong time to go AWOL.'

'Any clues?'

'Major Mirza saw him in Shiraz this morning,' Betty said. 'Pete told him he would call me. Not a word.'

'That helps my hunch,' Keyes said. 'That's why I'm here.'

'May I hear it?'

'He's gone looking for Colonel Zenner.'

'How did you arrive at that?'

'From the way he talked about him. All day.'

'That's what Major Mirza believes, too.'

'What do you think?'

'As ridiculous as it sounds, I agree with you,' she said. 'He has no sense.'

'But a lot of guts,' Keyes said. 'If I knew where he was I'd join up with him.'

'Then you'd be AWOL, too,' Betty reminded him. 'Didn't you say General Andrews was a court-martial freak?'

'It would be worth it.'

'You've risked your neck once, Lieutenant Keyes,' she said. 'I was at the ceremony with the ambassador when you got the medal and the commission.'

'That was before a lot of good friends on those trucks and trains got it from the commandos.'

'So you want to be a hero twice,' Betty said. 'Dope springs eternal.'

'Maybe women don't get it.'

'I can understand your motivation,' she said. 'But as for Captain Peter Harvis, well, I don't get it.'

Lieutenant Keyes made ready to leave.

She asked, 'What will you put down on the worksheet?'

'Today will be okay,' Keyes said. 'But if he ain't around in the morning, I'll have to ask for help.'

'Naturally, Lieutenant Keyes. It's an important assignment for very important people.' She paid tribute to the picture of President Roosevelt on the wall. 'Veriest in the whole world.'

'The Big C-in-C himself.' Keyes started out slowly. 'Old Tom-Tom is going to massacre Pete.'

'If Ambassador Gordell gets to him first, there won't be much left for the general,' she said. 'I've never seen him so angry.'

'Good night, Miss Lanteri.'

'Let's have coffee in the morning and compare notes.'

As he started out, she had an afterthought. 'Oh, Lieutenant.

Next time, please call me Betty.'

'Thanks, you can call me George.'

She ventured, smiling. 'Now that we're on a first-name basis, I can ask you an impertinent question. You don't have to answer.'

Keyes checked his watch. 'Shoot.'

'It was something I thought of when you got the medal.'

Keyes grinned. 'Let me ask the question.'

'Shoot.'

'How come me, a nigger from a racist country in a Jim Crow army, is so gung-ho?'

'You're a mind reader.'

'That ain't it. It was the only question around, but nobody asked it,' he said. 'But I was ready.'

'So answer.'

'Nazis hate blacks, too. Remember what Hitler did to Jesse Owens in Berlin, in the 1936 Olympics. And don't forget the Max Schmeling–Joe Louis fight. The other thing was I didn't jump with the engineer because he was scared and I wasn't. He was yellow, I wasn't. I'm just a man,' he said. 'Okay?'

'No,' she said. 'That's only part of it.'

Keyes laughed. 'Your question was the "real" question. The one nobody would ask.'

'Or think of,' she said. 'Except me.'

'When this war ends, it ain't really over for me. It goes on for us blacks back home, right?'

'Right.'

'Meanwhile, back at the front Hitler is attacking the United States, and that's my country, right?'

'Right.'

'Good night, Betty,' he said. 'I liked your answers.'

He left the office.

It had been a long day, and Betty slipped off her shoes and stretched out on the big couch, thinking of Peter. Pitting himself against an experienced commando like Colonel Zenner was a simple self-immolation. A circus act. Martyrdom for an ideal was soft-minded foolishness, best understood in terms of Freud and not realpolitik. Fortresses were to be burrowed under, gone around, or starved out, never stormed. That was for kids who play general and generals who were kids.

'What about heroes?' Peter had once asked.

'I recognize two varieties of homo sap,' Betty had replied, knowing he was exploring his own sources of courage. 'Number one is a shmuck without brains in a corner with no way to go. Number two is a putz with brains who has another way to go but puts himself into a corner. He's worse off than the dummy because he thinks he thinks.'

'They still end up as heroes,' Peter had contended.

'The luck of crazies and madmen,' she had declared. 'Against the odds the first should surrender but fights. The second doesn't even think of surrendering. Neurotics, the two of them.'

Then she had let her smugness go. 'I lost my cherry with Spain.' She had sighed. 'La Pasionaria and Abraham Lincoln Brigade never had a chance.'

Betty dozed off, thinking her lover a fool. She couldn't abide fools.

36

The walk to the village of Madar-e Suleiman was in cool moonlight. Harvis carried the tomb smell of death with him. He required the astringent night air to cleanse his lungs, clear his mind, and ventilate his clothes.

He sauntered gaily, each step a reaffirmation of his existence. He began to whistle.

He thought of the walks he used to take around the reservoir in his neighbourhood when he had something to ponder. Back to the time he walked a newspaper route pulling a hand wagon. (Remember the money he made in the streets selling the Jack Dempsey–Gene Tunney fight extra. . . .)

Childhood in California. It seemed that stage in his life extended from Moreno to Pasargadae. He had sweated off his last ounce of baby fat on the tomb of Cyrus the Great.

Walking is what you did at home. The war was on jeep wheels. But it was natural to be walking now because the Persian peasant walked. That identified poverty with walking. An absence of transportation. He didn't feel poor walking, but rich. Right now he was convinced he could walk all the way home, gathering wealth, and when he reached Moreno, he'd be a millionaire.

What a surprise it would be if he walked in on his family. The look on his father's face would be priceless because he loved the unexpected. Especially his father because Harvis had been going for broke. A phrase his old man would use.

For the first time in his life he had acted like a gambler. The blue chips he had laid on the line were his flesh, blood, and bones, his very life. His father always took chances, mostly when the odds were against him. Shooting for the jackpot. Money was to spend. He was perpetually broke. There would be no estate. But destiny is what you inherit, if nothing else.

Did you ever really know your father? Or is he revealed a little at a time as your time goes on?

'You'll understand later,' his father had said. 'When you're older.'

To hear that in his teens, to have a mind that was agelessly adult – it was hatefuly humiliating. The patronizing sidestep that masked grown-up hypocrisy. But he knew now, walking away from the tomb of Cyrus, it wasn't his father's lie. It was the wisdom of the world.

Older now, Harvis understood that. Only now. The now in Persia at age twenty-five, having left a battlefield. Now about the 'thing' between them. This moment now he could name it because he had committed it himself – adultery.

What does a boy understand coming home from junior high too soon? He had been sent home by the nurse because of a headache. His father's car was outside the house, which was not unusual. His tennis shoes made no noise as he went inside. At the bathroom he heard the sounds in his parents' bedroom like their lovemaking. But he knew his mother was at work in the dress shop.

Something made Peter bolt out of the house, slamming the front door hard. He waited outside behind a tree, sick to his stomach, his mild illness now feverish.

His father emerged with his mother's divorced sister, who was visiting from Los Angeles. He looked about worriedly, but his aunt hadn't heard or didn't care. They drove away in the car.

For about a week afterwards Peter caught sidelong glances from his father, on the verge of speaking. Once at dinner he went into a lengthy anecdote about his own father that involved a comic chase by an armed husband for eight miles. Peter had loved his grandfather, whom he resembled.

'Grandpa was a ladies' man right up to the day he died.' His father laughed.

His mother seethed. 'Stop this chatter. He doesn't know what you're talking about!'

'He'll get it one of these days.'

He learned that all the arguments around the house weren't about gambling. The 'thing' brought him closer to his mother. He never verbalized the situation. For a long time afterwards he had the nervous habit of clearing his throat. His mother continued to laugh and play the guitar.

He realized now he was victimized for ever by sympathy for his mother's complaints against her husband. What about familial jealousies? He could ask himself at last how much of the unhappiness was his mother's doing. Something drove his father to gambling and urgent business at the home office of the insurance company in Los Angeles.

Man to man, Dad. Tell me about Ma.

When he walked into the village, it was dark but the chaikhana was still open; it was early evening. His watch had stopped through neglect. Harvis was dishevelled and needed a shave. His uniform was wrinkled, dirty, and clammy.

The owner of the teahouse and a handful of his customers stared in awed puzzlement at the armed American soldier, who came in and spoke their language. They had never seen Europeans travel on foot, but the owner remained discreetly courteous.

Besides refreshments for Harvis, the owner arranged a ride on a truck going to Abadeh, which was halfway to Isfahan. Would the honourable guest like a bath?

It was as if the owner had read his mind because his desire for a bath went deeper than his need for cleanliness. But Harvis wasn't thinking of the village bathhouse. Ah, but there was a surprise in store for him. The owner took him to the rear of the building where there was a bathtub. An antiseptic British team of archaeologists had installed one for their own use and left it behind.

He had at least four hours. Harvis figured to spend it all in the warm water. At home he called a bathtub 'an enamel womb' because he received nervous revival and all varieties of inspiration in it. Stand-up showers merely washed. A tub got beneath the skin and soaked the soul.

Alone in the naked universality of a bathroom, it was all steam and soothing submersion. His numbness dissolved. At last retrospection was possible. His gunfight with Colonel Konrad Zenner emerged surprisingly as a two-character drama played in a historical setting. He projected himself as a romantic film star, large screen size. He saw the billboards advertising it: 'Dangerous Detours! Bold Adventure! Courageous Gambles!'

'I'm a smoked ham.' He laughed softly, thinking of the burning jeep, delighted to own the defence of humour against horror.

If the notorious German commando chief took on mythic proportions, so did he. Hadn't it been a standoff?

Wisdom begins with a smile, he observed. Had he read it someplace or just created it? He could always recall the idea and style of an author but not the exact quote. Now something inside him had cracked, like a concrete band around his brain, releasing a dam of ideas. He decided the aphorism was his own. Temerity seemed a permanent part of his newly organized ego.

He had gone after the enemy with all the proper war pennants and slogans. They had not sustained him in the smoke-choked tomb. He found that the fear of dying murdered all motivations except the will to live. The lesson came in the instant of his dive for survival in the doorway of the tomb. The heat of battle melted the soft sentiments of family, country, honour. The hard nugget of self was left. Alone. Harvis supposed it was because of his youth. Maybe it took the knowledge of a man like Professor Rudolph Berger to have the strength and bravery for political martyrdom.

Harvis laughed louder this time. It sounded a lot like the survivor's glee of Colonel Boris Artukin.

He had taken a test. A final. And he hadn't flunked it.

'I'll have to stop thinking like a schoolteacher, he told himself. But what am I? I'm Alexander the Great (in bed) because a Persian girl says so.

Only five times with her. Ali be praised.

Mirza must have been counting, too. But who'll be spying in the United States, old friend? When I go home to Moreno, California. And your daughter is living in Los Angeles. Her cross, your double cross, and my triple cross.

Where should I stay? Faraj asked.

Near me, of course.

That would not be nice. She blushed.

Three hundred miles away.

In Hollywood!

I have a friend who works in a studio, he said. He'll get you in.

What a wonderful thing to be an American girl!

The five times became one in his mind. His white arms around her dark body. The dark nipples against his white chest. His white stomach over her dark pubescence.

There was something primeval about it. Her body was a history and her eyes storied. The fascination of difference worked both ways. Her eyes devoured his nudity.

Once Harvis was in a sleep of sexual exhaustion, and something made him open his eyes. Faraj was holding his penis, studying it. She was an artist sensitive to colour, form, and texture.

How pink it is? She exclaimed like a child.

He laughed, aroused again. Kiss it!

And so she learned about that, too, and he learned the taste of her.

It's salty, she said.

He said, You are sweet.

Alone in his apartment for the first time. They used words but their eyes told more. Harvis and Faraj were soon drawn together, sucked in by the gravitational pull of Venus. Their clothes flew off into space, finding themselves in fellow nakedness. Then embracing in a free fall of love.

What are you putting on? she asked.

He replied, Do you want a baby?

Limp and unresisting towards him, Harvis waited for her trembling to cease. The suspended moment was important for him, too. If he was to guide, he'd better be in control. In the fiercest heat he kept cool. And so he was aware of the involuntary start and the little shudder and the closed eyes like some kind of flight. She said nothing as if knowing the cry of a virgin would be like a slap.

Then there was his pounding blood.

And her blood on the sheet.

Afterwards he thought, Is that how a man and a woman got into each other's blood? Blood is a mysterious river that runs us. Blood has its own laws.

Thoughts of home, the war, Mirza's omniscience. Now deep into the Persian girl. And then it didn't matter about the world because the past was dead, the future didn't exist, and only the everlasting moment was alive.

He would be travelling to see Faraj in Los Angeles. Picking up where his father had left off a long time ago. And his grandfather before that. Harvis possessed a family sin-drome.

He heard the bells of wandering animals as Harvis drowsed off in the bathtub....

... and then came a dim idea for the title of his book. Or maybe it would be better as the first line: 'Once upon a time there was a good war....'

37

The white Mercedes came to a halt at a crossroads outside Isfahan sometime before midnight. Nadiri stepped out on the road, leaving Colonel Konrad Zenner and the woman in the black chador in the car.

The young Iranian commando didn't have long to wait. A truck with a shipment of rugs drove out of a dark side road and pulled up behind the Mercedes. The truck driver got out to join Nadiri. He was handed a packet of money. Also a palmed note from Nadiri unseen by the others.

The completed transaction brought the presence of the colonel. He carried his custom gun case, now protected by a waterproof canvas cover, and a handbag to the trunk of the car, after removing a flashlight from it.

Zenner climbed into the back of the truck. Nadiri hid him comfortably under some rugs. Then the Iranian took over the wheel of the truck and drove it away, going in the direction of Tehran.

Intending to hitch a ride in the Mercedes, the truck driver reached for the door, but the woman in the black chador suddenly drove off, heading for Isfahan.

The truck driver shrugged, sighed, and began to walk.

38

When Ambassador Philip Gordell returned to his office, Betty was asleep on the couch. At first glance, in this hour of his rocketing career, the sight annoyed him. He had entered briskly with a briefcase of anxieties, but then restrained an irritable impulse to rouse his secretary, caught by something in her repose, struck in a dormant and vulnerable part of his being.

He fixed a drink, then sank into a soft leather chair like a deflating balloon, to contemplate this felinely arranged female as if she were a Matisse on the wall. She lay like an artist's model, he thought, seductively placed on her back in an abandon of exhaustion. Left knee up, baring most of a leg suggesting more, limp right hand, from which her glasses had slipped, just touching the floor with her fingertips.

Gordell had an eye for painter's detail like a connoisseur of art. He had never seen her before as anything but an employee in motion. Now she was a woman at rest. He sipped his scotch and judged the pleasures and possibilities – and the lost opportunities – of the body before him.

His wife was in Pennsylvania for the birth of a grandchild. In anticipation of his retirement, they had decided she would remain to arrange for their new life. By now in their long marriage sex was not a requirement for love. The book he was writing would fill all his extra time and thoughts and sublimate much. The woman on the couch was becoming an important part of the book. A part of him. He was flinging the book against a governmental Goliath that was declaring him useless. Betty Lanteri had become an ally in the battle.

She stirred, and Gordell hoped she wouldn't wake. A small moan escaped from a troubled dream. She writhed, then licked her lips, as though disturbed by dryness, or the aftertaste of a satisfaction. Then she rolled over luxuriantly on her stomach, hiking up her dress, and revealing an expanse of panties.

Gordell bolted his drink and propelled himself to the bar for replenishment. There was a mirror, and he couldn't resist checking his assets, like totalling the chemical count on himself, to offer someone. It was undeniable he was pushing sixty, but the grey in his temples was late. He had nonfat features, crisp and classic, composing a really handsome man. And he kept in shape with tennis, he was reminded by the trophies in the room. It was all in the mind, he thought, trying to see through the looking glass. But he saw no wonderland of youth.

'Oh, I'm sorry,' Betty exclaimed, sitting up.

He went to her. 'What for?'

'There's such a thing as secretarial decorum.'

'I'm supposed to have diplomatic reserve,' he told her. 'But I've been a Peeping Tom.'

'How did I do?'

'You drove me to drink. How about one?'

'Thanks, I'm parched.'

Betty rose, slipped into her shoes, straightened her dress, and put on her glasses, ready for work.

'Please,' he insisted. 'As you were.'

'Don't we have a meeting?'

'We're all to wait in our embassies for a courier from Cairo. Then we'll get together. An hour or so.'

'It seems like this is it?'

'I expect Mike Callahan to come himself.'

'Trailbreaking for the Boss.'

Betty returned to the couch, kicked off her shoes, and sat on her feet comfortably. Like a secretary sensitive to her employer's mood, Betty was responding to a manner and tone she had never heard. Romantic. She took off her glasses; they were for work only. But these new vibrations in his voice surely were a withdrawal from tension, the calm before the political storm of the Tehran Conference. They had always worked closely, but familiarity had not bred attempt, as in Betty's previous jobs. He was always correct, the ambassador who dealt with great events. He looked the part.

'What time is it?' she asked. 'I lost consciousness at eight after Lieutenant Keyes left.'

He arrived with her drink. 'Nine o'clock.'

She took the glass. 'My finest hour.'

'I couldn't agree more,' he said meaningfully. 'Let's drink to that.'

'I must learn to sleep in public more often.'

They touched glasses. He returned to the seat opposite her like an observation post. They took their first taste savouringly, smiling across their drinks, wondering: How young was fifty-eight? How old was twenty-four?

Something had melted down all the hard matters of state he usually brought into the office, she thought. Her intuition reported the chemical change had transpired while she slept. (It had been an unhappy dream of Peter.) Now it was her turn for speculation. She had always half joked about a 'rich, wise man' for a mate. At last there was one before her sending love messages in diplomatic code she could easily unscramble.

'What was Lieutenant Keyes after?' Gordell asked.

She told him.

'So he wanted to protect our Captain Peter Harvis,' he said without vehemence. 'Well, it's too late. It wasn't easy, but I told General Andrews he had disappeared. Tom-Tom beat his chest like a gloating gorilla, but the matter was too important to cover up.' Then he riveted Betty's eyes. 'I'm finished with our Captain Peter Harvis.'

She knew he was trying to divine her thoughts about Peter. He was aware of their relationship. The finality of his last words were meant to clear the obstacles between them. It was now up to Betty to drop any impedimenta as they advanced emotionally towards each other.

'I need a fresh-up,' she said, holding out her glass. He knew she was bidding for time as he went to the bar.

Her mind raced: She had this man at her mercy. With Peter she had reached the limitations of immaturity; like this childish wild-goose chase she had warned him against. Unlike Peter, there was nothing she could teach the ambassador (would she call him Phil?) in bed or out. She supposed there would be a sacrifice of quantity for quality. But what did she really want from life? Politics, prestige, money. Power, of course.

'Our Captain Peter Harvis,' she said as Gordell brought back the drinks, 'is a silly boy.'

He stood over her with two glasses.

'Let's consider the book a beginning for us,' he said. 'A real collaboration.'

In the euphemism of his profession he was asking Betty to share his life. He knew her ambitions to write.

'That's exciting!' She was genuinely overjoyed. She had talent and was already performing what amounted to ghost-writing. It meant equal credit – equal money. 'You're being too nice.'

Impulsively, she moved from the couch to hug him between his outstretched arms, holding the drinks. Then she clung and kissed him on the mouth. His arms went around her, spilling the liquor over the back of her dress.

'I'm sorry,' he said in polite distress, somehow shattering a mood. 'Let me do something —'

'Forget it,' she told him gaily. 'I hate to make love in a wet dress.'

She proceeded to take off her garments. Gordell put down the drinks and began to remove his clothes.

She was ready first, lying down on the couch in the position in which she had slept, thinking how words can kill sex. The diffident man would have talked on, talking himself out of it. The affair would be good, she thought. Victimless.

39

It was dawn when Nadiri stopped his truck at a qanat, about a mile out of Tehran. He went to the back and removed the rugs that hid Colonel Zenner. The two men left the truck.

A muqanni, a qanat caretaker, stood waiting for them on the mound. On of the water sources of Tehran was this ancient underground system. It emptied into the suburbs of the poor where water wagons came to fill their tanks. The muqanni was reluctant to descend the piled dirt of the qanat shaft.

Nadiri called out and jingled a bag of money. After some hesitation, the independent muqanni came down.

The payment was made.

Suddenly they heard the sound of oncoming jeeps that had spotted the truck.

The muqanni darted to the qanat shaft. Nadiri started in the opposite direction. With a swift draw of his handgun, Zenner put two bullets into the back of the fleeing young man.

Just before the jeeps arrived, the colonel ran to the shaft. He climbed down the rope ladder that hung from a wooden wheel. Slightly impeded by the gun case, Zenner followed the descent of the muqanni, deep in the well, towards a bottom blackness.

'Halt!' An English voice commanded.

Then a warning shot followed.

It was an Allied patrol of Russians and British in two jeeps. The Russians took the truck and the Iranian, while the English captain and his men headed for the shaft. They tried to raise the rope with the wheel, but it was a losing tug-of-war against the weight and resistance from the dark hole. The rope ladder came up empty.

'It's a hundred feet down,' the English officer said knowledgeably. 'Into the bowels of hell.'

'It ain't the River Styx, sir,' his sergeant demured. 'It's just the native underground stream.'

'They call these qanats "the murderers",' the captain said. 'They have a lot of respect for the people who work in them.'

'If you say so, sir,' the sergeant said. 'I'm not acquainted with the language.'

The Russian lieutenant joined them and reported a mysteriously murdered man and a load of rugs. Most likely a falling out of opium smugglers.

They didn't appear to be the German commandos the Allies were looking for, the Englishman judged.

'Let's drop the rope,' he said. 'Maybe they'll take the bait.'

Two men were left to watch the truck and the shaft. The patrol proceeded on their rounds, planning to return later. Some suspicious circumstances were better than nothing for a dull night's work. You never could tell.

40

It was five o'clock in the morning when Captain Peter Harvis was dropped off in front of the Friday Mosque in Isfahan. He had been given a ride on a truck delivering the elegantly carved utensils of fruitwood they made in Abadeh.

The driver was long overdue at the bazaar or he would have brought the American directly to his destination in the Yahudieh, or Jewish ghetto. The lengthy journey had been of tedious waits for the engine to cool and ragged tyres to be repaired. Parts were hard to get in wartime and expensive. Harvis gave the machine-maddened man, who came from a long and honourable line of camel drivers, a therapeutic tip.

Harvis stood before the eleventh-century religious edifice and collected himself. Six months before he had visited Isfahan with Farsai, who had lapsed into a cultural ecstasy in the ancient and beautiful city. The embassy interpreter had been a perfect guide. In a letter to his wife, Harvis promised to bring her here after the war. He was in Iran as a GI tourist, it seemed, and the idea carried over into an appealing avocation for the rest of his life.

Returning, however, by way of the murders in Shiraz, the killings of Persepolis, and the shooting at Pasargadae had undermined his confidence in immortality, Harvis thought wryly. He wondered if he would imagine the smell of smoke in his nostrils always.

Mirza had told him the suspected house was across from the minarets of Sareban, a short walk from the Friday Mosque. Harvis knew all the landmarks. Though all the houses were mud-built and looked alike, there was one with Russian and British jeeps and soldiers waiting outside it.

As he approached the captured house, Harvis prepared himself for Artukin and Skeene. When last seen – was it two days, two weeks, two years, a lifetime? – they were unfriendly allies. Now he was showing up with a story that was completely exposed to disbelief. The fact remained that Colonel Konrad Zenner was still in the commando business.

'Bloody bullshit!' Skeene would say. Then his narcotic-lidded eyes would shut as if to block out a boor. Artukin would say nothing, but his insulting thoughts could easily be read in his boozy grin. The pricks!

Yet even in his own mind there was the creeping mistiness of unreality. It was an effort to visualize himself in that perilous position of twelve hours ago. He recognized the healing mind at work. But he had acquired a past he was proud of, a true and irrevocable happening.

There was truth.

Harvis was an absolute end in himself (seen in his own possible end [death]). He was now a solitary man of unique nature, the sole judge of his own actions. There was no higher law.

Then why was he so anxious about the judgment of Colonel Boris Artukin and Major Sam Skeene when the only opinion that mattered was his own? Where were they when he was alone before eternity? Therefore, gentlemen, he was taking no shit today, tomorrow, or for the duration.

He hesitated before entering the house like a bather on the brink of icy water. Inside, a soldier directed him to an open trapdoor. Descending the stairs, Harvis was amazed at the compact communications centre the Germans had installed. Skeene was in the last stages of dismantling it with one of his expert Sikhs. Artukin sprawled on a couch, deciding the fate of the two German radiomen, who sat glumly in a corner. A Russian soldier guarded the prisoners.

'Hi, fellas,' Harvis announced himself.

The heads of the Russian and the Englishman swivelled towards him. 'Petroushka!' 'Peter!'

They broke to greet him.

Artukin embraced Harvis, kissing him on the cheek. 'Our hero!'

Skeene pumped his hand. 'Our very own commando killer!'

Their sincere relief and delight left Harvis pleasurably speechless and touched almost to tears. He was no longer an ally, but a friend brought into their fighting men's club courageous. But how did they know?

A Russian sergeant entered; it was time to abandon the house. He led the German prisoners away. The Sikh left. Now Skeene solicitously sat Harvis down, while Artukin brought out a bottle of brandy, delaying their departure for him.

Harvis lingered with the warming liquor to regain his composure, noting that Skeene's eyes were like diamonds and there was nothing alcoholic about the Russian colonel. They were fighting men with all senses alert. He had miserably misjudged them and grinned foolishly.

Skeene filled him in. 'We've got their codebook, maps, roster lists, listening posts, and underground stations. We know precisely where Wolf Pack Numbers Three and Four —'

Artukin said, 'We will crush them like cockroaches!'

'We don't know the location of Wolf Pack Number One. That's Colonel Konrad Zenner. Also the leader of the underground, a man named Otto Gormann, who was in charge of this operation,' Skeene continued. 'For the moment they're not our concern. But there's one hell of a search on for those two lonely chaps.'

'Okay, okay,' Harvis said. 'But who told you about me?'

'Your friend Miss Lanteri,' Skeene said.

The insides of Harvis began to dissolve with the mention of her name. It had left his mind, the Big Three. He had been the only One. He felt a premonitory twinge.

'How did Betty know about me and Colonel Zenner?'

'We all knew you were after the bloody Kraut. Last night she came down in a plane with Lieutenant Keyes looking for you,' Skeene reported. 'She was disappointed and very upset because she thought we were protecting you. She wouldn't believe we didn't know where you were. Finally, she broke security and told us Churchill, Roosevelt, and —'

'Stalin,' Artukin murmured the name reverently.

'– are arriving in Tehran one o'clock today,' Skeene said. 'She called you all kinds of a fool, philosophically and personally —'

Artukin censured: 'She speaks like a soldier!'

'You're in a bit of trouble with your own people,' Skeene said. 'She claimed going back with her was your last chance. Lieutenant Keyes said General Andrews would "throw the book at you". You are officially AWOL.'

'It is very bad,' Artukin added. 'The military police are looking for you.'

Harvis fell back on the couch like a man receiving a sharp slap across the face from a friend, literally struck dumb. The embassy alert, then his quick punishment, like a reprisal attack of commandos at midnight.

'I'll be court-martialled sure as hell,' he said.

'Where have you been?' Skeene asked.

'You really don't know?'

Artukin said, 'Petroushka, your girl told us you went looking for this Nazi scum. You could get hurt.'

Harvis laughed. 'So you guys were just happy to see me

alive. You don't have any idea —'

'We know you made a bloody try, Peter,' Skeene said. 'That was enough for us.'

Harvis related the events of Pasargadae, observing mingled disbelief, astonishment, amusement, respect, and affection on their faces, but there was no joy in the telling. The blow from the embassy was stunning.

'Major Ali Mirza will thank you,' Skeene said. 'You either put off or put down the Qashqai revolt.'

'All by yourself, Petroushka!'

'What are you talking about?'

'The major contacted us just before you came,' Skeene said. 'The son of the Qashqai khan was flying the plane you shot down. It broke the old man's heart.'

'Reza was the pilot!'

'I suspect Wolf Pack Number One himself was going to meet with the khan for the big push,' Skeene said. 'Mirza is happy about it. He doesn't like civil wars.'

'How did he find out?'

'He didn't say, but I imagine it's your friend Nadiri. You said he was there in the white Mercedes. I have an idea he's Mirza's man now.'

Artukin's sergeant looked in, curious about the delay.

'You can use my jeep. And please take this bag with you to Tehran,' Skeene said. Like Artukin, he wore a field jacket and helmet. The bag contained his tunic and cap. Then he offered his hand, and Harvis grasped it. 'I'm glad one of my friends came back.'

The Englishman had lost too many friends in the war. Harvis understood why he couldn't invest emotions in new ones. His aloofness had been a protection against disappointment and hurt. He had held the American at arm's length.

With his unjoyous laugh, the Russian made it a three-way handshake. 'It is good you are no more a war virgin.'

Then they left him alone.

41

Harvis pushed the borrowed British jeep hard to Tehran. It was five hours from Isfahan. Without incidents on the road he might arrive in about two hours before the Big Three landed in Mehrabad airport. Plenty of time, he thought. But time had been playing games with him lately. Time was a clown that struck from behind with a big bladder for laughs.

Artukin and Skeene had tried to talk him out of leaving Isfahan. He had vaulted the stairs and was on his way even before they had left the house for the merry massacre of the unsuspecting German commando teams. His manic rush towards the arms of the MP's and a court-martial amazed them; moments before, he had seemed sunk in depression.

Let them come out and arrest him with an empty bottle or two of well-earned brandy under his belt, the two battle-scarred men reasoned. They'd find him soon enough. Only shellshocked men went asking for it. He was like a man bringing nails to his own crucifixion, Skeene thought. Artukin shook his head sadly. It was love craziness for Betty, he decided. No woman on earth was worth a stockade.

Was he foolishly thinking of tracking the Nazi commando again? That would be pushing his luck too far!

Harvis had brushed by them without a word, taking off in the Englishman's jeep. Now he drove it fast with the usual hazards of road travel in Iran. He had to avoid potholes, walking people, crossing animals, and slower vehicles.

He saw trouble ahead and began to slow down. The road was impassable because a Rolls-Royce sedan had rear-ended a bus loaded with people and produce. There was no getting around the accident, and Harvis was forced to stop. He sat back and counted the minutes, while the leading contenders, a chauffeur and a bus driver, shouted accusations and insults. The passengers contributed what they could to the argument.

There was hope when an officer of the Imperial Iranian Gendarmerie arrived in the car with a driver. He was a handsome man in his forties, with an authoritative mustache. He didn't like being stuck behind the bus. It was all soon settled; everyone saved the proper amount of face.

The bus took off.

The Rolls-Royce couldn't move because a fender was bent

against a wheel. The chauffeur tugged at it. As Harvis started up, the officer signalled for him to wait. He pretended not to understand. Without hesitation, the officer pulled out his side-arm and sent a bullet over the jeep. Harvis turned off the motor, furious.

The officer opened the door of the car. An attractive woman of forty and a ten-year-old boy emerged, leaving it to their struggling chauffeur. Harvis recognized her as a famous entertainer, the mistress of a Cabinet member. It was officer club gossip. There were few sexual secrets in their society.

The officer, who had put down a crowd and threatened Harvis, was now all charm and servility. He brought the mother and son to the jeep. The boy jumped into the back, considering this a jolly improvement. His mother sat down beside him, regally. Then the officer informed Harvis in Persian that this very important lady wished to be taken to Delijan, halfway on the road to Tehran. They were police instructions, given with a tight smile, daring the foreigner not to co-operate.

'I don't speak Farsi,' Harvis said in English, bowing to the inevitable. If he didn't have to make conversation, the pair would not be an imposition. He desired no intrusion into his thoughts. 'But it's okay with me.'

He knew at once claiming ignorance was a tactical mistake from their sudden reticence. The officer had assumed he knew the language. Also, Harvis should have shown a bit more grace. But time was now a coiled spring in his stomach.

As the officer stood on the road, his eyes flicked from the British markings on the jeep to the American's uniform, dubiously. Harvis hadn't realized the incongruity. He listened while the officer told the woman it was imperative that he accompany her to assure maximum security and comfort, since there was no language communication. She protested politely but invitingly, apologizing for her lack of English.

The overbearing bastard, Harvis thought, unable to indicate he understood.

The officer shouted to the driver of his car to continue to Isfahan. Then he sat down beside Harvis, gesturing for him to get going, as if he didn't speak English and sign language was all they had.

Harvis started off towards Tehran.

The officer's gallantry in action would be rewarded in a high place. Harvis could see he was proud to be in the presence of this talented and popular woman. But Harvis detected an undercurrent directed at him as a foreigner. He suspected the officer knew English; language came easy to Iranians. It was a rare opportunity for him to assert his sovereign rights and demonstrate his modern lack of colonial mentality.

Along with the officer's courtesy the woman could also report to a certain nationalist Cabinet minister the style with which he had put a foreigner in his place....

The MP's were looking for him because of the ambassador's personal pique and the malice of General Tom-Tom Andrews, the court-martial maniac, Harvis thought. He had been a pawn in the long-standing feud between them. The general would now be in sole command of security, including the American embassy, leaving Ambassador Gordell unrepresented in that aspect of the historic moment because Harvis had disappeared. Gordell had made an issue about getting the assignment for him because President Roosevelt was staying in the embassy. And Callahan, his old friend, had recognized his right of domain.

Technically, it should have been the responsibility of General Andrews, but Gordell didn't want him trespassing in his embassy. Old Tom-Tom had been furious and vengeful. He would undoubtedly court-martial Harvis, and the ambassador didn't have to co-operate, but would. For with his defeat by the general, Gordell would lose the trust of the tough bodyguard of Roosevelt. Crossing Callahan was serious political business.

Duty demanded the appearance of Captain Peter Harvis in Tehran as an AWOL whipping boy. Three men on a warhorse were after him.

What about Betty Lanteri? It seemed as if he knew her better than anybody he had ever known. She was honest in her loves and hatreds. Betty had ambitions she never hid from him. Some of them were suddenly bound up in the Tehran Conference, giving her as much of a personal stake in it as the ambassador.

The arrival of the Big Three was a diplomatic coup and a perfect career booster for Gordell, who always thought he deserved better than he had received from the State Department. Betty was helping him make the most of it. She was a brilliant organizer of material and collector of significant notes, going to the heart of a matter. She wanted to write on her own, hating to have her talent and brains picked as a secretary. So she had a strong interest in the ambassador's success. Now Harvis had marred it by going AWOL. She had to be finished with him.

And yet she had flown to Isfahan with Lieutenant Keyes to help him. Or was it to detail the incident for the book? Betty had prescience. Harvis could be beginning something big.

Either way, she and Ambassador Philip Gordell were now a formidable team. They had no more use for him. Both now had potent personal motivations for wanting Captain Peter Harvis out of the way. His relationship with Betty was no secret at the embassy. Just as it would become known the moment she became more than just a secretary to the ambassador. The American and Iranian personnel of the mission were cliquish, inbred, and given to gossip. There had been some early resentment towards Harvis because Gordell had shown immediate favouritism. His downfall would provide a field day of sly jokes and raised eyebrows at the coffee breaks.

There was his own embarrassment to consider, and Harvis knew it would be better all around if he took his medicine like a good boy, the victim of military, political, and bedroom diplomacy.

Then why was he driving to Tehran at a reckless speed?

When Boris and Sam had questioned his rush towards the Tehran trap, Harvis had no reply. Now something Mirza had said returned with the mystical force of myth. The Persian had smiled as though seeing the phantoms of Shiraz, the place of Sufi poets, saying, 'You have an appointment in Tehran.' It had only reminded Harvis of a book title by John O'Hara. But Mirza was foreseeing a rendezvous with destiny.

The American author had borrowed the idea from Somerset Maugham for a book about his Gibbsville, USA, an enfeebling transplant of a tale from the exotic East. But here, where it was born, it had the truth of folklore. It was in the air Harvis breathed. He was walking on it, touching it, feeling it.

His jeep was a Detroit-made tumbril to his execution.

By whom?

Mirza?

Zenner?

Faster....

42

The muqanni carried a primitive lamp with a guttering light, and Colonel Konrad Zenner used the sharp beam of his flashlight as they moved away from the bottom of the qanat shaft. Walking in a foot of flowing water, they carried shoes tied around their necks.

Zenner had been briefed by the underground on the technical aspects of a qanat. There would be a shaft for ventilation and cleaning about every hundred and fifty feet, thirty-five or more of them, each diminishing in depth, in the mile of tunnel to Tehran. At the end lay the only unguarded entrance into the city. If all went well, he would find a white Mercedes waiting for him.

The muqanni stopped.

Though they had no common language, it was plain the Iranian had a change of heart. He was a poor man, but he offered to return the money; he wanted no part of the warring strangers in his hand. He had simply hired himself as a guide. Now he intended to turn back and accept the invitation of the dangling rope ladder and climb up to the Allied soldiers aboveground.

Zenner shot him.

The muqanni didn't see the handgun in the Stygian darkness. He heard only the echoing explosion that shattered the deep silence before he died.

Picking up the dead man's shovel, the SS colonel waded forward in the subterranean stream.

43

Harvis drove his jeep towards Tehran flat out, completely unconscious of his three Iranian passengers. His troubling thoughts were his own, and their conversation didn't penetrate. Not only had he blocked them out, but their voices had blended with the engine sound.

Was he a rebel? he asked himself.

The word and its implications scared him. He thought of his grandfather, whose character suddenly didn't seem merely eccentric. He was outspokenly anticapitalist and swore shockingly at family gatherings. He had a bemused and skeptical gaze that made people uncomfortable, as if he had seen moral flaws in their skeleton. Kids loved him because they had nothing to hide and recognized his honesty.

'Son,' he said once to Harvis as to imprint it, 'I'm your Grandpopulist!'

He called himself a Wobbly, hated anything 'big', William Randolph Hearst, Rockefeller, J. P. Morgan, 'jingoes', and war profiteers. He quoted Mark Twain and Clarence Darrow and voted for Eugene V. Debs and Norman Thomas. He doted on the time he got drunk with Jack London in Oakland. He embarrassed his family at picnics in the park by putting up signs and standing on a soapbox, shouting, 'Save Sacco-Vanzetti'. Another time it was 'Free Tom Mooney'.

Grandpa took him on a weekend camping trip to Yosemite National Park, which was near Moreno. Peter was ten years old and wasn't aware the old man was dying. It was his way of bidding him farewell.

'Your Pa wouldn't listen to me,' he told his grandson. 'He liked a good time.'

He spoke of a whole grammar of American motives Peter was too young to assimilate. He brought him to some rocks on the Tioga Pass Road on which he had painted anti-World War I slogans. Peter got the impression he had once hidden out there to avoid political persecution. His parents never talked about it, like a taboo subject.

Grandpa Harvis wasn't afraid of anything, a fistfight or a fuck. But his grandson reflected none of this influence when he went to college. The campus radicals were there with plans for remaking people, the country, and the world, no less. His best friend, the Composer, was one of them. He had introduced him to Billie Holiday singing 'Strange Fruit', the pool tax, John L. Lewis and the CIO, and the Soviet Union. Peter was asked by the Composer to attend private political-Marxist meetings. But he was no joiner (no trouble, no sweat, please. I'm here to prepare myself for a job), though Harvis had gained a social sense from the plight of the migrant Okies who came to starve on the roads of the San Joaquin Valley.

He had come of age in time of economic breakdown. His father had a fixed feeling of failure in the Depression he blamed on bad luck and not the government. 'Your Grandpa saw it coming....' Politicians and professors held out hope. But the Composer's predictions of things to come were better than most because, like the other campus Cassandras, he had correctly divined the oncoming war. It had proved out through his theory of economic crisis and necessity.

Harvis used to needle his doomsaying classmates, chiefly for their lack of humour. The loss of boyish and girlish laughter seemed a high price to pay. He agreed now the world was not a funny place. And now, confronted by a court-martial, his postwar situation would be no laughing matter either.

There was a teaching job waiting for him in Moreno after the war. Veterans had assurances from the schoolboard. But as Harvis considered the sentiments of his hometown, he was certain the three members would not rehire a man with a military prison record. Anyone who resisted Army authority was clearly against the war. It was not a popular stance for a teacher these days.

If the schoolboard was visibly more patriotic, being the guardians of the book, the rest of the citizens of Moreno were close behind in their zeal to win the war against the formidable military might of Germany, Italy, and Japan. The town was as close to being perfectly mobilized for the war effort as could be expected in a diverse and complex country like the United States of America. There were 'towns' within the town – Chinatown, Little Tokyo, Mexican barrio, Negro community. Despite minority problems, grumbling, and the American dissent, Pearl Harbor had united everyone, at least for the duration.

Harvis didn't know any draft dodgers, nor had he heard of any. Of course, there were 4 F's. And you wondered why some guys didn't go. But morale was high. People bought war bonds. Victory gardens flourished. Citizens tolerated the various shortages like sugar, meat, gasoline, cigarettes, liquor. Moreno already had its quota of dead and wounded in the conflict.

The schoolboard reflected perfectly the prevailing temper of Moreno. Harvis knew them well. After graduation he and the Composer went before them for employment. The three members were Mr Dickey, the Bank; Mrs Hunt, the Department Store; and Mr Witt, the Big Ranch. It was the final interview, the oral.

Harvis, the Tennis Star, passed with cordial ease. But the Composer, the Talent, was questioned about his campus political activities. His chances seemed nonexistent. Impulsively, he began to improvise obscene jingles on their names to the tune of 'Three Blind Mice' and walked out in the midst of shocked outrage. One year later he was in New York City with a hit tune. The town of Moreno was proud of its royalty-rich native son. He should have been grateful but never forgave them.

The reflexes of the Three Blind Mice were as predictable as a biology class experiment: They would not take back a man who came out of a military prison. After they finished with him, Harvis would be left to his own resources in Moreno. And with a wife and kid to support.

It was all a long way off, but he flinched from the dreary outlook. Harvis thought of Mike Callahan, the ambasador, the general, the military police, the stockade, and the court-martial. Why not make peace? Come home deloused and antiseptic.

Perhaps how the Composer described him was accurate: Pete Harvis had the traditionally timid soul of a schoolteacher. He was alone, far from home. An isolated, shrinking man.

I'm the insignificant size of an insect, he thought. A cockroach, that's me!

The regression from humanity into entymology was accompanied by a deep sigh of depression. Rallying, Harvis made up his mind he would not be Kafka's kind of meek cockroach. There was Pancho Villa's. Every California kid knew the song, 'La Cucaracha'.

Singing the Spanish words raised his spirits somewhat. He repeated them, louder each time, until he was shouting at the top of his voice. It was the battle song of cockroaches like himself. From Mexico to Persia a horse had metamorphosed into a jeep.

Ay hombre!

Harvis felt the gendarmerie officer's hand on his shoulder and realized he had obliterated the presence of the people riding with him. They were smiling, having obviously enjoyed his singing. The song was not unknown to them, and the boy echoed 'La Cucaracha, La Cucaracha'. His mother applauded with professional appreciation. But the officer thought he had been carried away beyond their idea of speed.

'Slow, slow,' the officer said in Persian.

Harvis replied in English, 'Late, late,' he held up his wrist-watch, without slackening the jeep.

The officer wagged his head sternly and squeezed his shoulder again. Harvis knew he was following the desires of the woman. He dared not prick the balloon of politics and vanity the gendarme was showing off. The foreigner's inferiority and the woman's honour were a perfect provocation. He had a powerful grip. Humiliated, Harvis brought the pedal up.

'Thank you, *merci*, *tashakkor*,' the woman said musically.

The boy set up a sudden clamour. He demanded speed, leaning over Harvis, shrieking in his ear, and flagging him forward, like a pampered child used to servants.

His impulse was to swat the boy's hand away; instead, Harvis used him as a compromise and restored some speed. The boy was satisfied. But Harvis was losing time, important, precious. He had become the prisoner of these three. I have to dump them, he began to think as a captive plotting escape.

Then, as a reward, or to match the American, the woman began to sing beautifully. It was a melancholy song that brought tears to the officer's eyes. Her son was enraptured. It was always the same response from her audiences.

Harvis wanted to weep, too....

In a bathtub behind the chaikhana Harvis had celebrated being alive after Pasargadae. He had broken even with Zenner, a draw with a champion. He had considered it a kind of triumph. Actually, it was a defeat. He was the loser. Zenner was still free, and Harvis was destined for a stockade.

That was bad enough. It would be worse if the German commando got through to Roosevelt. Harvis would be a scapegoat. He should have shot the SS colonel or died in the attempt. Kill or be killed.

He would be court-martialled for failing to die. The judging officers would correct this error of survival. Mike Callahan, the powerful protector of the Commander-in-Chief, would cut the rope, wield the axe, or pull the trigger. The bodyguard would kill for the Boss. That was his job.

'Captain Peter Harvis, before we drum you out, strip your

bars, and give you hard labour, what do you have to say in your behalf?'

'I had personal reasons, sir.'

There was nothing to be gained in explanations to them. Or even to himself. A man was what he does, not what he says. No matter what dream motivation, psychic necessity, or conscious desire, Harvis was faced with hard fists of fact: dereliction of duty and the stockade.

Okay, he was guilty. But it was a stiff price to pay for a little fun. The Army allowed for vacation from war. Rest and recreation, it was designated. And he had discovered on the hunt that there was joy in the chase, not the kill. It was a beautiful fantasy in the spirit of Persepolis and Alexander the Great that Zenner spoiled by materializing at Pasargadae. Then time, the clown, tripped him up with the sudden appearance of the Great Leaders of Our Side. Otherwise, arriving late in Tehran would be in the order of a martini-lengthened lunch or an unscheduled afternoon lay.

And now he was speeding (he had edged up the speedometer) to Tehran because he had gambled and lost and wished to pay his honourable debts. The way his father would....

They were approaching a village, and Harvis knew they would want refreshment. The officer was turned around, talking low to the woman. They had reached a flirtatious stage, unaware that Harvis was going full speed again. There was a chance he could race through the village, but the boy let out a howl. The officer went into action, and Harvis had to jam on the brakes. He wanted to kill the kid.

Harvis resignedly stopped before an open-front roadside shop. It had fruit and thin bread and a cook grilling strips of mutton on a bed of charcoal, which was his favourite Iranian food.

The boy jumped out, opened his pants, and urgently watered a wheel of the jeep. The woman waited for the officer's hand and went to the fruit stand. Harvis didn't budge, hoping this might discourage dallying. But the officer bowed like an inviting host in the best tradition of Persian hospitality. It was a dumb show. Harvis shook his head, as a new reason for stubbornness occurred to him. It seemed a perfect time to make a get-away.

As if reading the foreigner's intent, the officer shrugged and took the key from the jeep. Then he went to join the woman and her son.

I'm an open book, Harvis thought, having lost the game of charades. Easily read by Americans, Russians, Englishmen, and Iranians. Perhaps he was printed in some common language. Maybe he was Everyman in Anyland. He didn't have a patois to piss in.

Then the smell of burning mutton from the shop brought back pungent memories of a California barbecue. Harvis was drawn towards the food in blind nostalgia, getting out of the jeep. He bought a kebab.

'The condemned man ate a hearty meal of his own choosing,' he reported to the world.

And died thinking of home.

44

The information collected for Colonel Konrad Zenner on qanats said they often changed and detoured because of cave-ins, flash floods, and earthquakes. He wasn't told about the snakes, bats, ants, and strange fish that inhabited this nether region.

He carried the gun case and a flashlight, shoes hung from his neck. It was slow progress underground, moving over muddy bottoms and deep silt in the uneven passageway that sometimes narrowed to the width of his body.

When he brushed against the ancient cavern walls, choking dust fell. Another time pebbles rained down and stunned him. Once he was startled by the snarl of a crazed dog that had fallen into the shaft. Zenner had to shoot the attacking animal.

He stumbled and swore, then lost his shoes.

His natural habitat was the air and the sun and the moon. This place was perfect for the punishment of red rats and black moles, Zenner thought. Communists and Catholics. A new kind of concentration camp.

Mostly the big commando could walk erect in the cold water that varied from ankle-deep to waist-high. Often he was forced to hunch over or crawl on his hands and knees. His wristwatch became waterlogged. He knew the passing of time by looking up the shafts, noting the stars fade into daylight.

For a moment his disciplined mind slipped, and he thought of his mother. She believed in hell. There was no hope in heaven for her son since he gave up his belief in Christianity because Jesus was a Jew, a rabbi from Nazareth. Hitler had tortured the cross into a swastika with his horoscopes, mediaeval occultism, and ritual magic. She had prayed hard to save her Konrad from hell.

Now I'm in it, Zenner thought.

He had no concept of the distance he had travelled in the tunnel until he found a thirty-foot wood ladder left by some working muqannis. They might be topside. But he had to get out.

Zenner climbed cautiously, gun ready. He emerged to the dirt mound of the shaft, blinded by the sun, dripping with slime like a thing from the deep. He was alone. It was about nine o'clock in the morning, he judged.

He could see Tehran a quarter of a mile away. Then he saw the Allied patrol.

Zenner went back down the ladder, returning to the lower depths, retreating like a mole to its burrow.

45

The six Nazi commandos left the old fort in an American jeep. It was the trophy from their raid on the truck convoy. Their action had been celebrated in Berlin, and Wolf Pack Number Four had promotions and medals from Hitler himself waiting when they returned. When they talked about the event, it wasn't the enemy-smashed matérial they recalled but the look on the Allied soldiers' faces when they saw who was behind them. It was the last look of their lives.

They had received orders from the underground station in Isfahan to break camp and join the other team at the ancient caravanserai, ten miles away. Travelling now towards greater glories, they sang songs of their Hitler Youth days on the isolated road. Today they had an appointment in Tehran, tomorrow the world. Young SS men never entertained doubts.

It was midmorning when they saw a camel caravan of Arabs crossing the road ahead. One of the fifteen camels stopped and sat down to rest in the middle of the road. It was not an uncommon sight in Persia, the land of moving animals.

The jeepload of Germans was forced to a halt.

The driver of the camel couldn't budge it. The commando at the wheel tried to influence the tired beast by sounding his horn. The rest of the caravan waited for the stubborn camel, offering no help to the angry camel driver. Then two of the German soldiers left the jeep to help push the camel off the road. Their comrades cheered them on.

The young Nazis considered this a test of their considerable strength. They gestured the camel driver to get behind them and watch how they removed the smelly animal. As they bent to the odorous task, the camel driver brought out an automatic gun from under his robes and shot the two Germans in the back, killing them instantly.

The other Arabs, who had unobtrusively encircled the jeep, uncovered guns of the same manufacture and wiped out the four remaining commandos in the jeep, while they were laughing at their two comrades. The final glances of their lives was something for the Arabs to remember.

Observing this action from a jeep a short distance away was a two-man team with binoculars, a Russian and a Sikh, representatives of Artukin and Skeene. Having divided the assignment, they had wagered a month's salary on which would accomplish it with the most efficiency and daring, taking few, or no, casualties. It would be poetic justice, the Englishman declared, to outwit them at their own devices. 'Crush them like cockroaches!' the Russian contended. Anything less than total demolition was abject compromise to him.

Having made notes of the elapsed time and the Arab disguises used, the two observers drove off to report to Colonel Artukin. They would tell him Major Skeene, with a blackened face, got the first two kills in the ambush. Their other Nazis were finished off by the Sikhs.

Now it was the turn of the Russians.

Colonel Boris Artukin lay in waiting beside the qanat like a hunter at a water hole. At any moment members of Wolf Pack Number Three would come from their camp in the ancient caravanserai, about a mile away.

Prone in the heat of the sun by himself, Artukin was visible to his watching men. The dozen Russian soldiers and their jeeps were hidden from view a short distance away. Their colonel was about to attempt a solo performance of military grace in the best traditions of the Bolshoi Ballet, inspired not by Tchaikovsky, but because of a bet with an Englishman, Major Sam Skeene. What a way for their thirty-five-year-old commander to go, they thought. Like a dying swan.

Maintaining their own cover, the objective two-man team of observers prepared to clock and record Artukin's efforts. They had informed him of the Englishman's style and daring as a camel driver. It behooved Artukin to improve on it, with the tacit understanding that his men intervene only in the most extreme conditions. Skeene had done well, but he had required his Sikhs to shoot. Exposing his men, tch, tch.

It was nearing noon, and Artukin grew impatient, though he was certain the Germans would follow the orders. It was what they did best, follow orders. Orders were orders.

The orders had come to Wolf Pack Number Three not directly from Colonel Zenner but through central control in Isfahan, now in Allied hands. They were to get ready for the arrival of their comrades from the old fort. It would be the first time the two teams, totalling twelve men, would be together since training camp. The big drive was on. The train they had destroyed was mere practice. The Führer would be watching.

Two of the Nazi commandos left the camp to get water, having been told their comrades were coming without it. Lack of water was a common problem in guerrilla warfare in Iran. They drove a British jeep stolen for them by the underground.

En route to the qanat, the Germans noted a slow-moving camel caravan coming towards them but thought nothing of it. They had been told the caravanserai was on an old camel road, though it was their first sight of one. It was like a shimmering mirage. There was no one to warn them of these illusions of innocence since Wolf Pack Number Four was no more.

They came to the qanat and left the jeep with water cans. Artukin rose from the ground and blasted the two SS men to oblivion with his automatic weapon.

He waved towards his gallery of soldiers, and his sergeant came running at full speed because the observers were timing them. They stripped off the shirts and put on the caps of the dead enemy. It was meagre disguise but enough. Then the sergeant drove the recaptured jeep with Artukin towards the caravanserai.

It was the signal for the Russians and the observers to follow should their services become necessary.

Inside the caravanserai camp the four remaining men of Wolf Pack Number Three hardly took notice of the returning jeep from the water detail. It was too late when the two men with the odd uniforms leaped from the vehicle with guns and began blazing away. There was no time for defence.

The Nazis died where they stood.

Inevitably, there was dispute about who won the contest of killing, despite the notebooks of the observers. Both sides joined in the arguments when the camel caravan arrived at the caravanserai like old times.

The Englishman had accomplished his stratagem quicker, but the Russian's ingenuity got more of the enemy by himself. Both had used subterfuge. But it was the kind of debate that would not injure friendships, even if no money passed hands.

Still wearing his Arab costume, Skeene said, 'Too bad we won't get to see the parade of the Big Three.'

Artukin, the German imposter, said, 'They won't miss us.'

46

The officer of the Imperial Iranian Gendarmerie was no longer sitting beside Harvis in the jeep. After their food stop he had moved to the back seat, ostensibly to relieve the mother of her sleeping child. With this avuncular feeling towards her son came the unavoidable opportunity to touch the woman out of the foreigner's sight.

Harvis had overheard enough to know they would end up in bed together in Delijan. One word had led to another, he concluded, because they thought he didn't understand Persian. It was daring of the handsome officer to enter the territory of a powerful Cabinet minister. The singer was taking her chances, too, being the mistress of a millionaire.

By himself at the wheel, Harvis was enveloped in a bleak feeling of loneliness, driving to Tehran on the rough Iranian road amid a treeless landscape. It seemed he was only now discovering the entire country was primarily an arid plain.

The grinding jeep became a dull drone that gave Harvis a sense of suspended animation. The jeep stood still, moving on a treadmill highway to a dead end. He was helpless, or unwilling, to get off. What was the source that powered his automation? Parental blood? Environmental influence? Educational advantage? Tragic flaw? Hubris? Casting about for his own scapegoat, Harvis caught an answer. It was something outside himself. Not under his control. Imposed by people at the top, politicians. It was the unnatural state, the insanity of war. Not *the* war. Or the 'good' war. Any war!

The military was going to 'crush him like a cockroach', Artukin's favourite phrase. Harvis suddenly identified himself with the leading character in Kafka's *Metamorphosis* who woke up one morning to find he had turned into a cockroach the size of a human being. Harvis shivered with revulsion and degradation. It was what the military did to a man psychologically, physically, and spiritually. It twisted humans into grotesque and obscene metal sculpture, like wrecked machines after a battle. An army was an enemy of people, all people, its own and the enemy's.

It was cockeyed and absurd beyond belief, but he was at war with his own country. A war within a war within. Crazy!

Look, General Andrews, and other officers and gentlemen of

this court-martial, the proceedings all went by the numbers, in correct GI order, and no problems, right? So I hate to prolong this because I know you can't wait to get back to your booze, broads, and blackmarket, but I have a final statement, really. You may blink and cough politely while I talk so I don't think those are well decorated, but empty, uniforms. Listen, a man's country should exist for the preservation of its people. Not the persecution or destruction of them. Understand, sirs? Because people are more important than the state and always outlast it. Gentlemen, stop doodling on those pads and take notes. I'm about to illustrate my point with something familiar to all of us. Persia, look at it. Not out the window, Major, but at the map we used to follow my trail past the old stuff standing around. The many cultures of Persia are dead. Only its individuals continue. So a person is precious because he alone is the link with the past and the future of his country. Captain, please wake up the colonel. You snored, sir! Societies change, but the individual is always the same, with dreams, worries, sickness, hunger, oppression, and joy. Name your own. General, stop playing with yourself and pay attention. War is the ultimate indecency to the dignity of man because it murders people who connect us with yesterday. And it reverses values and words. Okay, you officers and gentlemen, which one of you let go that big fart? People cannot communicate if some ideas aren't for all time and all places, through war and peace, in any system of government. There have to be self-evident truths for all mankind. Now, men, eyes front, chin up, and chest out for this: We must have universally acceptable definitions of good and evil and love. A moral reality that would obtain for the world's allegiance. Thank you for listening, and kiss my ass, gentlemen!

Harvis exploded into laughter at his fantasy of defiance and couldn't stop. As a missionary among the pagan cannibal officers he wouldn't have lasted beyond the first line before being devoured. The military was not interested in justice; it wanted scapegoats.

The outburst startled his passengers just as the jeep hit a rock and bounced everybody around. The boy woke up. The officer and the woman made a discreet distance between themselves.

Harvis brought his laughter and erratic driving under control, while passing traffic swerved out of the way. The boy wailed that he was thirsty. His mother said it was not a good time to ask the foreigner for anything. The officer advised patience because they were approaching Delijan and a proper meal in the best hotel.

'He is crazy,' the officer whispered to the boy, touching his temple. The boy shut up.

They were afraid of him now, and Harvis enjoyed the subtle change. The mental masturbation of idealism had brought comic relief. Together it was small comfort. There still remained a one man-person-individual to preserve, himself, Captain Peter Harvis.

Or what was left of him.

Pasargadae had been a maturation ceremony for Harvis, confirmed by his masters, Artukin and Skeene. Somehow he had forged a 'self' in the heat and smoke inside the tomb of Cyrus. Like fired glass, it would be impervious to the Army. But being imprisoned in a stockade meant the military for an interminable time. He wondered if the shell of a cockroach was tough enough for that.

And then Harvis was reminded of lines by Yeats he couldn't forget: 'the unfinished man and his pain/brought face to face/with his clumsiness. . . .'

'Okay, folks,' Captain Peter Harvis announced, having decided they had cost him enough time. 'End of the line!'

He had stopped the jeep on the outskirts of Delijan but kept the motor running. They would have to walk the remaining distance into the centre of the town, more than a mile away. To take them further would consume more minutes he couldn't spare. 'Get out, please.'

It might have been his use of English, but the Iranians appeared puzzled by this unscheduled halt. The boy had been promised a sherbet at the hotel. The singer and the officer had their own delicious anticipations. The American should turn left, the gendarme indicated.

Harvis addressed himself to the woman, speaking Persian. 'Madame,' he said, 'I have enjoyed your singing in a nightclub, on the radio, and now in my jeep. It has been a great privilege, but—'

She began to blush, then the woman swept up her son in consternation and left the jeep, without a glance at the officer. The affair had ended.

'He speaks our language!' the boy shouted with lusty delight as his mother dragged him away.

Livid with rage and frustration, the officer didn't budge but pulled out his gun. The man's dignity was damaged, and that justified homicide in this country, Harvis was aware. It was a chancy manoeuvre he had to risk.

With the gun in his face, Harvis smiled. 'I don't think she's coming back,' he continued in English. 'Do you?'

'You heard everything,' the officer said with almost unaccented English. 'You listened —'

'Only to the sexy parts,' Harvis said.

'You spy!'

'They'll love it at the Iranian officers' club when I tell them how one of their boys was making out with a girlfriend of a member of the Cabinet.'

The officer holstered his gun but sat uncertainly. The American knew what Persian buttons to push. Meanwhile, mother and son were moving out of sight.

'Hurry up,' Harvis urged. 'Or hotpants will cool off.'

The officer got out, deflated.

'You loused it up,' he said. 'But if you stool on me, I'll cut up your balls and mail them to your mother!'

Harvis held up three fingers. 'Scout's honour.' Then he wondered. 'Hey, where did you go to school in the States?'

'University of Chicago, you prick!'

'That figures.'

Harvis gunned the jeep in a getaway.

He was midway to Tehran. The chauffeur service had lost him about an hour. There was still hope. He could get to his post on the parade route just in time to salute the Great Men. The ambassador would glance at his watch and cluck in mock severity to emphasize his silly tardiness, smile benevolently towards his tennis partner, and wiggle a discreet forefinger of mild reproach.

Bullshit!

47

Zenner was six feet five and had to walk in the water of the qanat bent over. Later because the underground waterway was shaped like a funnel, he would have to crawl, then float to the mouth of the tunnel into the outskirts of Tehran.

The shafts were shorter now.

He stopped when he saw two muqannis cleaning ahead of him, excavating silt and sending it up in goatskin bags by a wooden wheel. Zenner waited until they went up the ladder themselves to work aboveground.

He came to a sandy spot. What seemed like shallow water slipped into a pool up to his chest. He climbed back over the muddy bank, realizing there was no outlet for the pool. His flashlight picked out a collapsed wall.

He put down his guncase, then propped the flashlight for illumination. Zenner waded across the pool, barely keeping his head abovewater. The air was bad. He began to dig with the muqanni's short-handled shovel. He discovered a dislodged boulder had created a dam. He worked until he hit a pocket of poisonous gas. He was forced to swim back to relieve his lungs.

He rested, thinking of the two muqannis behind him. The Allied patrol was above. The way ahead was blocked.

After filling his lungs with good air, the colonel summoned himself for another effort. The boulder gave a little. The pressure of the pool did the rest. Zenner was caught in a cataract of rushing water and found himself tumbling helplessly downstream.

He was knocked unconscious.

The two muqannis found the foreigner when they went to investigate why their stagnant shaft had suddenly become a moving stream. The stunned giant wasn't dead, but he would be a tough task to raise out of the qanat.

It was mysterious. But there might be a reward in it.

48

Mike Callahan came down the steps of the Air Transport Command C-54 at Mehrabad airport in Tehran on a grey November morning looking august. He was followed by two American soldiers carrying a wheelchair out of the plane.

Ambassador Philip Gordell and General Tom Andrews waited for the President's bodyguard beside the embassy car on the runway. The driver was ready at the wheel.

They could see the carpenters completing the reception stand built for the British, Russian, American, and Iranian officials who would be there later for the arrival of Roosevelt, Churchill, and Stalin. Representative bunting was about to be draped on it. Various technicians were showing up early for the planned airport ceremony. The Iranian National Band had collected to practise their instruments. It was an important time in the history of Iran, and the Shah was sparing nothing by way of pomp and circumstance.

Mike Callahan shook hands with them and then sat between Gordell and Andrews in the car. The wheelchair was placed in an Army truck to follow him. The two American vehicles moved off the runway.

'There's breakfast waiting for you at the embassy, Mike,' Gordell said.

'I never eat till the Boss is settled down,' Callahan said. 'He'll be on schedule. That gives me five hours to make all the rounds.'

The general said, 'My troops are already on the streets, spit and polish, for your inspection, Mike.'

'That's great, Tom.'

'You'll find that wheelchair will move freely in a very fireproof American embassy, Mike,' Gordell added. 'The President will be absolutely comfortable.'

'Thanks, Phil.'

Callahan patted both men on the knees. Their voices had carried no hint of their personal animosities. It was time to rally round the flag.

'I don't have to worry with you guys on the job,' the bodyguard said. 'All I'm thinking about now is that Colonel Konrad Zenner. What's the word?'

'They knocked off his men, but the bastard is still loose,'

General Andrews reported.

'It seems easier to stop an army than one man,' Gordell observed.

'We'll have to button up the Boss pretty good,' Callahan said grimly. 'Did you hear from that jerk tennis player?'

Gordell said, 'Still chasing a wild goose.'

'I'd like to give him one hell of a goose,' Callahan said.

The general vowed. 'We'll be coming down real hard on that fuckoff, Mike.'

'Mercilessly,' the ambassador promised.

Mike Callahan snapped his fingers like a reminder. 'I'll begin with the President's car!'

It meant a change of direction, and Gordell told the driver where to go. He drove them to the motor pool behind the American embassy. The automobile the President of the United States would ride in from the airport was parked in the yard, guarded by soldiers in battle dress. Lieutenant George Keyes was in command of the Presidential detail.

The truck delivering the wheelchair also brought Callahan's Geiger counter. He held the tube, using it methodically on the vehicle, trusting no one else with this work. Inch by inch, under and over, unmindful of his clothes.

It was a Packard with American flags on the front fenders. The top was folded down, exposing the interior for the visual appreciation of heads of state. This custom model was especially built for such grand occasions.

It was a car like this in Sarajevo that started World War I, Betty Lanteri thought. So convenient for assassins.

She was among the embassy personnel who came out to watch the President's bodyguard inspect the car Roosevelt would use. It was an occasion. The historic hush among the Americans in the yard was broken when Callahan howled as he stubbed his toe on a tyre.

'Jesus, my corn!'

Gordell and Andrews moved sympathetically towards his outcry of pain, but Callahan waved them off. He motioned to the soldiers.

'Let's shake it,' he directed. 'If there's a plastic bomb stuck in it, we go first!'

Callahan began to rock the machine and was joined by the guard detail. The ambassador, the general, and the driver, who would be riding in it, helped out in their own best interests.

The Packard passed the test.

'Okay, let's give it a run,' Callahan said.

The embassy driver took over as if it were a chariot of the gods. Mike Callahan slumped down beside him, wearily. The ambassador and the general took their places on the back seat, flushed and proud, as if President Roosevelt already sat between them. It was a routine historic day for the bodyguard. But the others were entering the chronicles of the Great War.

As the assembled citizens cheered, the Packard moved out of the embassy grounds, where the American flags caught the wind.

49

Harvis could see the checkpoint outside Tehran when he stopped beside the road. He knew the procedure well, and crossing unnoticed would be impossible. Among the Allied MP's, the American eagle-eyed one would have his name on a clipboard to be taken into custody. A Yank in a Limey jeep would have to explain himself.

He was mentally unprepared to be picked up, Harvis was thinking when the idea struck him. He opened Skeene's bag and took out his neatly packed tunic and cap. The Englishman was a meticulous fellow who dressed properly for each occasion. It might work, he thought, removing his jacket and cap.

Skeene was a smaller man, and his clothes were a tight fit but passable – and ludicrous. He put the bag away with his own uniform and started off. Soldiers had always been issued ill-fitting garments, and not every officer could afford a tailor, he thought. At least the garb related to the British vehicle and would be customarily ignored by the other MP's, except the British. He would present a proper military balance.

He hoped they wouldn't ask questions. His English accent was for comedy purposes only.

The checkpoint was a bottleneck of protesting people. The stream of commerce and humanity into the thriving city had been forced into a slow trickle by Russian, British, American, and Iranian guards. The goods and produce for the bazaars were hours late because the MP's, anticipating the arrival of the VIP's, had to inspect everyone on foot and everything on wheels, horse-drawn, people-pulled, or motor-driven. They worked with the knowledge that their duty for the day was the most important in the war. Saboteurs and assassins came in all sizes, shapes, and colours, they had been warned.

Last in the long line, Harvis was swept by a wave of weariness after the hard ride from Isfahan. He fought off drowsiness. Or was that the torpor that precedes terror?

The epiphany was behind him now. He felt committed, but it was the waiting that wore him down. Time was his nemesis.

Eleven thirty. At one o'clock Franklin Delano Roosevelt, Winston Churchill, and Joseph Stalin would fly in for the historic start of the Tehran meeting. The date was 27 November 1943.

Thus descending from Olympus, the three gods acquired human proportions in his mind. The conference table became cocktail-table size because Harvis knew they were admirable drinkers.

'Gentlemen, we all have an appointment,' Harvis announced himself. 'It was made in a high and lonely place a long time ago.'

'We'll toast to that,' the gods said together.

His fate was bound up with theirs, which was not a ridiculous or egotistical conceit or a cocktail bar brag, but a naked fact of life and death.

'Do you guys know what I'm doing for you?'

Each of the gods sang his national anthem simultaneously.

'Okay, what have you done for me lately?'

The gods chorused: 'Trust us!'

He was being funny. It was not a funny war. But a man has a right to joke at his own funeral dressed in another man's small hat and short-sleeved jacket. It was an enjoyable way to pass time that was now gnawing away at his spirit and resolve....

The truck in front of him moved closer to the guard post and the Allied team of MP's. Harvis started up and followed, then turned off the motor to wait. There was another truck behind his jeep. The line of vehicles had grown.

He tried not to think about the time lost. He made an effort not to think at all because his thoughts were becoming intolerable.

His mind refused to go blank.

The entire world from the great cities to the remote jungles watched the outcome of the conference. It was a turning point in the great war. A crossroads for Harvis, too. The lives of millions of people would be changed by the decisions made in Tehran. His life had already been altered for ever by the meeting before it began.

Harvis felt immeasurably aged.

Tehran.

Coming to the checkpoint, he had known it was his last entry into the city. It would never again be like the first time he saw Tehran by air. The fantastic capital of the fairy-tale Persia of his mind. The gay adventure was gone. He was no longer playing a part in an Eastern fable.

Abandoning the books of the *Arabian Nights*, he was returning to the Greek myths he knew best. The grim ones that taught man learns through tragedy. Tehran was now Troy in his eyes. A massive armed camp. A fortress he had to penetrate.

50

Mike Callahan's orders to the Presidential guard detail at the American embassy under Lieutenant George Keyes were to maintain a constant security movement through the building until Roosevelt arrived from the airport. There was a standing guard outside the embassy, while another unit patrolled the streets in the vicinity.

The employees of the embassy had been given a holiday; they could either go to the airport or swell the crowds in the streets waving American flags when the President rode by. Checking out the rooms for interior protection, Lieutenant Keyes was startled and chagrined to come upon Betty Lanteri in the ambassador's office.

She sat behind Gordell's desk with a drink in her hand, despondently. The office was half-lit, and she was shadowed gloomily. She didn't greet him, staring into the drink.

'Hey, Betty! ?'

'I'm waiting for a telephone call,' she said obstinately.

'The switchboard is off.'

'I'm using the ambassador's private line.'

'Nobody, but nobody, is supposed to be in this building except us chickens in uniform,' Keyes said. 'Let's go —'

The phone rang, and she took it.

'This is she. . . . Hi, Sergeant Mostaffa. . . . Oh, thank you.' She hung up, like a last hope gone. 'He might have had some information, but Major Ali Mirza is at the airport for the big show. Everybody is at the airport. What do you say we hit the palace and steal the crown jewels, George?'

'Please, Betty —'

'I'm sick,' she said despairingly.

It worried him. 'It's the booze. I thought you didn't drink alone.'

'It's the sickness a psychic gets when she sees something terrible coming.'

'Can you walk okay?'

Keyes moved to help her out of the office. Betty recoiled, slyly.

'Touch me and I'll holler rape.' She smiled wickedly. 'You know what those red-necks in the hall would do to their black lieutenant.'

Keyes retreated, furious.

'What kind of gag is this? You're not sick. If you don't get out of here, I'll be in trouble,' he pleaded.

'Roosevelt won't be here for an hour,' she said. 'I'm waiting for Captain Peter Harvis.'

'So that's it!' Keyes burst out. 'I'm not worrying anymore, why should you? So he's late. Didn't you hear they got this Colonel Zenner?'

'That an unconfirmed rumour. I believe they're setting up a cover story.' She stood up and held her stomach. 'I ache all over with premonitions.'

His curiosity was piqued. 'Like what?'

'There are many possibilities. But I've followed through only on Peter. I called him a fool for starting. I didn't say he was stupid. He *is* on the trail of Colonel Zenner. For whatever legitimate reasons he wants to do it alone. But if he gets the commando, what happens?'

'He's a hero!'

Betty shook her head dolefully.

'No?' He hadn't forgotten his urgent duties, but Keyes was fascinated by this prophetess of doom and worried about his friend. 'I don't get it.'

'Peter will be the patsy. He's AWOL. They're looking for him —'

Keyes touched the handcuffs on his web belt. 'If he shows up, I'm supposed to put these on him.'

'If Zenner gets through these fantastic defences, it will mean somebody failed. Both men are outlaws. Therefore, Peter against the colonel are two inadmissible facts. If he kills the Nazi, they'll never let it out. Callahan will get the credit, and Peter goes to jail.'

'How could they cover up a thing like that?'

'They're on top. More powerful than us, a black man and a woman like me. We have an embassy file of things not for the public eye.' She breathed revolt. 'If anything happens that stinks, I'll do something about it!'

Her tragic foreboding had overwhelmed him. 'There's no way he could win —'

'That's right,' she said, then gathered his dispersed emotions into anger: 'He's one of those "good guys", like my first boy friend, who went to Spain.'

'Zenner could get him.'

It was not an alternative Betty could face. She broke into

tears and ran out of the office.

She left part of her drink, and Lieutenant Keyes, who didn't care for whisky, finished it, thinking, I hope to God they have that Nazi son of a bitch for sure.

51

Zenner opened his eyes.

He was lying on the mound of the shaft in the noonday sun. The two muqannis beamed down on the man they had rescued. They had retrieved his gun case and shoes. He sat up, then swayed unsteadily to his feet.

The muqannis tried to support him, solicitously. The colonel brushed them aside, pulling out the gun in his belt. The astonished muqannis retreated from this breach of gratitude. The foreigner must be crazed.

Zenner could see Tehran, one shaft away, three hundred yards distant. Then he saw the white Mercedes cruising along the qanat in search of him.

Zenner waved to the German car.

With his attention momentarily diverted, the pair of Iranians fled to the safety of the shaft. Zenner sent a wild shot after them.

In a few moments the woman in the black chador helped Zenner into the back of the car and hid him under a blanket. Then she drove in the direction of Tehran, driving parallel to the qanat.

He lay limply on the floor of the car, a powerless giant. It was the only time in his life in the German Army that Colonel Konrad Zenner could have been taken without a fight.

52

Moving up the line of vehicles towards the guard post, Harvis grew tense with apprehension. Wearing Skeene's clothes was no longer a joke or gave him comfort. He was too angry now with the necessity of masquerade to find it humorous.

He was close enough to the checkpoint to see beyond it. While Allied teams policed every entrance to the city, jeeps raced around the streets like fierce ferrets in search of real and potential threats to the conference. The final alert in defence of the Big Three was in full active force. Dubious and innocent alike would be detained for the week of the meeting. There were enough foreigners in Tehran to make all credentials suspect. Every alarm or rumour would be tracked down.

Thinking of himself, Harvis knew it was not a time for subtle interrogation or the strict observance of rules. If his camouflage as an English officer failed, he'd be jumped on all sides. What if by chance the American MP recognized him? It was not inconceivable.

He left unmoored, adrift in the British jeep.

The past seemed precious. Childhood was delicious. What did one bring from then to now?

Once his father brought home a tennis racket and balls. It was a day deep in the Depression. He had also arranged credit at the tennis shop for a complete outfit he was to try on. Things had to fit right for his old man. He had a ruinous theory of exorbitance that proclaimed what was begun must be finished, using only the best and the latest. It always meant a surplus cost for style and dash.

'Half-assed crooks get caught,' he would declare.

Tennis was his father's way of making Peter spend less time in the back bedroom (where he nurtured the cherished privacy of an only child) and more in the California sun. His dad's ideal was a balance of brains and brawn. 'Balls, too,' he added later.

Peter resisted his father and his mother sided with him. It was enough that her sensitive son did 'want to'. Also, it would take from his studies and his guitar lessons. The music was recent. Expensive. Each time he played for her, it brought tears to his mother's eyes.

His father prevailed. At twelve years music was a chore and

tennis was fun. She was hurt but recognized the outdoors value. After all, his father said, he was not banishing his boy to a coal mine.

He played with his father on weekends until he overcame the embarrassment of awkwardness. Then he took lessons from the 'best' coach, a high-priced man. It came from meagre savings. By the time he reached high school Peter was good enough to make the team. One afternoon his father came to watch him compete in a league match. Self-consciously, Peter flubbed an easy put-away, losing the game and first set.

'I'll never be the champ you want, Dad.'

It was during the rest period. He was accepting defeat. Peter was off his game, and the presence of his father made it worse.

'Did I ever say that?' his father asked.

His old man looked wounded, as though wrongfully accused, his sincerity in question and the inevitable victim of the father-son problem.

'No,' Peter confirmed.

'All I ever wanted was for you not to be afraid to try something new. So you did it with tennis,' he said. 'Okay, now you started. Then all I ever asked was for you to do the best you can. It might turn out number one, two, ten, or zero. Only give it all you've got. You might have more than you know, or less than I think. Okay?'

'Okay.'

'That's what I've been gambling on. And a little luck,' his father said. 'One thing for sure, losers quit early.'

He gave his son a pat that was more like a shove into an arena. His father had done some boxing on the Moreno Athletic Club team.

'The game ain't over yet, laddie,' he said. 'I'd bet a bundle on you right now.'

Peter played hard, over his head, he thought, and won the next two sets. It was his best victory. With a wide grin, his father waved and walked away, appearing proud because he had gone all out. Not necessarily to win. Peter had begun a game for his father and ended playing for himself. His old man knew something.

It was a desperate reaching, far back to an early stage of self-confidence, but it sustained Harvis. It was little enough stability but necessary now, as the truck before him moved up for inspection. He was next. Harvis started the jeep and closed the gap, his palm sweating on the wheel.

When the Russian, British, American, and Iranian MP's advanced on the truck, Harvis noticed they carried a special flyer on Colonel Konrad Zenner issued by the Allied command. It had a full description. The MP's crawled over the truck, opening boxes, untying bales.

Harvis was certain the colonel was in the city. He would be somewhere along the route his targets would travel, his rifle ready. Assassination, the ultimate murder. It took a life and deprived a people. It was a cruel and calculating crime, not one of passion. Zenner was born to this work. Was I born to stop him? Harvis asked himself.

He was suddenly struck be the relieving possibility that Colonel Konrad Zenner was not in Tehran. Or even captured. How would he know? Who could he ask without being arrested?

The commando teams were smashed. Zenner was alone in Iran with a failed mission. The firepower protecting the Big Three was awesome. Wisely, Hitler would order his favourite killer brought back to Berlin by a special pickup. The war was far from over, and the SS colonel would have time enough to redeem his reputation.

Harvis was suffused with elation, as if a burden of responsibility had lifted. He thought of surrendering to the American MP. He looked for him. And then strangely the checkpoint loomed as some form of great gate. To what? To where? Who was waiting for him on the other side?

The truck was cleared and drove off into Tehran. The MP's signalled Harvis to drive forward. But he sat still, as if immobilized, his eyes fastened on some vision ahead, listening intently.

The impatient MP's ran to the jeep. They obligingly pushed the stalled British jeep with the stiff (was he doped up? or drunk?) English officer through the checkpoint to the side of the road and left it. They had work to do on another truck. The traffic was stacked up.

Harvis lurched into life.

He had seen his father beyond the checkpoint. He was holding out a tennis racket, saying, 'Shut up and serve, laddie. The game ain't over yet. Don't do a half-assed job.'

Would anyone believe grasping a tennis racket for the first time took as much guts as holding a gun against SS Colonel Konrad Zenner, the Nazi commando?

Harvis drove off whistling 'La Cucaracha'.

More than thirty minutes had been torn from Harvis at the checkpoint. Now his President, Franklin Delano Roosevelt, Number One (Callahan was right), and two other heads of state would arrive in a country ruled by a Shah in one hour. Driving his British jeep towards the house of Ebenezer Foster Waite, twenty minutes away, he raced recklessly. He had no idea what he would do if the American didn't co-operate or wasn't home.

But the road was irresistible. He imagined if he took his hands off the wheel the jeep would steer itself directly to the home of the poet-lawyer. The course had been set for him, inexorably. Harvis had a strong sense of having done this before, replaying a scene from the past. It was Mirza who had put the reincarnation and destiny crap in his head. He was receptive because all beliefs had possiblities in Persia.

But the metaphysical strain in him that responded to superstition and magic and curious coincidence angered Harvis now because he didn't like being a puppet. If ever he had to know who he was, where he was going, and why, it was now. He believed he was doing what decency, virtue, and reason demanded, not blind instinct. That was for charging tigers. Or mechanical soldiers whose duty was to do or die, no questions asked.

There was no US Army ribbon for the combat zone he was travelling, Harvis thought. On the other side of this no-man's-land, if he survived, a stockade was waiting for him. He wasn't looking for medals. He was in the service of a democracy which, despite its faults, was still worthy of his commitment.

Except for Shah Reza and Firdausi avenues, where the parade would pass, the city seemed eerily empty. It didn't smell, look, or sound like the Tehran he knew. Business had closed down, and most citizens stayed indoors, intimidated by the drumbeats of the conference (they didn't know *who*, but it was something *big*) and the roaming MP's. It was as though they had evacuated and declared an open city.

No-man's-land.

There was a squeal of brakes, skidding tyres, an angry horn. Harvis just avoided a collision with a crossing jeepload of American MP's.

'Fucking Limey!' they swore at him.

He gave them the finger.

Looking back at them in the jeep's mirror, Harvis caught sight of himself in Skeene's clothes as a comical figure. He was reminded of Betty's Jewish phallic description of a hero. He laughed. He should be dressed in white because his duelling partner would be wearing the Nazi basic black.

The match was classical because evil was unchanging. It was the same anytime, anywhere. If the war ended in the next minute, or should Zenner have escaped, it would not absolve the Nazi. He had murdered innocents. Unlike the sabotage of trains and trucks, which were within the rules of war, the killings were unwarranted. There had to be retribution, now or later.

Like Inspector Javert in *Les Misérables*, Harvis thought. The eternal chase.

He and Zenner were linked like executioner and victim. Unconditional surrender.

Since he was himself operating outside authority, on a loner's code, Harvis mentally stripped the German officer of rank. 'Colonel' Zenner was the Army's job; Harvis was only an embassy deskman. The Nazi wasn't merely an enemy but a malevolence to be destroyed. He was purely a foul force out of a place with no nationality.

It occurred to Harvis that he had crossed the checkpoint into another country. A land that belonged to his new state of being. One man, single-minded.

He had never felt so strong and unafraid in his life. It contrasted with the powerlessness of a young man subject to the whims of superiors when he left Tehran in quest of Colonel Konrad Zenner. In his first encounter with the commando Harvis had prayed for the intervention of Artukin and Skeene. No more. Cheerio, chap. *Spasibo, tovarich.*

He was making his will.

It was farewell to his father, too, who had got him across the checkpoint like a child's game of crack the whip. His old man had 'bet a bundle on the kid'. Good luck, Dad. I love tennis, and I love you.

You, too, Ma. For the gift of laughter and the ear for a tune. And for the way you treated those Filipino, Mexican, Asian, and black kids I brought home from the grape fields in the summer.

Good-bye, Betty Lanteri, the kosher pizza. You guided me out of the provinces of love. Where I came from, going to bed with a girl was a promise of marriage. You were having a 'serious affair', not just a lay. There were always three in a bed because morality made a triangle. I learned about father-love, mother-love, wife-love, son-love, you-love, love-love. And your fairness to fairies. Prone or upright, you're a revolutionary. Come to my hometown, and scatter the hypocrites and free the women. But I warn you, the citizens will always think homos are disgusting and throw them in jail. With other men.

Adieu, Mr Ambassador. With your self-perpetuating diplomacy that creates crisis so you can conference to create another crisis so you can conference to create another crisis. Thanks for nothing.

Kho-Daw haw-FEZ, Major Ali Mirza. Thank you for Faraj, unlucky father. I bequeath you my good medicine, a rabbit's foot, four-leaf clover, and a horseshoe, all-American good-luck pieces, to improve your Iranian fortunes. They should supply power to your collection of rubbing beads and other amulets. I'm keeping my two-dollar bill not as a talisman, but as an investment in the curio market. Honest Injun.

I save you for last, my good wife, whom I love in my imperfect fashion, and thank you for your patient love and then giving me a son. A stake in tomorrow. A tree in my mind. Maybe the true reason for everything.

Harvis had entered the neighbourhood of Ebenezer Foster Waite, a fine residential area. It was disturbingly as he had foreseen. The white Mercedes, in need of a wash job, was parked outside the wall of the house.

Again there was the sense of a preordained path, and he hated it. Right did not always prevail. The good have been known to die young. And look what happened to Hamlet.

He stopped behind the German car. Then he jumped on it to get over the wall, gun in hand. He left the carbine behind as unwieldly. The front door wasn't locked, but he would have broken in.

He heard laughter inside the house. He followed it to the bathroom. A male servant saw him and scurried away, perceiving trouble. There was a blond man in his thirties in the tub. Mario, the black-haired one, was washing his back. He was naked. Standing without clothes was grey-haired Waite.

On a chair was a man's shirt, pants, and a woman's black chador. It was like a dropped veil to Harvis.

The three bare men were transfixed in terror before the unswerving weapon aimed at them. There was no doubt of the deadly intent of this American materialization. The lawyer recognized Harvis despite his mixed uniform.

'Are you Otto Gormann?' Harvis asked.

Skeene had given Harvis the name as the missing leader of the underground. The car outside and the woman's clothes in this homosexual household fitted in with Waite's story of political and sexual intrigue. The scene shocked him.

The German in the bath nodded, one hand at his constricting throat. The Italian was still on his knees beside the tub.

'Where's Zenner?'

Gormann shook his head, unable to utter words.

Waite broke in. 'He can't speak English, Captain Harvis.'

'He understood me. So did you,' Harvis demanded. 'Make it fast.'

'I don't know what you mean.' Waite breathed hard for control. 'Tell me.'

'Did you know he's the head of the underground?'

Waite shook. The structure of the middle-aged expatriate seemed about to collapse from converging strains.

'I only represent him legally.' His rich voice was hoarse.

Harvis couldn't deny the American lawyer managed the abandoned interests of the banished Germans.

He turned to the delicate Italian. 'Okay, Mario. What do you know about Zenner?'

Mario's head quivered denials.

He was only a camp follower, Harvis thought. Time was running out. He swept his gun across them.

'Somebody here knows something,' he said. Then meaning it: 'I could kill you guys.'

Mario stood up, as though to accept a bullet on his feet. Gormann was ready to die. Looking at Waite, Harvis thought of the cat he had shot as a kid. What did cat hating have to do with homos? It was treason he had against the man. Yet it wasn't easy for him to accept an American as a collaborator, though Waite had often broadcast against his country. He was especially obsessed with Roosevelt and the 'Jew deal'.

Harvis steeled himself to shoot one of them. He chose Mario because he didn't know anything.

The terrified Italian pointed at Gormann.

'He here ten minutes. Him give Neezie key. That is what I know. Nothing more. I swear it,' Mario pleaded. 'Them mean nothing. I wish only visa. Italy is dead!'

'He lives,' Harvis said, pointing the gun at him. 'How about you, Mr Waite?'

The lawyer brought out a key with frantic fumbling; it was

plain Harvis was aching to shoot him now.

'It's from my office on Firdausi Street,' he said. 'I don't know why Gormann borrowed it from me.'

The Nazi in the tub managed an oath.

'I really hope you don't. Because I do.' Harvis took the key wanting to believe Waite. The office was on the parade route. 'Thanks, Mr Waite.'

'I'm glad to be of service, sir.'

There wasn't time, but Harvis couldn't resist: 'Did you know who was coming to Tehran today?'

It was as if he had prodded an open wound.

Waite straightened, and his whole being blazed. 'A cripple, a drunk, and a tyrant!'

Then the naked man sat down and bent over, burned out.

'Let's go, Gormann,' Harvis commanded. 'You can drive me now.'

Gormann understood the gun. He got out of the tub, dripping water on the floor and venom at his friends.

53

Zenner made himself ready for murder in the legal offices of Ebenezer Foster Waite. Taking up the entire upper floor of a two-storey building, they were the working quarters of a cultivated collector of books, art objects, and pictures, a person more poet than businessman.

Seeing nothing but the ends of his mission, Zenner took no notice of the rich decor, acting as though in the spare cell of a monk. His faithful mind eliminated all else. There was a samurai ritualism about his movements that was like seppuku, yet Teutonic in origin.

He emerged from the bathroom towelling himself, cleansed inside and out of the muck from the qanat. He showed a powerful frame without clothing, his disciplined muscles revealing the results of cultish care. The diamond and gold decoration from Adolf Hitler gleamed wet from the shower bath.

After his body, he used the towel to wipe off his shoes, then folded it among his discarded clothes. Out of the bag he had brought from Berlin, Zenner took fresh underwear, shirt, cotton pants, and socks. He dressed with deliberation, as if the details were decisive and had special significance.

Then Zenner stood at attention with his eyes closed in momentary meditation. The scar was white on his tanned face, and his hair seemed more blond. He touched the Führer's reward to his lips like a religious medal, thus ending the self-communion. He glanced at the clock on Waite's desk, having ruined his watch in the qanat. Prepared now for the rifle, he removed it with reverence, like an icon, and began to assemble his weapon.

The bag also contained his ammunition. He loaded the rifle and then went to the office window. He peered cautiously through the corner of the drawn curtain to the street below. The crowds had already collected for the parade. Military police were as plentiful as civilians. Each of the occupying powers and the Iranians supplied guards, and more Allied troops in jeeps patrolled the streets.

There was the distant wail of a siren.

It was time.

As he moved into position at the window, Zenner heard a tapping on the office door. He straightened. The sound persisted. He went across the room and asked in German, 'Who is it?'

The reply was a heavy whisper. 'Gormann.'

Zenner shifted the rifle to his left hand, keeping his finger on the trigger, and unlocked the door. He recognized the familiar black chador that covered a man's face.

'Gormann!'

In that instant an American forty-five appeared from the ample sleeve and exploded directly towards the German's heart. Harvis knew he had killed Zenner, but the big man didn't fall, standing with a death mask of surprise fixed on his face. With the gun burst echoing in his ears, Harvis fired until his weapon was emptied.

Zenner collapsed.

When the German hit the floor, his rifle went off in a final salute, the bullet striking Harvis in the stomach like a blow from a baseball bat. He fell back in the corridor against the wall and slid down to a sitting position.

The sound of sirens swelled outside and waned.

After the initial impact of pain and incredulity, Harvis felt nothing, numbly. He could wonder which of the Big Three passed through, hoping it was Roosevelt who had led the procession. He had shot a man and might himself be dying to save the life of the President of his country.

He held his wound, throbbing with pain now, realizing he was drooling blood as it stained the chador. That's what you get for being an irregular soldier, he thought ironically. You can't call for a medic.

Yet he felt no regrets. And no self-pity because he had understood the rules. It had been a cold act, Harvis thought, even as he touched his own warm blood. He had been clearly conscious when he killed, though dizziness was setting in. Also, sadness where he had been unemotional.

His only unreality had been en route, leaving Waite's house with a feeling of stepping off the flat earth into the one-way black void of space, sitting on the back seat of a white Mercedes with his gun against the skull of Gormann. It was beyond belief that with all his knowledge he had no power to turn back from peril. Was that Peter Harvis, age twenty-five, affecting his own fate? A lousy volunteer, for chrissake.

I could bleed to death, he thought desperately, before anyone showed up.

He made an effort to raise himself, to get out of the hallway to the stairs. He had stripped Gormann and left him in the car behind the building after smashing the distributor with his gun butt; at the last moment Harvis had changed his plan to use Gormann at the door. The German might help, he thought, lifting slowly, very slowly, like an old man with a load of bricks on his back. But it was no use. He was too weak. He couldn't even crawl away. He sank down like a marionette that would topple with a touch.

Was this the end of Peter Quixote Hamlet Sir Galahad Casanova Harvis? Also doing business as Cockroach. Where did he get the idea that insects were so hardy, that they would inherit the earth?

Out with a bang. But not a whimper, eh, T.S.? He thought of a quote from the *Shah Namah*: 'Calamity be thy reward.'

This was the situation where one reviewed his life. But he had already done that all over Iran. Yet he had to think to keep from passing out and fought for sentience.

A sudden feverish thirst flared and made him lick his lips. The water in the office was across a Sahara. Or on the other side of a mountain.

He found his foot was touching the outstretched fingers of Zenner like the last clutch of murder. Harvis had only glimpsed parts of him before in the way he had zeroed in on the German's heart for the kill. So he was huge and handsome, this dead man. We were born at the same time, six thousand miles apart, he thought. Now we meet.

There was nothing to distinguish him as a German soldier, an SS Colonel, no uniform, no insignia. Only Hitler's medal that had somehow come to rest on Zenner's scar. But neither did Harvis wear warrior's raiment. Just a couple of guys settling an argument.

Staring at the inert human bulk weltering in blood, Harvis oddly felt no malice. It was a disturbing sense of nothingness he attempted to comprehend. How he had hated this man, this merciless killer who had shot him.

But it was the gun that got me, he thought, marvelling as if it were a moment of supreme revelation to the accompaniment of imbecile laughter. It pacified his pain. I am the instrument of a message!

The gun wasn't really an inanimate object. Weapons had roles of their own. When you see a rifle over the mantel, a drama critic once wrote, it'll be used in the play. It's character. So me, Zenner, and the gun were a triangle.

Of what?

There had to be some transcendental significance to the absurd accident. Why must I have meaning? Maybe it was merely bad luck. Fuck it all, the big and the small, the profound and the trite, the deep and the shallow.

Funny how what might be his last thoughts concerned symbols. . . .

He felt faint.

Then there was a surge through Harvis he defined as either simple pride or something as corny as patriotism, both threaded with pain. He had done a terrible thing in killing, but for a fleeting moment it was sublime.

Now he began to black out.

The sound of pounding boots on the stairway of the building roused him. Two American MP's came running with guns drawn, having heard the shots. They came upon a dead man and an Iranian woman in a chador on the floor.

'This dame just knocked off her boyfriend,' the first MP decided. 'Gave him every bullet in the barrel.'

The second one cautioned. 'It could be none of our business.'

'She could've missed and got Roosevelt.'

'Funny guy.'

Harvis opened his jaws and released the masking chador clenched in his teeth. Now he could whistle 'La Cucaracha'. It revealed his face.

At midnight of the same day General Tom Andrews entered the office of the ambassador in the American embassy of Iran. Philip Gordell was waiting for him, walking nervously, and with a scotch and water in his hand.

'Drink?'

'I'll make my own, Phil,' the general said, going to the liquor cabinet. 'Any news?'

'They extracted the bullet. He'll be okay. But they're not allowing visitors,' Gordell said. 'Not even me.'

'I couldn't get in either,' the general told him. 'It's orders.'

'From where?'

The general came forward with his own drink. 'From people who outrank us.'

'Do you know of any more such "orders"?'

'I've got the whole picture.'

'It can't be a pretty one.'

'What's bothering you?'

'That boy might have died,' Gordell said. 'He acted improperly and deserved to be punished. But not with his life.' Then added with admiration and awe: 'After all, he did track down and kill SS Colonel Konrad Zenner.'

The general spoke with slow emphasis. 'Sounds like a German name. I never heard of him.'

Their eyes held for a moment, and the ambassador chuckled. 'So that's the picture.'

'Half of it.'

'So to save all of us embarrassment the Nazi becomes a nonperson, a war mystery,' Gordell said. 'But what about the living half? He has every proud reason to talk his head off.'

'Aren't you forgetting something?'

'The court-martial!'

'I didn't get it right away, either,' General Andrews said. 'But the people who outrank us —'

'Think of everything.'

'First there's no visitors, no friends, no reporters. When he gets better, Harvis is shipped out. In the States he's given a choice: ten years' hard labour or an honourable discharge – if he keeps his mouth shut. I'd say that gets him out of the hero business, all right.'

Gordell's laughter was largely relief. 'Captain Harvis, if you won't talk, we won't!'

Hearing his own facile words, the ambassador felt a long-absent flush of shame. He hadn't intended to make light of this near tragedy. Peter's success was really Gordell's failure. The young man wasn't a precocious pupil but the ambassador's master. He had broken the rules because he loved his country. Gordell should have abandoned the State Department long ago to bring out his ideas for the nation's welfare.

There was something of value everyone could salvage from the incident that Gordell planned to express. Instead, he had uttered something unworthy of Harvis' bravery because he couldn't break the habit of diplomatic accommodation before the general, who reported to their superiors. It was after the fact, like the book he was writing, Gordell thought bitterly.

When it was all over, he would travel to California just to play tennis with Peter Harvis again. Also to pay homage. The ambassador would understand if he weren't welcomed.